PRAISE F

"Great follow on to the Hi〔 reality into a really enjoyable novel. Worth your time."

D. L. Olson

"The adventure shifts from small town Tennessee to the campus of Georgia Tech. Our young detectives move on to college as they take advantage of an SJW scholarship to further infiltrate the enemy. The book is an interesting mix of detailed science and vacuous social justice nonsense."

Dave Carver

"Captivating, complex and utterly gripping. I highly recommend this book for all readers of hard science fiction. This book incorporates the real world and fiction so well I have to remind myself that it's fiction."

Lisa Phillips

"A vast conspiracy to control history in an alternate timeline very similar to the 'reality' we all know and love is uncovered in the suppression of obscure discoveries in the physics of electromagnetics in the past. Written by a Ph.D. in theoretical physics and an antenna expert in the vein of the classical libertarianism of Robert Heinlein, this volume two of the "Hidden Truth" series is great fun for fans of alternate reality SciFi stories."

MX_Cat

"Very tightly plotted with well-defined characters. A self-contained story which leaves you wanting more."

md

"Great fun and a good read. Hans joins the short list of physicists who can write enjoyable fiction. Go Jackets!"

Jim Stratigos

"This series is a bit of Golden Age science fiction which somehow dropped into the early 21st century. It is a story of mystery, adventure, heroes, and villains, with interesting ideas and technical details which are plausible. The characters are interesting and grow as they are tested and learn from their experiences. And the story is related with a light touch, with plenty of smiles and laughs at the expense of those who richly deserve mockery and scorn. This book is superbly done and a worthy sequel to the first."

John Walker

Books by Hans G. Schantz

The Art and Science of Ultrawideband Antennas,
2nd edition, Artech House, 2015
1st edition, Artech House, 2005

The Biographies of John Charles Fremont,
Kindle Direct Publishing, 2015

The Hidden Truth:
A Science-Fiction Techno-Thriller,
Kindle Direct Publishing, 2016

A Rambling Wreck:
Book 2 of The Hidden Truth,
Kindle Direct Publishing, 2017

The Brave and the Bold:
Book 3 of The Hidden Truth,
Kindle Direct Publishing, 2018

A RAMBLING WRECK

BOOK 2 OF THE HIDDEN TRUTH

HANS G. SCHANTZ

2017

www.aetherczar.com

A Rambling Wreck
Book 2 of The Hidden Truth

by Hans G. Schantz

ISBN-13: 978-1548201425
ISBN-10: 1548201421

Cover Design by Steve Beaulieu at Beaulistic Book Services

10 9 8 7

To those who guide in truth and teach

TABLE OF CONTENTS

CHAPTER 1: WHATEVER HAPPENED TO ANGUS MACGUFFIN?

It was Angus MacGuffin's last day on earth, but he didn't realize it until too late.

Between the salacious speculation why a missionary might frequent so seedy a neighborhood and the ample amounts of blood from the slaying, the Atlanta press was all over the case. "Missionary Slain," the headline proclaimed from just below the front-page fold of the next morning's Atlanta Constitution, displaced by the details of Hitler's latest aggression. The account, by reporter Jack Sweeney, made hard-boiled pulp out of newsprint, describing in breathless terms how MacGuffin almost ended up an unknown John Doe in a pauper's grave. A fellow Presbyterian had recognized MacGuffin's picture in the evening's Atlanta Journal from a church "Jubilee" held in 1913, and church leaders confirmed the identification. Was it just a random slaying? Who would want to kill a humble missionary back in the country after a quarter century abroad? Why was MacGuffin living under an assumed name at a hotel? Sweeney clearly knew there was more to it. His article had more questions and speculation than answers.

I already knew much more than appeared in Sweeney's decades-old article. In the weeks before his brutal demise, MacGuffin had completed a manuscript, "*Suan Ming or the Art of Chinese Fortune Telling.*" The fire that "coincidentally" consumed the Magnolia Publishing Company the day MacGuffin's body was found accounted for most of the copies. The Civic Circle's "Technology Containment Team," or whatever they were calling it way back then, must soon have secured any remaining copies or notes.

All but one.

Forgotten over sixty years in my hometown up in the mountains of Eastern Tennessee, that last remaining copy, a bound proof inscribed to his friend, "Bill," at the Tolliver Technical Institute gathered dust on a shelf in the Tolliver Library, until that library, too, burned to the ground last year. Only we got there first, and preserved MacGuffin's legacy. Now, I was trying to piece together the puzzle of whatever happened to Angus MacGuffin and why.

Because the people who murdered Angus MacGuffin also killed my parents.

Of course, I doubt the same individuals were involved – they cut up MacGuffin in 1940, after all, and they ran my parents off the road and shot them in "an unfortunate drunk driving accident" just last year. Different players, but on the same team. If I was going to take down my parents' killers, I needed to know more about who they really were and what secrets they were hiding. The MacGuffin slaying might be the key to unlocking the mystery. Like me, MacGuffin had discovered parts of the hidden truth. I needed to discover what MacGuffin knew and what it meant, while avoiding his fate.

I'd already figured out that Jack Sweeney wasn't the usual police-beat hack. He was one of the top reporters for the Atlanta Constitution. Throughout 1940, Sweeney filed an article nearly every day. I'd read them. Good, sometimes even thoughtful stuff. Not so after the MacGuffin slaying. Nothing from Sweeney for over a week. Now maybe it just so happened that Sweeney took a vacation right after filing his MacGuffin piece. Maybe. Or maybe he spent the week digging for more information. Perhaps he didn't find anything of note, but it's hard to imagine his editor turning him loose for an entire week unless they both thought he was on to something. Sweeney had a long career in Atlanta journalism, and his widow donated his papers to the Atlanta-Fulton County Public Library on his death in 1972. Perhaps there was nothing to find. Or perhaps he'd written additional details in his personal notes that didn't appear in the paper. That was a long string of maybes and perhaps, but I'd learned to trust my instincts. I had a hunch there might be something there.

My hunch was why we were here in a hotel conveniently across the street from the library.

"That's him, Pete!" Amit exclaimed, peering through the hotel room window with binoculars. I peeked through the curtain and saw a man going into the Atlanta-Fulton County Public Library. I couldn't tell for sure from our vantage point, across the street and several stories up. I had to trust Amit's confirmation that the same man who we saw entering the library was the same one who'd picked up our payment and instructions yesterday. Next time we did something like this, we really ought to bring two pairs of binoculars.

We'd been taking turns as lookout. Amit's fifteen minute shift was almost over, anyway. "You may as well make that coffee run now," I suggested. "I'll keep an eye on the library by myself. He's not likely to be out any time soon." Now we just needed to wait patiently. Either the man would eventually emerge, or the police would show up, and we'd retreat quickly down the fire stairs and out the back of the hotel to Amit's car a few blocks away. Amit handed me the binoculars, and he headed out of the hotel room to get more coffee.

Why didn't we just walk on into the library and ask to look at the papers, ourselves? Why had we anonymously hired a researcher through Craigslist who called himself "Petrel," paid him cash in an anonymous drop, asked him to take a look through the papers, and told him to report back via encrypted email to an anonymous account? Why were we keeping a close eye on him, half expecting a police tactical team to descend upon the library? It's a long story. Sit down. Relax. Make yourself comfortable. I'll explain.

Have you ever stopped to consider how difficult it is to protect your privacy?

In the years since the 9/11 terrorists killed President Gore and a good chunk of the Congress, President Lieberman and Vice President McCain had pushed through a draconian cyber-surveillance law to "help prevent future terror attacks." All phone calls, emails, and online searches were screened and stored as a matter of routine. They nationalized the Internet into a government-run public utility called "Omnitia." The information was only supposed to be used to catch terrorists, but civil liberties activists insisted that soon everyone would be under scrutiny and no one was safe.

They were right.

No doubt, the people running the surveillance were patriots: loyal Americans who swore to uphold and defend the Constitution. But the data was there. It had other uses. The temptation was too great. Suppose a deranged student was planning on shooting up his school. Would you stand on some abstract principle, refuse to stop him, and let children be killed? Would you let a man plot to murder his wife and do nothing? What about thieves? Child pornographers? Pimps? Drug dealers? Gang members? Obnoxious people who let their dogs poop on your impossibly green and beautiful lawn? Where does it stop? Where do you draw the line?

"Actionable intelligence" from this haul of data was already making its way into police hands in the form of "anonymous" tips. The police would concoct an excuse to justify a warrant. They'd use the warrant to secure the evidence they already knew was there. No one needed to know the actual source of the original tip was a constitutionally dubious surveillance. "Parallel construction," they called it.

And if some stuffy judge or politician wants to adopt an old fashioned attitude on privacy, and stop all the good the police are doing? There's a complete record of their every indiscretion, every questionable activity, every bit of dirt they might not want the public to see. What a wonderful tool to make those constitutional literalists see the benefits of a more flexible interpretation of "rights."

Worse, what if someone else had access to all that information? What if they were even less scrupulous? What if they weren't afraid to use that information to secure their hold on the corridors of power? What if they'd already been in the business of pulling the strings, running the show, and calling the shots for a very, very long time?

Meet the Civic Circle.

They keep a low profile, and have only become public in the last few years. If you've heard of them at all, you know they're all captains of industry, political leaders, top financiers, media moguls, and leading academics, who aim "to serve society." For decades, probably longer, they've met periodically to discuss how "we" can make the world a better place. Then, they go off and do it, whether the rest of "we" like it or not. The "Preserving our Planet's Future" act, which imposed those steep carbon taxes to slow global warming, the Gore Tax, is just one of their more recent accomplishments. No doubt, many in the Civic Circle are sincere and mean well. Some are merely corrupt and venal, like my uncle, Larry Tolliver, who's been trying to worm his way deeper into the Civic Circle to twist the national agenda for private advantage.

Then, there are the others.

Somewhere within the Civic Circle lies an inner circle even more reclusive and secretive. They're a sort of parallel global government. They dispatch "FBI agents" who aren't really FBI agents whenever anyone gets close to the hidden truth of their existence or learns secrets they wish to hide. They appear to be firm believers in the maxim, "Three can keep a secret if we kill them all, destroy their records, burn their house to the ground, and then do the same to any associates who might have an inkling what the three were up to."

I know. I learned the hidden truth last year. I love puzzles. I love figuring things out. I love understanding the subtleties most people overlook.

I found a physics book in the Tolliver library that didn't match the Omnitia scans. I began to dig. I found an electromagnetic breakthrough by a 19th century physicist named Oliver Heaviside. Someone had suppressed his discovery and stricken every mention of it from period texts. As I dug further, I found other scientists killed in their prime before they could complete their life's work. I uncovered evidence that the course of history itself had been twisted and altered to serve someone else's purposes.

When the Circle's agents stayed at his family's hotel, Amit had broken into some of their emails. The Circle had rewritten and suppressed old books for over a century, but somehow they forgot to sanitize the old Tolliver Library. Amit uncovered a list of books they were after, including the MacGuffin proof. Amit and I and my Uncle Rob snuck into the Tolliver Library and stole them all before the Circle could show up to take the books themselves, and just before the library mysteriously burned down.

Amit and I took every precaution we could, but the Circle still tracked us down. They fingered Jim Burleson, a friend of my father, as the culprit and killed my parents just to be sure their secrets were safe. The Tollivers never forgave my father for "stealing" my mother away from them, but with the help of Uncle Larry on my mother's side and Uncle Rob on my father's side, my family came together to help save me. Uncle Rob worked with Dad's lawyer, Mr. Burke, to get me through the Circle's interrogation, and Uncle Larry's ties to the Civic Circle meant they gave me the benefit of the doubt. The wild card was Sheriff Gunn. He figured out we were up to something, but he also saw through the Civic Circle's lies. By tilting the scales of justice in my favor, he saved my life and threw the Civic Circle off my trail. It was a close call. I learned the Civic Circle's hidden truth, but at the price of my parents' lives.

I swore I would bring the Circle down, but I was going to need help.

Amit delighted in outwitting the Circle and tapping their communications. Sometimes he seemed to treat it all as if it were just a game, but at least it was a game he was determined to win. Also, if the Circle caught me, it would lead back to him.

Amit and I could probably count on some help from Sheriff Gunn, and from Mr. Burke, but our true mentor was Uncle Rob. My Uncle Rob was a wealth of information in what he called tradecraft – keeping out of sight, avoiding surveillance, sending secret messages. After the Circle killed my parents, Uncle Rob taught me and Amit how to avoid trouble. There was only so much that Uncle Rob could do to prepare me, however. Amit and I both needed more education and more training to understand the Civic Circle's history and to unlock the technical secrets they were hiding. Soon, we'd be off to Georgia Tech to get ready for round two. For now, we had a promising lead to follow.

And that was why Amit and I were spending the day before freshman orientation watching "Petrel" research Angus MacGuffin's last day on earth.

We knew the Circle was hypersensitive about MacGuffin. Back when we first began researching the Circle, we were trying to find out about Xueshu Quan, a book collector chasing the same books we were after. A web page about him had an exploit – a sneaky little tangle of code that made our computer ping the Circle's server directly, bypassing the anonymous connection we were using to hide our identity through TOR – The Onion Router. Only the fact we were logged in wirelessly from a vantage point across the Interstate saved us when Homeland Security and the Tennessee State Troopers converged on the truck stop whose wireless network we were using. "Cyber-Terror Plot Foiled by Homeland Security" explained the headlines and pundits, never questioning why cyber-terrorists sophisticated enough to hack into a nuclear plant and try to induce a meltdown would be stupid enough to do so from a truck stop only ten miles away.

There was a web page about MacGuffin with the same exploit.

Once we knew what the Circle was doing, it was actually quite informative to go searching for that particular exploit. The presence of the Circle's exploit on a web page indicated a sensitive topic. If they were that interested in MacGuffin, they just might go to the trouble of laying another trap in the papers of the journalist who'd written about him. Or perhaps, they'd leaned on Sweeney and his paper to suppress his further reporting and then failed to follow through decades later when Sweeney's widow donated his papers to the library. I was hoping for the latter, but we needed precautions against the former.

"Anything happen yet?" Amit was back from Dunkin Donuts with coffee and some pastries.

"Nope," I acknowledged continuing to keep my eye on the library.

"See?" Amit said triumphantly. "You were all worried for nothing."

"Petrel's not out yet," I cautioned him. "It takes time to assemble a strike team."

"Bah," Amit snorted. "They sent the strike team after us at the truck stop because they'd already traced our activity to the area. If there's a trap here, they'd have dispatched the Atlanta police to deal with it. Petrel knows not to tell anyone he's even interested in Sweeney. He's got a solid cover story all planned out – he's researching how Atlanta journalism reacted to the outbreak of World War II. Even if there were a trap, it would look like an obvious false alarm."

I hoped Amit was right, but I still wasn't comfortable sending someone else in the line of fire. He took over the watch, and while he kept an eye on the library, I reread Angus MacGuffin's *Suan Ming or the Art of Chinese Fortune Telling*.

The book was part history, part mysticism, part folklore, and part memoir. MacGuffin wove his experience as a missionary in China in the 1920s and 1930s into the story. His book described fortune-telling methods, their use in Chinese history, and the underlying Chinese philosophy:

"Non-polarity and yet Supreme Polarity! The Supreme Polarity in activity generates yang; yet at the limit of activity it is still. In stillness it generates yin; yet at the limit of stillness it is also active. Activity and stillness alternate; each is the basis of the other. When the Supreme Polarity is Non-Polar, there is a balance of yin and yang. Each contains its own beginning and its own ending, and together they flow harmoniously. In imbalance, yin exceeds yang or yang exceeds yin. Yin no longer begins at the end when there is stillness without activity."

I could only read a paragraph or two of MacGuffin's Taoist mysticism before my eyes would begin to glaze over. Many of the fortune telling techniques he described seemed unremarkable: face reading, palm reading, astrology, and the like. One caught my eye, a "rod of divination:"

"The Lord our Father revealed his words, wisdom, and laws through a burning bush. Not so with these Chinese. Their gods impart wisdom of a more subtle nature through the agency of a rod of divination. This rod does not foretell the future. Rather, it identifies the time and place where the mandate of heaven will soon be revealed."

We knew that the Civic Circle had what they called a "Nexus Detector," a device that let them identify the turning points where a few critical players and crucial decisions change the world. MacGuffin's "rod of divination" sounded an awful lot like the Civic Circle's Nexus Detector.

MacGuffin's memoirs described the violence and chaos he witnessed in China. The Japanese invaded Manchuria and warlords ruled the interior. MacGuffin taught his Chinese neighbors about Christianity, and his Chinese neighbors introduced him to Confucian thought and Taoist mysticism. When conflict came to their province, MacGuffin's desperate Chinese friends entrusted him to hide some sacred scrolls and the rod of divination. An unknown gang killed his friends and burned the mission. MacGuffin barely escaped, fleeing with the scrolls and rod. The same mysterious yet implacable foe pursued MacGuffin for months as he fled China. Finally, MacGuffin laid a false trail to make it appear he'd taken a boat to San Francisco. Instead he travelled under a false identity to Buenos Aires, via South Africa.

MacGuffin spent years hiding out in Buenos Aires, translating his scrolls and writing his memoirs. He sought out assistance in understanding his results.

"Discreet inquiries led me to the Dominicans at the Convent of Santo Domingo. They called themselves the Ordo Alberti. 'Investigare, cognoscere, defendere,' these Albertian Brothers like to chant: investigate, know, defend. Although such mummery merely obscures the power of God's word, they nevertheless showed an interest in those aspects of my work I shared with them. They introduced me to an intense young Italian, Mr. Bini – a scientist of sorts, although his background was never quite clear to me."

Mr. Bini convinced MacGuffin that there were technical secrets within his pages of mysticism. "He showed me how the curious yin-yang symbol followed from the calculations of 'a Russian mathematician' and an American named Smith, though I could not understand the mathematics behind his calculation," MacGuffin explained. The manuscript had a peculiar drawing of a yin-yang symbol, with a single line through it.

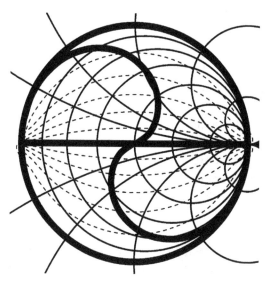

The diagram had a number of curious arcs and circles to it as well. Overwhelmed by the Taoist mysticism and confused by the diagram, the first time I'd read the book, I was ready to give up on it right there. Then, I read MacGuffin's next paragraph.

"Mr. Bini was convinced that my pursuers were connected to the men who drove him out of Europe. 'I came too close to their secrets,' Mr. Bini explained. 'I derived the heavy-side theory they thought they had hidden. They pressured me to join them. They burned my poor little cousin to death when I refused, and they threatened others in my family. That's when I knew I had to flee.' Mr. Bini had found shelter with the Albertian Order at the Convent of Santo Domingo."

"Heavy-side" as in Heaviside? It was a suppressed electromagnetic discovery by Oliver Heaviside that led me to discover the Circle's hidden truth. That sounded promising. But a Russian mathematician and an American named Smith? Could it possibly be more ambiguous? It seemed a dead end.

Finally, with war having broken out in Europe, MacGuffin chose to return home to the United States. Something gave him away, however. Sweeney's article described the brutal result. All we had was MacGuffin's proof and the inscription on the title page. "To my friend Bill, Angus," it read.

"Bill" was tough to track down, because there were several Bill's or William's at Tolliver Tech in the 1930s. The most likely candidate appeared to be a professor of Oriental languages who enlisted in 1940. The Army sent him to the Philippines to work as a translator, and he did not survive the Bataan Death March. Quite possibly, he never saw the MacGuffin proof. Another dead end. Tolliver Tech was taken over as a military training facility in the war, and never did regain its pre-war stature. Somehow in all the chaos, the proof ended up in the Tolliver library, the only legacy of the life of Angus MacGuffin.

I felt a strange kinship to this forgotten man, dead decades before I was born. Like me, MacGuffin tried to discover secrets that the Civic Circle wanted to hide. It cost him his life. I intended to pick up where he left off, and avoid his mistakes.

"There he goes!" Amit exclaimed, hours later. The two of us watched the man who called himself Petrel emerge from the library and walk off unmolested in the direction of the MARTA station. "Unless they made him in the library, he should be home free," Amit observed.

"Let's get going," I replied. "We need to be checking in at Tech."

I'd driven past the school any number of times – it's right off I-75/I-85, the downtown connector in Atlanta. Now, Amit and I were about to get an in-depth introduction by attending freshman orientation: "FASET" – Familiarization and Adaptation to the Surroundings and Environs of Tech. We were to stay in the dorms a couple of days, do tours, attend orientation lectures, and get signed up for classes.

Amit had been waiting for this moment for a couple of years. He'd been reading online about what he called "pick-up-artists" and their "secret methods" for attracting girls. I was skeptical that conversational and behavioral tricks could have that much impact. On the other hand, I'd seen how Amit landed a girlfriend our senior year using some of his methods. Emma was fun, smart, and cute, but Amit was eager to apply his ideas at the much larger hunting grounds of the Tech campus. Amit proposed what he called an "open relationship" to Emma. That basically meant that they could go ahead and date other people at school while remaining "friends." Emma would have nothing of it, and she broke up with him. Undaunted, Amit was ready to make his mark on the young women at Tech.

He forced himself to be outgoing, the center of attention, eagerly greeting girls and guys alike. "Just laying the groundwork, Pete," he explained. "First impressions are important." At one point, our rather attractive guide suggested if we had any questions, we could write them on the board of the lecture hall, and she'd answer them after lunch. Amit made his way promptly to the front and wrote: "Where are the best places on campus to make out with girls?" He got hoots and giggles from the class, and I swear the guide was blushing a bit when she came back from lunch, saw the question, and said, "You'll have to find out for yourself."

We learned Georgia Tech history and the school song, "I'm a ramblin' wreck from Georgia Tech and a hell of an engineer..." Since Burdell is my family name, one school tradition made a real impression on me: the legend of George P. Burdell. Back in 1927, a resourceful engineering student found himself with a duplicate enrollment form. He signed up the fictitious Burdell for a full load of classes. He and his friends turned in duplicate homework and submitted multiple versions of the same tests, enabling George P. Burdell to graduate with a Bachelor's degree in 1930. George P. Burdell served in World War II, was on the Board of

Directors of Mad Magazine, and is often paged over public address systems wherever Georgia Tech students and alums congregate. He may have been a made-up character, but as a Burdell myself, I took some satisfaction in knowing Georgia Tech's most famous alumnus was, in a sense, a member of my family.

We couldn't wait until we got home to learn what Petrel had found. We'd promised him another payment for his report. That night we used a directional antenna to tap into the Wi-Fi at a hotel on the other side of the Interstate from our dorm. Then, we connected to our encrypted email account using TOR – The Onion Router – to hide our IP address.

Petrel had struck pay dirt: Sweeney had a file on Angus MacGuffin. "G-men say: 'Nothing to it; some reefered up jigs had a razor party,'" read Sweeney's notes. That quote prompted another search to discover "G-men" were federal agents, "reefer" was slang for marijuana, and "jigs" was a racial slur for black people, not a dance. I must live a sheltered life. "They're hiding something," Sweeney's notes continued. "McG agrees."

"Maybe Ralph McGill, editor at the Atlanta Constitution?" Petrel helpfully added.

The notes were fascinating. Sweeney "slipped a fin" to a bell hop to get into MacGuffin's hotel room. He found a pad of paper MacGuffin had used. Rubbing a pencil over the sheet underneath to draw out the impression of the letters yielded a cryptic message: "Bill, please keep this safe! Our thorny friend helped me hide the scrolls and the rod where they won't find them. Angus." A cover letter for the proof MacGuffin sent to his friend Bill up at Tolliver Tech? But who was this "thorny friend?" Sweeney also managed to tie MacGuffin's death into the mysterious fire at the Magnolia Press, but the Magnolia Press editor who worked with MacGuffin was dead, and Sweeney couldn't pursue the lead further. Finally the G-men prevailed on "McG," and McG made Sweeney drop the story.

"I'm not sure it was worth the risk," Amit opined. "We knew everything already, except the bit about the thorny friend."

"Another piece of the puzzle," I countered. "Now we know a bit more about how the Circle was operating as early as 1940. Also, we have a clue that the Circle either got their Nexus Detector from MacGuffin, or at least that it probably came from China, too. Maybe MacGuffin's rod of divination and those scrolls are hidden away somewhere, so we can find them."

"We're David, and the Civic Circle is Goliath," Amit argued. "I just don't see how this information gives us a bigger rock to throw or a more accurate sling."

"It's more like an army of Goliaths backed by comprehensive cyber-surveillance," I agreed. "Someone burned down the Tolliver Library before the Circle's Technology Containment Team could arrive," I reminded Amit. "The Civic Circle has enemies. If we can figure out who they are, maybe we can ally with them. We need all the help we can get."

"True," Amit acknowledged. "But a missionary and his Chinese friends dead sixty-five years probably didn't burn down the Tolliver Library and won't be good allies. And you know exactly what your uncle would have to say about it."

"China's a big place. Maybe some of MacGuffin's Chinese associates are still around," I speculated. "Eventually Uncle Rob is going to have to let us reach out and recruit some more allies."

"Our job for now is to prepare ourselves," Amit replied in an excellent parody of my uncle, "to make ready for the battle to come."

"He was out of town," I insisted, "so we had to take the initiative without him, and we were successful."

"You don't have to persuade me," Amit agreed. "It was my money you spent on the researcher. I'm on your side. Save it for your uncle."

The next morning we signed up for classes.

We wrangled our schedules so Amit and I were in the same section of Introduction to Programming – not that either of us really needed the class. We'd both taken a basic course in programming at our high school back in Sherman, Tennessee, as well as an additional class at the local community college. Amit took programming to the next level – his passion, second only to girls. He'd written a script for policing the network at his parents' hotel. Amit's code monitored the IP addresses of all the traffic, so if any of the guests used the network for downloading child pornography or other illicit purposes, he could check the logs and tell the police which guest was responsible. He'd put a graphical user interface on top of it, drawing on his experience helping his folks run their hotel, and it had been adopted in lots of other hotels in the Berkshire Hotels chain.

When the Circle's agents came to town, they stayed at his family's hotel. Amit forked their traffic and figured out how to decrypt some of it. With Amit's manipulation, the Circle's agents made it to Double Platinum in the Berkshire Rewards program in record time. Apparently, they liked taking advantage of the upgrades, because they were staying in Berkshire Hotels whenever they were on the road. Amit included routines in his software to capture their traffic wherever possible, giving us insights to their activity.

In addition, he'd included an encrypted Virtual Private Network or VPN capability using his software that let us make it look as though our Internet traffic came from someone at one of the hotels running his software. If the Circle managed to bypass TOR, trace our IP address, and hunt us down again, Amit was determined they'd lose our trail back at a random hotel on the other side of the country.

Unfortunately, none of this expertise mattered to the folks at Georgia Tech – not that we told them all the details! Our high school and community college classes didn't meet their requirements, so we were back in the most basic, introductory class.

For my major, I was undecided between electrical engineering and physics. For my first year, I could take classes from both schools. Once I'd chosen a major, I could use the classes from the other school as electives. For my first semester, I signed up for an electrical engineering class, linear circuits, and an electromagnetics class from the physics department. I already had credit for calculus, so I took an introduction to differential equations class. I had to take freshman chemistry for both programs, too.

I was more convinced than ever that MacGuffin's work was key to figuring out the Circle and the rest of their technical secrets. MacGuffin reported that "Mr. Bini," an Italian scientist, told him there was a link to Heaviside's suppressed electromagnetic discoveries. MacGuffin's Chinese associates also had a Nexus Detector or something very much like it. I found MacGuffin's Chinese mysticism and history overwhelming, though. There was simply too much he was taking for granted due to his familiarity with Chinese society. I thought that taking a class or two in Chinese language or culture might help me better understand his work. I planned to take a suitable elective, but other events intervened.

When I got into Tech, the school calculated my "need" based on my parent's income. Other than being ruthlessly murdered last November, Dad had had a great year, financially. The folks in the Financial Aid Office figured he could pay a big slice of my hefty out-of-state tuition. The problem was that my parents' estate was still tied up between probate and the asset forfeiture the Circle's agents had arranged. No amount of reasoning with the Financial Aid Office that I could not pay tuition with assets I did not control seemed to work. Uncle Rob said he'd help. He'd bought me a truck and was paying for the insurance, but even with his business doing well, he couldn't afford the full cost of out-of-state tuition payments either. I'd reconciled myself to saving up money, another year of community college, and transferring into Tech as a junior. Then, Uncle Larry came to my "rescue."

He'd hinted "times were a-changing" at Georgia Tech. The school had begun a "Social Justice Initiative" funded by the Tollivers and Uncle Larry's friends at the Civic Circle. In the first phase, launching this year, the Civic Circle offered a select cadre of students full-ride scholarships to serve as "social justice ambassadors" to the Tech community. Instead of the usual humanities elective, we had to enroll in a special class: "Introduction to Social Justice Studies," and we were supposed to share the ideals of social justice with the broader Tech community.

Uncle Rob didn't like the idea. "You're playing with fire. You barely got away from them last time, and now you're going right back in again, drawing yourself to their attention."

"We're planning on fighting them, Uncle Rob," I pointed out. "I'm going to be drawing their attention anyway, one way or another. Better to do so from the position of trusted insider and protégé of Uncle Larry."

"You don't have to be in the Civic Circle to study the MacGuffin manuscript and all the other clues we've acquired. That's what you need to be doing, not running off trying to play spy."

"It's going to be a lot easier to figure out what's going on from inside the periphery of the Circle than from a distance. Plus, the Circle's planning on re-investigating me in a few years, anyway. I'll be safer with a clean bill of health as a trusted junior member than if they discover I've holed up somewhere and start wondering what I'm up to." Then, I played my trump card. "I need a first rate education to understand those clues and to figure out who's really behind the Civic Circle and what they want. Are you going to pay for it?"

Uncle Rob had no good answer or alternative. I got one of the social justice slots. I figured Uncle Larry pulled some strings on my behalf to get me in.

Amit found out about the opportunity when I submitted my application. He promptly submitted an application of his own. His essay, "Growing Up Colored in Appalachia," spun a couple incidents of bullying into a heroic tale of surviving pervasive white oppression amid the hillbillies and rednecks of Tennessee. "It's what they want to hear," he explained smugly as I rolled my eyes at his gross exaggerations. He was clearly on to something, though, because he won a spot in the program, too.

The upshot of it was instead of a free elective I could use to study Chinese language and culture, I now had to suffer through what looked like a class in political indoctrination. At least I had Amit as an ally. "Look on the bright side," Amit pointed out. "The Civic Circle is trying to subvert Tech. This gives us the perfect opportunity to subvert them." We had a good idea of their political agenda, thanks to Uncle Larry's attempts to recruit me. I'd already planned on stringing Uncle Larry along as best I could to try to get more information, so Amit's plan made good sense. We both agreed to play along and parrot back the social justice ideology. We aimed to use the class as an opportunity to establish credibility, so we could better infiltrate the Civic Circle.

With orientation over, we hid Petrel's final payment, logged on yet again to tell him where to go to collect it, and we returned home to Tennessee. After a long day's drive we pulled into town at dusk. Amit drove through town and then up into the mountains to my home at Uncle Rob's place. The gate was locked, as usual, with a no trespassing sign. I used my key to unlock the gate, Amit drove through, and then I locked the gate back up behind us. We drove under the sign that labeled the property, "Robber Dell." Uncle Rob was proud of the legend that his little cove had once sheltered Unionist guerillas. Then, we drove up the narrow incline to the old abandoned farmhouse, then across the knee-high corn field to Uncle Rob's trailer. He was sitting on the porch in front of his double-wide trailer when we drove up.

Uncle Rob and my father built a hidden complex underneath the new barn last year, but he was adamant that even Amit was not to know anything about his underground refuge. Rob maintained the illusion that he lived in his old, rundown trailer, or in the small apartment he'd built out on one side of the garage. Getting trucks up and down the narrow incline to his property was a real pain, so he'd moved his business to another nearby location.

"Welcome back, boys," Uncle Rob said cheerfully. "I just got in myself, not long ago."

"Did the shop rats keep the operation running well while you were gone?" They were some friends of mine from high school who'd decided to bypass college and go straight to work. Uncle Rob had taken them on to work with him.

"I left Bud Garrety in charge of the boys," he confirmed. "Nice getting to the point where I can be away a few days."

"How was your trip?" I asked.

"There's lots of potential down in Texas. They have even more idled gas fields than we do up here."

The Preserving our Planet's Future Act was passed as a memorial to President Gore, not long after his death. In addition to imposing steep taxes on carbon, it included "safety" regulations specially crafted by lobbyists for the Tolliver Company and other large producers of natural gas. Although it was perfectly safe to drive tanker trucks of natural gas from a railhead to a distributor or from a distributor to a customer, it was terribly dangerous to fill up the tanker truck at a gas field and transport it to market. The result was only large gas fields with railheads could ship natural gas to market, idling the gas fields of many small independent producers and driving up the cost of natural gas.

My father and Uncle Rob had an idea to do something about that. They designed and built a truck-mounted rig that could be hauled up to a gas field. Their rig burned the gas on site to compress and liquefy air. Then, they transported and sold the liquefied air. The gas owner got a return on an otherwise idle field, and my father and Uncle Rob got a cut-rate price on the gas, which let them undercut traditional liquefied air suppliers. Uncle Rob had been "bootlegging" liquid air for over a year now, with the help of the shop rats and a number of free-lance truckers and wildcatters who'd been left idle by the devastation caused by the new regulations. Nothing illegal in it. The regulations that throttled independents from transporting natural gas said nothing about liquefied air. Of course, if the regulators who were in the pockets of the big producers realized how Uncle Rob was exploiting this loophole, they'd probably figure out a way to shut down his lucrative business.

Uncle Rob described his plans to expand production and his ideas for other energy intensive processes that might burn natural gas on site. The ideas seemed to have lots of potential, but in the end, his business was only really viable because of a loophole that could be closed at any minute. The challenge was to grow the business, but to do so in such a way that if it ever got shut down on short notice he wouldn't lose money. Uncle Rob seemed in a good mood, so I figured it was as good a time as any to break our news.

"We discovered something interesting when we were in Atlanta." I explained how we'd anonymously hired Petrel to check on Sweeney's papers, and how we'd confirmed that MacGuffin had hidden the "rod of divination" with his "thorny friend."

I could see the good mood evaporating from Uncle Rob's face. "I thought we agreed that you boys would not be engaging in any tactical operations without my approval."

"We realized the opportunity was there, and since you weren't available to discuss it, we decided to go ahead," I explained.

"The risk was very low," Amit argued. "We used an anonymous researcher we found on Craigslist. He calls himself 'Petrel.'"

"Petrol, as in British gasoline?"

"No, Petrel with an ee-ell as in the sea bird," Amit explained. "We laid out all the risks for him. We told him that the information was important and people might kill for it.

He had a cover story to explain why he was accessing the papers."

"Did you provide him with a false ID?" Rob asked. "Was he using gloves to handle the papers so he wouldn't leave fingerprints?"

"No," I acknowledged weakly. That hadn't occurred to me.

"Suppose they got your Petrel. He talks. Then, what?"

"We paid him in a dead drop, and we used a throwaway encrypted email for communication with him. They couldn't trace him back to us," Amit insisted.

"Let's take a closer look at your assumptions." I could hear the skepticism in Rob's voice. "First off, you may have isolated yourselves from this Petrel, but if there was a trap, you'd have thrown your researcher in it. You know how hypersensitive the Circle is. He'd be dead, and it would have been your fault. If they killed a few people to protect the Heaviside secret, they'd think nothing of killing everyone in the library and your hotel alike if they had reason to believe they might catch someone there who knew the MacGuffin secrets."

Rob was shaking his head. "What was your contingency plan to get Petrel out if they were interrogating him?"

Amit and I could only look guiltily at each other.

"Pete, the reason you got away from the Circle's agents last year was because your father had been working with an ace of a lawyer. Mr. Burke got in the middle of their interrogation of you and kept them from going anywhere with it. What's more, you had Sheriff Gunn pulling strings behind the scene as well. You don't just plan how to avoid trouble. You have to have a plan for what to do when trouble finds you."

"Suppose the Circle was more restrained in their response," he continued. "They'd have concocted another terror fantasy, and they'd have the real FBI, the Atlanta police, and the Georgia Bureau of Investigation looking through every bit of security camera footage, interviewing the desk clerk at your hotel, and anyone else in the area. People saw you, and they'd have a good chance at catching you in their dragnet. You were there most of the morning?"

"That hotel runs my network software," Amit explained. "I got in and flagged that room as having broken AC. I got the key code. There's no record of us at the hotel, and we never even had to talk with the desk clerk."

"Clever. But they do have video surveillance at the hotel, right? If they really looked hard, they'd see you going into and out of the flagged room. Or an overly efficient clerk could have sent maintenance up there to check on it while you were in the room. Did you bring all your food with you or did you go out to get something to eat?"

Amit looked at me and Rob guiltily. "I got us something at Dunkin Donuts, down the block."

"And you flirted with the cashier?"

"It was a guy." Amit was defensive, but we all knew if it had been an attractive girl he'd have tried.

"And they probably had video surveillance at the donut shop as well. This is why I plan any of our ops," Rob said patiently. "Your plan sucked, plain and simple. True stealth is way difficult to achieve. Get in and get out without anyone realizing you were ever there. You have to do everything right. One mistake and you leave yourself vulnerable. You have to be prepared for when things go wrong, also. You confirmed what you already knew – that MacGuffin's death was probably another Circle hit. Maybe this thorny friend bit is something of a lead. None of it was worth the risks you ran.

"I went over Amit's protocol for intercepting the emails of Circle agents when they stay at hotels that use his software. That's solid and secure, and it's giving us good intel."

"We already have so many of the Circle's secrets." I was frustrated at Uncle Rob's enforced inaction. "We should be doing something with them. Releasing them to the world. Or acting on the information. Or seeking out the people who burned down the library. We know the Circle didn't do it. Their enemy may be a potential ally."

"I'm sure Amit could release the MacGuffin text anonymously, and no one could trace it back to us directly. The problem is the Circle would realize that the last hint they had of the MacGuffin text's existence was in the Tolliver Library," Rob explained. "That would bring them right back to taking another hard look at just what happened that night. They accepted that the book burned up in the Tolliver Library fire, and they overlooked the problems and loose ends. They lost a couple of agents and almost exposed their whole operation what with Sheriff Gunn poking around. They didn't come after you, Pete, between Mr. Burke throwing a legal monkey wrench into your interrogation, Sheriff Gunn's protection, and your Uncle Larry having ties to the Civic Circle.

"Last thing we want is for them to reopen that investigation and take a cold hard look at what happened. If they do, they'll figure out there was something screwy and they'll be looking to interrogate you again. That will lead straight back to me and Amit as well. If you boys don't get it through your heads how dangerous this is, we're going to have more victims."

"Victims like Robb LeChevalier?" I asked.

LeChevalier was still a sore spot with me. The man was a brilliant physicist in Colorado who invented a way to make a miniature particle accelerator on a semiconductor chip. His system could be used as an ion propulsion drive or as a cheap and safe way to build a fusion power source. Instead of one big expensive reactor, he'd prototyped an array of miniature reactors on a chip. He was convinced he could take advantage of Moore's Law and existing semiconductor manufacturing technology to make limitless cheap power available to everyone.

It was a work of genius.

It was also, apparently, a threat to the Circle's plans.

LeChevalier's research funding was placed on bureaucratic hold, slowing, and then stopping his work. Amit intercepted orders to a Circle action team dispatched to

Colorado to deal with "the situation." A week later we intercepted the team's reports describing how they set up a plan to ambush LeChevalier and subject him to an intense beam of radiation.

It was like watching a slow motion train wreck, knowing exactly what disaster was about to happen and hoping against hope that something, anything, would happen to change the obvious outcome of the events. At any point over the course of a few weeks, we could have intervened. We could have tried to save him. I begged Uncle Rob to do something. I begged him to let Amit and me warn LeChevalier. We weren't ready to undertake such an operation, Uncle Rob insisted. It could lead right back to us. The risks were too high. He wouldn't believe our warning anyway. What could he do?

Then, it was too late.

A few months later, LeChevalier began suffering from seizures. A few weeks after that, his doctors diagnosed him with a particularly aggressive glioblastoma – a brain tumor – and gave him a few months to live. I was still furious with my uncle at our forced inaction.

"If we don't act sooner rather than later," I continued, "there won't be anything left to save."

"If we act prematurely and expose ourselves," Rob countered, "there won't be anyone left to save them. Besides, you must not have been keeping up with Amit's online monitoring. LeChevalier went to a cancer clinic in Tijuana, Mexico. Apparently, he's found an old-fashioned cancer remedy that appears to be helping – Coley's Fluid. He may yet pull through."

"That's good news," I acknowledged, "but it doesn't change the point. If we continue to do nothing, if we refuse to act at all, before long there won't be anything left to protect, because the Circle will have completely taken over. You need to stop shielding Amit and me and start helping us take them on."

"We are doing something," Rob insisted. "We're getting you ready to figure out the technical secrets of the Circle. As for the Tolliver Library fire," Rob was shaking his head. "You simply cannot go poking around the library fire. This is a very dangerous game we're all playing. The Circle is enough of a threat without risking contact with yet another player. I don't think you fully realize how much of a risk we're all running."

He looked away as if thinking about something. Finally, he continued. "I guess Amit needs to hear this, too, Pete. I stopped by Nashville to see Kira," Rob said. "Your sister still blames you for your folks' death. She knows intellectually that it was the Circle's doing, but she can't shake the feeling that if it weren't for you and your curiosity, none of this would have happened. I considered intervening, trying to patch things up between the two of you. Honestly though? I figure it may well be for the best."

I was shocked. I'd lost my parents, and now he was deliberately driving a wedge between me and my sister, too? "Why would you say such a thing?"

"Because you two are just like Kira. You understand intellectually that the Civic Circle is a threat, but you feel invincible and you act accordingly. You feel that since they didn't get you the last time, you're too smart for them to get you ever. That disconnect between what you know and what you feel is going to get all of us killed. The way I see it, the more distant Kira is from us and from our secrets, and from our battle with the Circle, the safer she'll be. I owe it to your folks to try to see that at least one of their offspring survives."

He looked at me as he let that sink in. I could feel my sister, the last member of my immediate family, slipping away from me, and there was nothing I could do about it.

"Your father was great man, Pete: hardworking, talented, and proud of it. He wasn't about to bow down to the Tollivers, or to the Civic Circle, or to anyone. Your mother made a matched set. She turned her back on the Tollivers to live life on her own terms with the man she loved. Beautiful, brainy, full of spunk. She was a real firecracker," he added wistfully. Then, he continued. "Now they're gone, killed by the Circle. That leaves me here, trying to fill their shoes and look after you. You know how I envied your father? There was a time I thought I'd find the right woman and start a family of my own, just like my big brother. I can't do that now. We're in a fight to the death with the Circle. I can't expose anyone else to the risks involved. I've had to give up my dream.

"I've been shielding you and Amit. Protecting you. Guilty as charged. I don't think you have the least idea what you're up against. You, me, and Amit are going to tangle with the Civic Circle? Try to take down the group that pretty much runs the country and maybe as much of the entire globe as matters? What happened to your parents should serve as a lesson to you. Unless we are all very, very careful and very, very lucky, that's going to happen to us, too.

"We'll have a little help – Burke knows the score, and he'll provide some legal cover. Sheriff Gunn is on our side, so we have some help from our local law enforcement. Your father's friends, men like Dr. Krueger, may not know the score yet, but they'll lend a hand if asked. In the end, though, it all comes down to the three of us: me and you two boys to draw a line, to stand against the darkness, to defy a vast conspiracy with the power to crush us like bugs.

"We escaped in our first encounter. We know a bit about our enemy. We have a few of their secrets and leads to more. We paid full price for that 'victory' with your folks' blood. We simply can't afford another 'victory' like that. The war is just beginning. I don't much like our odds, but we each have a job to do. I have to get you boys ready for the ordeal to come. You need to work hard to prepare yourselves. Together, we have to learn more about our enemy. We have to identify pressure points where our modest capabilities might throw some sand in the Civic Circle's gears. We have to find the Inner Circle – the bastards calling the shots. We have a debt to pay – in blood. I don't know how we're going to be able to accomplish it all, but we are – the three of us – going to try to teach the horse to sing."

"Teach the horse to sing?" That didn't make any sense to me.

"There's a story I read somewhere about a thief captured trying to steal the Emperor's horse," Uncle Rob explained. "The Emperor sentenced him to death. 'Oh great Emperor,' beseeched the thief, 'if you will but spare me, I promise you that before the year is out, I will teach your horse to sing.'

"'Teach a horse to sing?' The Emperor was incredulous. But what did he have to lose? He accepted the thief's proposal.

"Day after day the thief spent his time in the stable teaching the horse. Day after day the horse ignored him. Finally a stable boy said to the thief, 'You fool! Why did you promise to teach the horse to sing? The Emperor will only torture you worse at the end of the year when it becomes obvious you've failed. What have you accomplished with your lies?'

"The thief turned to the stable boy and replied, 'I've accomplished much. I have another year. Who knows what might happen. The Emperor might die. I might die. Or maybe, just maybe, the horse will learn to sing.'

"We, all three of us, are going to have to teach the horse to sing."

CHAPTER 2: RAMBLING TO TECH

Maybe Uncle Rob was right. Maybe our fight against the Civic Circle was a noble but probably doomed crusade. Maybe he was making sense. His fatalistic wisdom just didn't make an impression on me, though. I was in the fight to win. I had no interest in dying heroically for our cause. I was committed to making the Circle and their minions die heroically for their cause. I didn't want to throw sand in their gears. I wanted to wreck their whole miserable machine.

The Civic Circle seemed invincible, but their power rested on their secrets. Uncle Rob was right: we couldn't reveal those secrets without it leading back to us. For now. Eventually though, we should be able to construct a plausible way to reveal the Circle's secrets – a way that didn't lead directly to the Tolliver Library and to us. In the meantime, we had to figure out the rest of what the Circle was hiding and why. Amit and I would need a good education from Georgia Tech to understand and uncover the Circle's secrets. A few weeks later, Amit and I were back on campus in our first class, Introduction to Computer Programming, eager to take our first steps on this new path toward saving the world.

What a disappointment!

Our instructor droned on and on in a monotone explaining "what is a computer." We sat in the back of the class and Amit kept distracting me by rolling his eyes at the ridiculous simplicity of the material. Probably just as well with Amit studying computer science and me trying to make up my mind between physics and electrical engineering we didn't have many classes together. Amit's attention span was even shorter than mine.

My next class, Linear Circuits, had me appreciating the simplicity of programming. I'd taken an electronics class in high school, but it was basic stuff. I knew resistors from capacitors and inductors, Ohm's Law, and the basics of analyzing direct current (DC) and alternating current (AC) circuits. We'd even taken apart a telephone, a television, and an ink jet printer, and worked through some simple digital and analog electronics to reverse engineer how they work. Despite my experience, I was already struggling in the first class. Linear Circuits was AC electronics on steroids.

The teacher, Professor Muldoon, was a no-nonsense type who assumed if he told you something once and you didn't get it, it was all your fault for being stupid. Someone told me he'd been recruited because the School of Electrical Engineering had been looking for professors with more practical experience in industry. I wish they'd recruited someone with expertise in teaching instead! He handed out a syllabus and immediately launched into something called phasors without any other preliminaries. These phasors combined imaginary numbers and polar notation to describe AC circuits. The complex numbers and trigonometry were flying fast and furious. Professor Muldoon would work an example on the board, stare intently at some complicated trigonometric expression, and then calculate the answer – in his head – and write it on the board faster than I could key it in my calculator! Whoever coined the phrase "set phasors to stun" must have taken linear circuits. It was overwhelming and deeply humbling.

The class I was most looking forward to, though, was Electromagnetics. My life turned upside down last year when I found a curious anomaly – a difference between the online scanned version of a book and the physical copy in the Tolliver Library in my hometown. Working with Amit, I learned that the electrical pioneer, Oliver Heaviside, had discovered some unappreciated aspects of electricity and magnetism. Electromagnetic waves normally have a balance of electric and magnetic energy. When two electromagnetic waves coincide or interfere, they upset that balance. The fields add together normally, like 1 + 1 = 2. The energy, though, goes as the square of the field, so if 1 + 1 = 2 for the fields, then 1 + 1 = 4 for the energy. It took some time for me to wrap my head around the geometry of what Heaviside described. In constructive interference, you double the electric field and get four times the electric energy. But that's because when you double the electric field "**E**", you cancel out the magnetic field "**H**," so all the magnetic energy becomes electric energy. The total energy is actually conserved. It works the other way in destructive interference. The geometry looks like this:

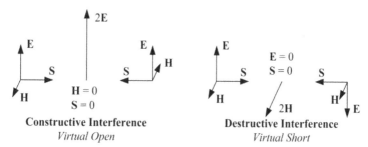

Constructive Interference
Virtual Open

Destructive Interference
Virtual Short

Something called a Poynting vector, "**S**," describes the energy flow. When one field or the other goes to zero, the energy in the waves slows down. In a perfect constructive or destructive interference, the fields become momentarily magnetostatic or electrostatic, respectively. Energy is stationary in static fields. Yet, the waves continue moving through each other at the speed of light. The waves exchange energy with each other. It's like the energy in one wave bounces off the other as the two waves pass through each other. It took some time for me to understand Heaviside's discovery. What still didn't make any sense was why the Circle suppressed his discovery and why FBI agents who weren't really FBI agents showed up to kill anyone who got too close to the secret.

Electromagnetics had a bad reputation among freshmen – "E-Mag, Re-Mag, Three-Mag, Out!" And that was the introductory emag class. I was taking a more difficult intermediate level class, since Tech actually did recognize my community college transfer credit in physics. Still, I was looking forward to the class. I hoped studying electromagnetics would help me better understand Heaviside's discovery and what motivated those who were trying to suppress it.

The subject matter was not the only challenge, however. In fact, the introductory lecture was straightforward. Professor Graf reviewed the electromagnetic spectrum, from audio frequencies, through radio waves, infrared, visible light, ultra-violet, X-rays, and gamma rays. I found it difficult keeping my mind on the subject matter and my eyes off Professor Graf's rather shapely figure. Finally, she was explaining the difference between x-rays and gamma rays.

"There isn't an exact cutoff between x-rays and gamma rays," she explained. "Certain high energy x-rays actually have shorter wavelengths, higher frequencies, and higher energies than certain low energy gamma rays. So, there's actually some overlap. The distinction lies in their origin. X-rays are atomic – they are emitted from strongly accelerated electrons or from transitions of electrons in atomic orbitals. Gamma rays are nuclear. They are emitted from radioactive decay processes within the nucleus of an atom. Those radioactive decays are nuclear phenomena – inside the nucleus – completely independent from atomic phenomena in the electron orbitals outside the nucleus. That's why we make the distinction between x-rays and gamma rays. It's based on the origin, and not, strictly speaking, the energy levels, although gamma rays generally have higher energies than x-rays."

I had studied radioactive decay processes as part of my debate research on radioisotope thermal generation (RTG). I knew what Professor Graf said about radioactive decays being completely independent from atomic influences wasn't exactly true. Maybe she was oversimplifying, but I thought I'd ask her to clarify.

"Professor Graf?" I asked. "Aren't there certain beta decays whose decay rates can depend on temperature or on external fields?"

She looked puzzled. "No, I don't believe so. Nuclear processes are independent of atomic behavior." I didn't press the point.

At the end of the class she announced, "We're looking for an undergraduate research assistant to help us out in our mirror lab. If you're interested, you can check out the job posting for more information."

I had some time before my next class, so I looked at the link Professor Graf had provided. The job involved making mirrors for a gamma ray telescope – using a kiln to shape glass disks into optical shapes, and then depositing aluminum on them in a vacuum chamber. The work sounded interesting. I didn't know vacuum pumps, but I had helped my uncle with his compressed and liquefied air business. Until the legal mess surrounding my parents' estate was resolved, I was entirely dependent on my Social Justice Initiative Scholarship and on my Uncle Rob. It would be nice to have my own money. I updated my resume to emphasize the points that tied into the job posting. Then, I turned to explaining the question I'd asked in class.

Certain kinds of beta decays involve an electron being captured by a proton in the nucleus and transforming into a neutron. These "electron–capture" beta decays can be influenced by strong electric fields or possibly even by temperature – a rare case where phenomena on the atomic level can influence nuclear behavior. I wrote a cover letter summarizing my qualifications for the job and I "Omnied" for some links to information on the temperature dependence of beta decays. I sent my email to Professor Graf, and went to the Student Center for lunch.

Funny how new words enter the English language. The government created Omnitia when they nationalized the Internet in the interest of public safety after the 9/11 attack. They formed Omnitia by consolidating Yahoo, Altavista, and a number of obscure start-ups, including one with a name like Googol. Then, they logged and correlated all searches looking for patterns that might suggest a future terror attack. In addition, they looked for anyone who searched on sensitive or restricted terms. To fire up your Omnibrowser and "Omni" for data was fast becoming a synonym for online search. Only a few online rebels insisted on using third-party search engines like Duck Duck Go that would protect your online privacy. What's more, a concern for online privacy threw a red flag that you were up to no good and invited further scrutiny. Those were exactly the online surveillance tools that had helped finger my research with Amit, which led to the deaths of my parents and too many others.

Amit and I had worked out our online protocol with Uncle Rob. Most of the time we were compliant young citizens who dutifully used the Omnitia infrastructure. When we needed to search for potentially sensitive data, we'd use a separate laptop that we never connected to our official online presence. Uncle Rob had even sourced us some surplus military laptops – ones without all the surveillance hooks the computer companies put in standard commercial gear for the public. We'd considered using an open-source Linux distribution, but Rob vetoed that. "Too easy for someone to slip in malware in one of the drivers." Instead, he had us using the military distribution of Windows XP. "DoD would never be stupid enough to allow the military version to have all the backdoors they put in the commercial distribution," he explained.

We'd access a public Wi-Fi node from a distance using directional antennas. Then, we'd use Amit's VPN code to route our encrypted query through one of the hotels using his network software. Amit would either borrow a recently checked out guest's profile or make up a reasonable but phony profile. From there, we'd use TOR to bounce our queries around the Internet in a way that was supposed to be untraceable. It was complicated to set up, and the resulting links were slow, but it let us make secure online searches.

Amit was my debate partner all through high school, and frankly, he was better at it than me. I was an excellent researcher. I could string together facts and evidence to prove, or at least support, almost any given point in an argument. I was a master of dialectic. Amit, on the other hand, was a master of rhetoric. He could speak with a passion and a conviction that made you want to believe him, and then the next round he'd be speaking with the same passion and conviction on the exactly opposite side of the debate question. We made a good team, but it was Amit's skill that usually carried the day for us. I had trouble turning my argumentation on a dime like Amit could. I was never quite sure whether it was just a skill I lacked, or whether it was something Amit lacked: a certain kind of reticence or consistency. Nothing in my long friendship with Amit prepared me for our first social justice class, however.

"Welcome to Introduction to Social Justice Studies," the professor said with a warm smile. "Social justice values our diversity and promotes a fair and equitable society. All people share a common humanity and deserve respect for their rights, equitable treatment, and a common share of community resources. Social justice commands us to comfort the afflicted, and afflict the comfortable."

Professor Gomulka introduced himself. "...but, this class isn't about me," he quickly added. "It's all about you. Let's introduce ourselves to each other. Tell us all your name and something about yourself – something relevant to your personal quest for social justice." He pointed to a girl in the front row.

"I'm Madison Grant," she introduced herself.

"Welcome to social justice, Madison," Professor Gomulka said warmly. "What challenges have you had to overcome to be with us here at Tech?"

"I grew up with a single mom, and I saw how hard she had to work to take care of me," Madison replied. "Many of her male coworkers had stay-at-home wives which gave them an unfair advantage in the workplace. I had to become a strong, independent woman, myself, to help my mother out," she said proudly. "I made extra money as a yoga instructor to support us."

"We live in a social system designed and built by men," Professor Gomulka confirmed. "Employers don't like to accommodate women who need time off to take care of their families. Your and your mother's heroic struggles highlight how all of us need to work to de-center masculinity and other elements of the dominant patriarchal perspective, so we can foster an environment that promotes equality through diversity and inclusion."

I noticed a common pattern as each student introduced him or herself and explained their family background. My classmates all came from modest circumstances and I doubt many would have been able to afford the tuition if they weren't in the program. Professor Gomulka encouraged each to speak of how they'd been oppressed by society, and had warm words of support for their heroic victimhood. Finally, the professor got around to Amit.

"Amit Patel," Amit said by way of introduction. "I grew up in a sea of white faces in Appalachia, a symbol to my classmates of 'the other' that threatened their nation and community after 9/11."

I recognized the phrase from his scholarship essay, but Professor Gomulka interrupted him before he could continue his colorful prose. "It's too easy to sacrifice our humanity, to give way to fear of the other," the professor explained. "The powerful have less empathy. We ignore how the domination of American economic and cultural imperialism offend the sensibilities of Muslims and others around the world. Then, we are surprised when the peoples we have oppressed strike back. Terror inspires fear, and fear inspires more terror.

Instead, we must recognize oppression and correct historic injustices."

I was still trying to figure out what his impressive sounding words actually meant in practice when he turned to me. "I'm Peter Burdell," I introduced myself. "My parents both died in a car accident, so I'm an orphan." Explaining the probable role of the Civic Circle in that "accident" would be counter-productive. "Their estate is still tied up in probate, so I appreciate how the social justice initiative is paying for my education."

"Anyone can fall into the vicious cycle of poverty and injustice," Professor Gomulka offered sympathetically. "That's why we have to ensure that even the least advantaged have access to goods and wealth adequate for free and equal people to live a complete and fulfilling life." I felt vaguely uncomfortable – as if Professor Gomulka were patting me on the head like a dog while slipping a collar around my neck. A brash voice next to me interrupted my introspection.

"My name is Marcus Brown," a black student sitting next to me declared proudly. "And where I come from doesn't matter near as much as where I'm going."

"Marcus, self-respect has a social basis," Professor Gomulka began with just the slightest hint of condescension. "Self-respect relies on basic institutions to allow an individual to advance their ends in harmony with society at large. Social justice is about the activism required to clear your way and make your self-respect possible."

"That's fine," Marcus acknowledged, though the skepticism in his voice was loud and clear, "but I'm not going to be waiting on some activist to tell me what to do and what to think. And my self-respect doesn't rely on anybody else's approval. I think..."

"For a colored man," Amit interrupted, "you're showing an amazing lack of gratitude for all your allies who've fought long and hard for social justice."

Amit's presumption shocked me until I realized what he was up to. He'd found the perfect opening to worm his way into Professor Gomulka's confidence. Without the benefit of my insight as to Amit's motives, the rest of the class, Marcus included, stared dumbfounded at his effrontery.

Finally, Marcus broke the silence. "Who the hell are you to talk to me about 'colored' people?" he asked Amit, indignantly.

"Social justice activists have been campaigning for your rights and mine for decades," Amit countered. "Why, fifty years ago, folks like you and me would have had to use different water fountains and restrooms, if we were allowed on campus at all. We activists are the only reason you and I have any civil rights. We did all this for you, and yet there you are, flaunting your self-respect, attacking those who made it possible, and supporting the racists who would love nothing better than to burn a cross on our campus and string you and me up on the nearest tree."

Marcus was furious, but Professor Gomulka cut him off before matters got out of hand.

"This is a safe space where we need to support each other," he said, patronizingly. "There's nothing wrong with being proud of who you are, Marcus. However, Amit is right that we're all indebted to the activists who've made our civil rights possible. There are reactionaries even here at Georgia Tech who see you and Amit as tokens that erase their guilt and complicity in oppression. You need to be careful in your choice of words not to reinforce that reactionary tokenism. If you don't want to acknowledge your allies, Marcus, well that's fine. We don't need your acknowledgement, but at least you really should abstain from undercutting our efforts on your behalf."

I could tell Marcus was no less angry, but he had his temper under control.

"I'm Ryan Morgan," the student beside Marcus said in a controlled voice that didn't do a good job hiding his contempt for Professor Gomulka. "I'm from Macon." Ryan didn't seem inclined to share a tale of victimhood. Good for him.

"You haven't experienced oppression firsthand?" Professor Gomulka asked. "It's more difficult to understand the fundamental dynamic between oppressed and oppressor without having experienced it first hand, but if you approach the class with an open mind and an open heart, I'm sure you can learn from your classmates."

"You all have great potential to become true ambassadors for social justice," Professor Gomulka beamed at the class as he handed out the syllabus. "Pay attention to the assigned readings, and the due dates. Next Monday, I will expect an essay from each one of you about the oppressions you've faced, and you'll be reading your essay aloud to the class, so we can share our experiences with each other."

Wonderful. The "oppressions" experienced by a class full of students privileged enough to have a free ride at Georgia Tech seemed a thin gruel from which to demonstrate an omnipresent environment of social injustice, but to hear Professor Gomulka talk, oppression was pervasive. Further, unless you identified how you were being oppressed, you were likely an evil oppressor, yourself.

He dismissed the class.

It was getting late as Amit and I walked out of the building. "I'm heading to west campus to look up some of the girls we met at orientation. Want to come?" he asked me.

I was troubled by the social-justice class experience, and my heart wasn't in it.

"Don't wait up for me," Amit said smugly. "I might get lucky!" He headed off.

It may have been just as well I had some time to myself. Amit seemed to brush off his attack on Marcus, but I was in turmoil. I hadn't thought through the consequences of my actions. I hadn't realized that trying to fit in with the Civic Circle and their social justice crowd might mean hurting other people: good people like Marcus or Ryan. Not that they couldn't take care of themselves against the likes of Amit and Gomulka, but I was beginning to see how the class was set up. Take a bunch of students whose college educations depended on their continuing participation in the social justice course work. Grade them according to how well they parrot back the dogma. Make them read their essays aloud to their fellow students for mutual reinforcement. To act like one of the social justice crowd was to become one. No matter how strong willed and independent you might be going into the process, four years of indoctrination would take a toll. And this was just a pilot program. If I understood the social justice initiative correctly, within a few years, every student at Georgia Tech would be required to take social justice in order to graduate.

I thought it over as I ate dinner by myself.

"Comfort the afflicted and afflict the comfortable," Professor Gomulka had said. That was right, only not in the way he intended. We needed a way to comfort the afflicted – to support and encourage students like Marcus and Ryan, to help them defend themselves against the Civic Circle's social justice indoctrination. We couldn't very well tell them about the Civic Circle's plan, though, without risking it getting back to the Civic Circle. Marcus in particular certainly wasn't going to want to pay any attention to anything Amit might have to say. I'd have to think on it.

I was equally determined to come up with a way to tackle the other half of Gomulka's motto, but I had even less idea how Amit and I might be able to "afflict the comfortable" Civic Circle and derail their plans to indoctrinate students at Tech.

I cleared my head and tackled the more tractable problems assigned by Professor Graf. I'd made it most of the way through my emag homework by the time Amit returned.

"I came this close," he said, holding his fingers a fraction of an inch apart. "But no, she didn't feel comfortable making out in front of her roommate, and she didn't want to come over to my place when she found out I had a roommate. Do you realize this whole system of student housing is designed to repress our sexuality by insuring everyone has to worry about the logistics of getting their roommate out of the way so they can have a little privacy? We have to find off campus housing where we can have our own private rooms."

"It's the buddy system, like in Boy Scouts," I explained. "Make sure you have a friend to look out for you so you don't get into trouble, and if you do, help get you out of it."

"Well, I didn't sign up to be a Boy Scout," Amit insisted, indignantly.

"There must be some dark corners on campus where you can take a girl and not be discovered," I pointed out. "Weren't you fond of libraries?"

"Yeah," he said with a smirk, probably recalling his adventures in the Tolliver Library with his girlfriend, Emma, "but I don't know the library here well enough yet."

Amit was tired and didn't want to talk social justice, so we agreed to discuss what to do about Professor Gomulka the following day.

Amit was off early to one of his classes. I had chemistry class in the morning, and a lab in the afternoon. That first chemistry class made an impression on me. "Look at the student to the left of you, and look at the student to the right," the professor said. "Of the three of you, one will not be here at the end of the year, and the other will not make it to graduation." I looked at my neighbors and resolved that I was going to be the one of us to graduate!

I'd studied calculus at the local community college and Georgia Tech accepted the transfer credits. The reward for my hard work was to be placed in differential equations with a bunch of sophomores and juniors. By the end of class, I regretted my initiative. "Diffy-q" was complicated, and the professor spoke with a thick accent that was hard to decipher. I saw Ryan was in my class, so I went over to speak with him.

"Hi Ryan," I held out my hand, "Pete from social justice."

He shook my hand, but didn't seem terribly thrilled to see me.

"I see you must have tested out of calculus, too."

"Yes, I did," he said.

"I was wondering if you'd like to exchange email addresses and phone numbers so we could compare notes or discuss the homework," I offered.

"I don't anticipate I'll be needing your help," he said levelly. "Good bye."

I wasn't sure what pissed him off, but clearly I was going to have to find another study partner.

After lunch, I had my chemistry lab. Mom was a chemist, and she always told me that the secret to success in chemistry was to be meticulous when you wash your glassware and then be even more meticulous when you wash it a second time. I missed Mom, but the press of activity getting checked into lab and inventorying the supplies soon took my mind off her.

I met Amit for dinner. He still didn't want to talk about Gomulka.

"You can't make saving the world your full-time obsession," he counselled me. "There's more to life. Like girls. I'll make you a deal. Come to the mixer tonight and be my wingman. You need to relax and unwind. We'll hit on girls for a while and then afterward we'll figure out what to do about Marcus and Gomulka."

"We need to go over the programming homework," I reminded him.

"Pete," Amit said, "I didn't rush a fraternity because we need to stay together and have more privacy as we work together to take down the Circle. That's seriously impacting my social life. The least you can do is help me out once in a while. Let's review the homework. Shouldn't take long. Then, off to the mixer for an hour. We can discuss social justice, after. Fair enough?"

I agreed. After dinner we went over the programming homework. It was a simple bubble-sort algorithm, and we cranked it out in about fifteen minutes. I started changing into something a little more formal for the mixer.

"No," Amit advised. "Makes you look too desperate. Go in what you have on."

I was still uncomfortable just going up and talking to girls. "I was, too," Amit confided in me. "I figure by the time you've done a hundred or so approaches, you get used to it. And tonight's low pressure. We're not going to actually try to pick anyone up. Just maybe get some numbers to try later."

We showed up fashionably late and began working our way around the room, introducing ourselves to guys and girls alike. Amit worked the room like a master, outgoing, enthusiastic, everyone's new best friend, but only taking a minute to talk before moving on to the next group. We watched a guy approach a gang of eight girls chatting together in the corner. He lasted half a minute before walking off with a dejected look on his face. "Tough nut to crack," Amit said. "Let's get warmed up and come back later. How about them?" he said, gesturing toward a pair of attractive girls chatting. "You've seen me do it. Your turn." I took a deep breath and approached the girls.

"Hey girls," I said full of confidence. "I'm Pete, and this is my friend Amit."

They turned out to be Jennifer and her friend Ashley.

"What brings you to Tech, Jennifer?" I asked the more attractive of the two who stood almost as tall as me in her spike heels.

"I'm studying architecture," she answered.

"It's going to be hard finding steel-toed boots with heels like those," I noted.

"It's mostly indoor work," she explained with a smile, "but I like the idea of getting to go out to a construction site."

"I used to work as an electrician's helper," I offered. "You'll have to be careful around job sites – some of those construction workers can be real wolves."

"I can handle myself," she said, confidently. "So what are you studying?"

"Electrical engineering," I answered.

"Oh, a real Brainiac," she teased me.

"I know enough not to let studying get in the way of my social life," I offered nonchalantly. "Speaking of which, what's your number? Maybe we could go out Friday?"

"I don't know," she said. "Ashley and I have plans."

"We can't go out Friday anyway," Amit lied. "We're going out with those cute psychology majors from the other dorm, remember?"

"Oh, yeah," I said. "Well, give me your number anyway, and maybe we can find some other time."

I hid my surprise at my success while Jennifer gave me her number.

While I was busy with Jennifer, Ashley said, "I know you," to Amit. "You're that guy at orientation who asked about make-out places on campus."

"Guilty as charged," he said. "If you give me your number, maybe we can go looking for one sometime."

"I don't know about that," she looked reluctant.

"Hey, maybe we could double with Pete and Jennifer," he offered. "You'll need an excuse to tag along and help protect her from this wolf here."

He got her number, too.

"See you around," I offered as Amit and I moved on.

"So how was that?" I asked him.

"Not bad," he acknowledged. "The bit about wolves was nicely ambiguous. You might have been saying you were one or that she was in danger from one, or both," he added knowingly as we ambled off. "What matters is we got their numbers and left a good impression."

We were so distracted by our after-action review that we didn't notice we were nearing Ryan standing with Marcus. "You better take this one," he suggested quietly before continuing on.

"Hi guys," I said. "You're both in this dorm?"

They looked impassively at me. Finally, Marcus spoke. "You're friends with that Amit?"

"He's my roommate," I said neutrally. There was another long pause.

"I don't have anything to say to him or to you," Marcus said, turning his back to me.

"See you around," I said.

I saw Amit already talking with a bunch of girls. "Hey girls," Amit exclaimed as I approached, "meet Pete. Don't let that Boy Scout demeanor fool you, though. They kicked him out for his bad behavior."

I wasn't happy Amit had shared that incident. I certainly wasn't proud of it. I was on my path to Eagle Scout when some campout pranking got out of hand. Another troop sabotaged our sleeping gear, so we cut their tent strings. Only they escaped undetected while I had the misfortune to be caught in the act by one of the scout leaders. Trustworthy? Helpful? Kind? Not exactly. They take the Scout Law seriously. That incident was the end of my career in scouting. I introduced myself to the girls.

"So what did you do to get kicked out of scouting?" one of the girls asked me.

"An unfortunate incident involving the scoutmaster's daughter," Amit jumped in before I could tell the truth. "Some girls just get carried away and start moaning too loudly at the most inopportune times."

This was going a bit too far for my taste. "All lies," I told the girls.

"Just goes to show the importance of a good gag," Amit said deadpan. "You should see the knots he can tie. Taught me everything I know. We'll be seeing you around," he added.

I followed his cue to escape the embarrassment and inevitable questions.

"What do you think you're doing spreading stories like that?" I asked him.

"Just helping you establish your bad-boy credentials," Amit explained. "You'll thank me later."

"I don't want to have to lie to a girl to date her," I explained.

"It's not a lie," Amit countered, "if no one's expecting the truth anyway. Like a politician saying what the voters want to hear, even though everybody knows he won't really follow through on it. How many times has a girl told you she's 'busy' when what she really means is she has no interest in you? Girls lie to us all the time. If you want to be successful with them, you have to lie preemptively; throw them off balance."

"It didn't work back there with that last group," I pointed out.

"You were fighting me too hard for me to risk going for their numbers. You need to just go with the flow. Let's finish up here. That last group will be tricky," he said, looking at the eight girls we'd bypassed earlier, hanging out in the corner of the room. "They've rebuffed a couple of guys who've approached them already, so their defenses are up. That really hot brunette with the glasses looks to be the ringleader."

My heart wasn't in it, and I just wanted this to be over, so I took the path of least resistance. "She's really smoking," I acknowledged. "You think you can interest her?"

"Not directly," Amit said ruefully. "But I have an idea for a quick hit and run." I saw one of the girls look our way. "Perfect," Amit said, "she's looking at us. Maintain eye contact, and follow my lead." We approached the group.

"Hey, Lisa!" Amit said exuberantly, boldly interrupting whatever conversation was underway, thrusting himself in the middle of the group with his back to the hot brunette. "Good to see you here!"

"I'm not Lisa," the girl looked confused. "My name is Michelle."

"Oh, I'm sorry," said Amit. "My name's Amit, but you do look an awful lot like Lisa."

"I'm Pete," I said, making a show of carefully looking her over. "Have to admit, there's a strong resemblance," I said to Amit.

"Well, anyway," Amit continued. "You're looking really great tonight in that dress, Michelle. I'm sure we'll be seeing you around. Good night, ladies." He pivoted neatly as he left the group to leave the group without ever facing or acknowledging the existence of the hot brunette.

"Help me out here," I said once we were out of earshot. "You ignored the brunette which is going to annoy her. Won't that make her more likely to shoot down any attempts to hook up with one of her clique?"

"Maybe," Amit acknowledged, "but it's better to be remembered than forgotten. She'll be wondering about us and why we ignored her in favor of her less attractive friend. She's the most beautiful girl in that clique, and she and all her friends know it. Besides Lisa's probably been in her shadow so long; it's nice to give her a moment in the spotlight. Aren't you Boy Scouts supposed to do a good turn daily?"

"Yes," I agreed. "But it's Michelle."

"Whatever," Amit said indifferently. "Michelle isn't bad looking, and she'll be favorably inclined in the future. That was probably the most exciting thing to happen to any of them all night, so they'll all remember us in the future."

We got up to our room and back to work.

I explained my concern that by playing along, we were helping Gomulka attack Marcus, Ryan, and the rest of the students in the class. "We're no better than the Civic Circle, if we help Gomulka indoctrinate our classmates."

"This is a war," Amit said. "There may be casualties. I don't see how we can infiltrate the Civic Circle without emulating what they do. And that means we have to be willing to bully and intimidate opponents of the Civic Circle using the same social justice ideology."

"I don't like it," I insisted.

"That's the way it is," Amit countered. "That's the way it has to be. We can't behave like Boy Scouts and expect to beat the Civic Circle."

We stared at each other in silence as he tried to intimidate me into submission. I returned the favor back at him. We were both working from the exact same playbook Uncle Rob had taught us. Finally, I smiled at the ridiculousness of playing dominance games with each other.

"Look Amit," I explained. "Just help me figure out a way to communicate anonymously with Marcus and Ryan. We ought to be supporting opponents of the Civic Circle not helping the Circle tear them down. Part of beating the Circle is providing aid and comfort to their enemies. We can explain to Marcus and Ryan a bit about what's going on so they can know how to play along without getting steamrollered."

Amit looked thoughtful. "I suppose we could send an email to them anonymously," he offered. "But anything we say could be read by the sysadmin."

"The who?" I asked.

"The sysadmin. System administrator," Amit explained. "The email may come from an untraceable source, but once it's in their gatech.edu inbox, the Tech sysadmin will be able to read it. We wouldn't be able to share anything of substance."

"What's that encrypted email service you set up for Uncle Rob and Mr. Burke?" I asked.

"Yeah, Lavabit," Amit replied. "Or we could help them get up to speed with an account to send and receive email. First, though we'd have to get them to sign in and make sure they understood how to use it."

"We could slide a note under Marcus's door. And Ryan's. And anyone else we want to approach," I suggested.

"That could work," Amit agreed, warming to the plan. "We might not be able to persuade them to go to all the hassle of signing up for encrypted email, though."

"It's worth a shot," I argued. "If they do sign up, we can help them. If they don't, well at least we tried."

"OK," Amit agreed. "Let's give it a try."

I wrote the cover letter on my secure laptop, explaining that we had information they needed to know. Conventional email was under continuous surveillance, so if they wanted to learn what we had to tell them, they'd have to follow the instructions Amit appended.

Amit connected his laptop to our printer. "Wait a sec," Amit said thoughtfully. "We can't use our printer."

"Oh, that's right," I replied, recalling how one of the pieces of evidence that tripped us up last year was microdots printed by a color laser printer to identify the serial number of the printer. They're included to help law enforcement trace people who try to counterfeit money on color printers. The Civic Circle's agents used the technology to trace our printouts of forbidden and suppressed technical books back to my dad's printer. "Do black-and-white laser printers do the microdot thing?" I asked.

"I don't know," Amit said. "Why take the chance? In any event, we're using this printer for homework so there will be lots of copies of our work printed on it, publically available. Any common idiosyncrasy, like a couple streaks from the toner cartridge in the same place, and these letters you want to print could be linked to us."

Amit copied the instructions to the flash drive we'd dedicated for exchanging files between our secure laptops. I copied his instructions to my secure laptop. "I'll burn your instructions and my cover letter to a CD and figure out where to print it later," I said.

"Who are you going to say the letter is from?" Amit asked.

I thought about that a moment. "How about George P. Burdell?"

Amit grinned. "Perfect!"

"See?" I pointed out, "You don't have to be a Boy Scout to do a good turn."

CHAPTER 3: A SERENDIPITOUS DISCOVERY

I found a place in the library where I could print out the letters for Marcus and Ryan. The computer there required me to log in using my password, which would spoil my anonymity. Fortunately, they left access to the power switch. I carefully donned rubber gloves before handling the computer. I turned it off, and as it was powering up, I pressed function keys, esc, delete, to try to interrupt the boot sequence and the BIOS settings screen popped up. I reset the BIOS to boot from the USB drive, entered my Linux boot flash drive, and let the computer finish booting up. Then, I loaded my CD, printed the letters, and closed them in envelopes – without licking them shut and leaving my DNA. Uncle Rob had drilled into me and Amit the importance of not leaving fingerprints or DNA evidence behind. I sealed the envelopes in a plastic bag, so they wouldn't pick up any contamination from me, power cycled the computer, and confirmed it booted up as normal. I left the BIOS settings alone in case I was ever in a hurry and wanted to use that particular computer again. Early the next morning, I slid the envelope under Ryan's and Marcus' respective doors.

Almost immediately, Amit began blowing off our Introduction to Computer Programming class, so he could sleep in later. I collected assignments and took notes. With Amit helping me on the programming assignments though, it was an easy class. I returned the favor by helping him out with his calculus and physics homework.

If there were such a thing as academic whiplash, I'd be suffering from an acute case of it by leaving programming and following up with linear circuits. The linear circuits material wasn't conceptually that difficult. I already knew basic AC electronics quite well. The problem was the tedious complexity of the homework. The problems all involved phasors – complex AC voltages and currents that could be expressed as a magnitude and phase angle, or as a real and imaginary part. The most difficult aspect of each problem was the vector analysis – using sines, cosines, and tangents to work out the missing components of the right triangles formed by the physical quantities.

My first inclination was to find a study partner to work with – someone to compare answers with and discuss the trickier problems. Unfortunately, the only student I knew in class was Ryan, and, of course, he wasn't talking with me.

Professor Muldoon was a ruthless and unforgiving instructor. One student asked if the homework deadline could be pushed back to accommodate the imminent football game. "Electrical engineering is not for everyone. Perhaps a transfer to the School of Management would better accommodate your active social life?"

Another student was confused about the professor's "solution" to a homework problem. "How did you go from the second line of that solution to the third?"

Muldoon showed how the third step followed, using an obscure trigonometric identity. Then he added, "Basic trigonometry is a prerequisite to the prerequisite for this class. Perhaps you were misinformed by the registrar?"

He seemed to take a particular dislike to me, though. When I dared ask a question, he answered me. Then he added, "Not nearly as easy as 'Introduction to Social Justice Studies,' now is it?" I had no idea how he knew I was in that class.

The challenge in emag continued to be keeping my mind on the subject matter and away from inappropriate daydreaming about what was under Professor Graf's blouse. She was very proper and very formal, almost too formal, as if deliberately trying to distance herself from the kind of attention she inspired in me, and probably others. Unfortunately, from my perspective, it just gave her an even more powerful sexy librarian vibe.

She stopped me as I was leaving class that first week.

"Peter," she said. I could get used to her saying my name like that, but I had to focus on what she was saying. "I looked at the links you sent on the temperature dependence of beta decays. Very interesting. I also passed your resume on to Dr. Chen. He's in charge of our research group, and he'd like to speak with you." I spent a few minutes discussing the research with her, and then we set up a time for the interview.

That Friday, I met with Dr. Chen. He was not what I expected – the polar opposite of Professor Graf. Where Professor Graf was formal, distant, and reserved, Professor Chen was more brash and outgoing. He wore a loud Hawaiian-style print shirt. As I was shaking his hand I saw a curious tattoo on his upper arm – a Yin-Yang symbol with a line through it. I didn't get a good look at it, but it sure resembled the diagram I'd seen in MacGuffin's book. I repressed my curiosity and focused on what he was saying.

"Peter, what's the difference between alpha, beta, and gamma radiation?" he asked. I answered dutifully. He continued questioning me on Cerenkov radiation.

"Cerenkov radiation happens when something travels faster than the speed of light in a medium, like in the water where nuclear fuel is stored." I'd actually seen it on a field trip to Oak Ridge National Lab. "It makes a beautiful blue glow, and it was actually first predicted by Oliver Heaviside," I added.

Dr. Chen raised an eyebrow. "Not many people know that. You're familiar with Heaviside?"

"A bit," I acknowledged. Then, he questioned me on some of the research I'd shared with Professor Graf, making sure I understood it. I became frustrated by all the grilling. "You know all this already," I pointed out. "And you know that I know it," I said looking to Professor Graf, "because I discussed all this with Professor Graf."

"Yes, Professor Graf reports you are quite knowledgeable for an undergrad," Dr. Chen confirmed. "However," he added with a smile, "a good scientist always prefers direct evidence to hearsay."

Dr. Chen explained his research involved studying high-energy cosmic rays. As they ripped through the upper atmosphere, they generated Cerenkov radiation: cascades of high energy light. "We use nature as our particle accelerator," Dr. Chen explained. "We build ultraviolet telescopes that capture and characterize the flashes to learn about the original cosmic ray that triggered the flash." He turned to Professor Graf. "Would you please show our guest the mirror lab?"

Professor Graf escorted me to the mirror lab around the corner from Dr. Chen's office. A vacuum chamber dominated the center of the lab. At one end there was a large sink and a pallet of circular disks – glass? At the other end of the room, there was a row of bookshelves, partitioning a small office area. There were two desks with a narrow gap to allow access to an old chalkboard. At one desk, there was what looked like a fishing tackle box, only it was purple with silvery sparkles. A cosmetics case? I noted it had a couple of Hello Kitty stickers. A girl looked up at us.

"Sarah," Professor Graf began, "I'd like to introduce you to Peter Burdell. He's interviewing to be our new student research assistant. Do you have time to show him what we do here?"

"Sure, Professor," she said, putting what looked like homework aside. "First stop on the tour is your desk." Sarah pointed at the other well-worn wooden desk. I'd worked for my father as an electrician's apprentice and for my uncle in his liquid air business, but this was the first time I might have an actual desk on a job. Sarah guided me around the lab. The central focus of the mirror lab was a large vacuum chamber. Professor Graf grabbed the control of an overhead hoist and lifted the four-foot diameter, five-foot-high bell a couple feet off the base of the vacuum chamber. Sarah had twisted a hundred or more small pieces of aluminum wire on heating coils on the base below the frame where a glass blank would fit in the chamber. Once the chamber was evacuated, the heating coils vaporized the aluminum, depositing a film of aluminum on the glass to make the mirror. I discussed with Professor Graf and Sarah the differences between the vacuum pump arrangement and the gas liquification equipment I'd worked on for my uncle. They seemed satisfied with my answers to their questions. The work didn't look difficult, and a lot of it was just babysitting the vacuum chamber while the pumps evacuated it over the course of a couple hours.

"Please show him the kiln, bring him back to Professor Chen, and then see me when you're done, alright?" Professor Graf left us and Sarah took me to the basement. She showed me the furnace which melted disks of glass. Finally, I was beginning to understand the mirror-making process. The kiln heated up one of the circular glass plates I saw up in the lab. The glass disk slumped into a stainless steel bowl machined to have the precise parabolic shape required. Each telescope they were building was an array of over a hundred of these mirrors. The disk in the kiln was still cooling. "We'll be coating that one in the chamber on Monday," she explained. Sarah patiently answered my questions, explaining the process and how it worked.

"So, what do you think?" Dr. Chen asked when Sarah left me with him.

"Looks like a great job." I asked a few more questions about the hours and the work. The research team had a weekly meeting but otherwise I could put in my ten hours a week whenever convenient, and at least some of the time I could just work on my homework. A few critical operations, like loading the vacuum chamber took two people. I'd have to coordinate my work schedule with Sarah. I saw Professor Graf enter the office and give a subtle nod. I must have passed muster.

"You're hired," Dr. Chen said, welcoming me to his group. Professor Graf walked me to the physics office where I completed the paperwork.

I actually started hanging out in the mirror lab even when I wasn't officially on the clock. Sarah was a real tinkerer. Her cosmetics case was actually a tool box, and she was working on a gamma ray sensor and payload for a balloon launch sometime in the spring. The project was part of her senior thesis. Sarah and her physics student friends often did their homework there. There was a group of them in the climbing club – they'd head out weekends to go rock climbing and rappelling. They invited me to join them, but I'd had my fill of that kind of thing in Boy Scouts. They tended to be generous with their time when I had a question about my diffy-q or emag homework, particularly when I'd volunteer to run over to the Student Center to grab dinner or to the Varsity to pick up some frosted oranges. Sometimes I'd invite Jack, James, and Josh, three of the guys from my emag class for a homework or study session.

Unfortunately, none of the physics majors were familiar with linear circuits. I'd struck out with Ryan, and tried to make friends with other linear circuits students, but none of the older students seemed much interested in collaborating with me. One evening, a couple weeks after I started working for Professor Graf, I was babysitting the vacuum chamber and working on my linear circuits homework when I spotted the pattern.

Every single triangle that came up in one of Professor Muldoon's problems was either a common case, like a 30-60-90 or a 45-45-90 right triangle, or a Pythagorean triple with sides like 3-4-5, 5-12-13, or 7-24-25. Oh, he camouflaged it very cleverly. In one problem it would be a 6-8-10 right triangle, in another it would be 12-16-20, in yet another it would be 15-20-25. Nevertheless, they were all just 3-4-5 triangles in disguise, scaled by some factor, with the exact same angles and trig relations. Every one of the twenty homework problems was really just a simple variation of a half dozen distinct trig problems.

Come to think of it, that was exactly how Professor Muldoon solved his example problems in class. That old faker! He wasn't solving arbitrary sines, cosines, and tangents in his head while we all raced to keep up with calculators. He had the answers memorized. He was writing down solutions he knew in advance because all his questions were drawn from a small pool of possible triangles. Two could play at that game. I made myself a study sheet and resolved to memorize the relations for all the basic triangles Professor Muldoon used. I realized that half the challenge in linear circuits was getting the problem set up and the other half was correctly solving the trigonometry of the vectors without screwing it up. By discovering Professor Muldoon's pattern, linear circuits became about half as difficult.

Once I began working for Professor Chen on his mirror project, I began learning more about Professor Chen's related research. In between teaching me how to run the vacuum chamber and make mirrors, Sarah was analyzing the data from a gamma ray observatory satellite for Professor Chen. Many other researchers had booked time slots in advance. She'd download Professor Chen's data, look through it, highlight any interesting signals, and then store it in our local archive for Professor Chen or Professor Graf to analyze later. I looked over her shoulder, watching what she was doing.

"Why don't you download this data, too?" I asked, pointing to some file names.

"That's not our data," Sarah explained. "See?" She selected the file I pointed at. A "permission denied" error popped up. "That lock icon means we don't have access. Other researchers use the satellite, too. Each research team gets exclusive access to their own data."

"What about those files?" I asked, pointing to some she'd skipped that didn't have the lock icon. "Why can't we access those?"

"We can access them," Sarah explained, "but it's garbage data. That's just the earth getting in the way of the target the observatory is imaging."

"Why don't they point the satellite in a different direction?" I asked. "I thought observing time was expensive."

"It is," Sarah confirmed, "but propellant is even more expensive. The gamma ray observatory only has so much propellant for its attitude-control jets. When it runs low on propellant, the satellite is dead: it won't be able to point at new targets. So, they let the earth eclipse it, and continue taking real data on the other side."

"Mind if I look at that garbage data?" I asked. Sarah shrugged and gave me the login information and set up a folder.

"Don't mix it up with the good data," she insisted.

I downloaded the data, and started taking a look through it. It may have been garbage data to Sarah, but the more I looked at it, the more I was convinced I was seeing real hits on the detectors. They all had this ramp up and ramp down behavior that was very similar. By then, Sarah had left for the evening. I printed out a bunch of the hits from the "garbage data," and set them aside, convinced there was something there. Then, I headed back to the dorm.

"Guess who I just heard from," Amit challenged me when I came in the room.

"Marcus," I speculated. "Or maybe Ryan."

"Got it in one," Amit acknowledged. "Particularly the 'maybe' part."

I looked at the note from Marcus. He'd followed the instructions and sent the note to Amit's encrypted email from the account Amit had set up for him. Like most of the public, he didn't think his own government would be spying on him. He didn't believe what we'd told him about all emails, texts, and phone calls being under surveillance, though. He'd checked with a smart friend of his who assured him that it would be impossible.

"The 'smart friend' has to be Ryan," Amit concluded. "They've been sitting together in social justice. We need some way to convince Marcus and Ryan that emails and texts truly are being monitored."

That social-justice class continued to be an ordeal. Professor Gomulka insisted on classroom participation. Failure to get involved in the conversation led to reminders that everyone was part of the problem or part of the solution; everyone was either oppressed or an oppressor, a victim or a victimizer. There was no middle ground in Gomulka's class, no innocent bystanders. He'd been hinting more strongly that perhaps Ryan and Marcus didn't have the best interests of the oppressed at heart.

"We need to persuade Ryan to send a message to Marcus," I offered. "A message that the monitors cannot ignore. A message that will make them show their hand."

"How about 'I'm going to blow up Tech Tower'? That would get a reaction," Amit suggested, the sarcasm thick in his voice.

"No," I countered, "it can't be anything that would get them in real legal trouble." I explained to Amit what I had in mind.

"That's inspired," he said. Amit added a few embellishments of his own. We sent a write-up of our idea to Uncle Rob, to get his tactical approval, and to Mr. Burke, our lawyer in Tennessee.

Somewhat to my surprise, Uncle Rob endorsed the idea, after chastising us for reaching out to Marcus and Ryan without his approval in the first place. He could find no flaw in the encrypted-email-communication concept, but he cautioned us to remind Marcus and Ryan to log in via anonymous Wi-Fi and TOR connections. "Security procedures only work if they're scrupulously followed." We'd heard it many times before, but he was right, it wouldn't hurt to remind Marcus and Ryan. Mr. Burke had some additional suggestions and the name of a lawyer in Atlanta that Marcus and Ryan could call for help if things got out of hand. A couple days later, we forwarded it all to Marcus and waited. If he and Ryan followed through, they should have all the evidence they'd need that their emails and texts were being monitored.

We were finally doing something – sounding out two potential new allies and perhaps even helping to expose the government's surveillance of online and phone communications. It seemed a pitifully small step compared to the larger forces at work, though. The Chief Justice of the U.S. Supreme Court, William Rehnquist, died. The Circle was moving, vetting President Lieberman's nominee to the court. The Circle's agents had dug up some dirt on the nominee's questionable behavior. One of Amit's hotels picked up a field report from one of the Circle's field agents confirming aspects of it. If the information came out, the new Chief Justice would be disgraced, disbarred, and impeached if he didn't resign in disgrace. The Civic Circle now had the perfect leverage over him to make sure any important cases on the closely divided court went their way.

I had the distinct impression we were in a race and losing badly. The Circle was securing their grip over the Supreme Court of the United States while we attempted a holding action in the Introduction to Social Justice Studies class at Georgia Tech. Amit and I sent the intercept on to Uncle Rob and Mr. Burke to be sure they'd seen it.

My depression was compounded by Professor Gomulka's latest initiative. He offered extra credit for attending a "Free-Speech-a-Thon" event by the Campanile (bell tower) one hot Friday afternoon in September, and more points for actually speaking. I was too uncomfortable to do more than just listen. My heart simply wasn't in it. A few other students made feeble attempts. The only two who really shined were Amit and Madison. Amit harangued passersby on their privilege, and Madison rambled on about the patriarchy and how the "I'm a ramblin' wreck from Georgia Tech" fight song was sexist.

"She's really good," Amit said approvingly of Madison. "It's like she actually believes it."

"I'm dehydrated, and I need a drink," I told him. "Let's head on back."

"I want to hear her finish," Amit insisted. He handed me a ten. "Drinks on me, if you bring me back a Coke, too."

When I got back with the drinks, Madison had finished.

"You know, guys paying for their date's dinner is just another form of patriarchal oppression," Amit was explaining. "It's a way of expressing power and dominance and creates the impression that sexual favors are owed as a quid pro quo. As a strong independent woman, you should pick up the tab when we go out."

"But, if I pick up the tab, doesn't that mean you're obligated to me?" she countered.

"True," Amit acknowledged, "but as a strong independent guy with lots of options, I'm probably better able to resist the pressure to reciprocate." He grabbed the Coke I got for him and offered it to Madison.

"I am not going out with you," Madison insisted.

"Who said anything about going out? I'm just offering a Coke to a thirsty fellow social justice ambassador." He popped it open and took a big swig in front of her. "But if you don't want it, fine. We're heading over to the Student Center. You can buy a drink of your own there, and then there are no obligations on either side."

We were supposed to be meeting Jennifer and Ashley at the Student Center and then going out on a double date. I figured Amit was up to some kind of game as usual. To my surprise, Madison joined us, but she continued to be critical of Amit.

"I see what you do," Madison insisted to Amit. "You don't fool me. You've been pretending like being Indian is the same as being African-American.

"You think we Indians don't know about oppression?" Amit replied indignantly. "For centuries the British ruled India with brutality, deposing our rulers, seizing our wealth, suppressing and expropriating our culture. Then adding insult to injury, you misapply our name to the native peoples of this continent." Madison seemed taken aback. "You teach yoga, right?"

"Yeah," she acknowledged, tentatively.

"Yoga is a holy ritual for us Indians," Amit explained. "To see it debased as mere exercise and stretching... well, it's a cultural appropriation, an insult, an ethnic affront, a symbol of Western imperialism and domination."

"I didn't know that," Madison looked shocked at the magnitude of her previously-unappreciated complicity in oppression.

"Well, you do now," declared Amit, as if putting her on notice. "However, we Indians are noted for our generosity as well. On behalf of my people, I am prepared to absolve you of your guilt for appropriating our traditions. If you're going to continue practicing yoga, though, you really ought to be instructed by a native about the deeper spiritual meaning of our rituals."

"What kind of rituals?" she asked tentatively.

"There are various tantric poses that can deliver profoundly satisfying spiritual bonds between two people," Amit explained. "I could demonstrate," he added, grasping her forearm.

She pulled her arm back. "You are so bad," she said. There was a smile on her face, though.

Just then Jennifer and Ashley showed up. "We have to go," Amit explained. He liked double booking girls to show each that he had options.

"Who was that?" Ashley asked him after Madison had departed.

"Just a friend of ours from class," Amit said nonchalantly. We took the girls out to dinner and a movie. I don't remember much about the movie, because Jennifer was very distracting. I was doing my best to distract her back. Amit pressed hard for them to come back to our room, but they demurred.

It was late and we were walking back to our dorm room. Amit had never much discussed his background or culture before. "So, how much of what you told Madison about British oppression is actually true?" I asked him later.

"Most all of it," he explained. "At times the British really were culturally oppressive as well as brutal and exploitative. On the other hand, they also invested in education, introduced the rule of law, and developed industry and a rail network. History is complicated. You know, one of the customs the British suppressed was "suttee." That's when a widow was expected to throw herself into her husband's funeral pyre. She'd be helped along if she was reluctant.

"This British officer heard that a suttee was about to take place, and he informed the priests that he would stop the sacrifice. The priests complained that suttee was their religious custom and that the British should respect their traditions. The officer replied, 'Be it so. This burning of widows is your custom; prepare the funeral pile. But my nation has also a custom. When men burn women alive we hang them, and confiscate all their property. My carpenters shall therefore erect gibbets on which to hang all concerned when the widow is consumed. Let us all act according to national customs.' In the spirit of cultural cooperation, the priests decided to compromise by indefinitely deferring both the immolation and the hanging."

The following day, Saturday, was an opportunity for me to catch up on my homework. Amit and I spent some time double-checking each other's code for the intro to programming homework. "Kids' stuff," was Amit's assessment. When we finished, Amit started working down his list of girls and finally found one ready to go out right then. It was still early, and one of those rare nights when I didn't have any homework to do. When Amit took off, I pulled out my secure laptop and started reviewing the text of an old book I'd downloaded on Chinese history.

The MacGuffin manuscript had me convinced that the conspiracy we were fighting had some Chinese ties. And there had to be some secret conspiracy out there opposing the Civic Circle. Someone had burned down the Tolliver Library just before the Circle's Technology Containment Team arrived. I set out to read the books looking for hints or indications of conspiracies being involved in Chinese events. My problem was not detecting the subtle signs of hidden conspiracies, but rather sorting through them all! It seemed that all of Chinese history could be interpreted as one conspiracy or another fighting against each other or against the central government. A clandestine community started the Boxer Rebellion of 1900. The nationalists and communists each had their own covert organizations. Modern-day secret societies continued aiming at political goals, enrichment of members, or mutual support. These "tongs" and "triads" were sometimes fraternal organizations to help Chinese immigrants in new countries. Others were of a more criminal nature – a kind of Chinese mafia, with activities including prostitution, drug dealing, gambling, and extortion. I worked my way through the history to a rather dry account of an attack on the Imperial Palace in 1814 by a coalition of covert groups including the "White Lotus," the "White Feather," the "Three Incense Sticks," the "Eight Diagrams," and the "Rationalists." Information on the specific nature of these secret societies was sparse because they were, after all, secret. Finding actual ties to the Civic Circle or a counter-Circle conspiracy among this complicated tangle did not appear a productive line of inquiry. I set it aside as a dead end.

Uncle Rob insisted I should be focusing on the Circle and not on whoever burned down the Tolliver Library. His attitude made no sense to me. Somehow, the Circle had some powerful opposition – adversaries who managed to burn down the Tolliver Library before the Circle's Technology Containment Team could recover the forbidden knowledge contained in its books. I could see Uncle Rob's point that these mysterious adversaries were dangerous, but that was exactly what we needed – allies who were dangerous to the Circle. Uncle Rob's insistence that I "leave it alone" only compounded my frustration.

I was making more progress in my physics research, however. I visited Professor Graf during her office hours the following week to talk about electricity and magnetism. I didn't dare tell her about the Heaviside discovery – people who started poking into it had a bad habit of suffering terminal cancers or fatal accidents. I asked her, though, in a general sense about what happened to classical electromagnetics and why so much of the work of folks like Hertz, Heaviside, Lodge, and FitzGerald had been forgotten.

"The original work in electromagnetics was all based on the notion of the 'aether' – a medium through which electromagnetic waves propagate," she explained. "The Michaelson-Morley experiment showed no evidence for this aether. When Einstein developed the special theory of relativity, which we'll be discussing next semester, he showed that no preferred reference frame was needed."

"Could there be something about the way electromagnetics works that gives rise to the relativity effect?" I asked. "Treating it as an axiom begs the question of how and why it works, questions that FitzGerald was looking into." I didn't add how FitzGerald died mysteriously just a couple of years before Einstein popped up out of nowhere to "solve" the problem.

"I suppose there could be some other, more fundamental reason for relativity," she acknowledged, "but if a tool works, use it. Physicists are a pragmatic bunch. We take ideas that work, and we use them. We don't necessarily care all that much about why it works."

"If there's no aether, then what's waving?" I asked.

"Our best understanding is that electromagnetics results from the wave-like behavior of little particles we call photons," she clarified. "Planck came up with the hypothesis that radiation is quantized to explain 'black-body' radiation, and Einstein showed it explains the photoelectric effect. You'll be getting a chance to learn all about this over the next couple of years.

"As physicists probed deep within the atom, they discovered that everyday concepts like definite locations and velocities no longer made any sense," Professor Graf continued. "Waves behave like particles, and particles like waves. The discoveries of atomic physics forced physicists to rethink their classical ideas about identity and causality."

That wasn't much immediate help, but she pointed me to some introductory modern physics and quantum mechanics books to look into.

My real success came when I presented the work I'd done analyzing the "garbage data" from the gamma ray observatory satellite at the Friday research team meeting. Professor Chen got excited looking at the samples I'd pulled. Although the earth was blocking the view of the satellite to the target it was supposed to be imaging, the sensor was picking up something. "Those are real detections!" he concluded. "Those patterns of hits are the aperture of the telescope sweeping past discrete sources of radiation on the ground. We could be seeing uranium deposits, nuclear test sites, or radioactive contamination!"

He and Professor Graf started discussing with Sarah and a couple of their graduate students how to calculate where on Earth the satellite was pointed based on the timestamps. The geometry quickly went over my head, but the upshot of it was that Professor Chen would be working through the weekend with Professor Graf to correlate the "garbage data" detections with their locations of origin on the surface.

As everyone left, I followed Professor Chen back to his office. He was in a good mood, and I figured I should take advantage of it.

"Outstanding work, Peter," he was saying. "Some of the best scientific discoveries come from accidental noticing things like that." Professor Chen's English could get a bit choppy at times. "There's a word for it. I do not recall."

"Serendipity," I offered.

"Ah," he said. "So many words, so little time. Was there something else you needed?"

"Actually, sir," I began, "I was just wondering about your tattoo. What is that?" I gestured to his forearm where the sleeve of his garish floral print shirt partially covered his tattoo.

"This shirt? I have an artist friend who lives in Buckhead," he explained, turning the tattooed arm away from my view. "She makes these shirts. I like to bring some color to our serious business of physics."

"No," I clarified. "I'm curious about your tattoo."

I was expecting him to show it to me. Uncle Rob had lots of friends with tattoos – it must be some kind of military social initiation thing to go out with your comrades to a tattoo parlor. When I'd hang out with Uncle Rob and his friends, they'd proudly show off their tattoos and launch into wild stories describing the circumstances of how, when, and where they got them.

Instead, Professor Chen left his tattoo under his sleeve. "Oh," he said, "that's just a taijitu, a yin-yang symbol. I really must be getting to work. The unknown won't discover itself. Anything else?" he asked dismissively.

"No, sir." I left. His evasiveness was... interesting. I'd gotten a bit better look at the tattoo, though, and I was even more confident that it matched the diagram in the MacGuffin proof.

* * *

By then, it was time for my midterms. Differential Equations was my most challenging class. The diffy-q midterm was grueling, but thanks to the coaching and tutoring I got from Sarah and her friends, I thought I did all right. Emag was similarly difficult, but I'd been studying it with such a passion for so long, that the jumble of "divs, grads, and curls" actually made sense to me. Chemistry was not terribly stressful, now that I was up to speed.

The midterm I was really looking forward to was Linear Circuits. I'd memorized all the common right triangles Professor Muldoon used in his problems, so I knew the answers for all the trigonometric relations without needing to key the problems into my calculator. I was ready.

"My Linear Circuits tests are extremely difficult," Professor Muldoon proclaimed on the day of the exam. The class was silent. Tension was in the air. "If past experience is any guide, no one will actually finish this exam in the allotted time. You should try to do as many problems as you can as quickly as you can. Do not allow yourself to get stuck on any particular problem. If you can't do it, skip it, and move on. Fortunately for you, the department requires me to grade on a curve."

I turned over the exam on his command, and got to work. As I'd anticipated, every problem involved one of Professor Muldoon's favorite triangles. Before long, I was completely in my zone, setting up the trig, writing down the answer, moving on to the next problem. Before I realized it, I'd completed the last problem. I looked at the time. I had twenty minutes left! I went back and double-checked my work. Without needing to write anything, I ripped through the problems even faster, confirming I'd set them up correctly, and had the right trigonometric answer. There were five minutes left. I couldn't help myself. I scraped my chair back noisily to draw attention to myself, stood up, walked over, and handed my exam to Professor Muldoon. He looked at me in surprise. "Oh. You shouldn't give up. You have five more minutes. Keep working on it and you may be able to earn a few more points."

"I'm done," I announced. "Thank you, sir." I handed him my test.

He looked incredulously at me, then I saw him out of the corner of my eye flipping through the pages of my exam. I saw Ryan looking at me in disbelief before focusing on his own exam and continuing with his furious scribbling. I grabbed my bag, walked out of the classroom, and headed over to my emag class.

My most challenging midterm turned out to be Introduction to Computer Programing – the class I thought was the easiest. I turned the exam sheet over. Question one – what is a computer? My programming class had essay questions?!? I answered that one as best I could. Question two – what are the four basic functions of a computer? I really wasn't sure about that one. Addition, subtraction, multiplication, and division? That made four. I wrote that down and moved on. I finished the essay questions and worked on the algorithms. At least I knew all the algorithm questions. I thought I wrote some decent pseudocode describing how to implement each one.

I compared notes with Amit after the test. The four basic functions of a computer? "You were thinking of conventional arithmetic," Amit corrected me. "Computers are digital. They use Boolean algebra. The four basic functions are AND, OR, XOR, and NOT." There went something like twenty points right there. Ouch. I was not looking forward to the grade.

* * *

The next morning a fire alarm woke us up at 5 am. Police were everywhere. "Another bottle bomb?" I speculated to Amit. Just a week before, some idiot had abandoned a few two-liter bottles filled with dry ice. The pressure builds as the dry ice turns to gas and then finally, a resounding boom! One had gone off next to a janitor, temporarily deafening him. Those things were dangerous, if not properly attended.

"Maybe," Amit acknowledged. "Might be Marcus and Ryan executing their plan, instead." I followed him as he made a point of circulating through the crowd looking unsuccessfully for them. Then, just to be thorough, Amit suggested we circulate through the groups of girls standing around in their pajamas. Amit happily spread gossip, shared rumors, and expressed his judgement on their choice of sleepwear. It was a couple of hours before we were allowed back into the dorms to get dressed and head off to class. In fact, we missed introduction to programming entirely. Ryan was not in linear circuits. He and I always sat near the front of the class, and I noticed his unusual absence. He didn't make it to social justice studies, either, and neither did Marcus. Amit looked knowingly at me. I nodded. They must have done it.

It took a few days to get the full story of what went down. The evening before, Ryan sent a text message to Marcus. "Got my Remington. Will shoot students in the commons this am. Want to help?" The commotion was the police arriving on an "anonymous tip." They searched Ryan's room and found his Remington. His Remington camera. Apparently they manufacture game cameras, and not just guns. Hunters stick them up on game trails to shoot, not bullets, but pictures of deer, so they have an idea of what they might be able to hunt later.

Marcus and Ryan had an uncomfortable day in custody. Fortunately, they'd followed George P.'s instructions. Ryan had suggested to the residence hall director that it would be really cool to have a time-lapse film of students coming in and out of the lobby to put up on the web page. They'd maneuvered the director into sending an email requesting that they do it. Then, they clammed up and refused to answer any questions when they were arrested and interrogated. Mr. Burke had figured the investigators would drop the case if all they had to go on was the text message, rather than admit that they were monitoring all text messages. They didn't, though. They charged Ryan with making a terroristic threat, and Marcus was facing conspiracy charges.

The lawyer Mr. Burke found for them had to arrange bail, and decided to call the prosecutors' bluff. The next day the news was full of the story how an intercepted text message and an unfortunate misunderstanding had led to the arrest of a couple of innocent college students. "The US government, with assistance from major telecommunications carriers, has engaged in massive, illegal dragnet surveillance of the domestic communications and communications records of millions of ordinary Americans," read the press release from the Electronic Frontier Foundation a few days later. "Bring government surveillance programs back within the law and the constitution." Charges were dropped, and Ryan and Marcus had to agree not to sue for false arrest, but the genie was out of the bottle.

"We've been looking for a trigger point like this," Mr. Burke confided in an encrypted email, later. He and his lawyer friends had been ready, and Ryan's arrest over a text message made a perfect smoking gun. Mr. Burke's allies at the Electronic Frontier Foundation and in the press made it a top story for several days. Even Uncle Rob complimented us on the outcome. It was our first real victory. We didn't know how deep the Civic Circle's influence went into the government. They could pose as FBI agents with impunity, and they clearly had access to all the data collected by the government's surveillance programs. Exposing that capability to public scrutiny delivered a solid black eye.

We got an email from Marcus the next day. "OK, George. I believe you now. What next?"

We explained to him and to Ryan how the social-justice class worked. "Play along," we suggested. "Use your experience with the police to spin your own tale of heroic oppression." In addition, we told Marcus and Ryan to be on the lookout for additional allies, and to educate them on how to use encrypted email. George P. Burdell could use all the friends he could get!

Marcus told the story at the next social-justice class and railed about the police assuming because he was black he had to be guilty. Ryan described how he and Marcus had struck a blow for civil liberties by standing on their right to remain silent until their lawyer could be present. Professor Gomulka just nodded and smiled. It seemed as if Ryan and Marcus had finally joined the rest of the class as courageous victims of oppression.

* * *

One evening, while I was wrestling with a particularly difficult initial value problem, Amit burst in carrying a box "It came!"

"What's that?" Amit ignored me and continued furiously unwrapping something. It looked like a digital alarm clock. "You already have an alarm clock."

"Look closer," he insisted.

I did. He was all excited... about a clock. A clock with a USB serial port? "I don't get it. Is it rechargeable or something?"

"It works!" he was as triumphant as I was confused. "At least the unobtrusive part. Now to check out the video quality on this baby." He plugged the USB cable into his computer and installed a program. In a minute, live video of our room displayed on his screen. Ah. It was a stealth video camera that looked like a clock. "See, you can set it to motion-detect, or to just start recording video when you push the snooze button."

"And why do you need a video camera?"

"So I can record and replay highlights of my exploits. With girls!"

I thought back. Unless he was way more discreet than I expected... "You haven't actually had any exploits, yet, have you?"

"No, not yet," he acknowledged, "but I'm getting really close! I want to be ready for it." He carefully positioned the clock in the corner of our room, so the wide-angle lens would capture any events that transpired.

I simply wasn't understanding my initial value problems. Time to set them aside and see if Sarah or one of my other physics friends could help me out tomorrow.

CHAPTER 4: AN UNORTHODOX SHORTCUT

I was not the only victim of the deceptive simplicity of Introduction to Computer Programming. Amit was correct that the four basic functions of a computer were not addition, subtraction, multiplication, and division. Only they weren't AND, OR, XOR, and NOT, either. The answer the instructor was looking for was input, output, processing, and storage. Amit got a C on his midterm and now had a B in this "easy" class. I'd have been more amused at his indignant outrage, but I now had a C in the class thanks to a bit more ineptitude on the algorithm and coding sections yielding a D on the midterm.

At least I had A's going in chemistry and electromagnetics. I felt fortunate to have a B in diffy-q. I found that class particularly challenging. I also had a B in social justice. Amit and Madison were the only students I knew of actually acing the class. Professor Gomulka just loved Amit's essays expounding on racism and oppression. Amit and Madison were both publishing weekly columns in the *Technique*, Georgia Tech's campus newspaper. I had trouble taking them seriously. One week, Madison had a diatribe on how demeaning it was for women to have to dress in a provocative fashion to attract male attention. The next week, she'd extolled how empowering it was for women to flaunt their sexuality. I read that last column and pointed out the contradiction to Amit.

"You need to stop trying to bring facts to a feel fight," was his response.

Amit's articles were even crazier. He had a long and genuinely touching piece on eating disorders, like bulimia and anorexia, and their tragic prevalence among college women. Then he argued that the physical differences in height and strength between males and females were due to malnutrition caused by systemic hetero-patriarchal oppression and pressure on girls to conform to archaic gender stereotypes. I pointed out to Amit that sexual dimorphism – asymmetries between male and female body sizes – was a common feature in many species and was not actually a function of nutrition.

"What did I tell you about bringing facts to a feel fight?" was his response.

The praise heaped upon Amit in social-justice class made it clear to me that humanity was not merely divided into victims and victimizers, oppressors and the oppressed. Amit had secured for himself a place in a third category – heroic champion of the victims. That left me feeling distinctly oppressed, not only at my own lack of obvious victimization, but also at my lack of enthusiasm for trumpeting patently ridiculous social justice ideology. I doubted, however, that was the kind of oppression Professor Gomulka would rate highly.

I was really looking forward to receiving my Linear Circuits midterm grade. I was absolutely confident I'd aced that test. That's why what happened to me was such a shock.

Zero.

A big fat zero was written across the top of my Linear Circuits midterm when Professor Muldoon returned my paper. As he reviewed the exam, I compared my work to his solutions. I had every problem correct. What was going on?

"What's this?" I asked Professor Muldoon after class.

"That? That is a zero," he replied as if I were innumerate.

"Every answer on this exam is correct," I insisted.

"I don't suffer fools in my class." Professor Muldoon began collecting his things. "I make fools suffer. It's too perfect. That's what gave you away. There is no way you could have completed that test in the allotted time. Therefore, you cheated. I have assigned you a zero. I don't know how you did it, but clearly I need to work on my exam security. In any event, if you waste my time by contesting my decision, I will insist on your expulsion from Georgia Tech."

"Professor Muldoon, I didn't cheat on your exam," I tried to explain. "You used..."

"A regrettable decision on your part," Professor Muldoon said, cutting me off. He stood up, walked to the door, and turned to face me. "So be it. You will receive a notification from the Office of Student Integrity of the time of your hearing." He shut the door decisively behind himself.

Great.

I tried being proactive, but no one would listen to me. "You'll just have to wait for your hearing," said the head of the School of Electrical Engineering. "We have a process we have to follow," said the not very helpful lady in the dean's office. "You're wasting your time," Professor Muldoon said smugly, as I continued to submit homework to him. He refused to grade it. I felt helpless. All I could do was treat myself to a frosted orange at the Varsity, carry on, and wait for "the process" to provide me an opportunity to tell my side of the story.

I read through the material on quantum mechanics that Professor Graf gave me. I did pretty well at understanding black-body radiation and the Bohr model, I thought. The photoelectric effect and Compton scattering weren't too bad. As I started looking at the Schrödinger equation, though, I began to get overwhelmed. I was beginning to master the "divs, grads, and curls," of vector calculus, but the Schrödinger equation was simply beyond me. My progress slowed and finally ground to a halt.

One of the critical clues I'd uncovered in understanding how Heaviside's work had been suppressed was the mysterious way in which so many of the key figures in electromagnetics died at an early age. Five scientists, "the Maxwellians," were most responsible for the modern theory of electricity and magnetism. James Clerk Maxwell died in 1879 at age 48, not long after his theory began to be widely recognized. Heinrich Hertz died in 1894 at age 36, within a year of publishing his book that described how he discovered the existence of radio waves. George FitzGerald died in 1901 at age 49 as he was deriving how electromagnetics led to what would be dubbed special relativity by Einstein a few years later.

Only two of the five electromagnetic pioneers lived into old age. Heaviside himself was an eccentric and hermit. He managed to publish his last book in 1912, but it was largely work he had completed years earlier. His work on wave interference never appeared in print, or if it did, was thoroughly suppressed and vanished. Only the few hints and mentions I'd found gave evidence of it.

The other electromagnetic pioneer was Oliver Lodge. He was deceived by spiritualists and became convinced that he could talk to the dead, a conviction that became even stronger following the tragic loss of his son in the first World War. He died in 1940 at age 89, but his best electromagnetic work all dated back to the nineteenth century. Here's a summary of the electromagnetic pioneers:

- James Clerk Maxwell (1831-1879) died at age 48
- George FitzGerald (1851-1901) died at age 49
- Heinrich Hertz (1857-1894) died at age 36
- Oliver Heaviside (1850-1925) died at age 75
- Oliver Lodge (1851-1940) died at age 89

As the nineteenth century ended and the twentieth century began, electromagnetics was dealt a staggering blow – its leading pioneers either dead or diverted from further progress. The clues were obvious once I opened my eyes to look at them.

Since it would be a while before I could master the math and physics of quantum mechanics, I chose to examine the history. I wondered if there might be a similar pattern among the founders of quantum mechanics. Here's a summary of what I found:

- J.J. Thompson (1856-1940) died at age 83
- Max Planck (1858-1947) died at age 89
- Albert Einstein (1879-1955) died at age 76
- Niels Bohr (1885-1962) died at age 77
- Erwin Schrödinger (1887-1961) died at age 73
- Louis de Broglie (1892-1987) died at age 94
- Werner Heisenberg (1901-1976) died at age 77
- Paul Dirac (1902-1984) died at age 82

Even the two who came closest to being contemporaries of the Maxwellians had no problem living into their eighties. Quantum mechanics was a much healthier line of inquiry than electromagnetics! Unlike their electromagnetic counterparts, none of the quantum mechanical pioneers died prematurely. The contrast was striking. Average age at death for the "Maxwellians" was 59; for the "quantum mechanics," it was 81!

Professor Graf had told me that discoveries in atomic physics led physicists to reject the classical or objective view of reality, to throw aside notions like causality and identity. The more I looked into the history of how quantum mechanics arose, the more convinced I became that she had it exactly backwards.

I traced a couple of intriguing mentions back to a 1971 article by Paul Foreman, "Weimar Culture, Causality, and Quantum Theory, 1918-1927." The philosophic spawning ground of quantum mechanics was the culture of Weimar Germany. This period was characterized by amazingly flagrant attacks on reason and causality. One Weimar government official proclaimed, for example, "The basic evil is the overvaluing of the purely intellectual in our cultural activity, the exclusive predominance of the rationalistic mode of thought, which had to lead, and has led, to egoism and materialism of the crassest form."

Even scientists commented on this cultural hostility. For instance, Nobel Laureate chemist, William Ostwald commented, "It is at present considered modern to speak all conceivable evil of the intellect." Science was viewed as the root cause of societal ills. "[Natural science] is represented as bearing the guilt for the world crisis in which we stand at present, and the whole of the intellectual and material misery bound up with that crisis is charged to natural science's account," observed Nobel Laureate physicist, Max von Laue. A conspicuous embodiment of reason and intellectual achievement, science came under particular assault. As Ostwald further noted, "In Germany today we suffer again from a rampant mysticism, which... turns against science and reason as its most dangerous enemies."

It was easy to see how quantum mechanics arose from a culture with a deep aversion to reason and intellect and an outright hostility to science – a culture that was already giving birth to National Socialism. I was stunned to see such tight coupling between culture, on the one hand, and science and politics on the other. I'd read an interview somewhere – some guy who worked with Matt Drudge – who claimed that "politics was downstream from culture." That's certainly true, but I came to realize it's only a part of the truth. Culture – or more fundamentally, the ideas, the "zeitgeist," the spirit of the times, the philosophy at a culture's roots – is tied not only into politics, but also into science and art.

One key principle came under particular assault in the Weimar era – the principle of causality. As an example, consider the diatribe from the prominent historian, Oswald Spengler:

> *I mean the opposition of the destiny-idea and the causality-principle, an opposition which, in its deep world-shaping necessity, has never hitherto been recognized as such.... Destiny is the word for an indescribable inner certainty. One makes the essence of*

the causal clear by means of a physical or epistemological system, by means of numbers, by means of conceptual analyses.... The one requires us to dismember, the other to create, and therein lies the relation of destiny to life and causality to death.

Scientists who opposed the wave of mysticism and irrationality washing over their field were often hindered by their own acceptance of their opponents' basic premises. Consider the efforts of Albert Einstein to uphold the existence of an objective reality:

The belief in an external world independent of the observing subject lies at the foundation of all natural science. However, since sense-perceptions only inform us about this external world, or physical reality, indirectly, it is only in a speculative way that it can be grasped by us.

If even the champions of "objective reality" acknowledged the impotence of reason, the battle was lost before it had begun.

I was depressed to see how so many scientists joined forces with their own destroyers. In a 1914 speech to a lay audience, Nobel Laureate physicist Wilhelm Wien proclaimed: "...causality... has nothing to do with the business [physics]." By the 1920's the list of the advocates of acausality sounded like an honor roll of German physics. They included among them Nobel Laureates like Max Born and Otto Stern, and (for a while at least) Erwin Schrödinger. These scientists were not some marginal or fringe group. They represented the mainstream of Weimar physics. They were among the leaders and innovators in the coming discoveries. Non-objective philosophy and in particular, the rejection of causality were firmly entrenched well before the discoveries of the 1920's.

Professor Graf was simply wrong. The anti-causal thinking came before the development of quantum mechanics in the 1920s. It was the cause, not the effect.

Quantum mechanics was the end result of a Beer Hall Putsch that, unlike the Nazi's failed attempt, succeeded in overthrowing the basic principles of science years before the discoveries of quantum mechanics were alleged to have demanded the change.

I thought I was going to have to wait a year or two for quantum mechanics to start showing up in my classes, so I could really begin to understand it. Boy, was I wrong! Professor Gomulka was reviewing the advocacy and lobbying that led to the Preserving Our Planet's Future Act. "Americans were whipped up into a fury at the 9/11 attacks," he explained. "They were ready to do something, anything to strike back. That's when a few of the surviving congressmen bundled together some of the most progressive environmental policy concepts – ideas that had previously gone nowhere. Repackaged as a tribute to the late President Gore, Congress enacted those policies by acclamation. That's a prime example of exploiting current events and the spirit of the moment to achieve policy goals entirely unrelated to the events themselves."

Ryan raised his hand, "Professor, the Gore Tax has devastated our economy. Coal and oil workers lost their jobs, and with gas over $5 a gallon, everything that has to be transported becomes more expensive."

"Carbon taxes, Ryan," Professor Gomulka corrected him, "not 'the Gore Tax.' That's reactionary rhetoric, and I will not tolerate hate-speech in my class. I'd like you to deconstruct that term in a one-page essay for Monday morning, focusing on how that right-wing propaganda only serves to avoid and redirect genuine interrogation of critical environmental issues."

Ryan had been getting lots of Professor Gomulka's special essay assignments.

"In answer to your question, though," the professor continued, "it all boils down to quantum mechanics."

Say, what?

"Everything is interrelated and connected to its polar opposite. As soon as we're born, we begin to die. To achieve peace, we must use violence. There's no utopia without a downside. To save the planet's future, we must destroy the personal futures of some among us. For every positive, there is a negative, and we cannot have the one without the other. We must embrace the contradiction, because it is fundamental to reality itself.

"Niels Bohr called this 'complementarity.' The natural harmony of reality manifests itself in contradiction, and when we have found what appears to our limited minds to be a contradiction, we are actually looking at a fundamental truth. Quantum mechanics swept away causality and certainty, and demonstrated that we can only look at the world in a probabilistic fashion.

"The duality inherent in quantum mechanics carries over into politics. One man's positive is another man's negative. Assessing political policy as either positive or negative is the act of a naïve amateur. You have to look at politics through the filter of quantum mechanics, like Saul Alinsky did in his *Rules for Radicals*."

I thought about what Professor Gomulka had said through the filter of Newtonian mechanics: action-reaction. I had to admire the evil genius behind the Circle's plans. They certainly derailed electromagnetics. How much of the anti-causal, anti-logic thinking of the 1920s was their handiwork? Were the anti-causal interpretations of quantum mechanics just intended to confuse scientists and throw them off the track? Or were these interpretations specifically designed to give the likes of this Alinsky and Gomulka the means to justify and evade the contradictions and consequences of their political policies?

Amit was too busy working on his hotel network security app to review what I'd found and discuss it. He'd licensed his software to another small hotel chain, and he was busy trying to fix compatibility issues in time for a hot date with Ashley he had planned for the evening. Jennifer had declined to make it a double date, citing homework. It was a Wednesday afternoon, and I was done with my classes. I thought I'd head to the physics building to put in a couple hours at the mirror lab, work on some homework, and maybe find Professor Graf. I got the kiln warming to slump a glass plate.

I found Professor Graf in her office and started asking her further about complementarity.

"Honestly, I don't think many physicists care about the philosophic details," she explained. "The equations work. When someone starts talking about philosophy, we tell them to 'shut up, and calculate.'"

Unfortunately, her office hours were about to begin for her pre-med physics students, and they were already lining up outside her office door. She'd reformed the pre-med physics curriculum to make it align with the MCAT exam that pre-med students have to take to get into med school. In addition to the usual stand-alone multiple-choice questions, the MCAT had essays about topics in physics and associated multiple-choice questions based on the content of the essays. She had reworked all her homework and exams to match the MCAT format. Professor Graf was very popular with the pre-med students, and her section of the class was full to overflowing – students in other professors' sections would attend her class instead. She had an exam coming up soon, and the hallway outside her office was getting crowded. I wouldn't be getting any time with her that afternoon.

Fortunately, I discovered Professor Chen in.

"Peter!" he greeted me cheerfully. "What brings you in this afternoon?"

"Just making another mirror and catching up on homework," I explained. "You?"

"This satellite gamma ray data is extraordinary," Professor Chen explained. "Professor Graf got the ephemeris data synched up and worked out the geometry, so we can correlate the time and orientation of the gamma ray observatory with specific locations on the ground."

He motioned me over to look at his screen and typed "1022," and a map of the Earth refreshed with different coloring. There were hot spots seemingly all over the place, but the strongest concentration appeared to be in central Africa.

"What's that?" I pointed to a bright spot over central Africa.

"1022 kilo-electron-volts is the energy associated with the annihilation of an electron and a positron," Professor Chen explained. "We're seeing the creation and destruction of antimatter."

"Antimatter exists in nature?" I hadn't heard anything like that before.

"It's another new discovery. Professor Graf figured it out. These hits correlate to thunderstorms. Apparently, the electric fields get so intense they actually generate an electron-positron pair. We're seeing the gamma rays from the annihilation of antimatter – natural antimatter being created in storms high up in the atmosphere."

"Wow," that sounded incredible.

Professor Chen typed "622" and the map refreshed yet again. He zoomed in the field of view. "Here's a map of Europe showing the locations of 662 keV hits." I must have looked puzzled. "That's the energy of the gamma ray emitted by cesium-137 when it decays," he clarified.

I looked at the map. There was a particular hot spot in Eastern Europe, no, further east. The Ukraine? Wispy tendrils of seemed to flow from that source. "Chernobyl?"

"Exactly!" Professor Chen said triumphantly. "The half-life of cesium-137 is thirty years, so over half the cesium-137 released in the accident is still there, in the soil, taken up by plants. Chemically, it tends to displace potassium. This is an unprecedented level of detail. No ground-based survey even begins to come close!"

Professor Chen slowly scrolled his map to the east. "What's this line here?" I pointed to a disconnected line of hits in central Russia.

"The Kyshtym disaster," Professor Chen explained. "Another major Soviet nuclear accident. It happened in 1957. Huge release of cesium-137 and strontium-90. The cloud didn't get up high into the atmosphere, so it wasn't as widely distributed as Chernobyl. Now we can see it from space fifty years later."

"This is amazing." I could understand his enthusiasm. "You can see a nuclear accident fifty years later from space." I looked closer. "These fainter collections of dots. Are they even older accidents?"

"It's hard to tell from this data," Professor Chen pointed out, "because of the decay process. A tiny concentration could be from a little cesium-137 released recently, or from a big release a long time ago. There's a certain background noise from nuclear testing fallout most everywhere. In any event, Professor Graf and I are submitting a rapid communication to Geophysical Letters on these preliminary results – the first detailed global survey of radiation data, not to mention the discovery of antimatter being created in the atmosphere. There's so much more, though, we can pull out of the data. If we compare the maps of different isotopes, we can actually date when the releases occurred."

I wasn't following. "How does that work?"

"When uranium fissions," Professor Chen explained, "it splits into two parts, one a bit larger than the other. You get a radioactive isotope with an atomic mass around 95 and another one around 137. Some of the isotopes, like Iodine-131, decay very quickly. Its half-life is 8 days, so in a few months, there's very little left. Cesium-137 has a half-life of 30 years. By comparing the concentrations of the fast-decaying isotopes to the slow-decaying isotopes, you can get an estimate of how long ago the source event occurred."

I think I actually understood that. "I see."

"Do you have plans for winter break?" Professor Chen asked. "We have lots of data, and we can afford to pay to have you help go through it."

"I can certainly work through some of the break," I replied. I wanted to get some quality time in the library running down leads, anyway. "Can you answer a question for me? I've been asking Professor Graf for help in understanding how quantum mechanics and electromagnetics work. She's pointed me to the Schrödinger equation, to the Dirac equation, and to Feynman's quantum electrodynamics. In each case, though, the math always includes charges. Is there a formulation more basic than that? An equation to describe just photons, without reference to any charges?"

Professor Chen raised an eyebrow. "That's an interesting question. You can't get photons of electromagnetic energy without some kind of accelerating charge. I'm not sure you actually can consider it in isolation." He looked thoughtfully. "I suppose you could use the my-your-anna equation." He wrote it out for me: Majorana. Then, he searched online a bit. "I found a few references for you," he said, copying and pasting links into an email. "Complicated stuff. You might not be able to understand it all just yet, but it's good to try." I asked him to send the references straight to the printer to avoid leaving any sort of email trail.

I headed back to the mirror lab and reviewed the papers Professor Chen printed until it was time to check on the kiln. After I loaded up a glass plate, I studied papers on the Majorana equation a while and finally set them aside as too complicated. I made a bit of progress on my homework, but I was too stressed to concentrate. Even my usual pick-me-up of a frosted orange at the Varsity held no appeal.

Something I didn't understand was happening behind the scenes of my academic dishonesty hearing. I'd thought that Professor Muldoon's complaint would be heard by the Student Honor Committee. Instead, the Office of the Dean of Students had escalated my case straight to a hearing in front of some professors and a new dean. I hadn't been able to find out much about this new dean.

Finally, I shut off the kiln to allow the kiln and the glass plate to cool, before heading home. Amit didn't show up. "Nailed her," he proclaimed proudly when I saw him the next morning. He recounted the particulars of the seduction in uncomfortably exquisite detail. Jennifer was not happy that Ashley and Amit had taken over the room for the evening. "She ended up sleeping in another friend's room," Amit explained. "You should have come with me and volunteered our room to do 'homework' with Jennifer. You might have scored, too!" My stress level was too high to care about Amit's antics, or even girls for that matter.

I showed up to my hearing at the appointed time and took a seat outside the closed room. Professor Muldoon was already there. He glared at me when I arrived, then turned away, studiously ignoring me. I heard noises from inside: crying and sobbing. The doors opened and a weeping girl walked past me. An older woman, maybe her mother, had her arm around her. She'd been expelled.

"Your turn," Professor Muldoon said calmly not deigning to look me in the eye as he walked past me to enter the hearing room.

I followed, taking my place at the table.

The hearing was a bit like a court, except I wasn't allowed to have a lawyer. That didn't seem particularly fair given that Professor Muldoon probably had way more experience at these things than I did. The dean began the hearing and asked Professor Muldoon to explain the complaint.

"This is my Linear Circuits midterm test," he said, handing out copies to the dean and the other professors at the head table. "No student has ever completed my Linear Circuits midterm in the allotted time. The best score I've ever awarded was in the high eighties, and the last student who accomplished that was Roger Thorn."

The name meant nothing to me, but apparently that impressed the professors.

"Here we have Mr. Peter Burdell, whose records lie before you: a student who's currently managing a "C" in

Introduction to Computer Programming, which is the easiest joke of a programming class this institution offers. Mister Burdell," he said as if "mister" were a term of contempt, "turned this in to me and walked out five minutes before the end of the allotted time. I often have students so demoralized by the difficulty of my tests that they give up. I encouraged Mister Burdell to take the full allotted time.

"'I'm done,' he said, strutting out of my classroom.

"To my surprise, I saw that he had actually completed the exam. To my further surprise, once I graded the test, I discovered that every problem was correct, in many cases with just the answer and a few scribbled numbers. I myself can only barely solve the test in the allotted time. There is no way a student could have done so.

"It was clear to me that Mister Burdell must somehow have acquired either an advance copy or the solution key to my exam," he continued. "The average on the test was a 53, and the high score was a 76. Were I to allow Mister Burdell to profit from his dishonesty, it would distort the curve and be unfair to the rest of the class. I generously offered Mister Burdell the option to take a zero on the test. He foolishly refused. I must, therefore, insist that he be expelled from this institution." Professor Muldoon sat down.

"Professor Muldoon has levelled some rather serious accusations at you Mr. Burdell," the dean began. "Before we hear what you have to tell us, I want to explain a few things to you." The dean looked at some notes, clearly reading a prepared statement. "This panel reviews cases of academic dishonesty. Too many times each year, we meet with students who insist that it was the first time they ever cheated, that they thought they could get away with it, that they didn't think they were hurting anybody by their actions."

I was appalled. I hadn't yet presented my side of the story, and the dean was busy lecturing me on the evils of academic dishonesty as if I'd already been found guilty.

"...When you cheat, you're really cheating yourself. Cheating not only gives you a grade you have not earned, but in a class in which grades are curved, your actions lower everyone else's grade," he droned on. "Degrees from Georgia Tech are a precious commodity, and cheating to obtain a false advantage shortchanges your fellow students. It cheapens the diploma so many work so hard to earn. It's the same as stealing something of great value. Now," he finally concluded, "do you have anything to say for yourself?"

"Yes, sir," I answered, rising to my feet. "I agree completely with what you just said."

"You acknowledge your guilt and accept responsibility for your actions?" the dean asked.

"No, and yes, respectively, sir." I said.

The dean looked confused. "What do you mean?"

"I mean, I do not acknowledge any guilt," I clarified, "because I did not engage in any academic dishonesty, and I do accept responsibility for my actions. Always. Please pardon my ignorance, but is there someplace on the agenda of this hearing where I will be allowed to present my side of the story?"

"This is not an adversarial proceeding in the formal sense," the dean said. "Think of it more as a counseling session in which members of the university come together to discuss academic dishonesty. If you have something to contribute, we will listen to you."

"Thank you, sir." I asked the members of the judicial board to take a closer look at the problems on Professor Muldoon's test. I pointed out that every problem involved the solution of a simple right triangle or a common Pythagorean triple. I saw Professor Muldoon's face go blank. He knew I had him. The members of the committee were not convinced, however.

Professor Fries frowned and interjected, "Would you please go to the board and solve this problem." He read from the exam. "The real component of the voltage is 21V, the reactive component is 72V. What are the phase angle and the power factor?"

I walked to the board. "Would you please time me also?"

The other professor looked at his watch. "OK." He paused a moment and said "Go."

I wrote "θ = 78.46°; PF = 28%" on the board and said "Stop! So how long did I take?"

"Five or six seconds," said the professor. "You may have a remarkable memory, but that's entirely consistent with having advance access to a copy of the exam, like Professor Muldoon claims."

"I did memorize certain solutions, sir," I answered, "but I had no access to the key. Actually, I worked it out while walking to the whiteboard."

I saw skeptical looks. "How did you memorize solutions and work out the answer so quickly if you didn't have access to the key?" the dean asked.

"That's a Pythagorean triple," I explained. "The problem is just a 7-24-25 Pythagorean right triangle scaled up by a factor of three: 21-72-75. The net voltage is 75V, and the power factor is the cosine of the phase angle. Adjacent over hypotenuse is 7/25 or 28/100 which is 28%. I did memorize the angles in a 7-24-25 right triangle. The skinny one is 11.54 degrees and the fat one 78.46 degrees. Memorizing fifty different problems would be very difficult. It's much easier to learn the half-dozen triangles Professor Muldoon uses and figure out how he applies them in each problem. You'll notice he likes using 7-24-25 triangles as well as 3-4-5 right triangles in problems involving power factors, because it's particularly easy to calculate percentages.

"Every single problem on the test has a simple, straightforward solution like that," I explained. "The reason the test was so difficult and time consuming for most students was they had to set up the problem and key the numbers into their calculators. It took the other students the better part of a minute to do what I could do in my head in seconds."

Professor Fries leafed thoughtfully through the exam. "I think he's right," he told the dean. Then, he looked at me. "Why didn't you explain this to Professor Muldoon?"

"I tried," I confirmed, "but Professor Muldoon refused to listen. He said, 'I do not suffer fools; I make fools suffer.'"

I saw the professors on the panel smile. Muldoon must have said something similar to them in the past. "Appears someone may have been a bit too hasty in accusing his student of cheating," Professor Fries said, dryly.

I felt relieved to have an ally on the committee. There was a long pause. Professor Muldoon finally spoke. "Mister Burdell has admitted his duplicity in employing a trick to give himself an unfair advantage over his fellow students. This is an open and shut case of academic dishonesty."

"Duplicity, Harmon?" Professor Fries countered. "I see no dishonesty or any reason he should be penalized. Mr. Burdell here merely figured out the shortcut you used to make it easier to grade your exams."

Professor Muldoon was not giving up so easily, though. "The dean is well aware that the policy of this institution is to give deference to the judgment of faculty to evaluate academic performance at their sole discretion," he countered. "In my opinion, even if Mister Burdell can be excused for applying an... an unorthodox shortcut to solving my exam questions, he showed insufficient work to justify his fortunate guesses."

"With respect, sir," I replied, "I correctly answered each question you posed, and I committed no acts of academic dishonesty to do so. Your specific instructions were to answer as many questions as quickly as possible, not to show work and justify each solution."

"I will be the judge of that," Professor Muldoon insisted.

"Harmon," said Professor Fries with an exasperated tone, "you got lazy. You got sloppy. You got caught. Don't take it out on your student. If there's any fault to be found, it's yours."

"My teaching is not on trial here," Professor Muldoon insisted smugly. "As the course instructor..."

"This is not a trial, Professor," I interrupted. I was angry at his intransigence. I couldn't believe he was still gunning for me. "Think of it more as a counseling session in which members of the university community come together to discuss academic dishonesty. After all, degrees from Georgia Tech are a precious commodity, and lazy or slipshod teaching shortchanges me and my fellow students. It cheapens the value of the diploma so many of us work so hard to earn. It's the same as stealing something of great value."

The professors on the review board were amused. Muldoon was angry. The dean looked strangely... smug?

"The evidence does not support the allegation of academic dishonesty," the dean concluded. "You've taught Linear Circuits, before, haven't you?" he asked Fries.

"I have," the professor acknowledged.

"Under the circumstances," the dean explained, "I'm going to have to ask you to take over as our young Mr. Burdell's instructor of record for Linear Circuits. I think a transfer would be in the best interests of both parties.

I met Professor Fries after the meeting. "I understand you're considering pursuing either physics or electrical engineering," he started off. "I hope you won't judge us engineers by the example of Professor Muldoon. You'll complete the same assignments and take the same final as the rest of the class, only I'll be grading them and assigning your grade." We exchanged contact information, and I made arrangements to get the homework to him that Professor Muldoon had refused to grade.

I hadn't realized the pressure Professor Muldoon had placed on me until I felt the enormous relief of its absence. I felt almost giddy with joy. Not only was I going to get through the semester, but our efforts continued to have repercussions, not just nationally, but also locally. A student named Erin McCracken wrote a brilliant column in the *Technique* about avoiding this new social media website called Facebook, and how it was tied into an NSA program called "Echelon" that monitored everything on the Internet.

The Tuesday before Thanksgiving break, I walked into chemistry with my head held high. I didn't have a particularly great aptitude for the subject, but I was getting a solid A, because I'd seen the material in high school. The first time I struggled through it, I thought my mother was an awful teacher, expecting me to know every atomic weight and ionic state. Finally, I'd begun to appreciate her perspective. There were certain basics all chemists knew and took for granted. Now, I had memorized them, too. Chemistry, for me, was just a matter of showing up, completing the homework, and taking the tests. It was my least stressful class. Also, it brought back so many memories of my mother. It was like she was there with me. It helped me be at peace with her loss.

Plus, there were so many amazingly cool demonstrations!

Today, for instance, our professor was demonstrating liquefied gases. He froze a hot dog in liquid nitrogen and shattered it. He froze a rose and did the same. I wish I'd known about all those tricks back when I was working for Uncle Rob in his liquefied gas business. Then, my chemistry professor brought out a Dewar of liquid oxygen and demonstrated how pouring liquid oxygen on objects made them highly flammable.

"It makes most anything burn with a particularly intense flame," my chemistry professor explained.

Whoosh! The burst of heat on my face punctuated a sudden epiphany.

I squinted at the brilliant flame greedily consuming the old textbook my professor was using for a prop. The puzzle pieces fell like dominos in a chain reaction. A particularly intense flame. A particularly intense fire. Consuming a book with amazing speed. Using liquid oxygen. Which my uncle had in abundance.

Suddenly the mysterious fire at the Tolliver Library did not seem quite so mysterious.

I didn't need some phantom ally who just happened to know the Civic Circle's Technology Containment Team was on the way to confiscate the proscribed books. I didn't need some mysterious counter-cabal with the ability to successfully execute the largest single arson Tennessee had seen in decades on incredibly short notice. All I needed was good old Uncle Rob. Occam's razor. The simplest explanation.

"Don't look into the fire," Rob had insisted. "Don't seek out the potential ally who burned down the library before the Civic Circle's Technology Containment Team could arrive. Keep your head down. Stay safe." And the cruelest manipulation of all, "Your carelessness killed your parents. You're not ready to join the fight."

That last one stung, because it was true, if only in part. He'd been using it as a club to pound me into submission whenever I started looking into the Tolliver Library fire. He took my love for my parents, my grief at their loss, and my guilt for contributing to their murder, and he fashioned it into weapon to use against me.

The bastard. My uncle lied to me. He looked me in the... well, come to think of it, he didn't lie directly. He deliberately deceived me by withholding information, though. A half-truth is a full lie. It was a lie of omission. He let me squander my valuable time researching this mysterious potential ally all the while he knew damn well who'd burned down the library. A lie that is half-truth is the darkest of all lies. He did it. He betrayed me. He had me chasing my tail for no good purpose.

He had the motive. I knew exactly what he was thinking. Keeping me in the dark would keep me safe. It would keep me out of trouble, and he probably didn't want some kid knowing he was guilty of arson, even if that kid was his nephew. No "need to know."

He had the opportunity. In my mind, I replayed the events of the night the Tolliver Library burned down, the night my parents were murdered. As soon as we got out of the library, Rob abandoned Amit and me, telling us to go to hide out at Amit's hotel while he stashed the books. Yes, hiding the books we stole from the library was important, but if the hotel was a safe enough place to hide me, it was safe enough to hide the books. It was all an excuse to get us out of the way.

He had the means: means my chemistry professor had just demonstrated. Rob drove back to his place, loaded up with liquid oxygen using the tunnels I had so helpfully shown him to avoid detection, and set the library on fire. That's why the fire was so intense. That's why the investigators couldn't prove arson – because there was no accelerant in the usual sense. No wonder the sprinklers couldn't stop the fire. He had already disabled the alarms when we entered the first time, and the way we rushed through the door back into the tunnel, he didn't have time to try to cover our trail by turning the alarms back on. He was already planning on returning. When he'd come back, he probably drained the sprinklers long before starting the fire. All the pieces of the puzzle were tumbling together in a vast cascade.

By then, class was over. I hoped my professor hadn't disclosed any additional aspects of liquefied gases, because I'd been completely lost in thought. I suppressed my first inclination to rush home immediately and confront Rob. I continued on to my Differential Equations class. I needed to complete my "OODA" loop: I'd Observed and Oriented. With Rob convinced he'd fooled me, I had all the time I wanted to take to Decide and Act. How would he respond? How would I counter his response? I needed to calm down and stay focused. Diffy-q was tough enough under ordinary circumstances. Also, I had chemistry lab after lunch, and the last thing I needed was to blow something up by mixing together the wrong chemicals. I left my school work distract me from my problems with Rob, so I could focus on them fresh, after class.

By the time I got back to the dorm room, Amit was already on his way home to Tennessee for Thanksgiving. Pity – it would have been helpful to discuss the situation with him, but there was no way I could discuss something this sensitive by phone. I needed time to think and time to plan. I had all day Wednesday, and not much happened in class with half the students taking off early for Thanksgiving, like Amit. I stayed Wednesday night in the nearly deserted dorm. I let

Uncle Rob know I'd be driving up first thing in the morning. I'd head to Uncle Larry's for Thanksgiving dinner mid-day before continuing on to Robber Dell to confront Uncle Rob.

CHAPTER 5: A TALE OF TWO UNCLES

I left campus first thing Thanksgiving morning for the drive up to Tennessee. I swung by the Berkshire Hotel on my way into town so I could tell Amit what I'd figured out. He didn't need much persuading. "Of course," he said. "I should have seen it before." We ran through our recollections of the night the library burned. Amit pointed out more evidence. "Come to think of it, it took your uncle a couple of minutes to pick the lock on the way into the library from the tunnels. He didn't bother taking the time to lock the door on the way out."

"Because he was already planning on returning," I drew the obvious conclusion. "I'll let you know how it goes with both my uncles."

I drove to Grandma Tolliver's house. The doorbell gonged when I pressed the button. Grandma's maid, Cookie, answered the door and almost bowled me over with her enthusiasm. "Mister Pete! So glad you could make it!"

"Hi Cookie, good to see you, too!" her zeal was infectious.

"You come right on in here, sir, and let me take your coat," she insisted, barring the way until I let her fulfill her mission.

"None of the other men have on suit jackets?" I asked, handing it to her.

"No, sir, none of that silliness this year," she said disdainfully.

Once Grandpa Jack died, Grandma Tolliver insisted on inviting her daughter, my mother, to Thanksgiving dinner over the obvious objections of Uncle Larry and Uncle Mike. Grandma Tolliver got her way, but the event was always a kind of social minefield. Larry and Mike seized every opportunity they could get to belittle or insult my father. One year, the Tolliver men all wore their best suits and ties to dinner, making my father seem to be an ill-dressed bumpkin. The next year, Dad wore a suit and tie, and the Tolliver men wore jeans and polo shirts, making my father seem like an over-dressed poser. I'd worn jeans and a nice dress shirt and brought along a tie in the pocket of my suit jacket, so I could dress up or down as needed.

"Sir," she said just standing there, holding my coat and beaming at me. "It's good to be calling you, 'sir.' All growed up and off to college, yes, sir!"

I was getting a bit uncomfortable with all the sirs. "Thank you, ma'am," I replied, returning her formality with my own.

"Pah," she exclaimed. "Don't you go gettin' so fancy with me."

The joy on her face evaporated, and she softened her voice, "I never did get to tell you how sorry I am for your mother and father. Your father was a good man. He was quality, no matter what some might say against him, or your mother would never have had him."

I thought she was about to cry. I reached out and gave her a hug. She sniffled and controlled herself. Truth be told, the room did seem to be getting just a bit dusty for me, too.

"Now you just walk on in there to the kitchen and hold your head high, you hear me?" she said, just like she used to lecture me when I was a boy. "Sir." She added with a smile.

"Yes, ma'am," I said deliberately, following her instruction. She stepped back to hang my coat up, yet somehow managed to get back in front of me in time to hold open the door to the kitchen and announce my entry.

"Mister Pete is here, ma'am," she said to Grandma.

Grandma pushed right past Uncle Mike, and Cookie slid right behind her to take Grandma's place at the stove. I noted Uncle Mike had made no move to greet me.

"Hello, Peter!" Grandma said, kissing me on my turned cheek. "Did you drive up all the way from Atlanta just this morning?"

"Yes, ma'am," I replied.

"You must be hungry. Don't be shy, help yourself to an appetizer," she insisted, sweeping her hand over a buffet loaded with sandwiches, cookies, and treats. "Would you like a cup of coffee?"

"Yes, ma'am. Thank you."

Grandma turned away to get a cup of coffee for me. "Michael," she said sternly to her still-motionless son, "greet your nephew."

"Hello, Peter," Uncle Mike said coolly, carefully timing his offer of a hand for just after I'd already picked up one of Grandma's little sandwiches. Jerk.

"Good to see you, Uncle Mike," I lied, transferring the sandwich to my other hand and shaking his. "How's business been?"

"Complicated," he replied. Too complicated for the likes of me to understand, apparently. He turned his back to me and walked off.

Grandma brought me a cup of coffee. "No cream, no sugar," she said. "Just like your father took it. My boys are to be on their best behavior today," she said. "And if anyone gives you a hard time, you let me know, you hear?"

"Yes ma'am," I replied. I heard her, but there was no way I would whine to her about my uncles or my cousins being mean to me. Mean was exactly the right word: not just nasty and spiteful, but in a particularly base or low way. Dad would never have come to Thanksgiving dinner at the Tollivers if Mom hadn't insisted on defending her place in the family. If Mom wanted to sit at the table as Grandma's daughter, Dad was going to back her up as best he could, even if it meant suffering the slings and arrows of Mom's brothers. Dad mentioned to me once that part of what got him through the annual ordeal was the realization that he and his family upheld much higher standards of courtesy and civility than those who thought themselves our superiors. I didn't much care for that kind of game playing, but if I had to be here anyway, Dad's game gave me a chance to turn the slights and snubs into a way of running up the score against the Tollivers. And I did have to be there.

Mom would have expected me to represent her to Grandma and the family, even though she was no longer with us. More importantly, last year's Thanksgiving dinner was deeply insightful. Uncle Larry had attempted to recruit me for the Circle. I hadn't realized there were layers and levels in the Circle's hierarchy. For all their pretensions, the Tollivers were merely big fish in the little pond of Eastern Tennessee. Working on up to the Inner Circle could take generations. Great Grandpa Tom Tolliver had apparently connected the family with the Circle back in the days when the Circle and their local allies were busy expropriating farms from small landowners (my family among them) to make Great Smoky Mountain National Park.

Ol' Tom Tolliver took a page from the Rockefellers' game plan. The Rockefellers formed a secret company to buy up land in Jackson Hole, Wyoming, then lobbied FDR to designate the area as a National Monument, running roughshod over the wishes of local ranchers. The approval removed the property from the tax rolls and greatly enhanced the value of the Rockefellers' remaining holdings. Ol' Tom actually did even better than that. Instead of donating land and taking the tax write-off, he successfully lobbied the state of Tennessee to buy up much of his timber holdings paying par value. Combined with the land holdings confiscated via eminent domain from small landowners without the political clout to secure a fair price, the state of Tennessee donated the land to the Federal government to make Great Smoky Mountain National Park. The Tollivers retained vast, valuable tracts around the emerging tourist meccas of Pigeon Forge and Gatlinburg and further enhanced their fortune during the following development boom.

Ol' Tom Tolliver and the Tennessee congressional delegation also successfully lobbied the New Deal Brain Trust to create the Tennessee Valley Authority and Oak Ridge National Lab, displacing still more "unenlightened hillbillies and rednecks" and paying off the politically powerless owners with a fraction of their homesteads' values. They were the aristocracy, and the rest of us were peasants to do the bidding of our betters. Tom Tolliver's son, Grandpa Jack, picked up where Tom left off, getting the family admitted to the Circle in a junior role. To his credit, he did a masterful job of diversifying the family's interests out of coal and into lumber, natural gas, chemicals, development, and tourism. Grandpa Jack had high hopes for marrying his daughter into one of the more senior families in the Circle, but his hopes were dashed when Mom took up with Dad instead. My existence was a reminder of the family's failure to procure a "suitable match" for Mom. As head of the family following Grandpa Jack's death, Larry was pushing to get the family accepted as full-fledged members of the Circle. I figured Uncle Larry's championing of the Circle's Social Justice Initiative at Georgia Tech was part of his campaign to ingratiate himself with higher-ups within the Civic Circle.

I wandered into the living room where my cousins, Abby and David, were sitting at opposite ends of the couch talking. They cut off their conversation and both looked at me. Neither deigned to offer a greeting. The social game playing was really getting old.

"Good afternoon," I said, settling myself into the chair facing the couch as if I were in charge and the two of them were my underlings.

"I hear you have a C in your programming class," Abby opened the conversation. "And you almost got kicked out of school for cheating." How the hell did she know that? My dear cousin Abby. Always looking for a back to stick a knife in.

"Gee," I replied, "now you're making me feel guilty I haven't cared enough about you to keep up with what you're doing."

"Cheating, huh?" David half grunted by way of rejoinder. This was a sore point for him, because I'd ratted out his debate partner, Shawn, for concocting fraudulent evidence back in high school.

"When you're as good as I am," I told David, "sometimes it just doesn't seem fair."

"Oh yeah?" See, the newbies and novices debating against David and Shawn would immediately begin countering one of David's stupid sounding yet subtle "oh yeah's" with some kind of dialectic response. They'd justify themselves, trying to prove the righteousness of their cause through keen reason and overwhelming logic. By doing so, however, they were immediately conceding that David was their judge and arbiter. Then, after they'd concoct their brilliant, perfectly clear and cogent reply, he'd just shake his head sadly and say "nope," implying that he'd weighed their arguments and they were inadequate. The really foolish would keep arguing as if with sufficient logic they could persuade him, and he'd just keep sadly shaking his head. I'd seen David reduce a freshman nearly to tears. It was devastating... unless you had a clue how to handle it.

"Yeah," I said authoritatively. No sense wasting any more substantive reply on him.

"So, how come you got a C in programming then?" he countered.

"All work and no play makes Peter a dull boy," I offered ambiguously. "So this is all going to be about me? Neither of you doing anything the least bit interesting you want to talk about? It's sad to see such promising futures go to waste." Their egos would hardly let them concede that point to me.

"I hear Emma broke up with Amit." Abby really hated Amit, but if she'd actually troubled herself to participate in debate, she'd never have left me an opening like that one.

"Yes, I'm sure Amit's playboy life is vastly more interesting than anything you or even I've been doing. I've lost track of how many girlfriends he's gone through. It's a new one every week or two. Not that Amit believes in anything as old-fashioned as serial monogamy."

"Come on," David said to Abby. "Grandma's sugar pecans will be out of the oven by now."

They left. Well, that was easy. Thanksgiving at Grandma's had become much more fun since I'd given up worrying what my cousins thought of me. Let them worry what I thought of them, instead! I toyed with pursuing them to the kitchen and rejoining the battle on friendlier turf with Grandma and Cookie as witnesses, but honestly, I was simply tired of the stupid social game playing. They were both just a couple of hens going peck, peck, peck to try to establish themselves at the top of the pecking order. I no longer cared.

Just then, Uncle Larry came into the living room. "Peter," he said warmly.

I rose and shook his hand. "Good to see you, Uncle Larry." Another social lie. The Tollivers were a bad influence on me.

"I've been hearing great things about you," he said. "Seems you had a run-in with a particularly reactionary professor and wiped the floor with him."

"One thing led to another," I said modestly, wondering how it was everyone knew the details of my fall semester.

"We had a review meeting for the Social Justice Initiative down in Atlanta the other day," Larry offered. "Your professor, Gomulka, speaks very highly of you."

Ah. That explained it. "He certainly keeps a close eye on all his social justice ambassadors," I acknowledged.

"It's almost time for dinner. Hang around. After Mike leaves, we'll talk more."

"OK." This ought to be interesting. I gave him a minute or two, and then followed him back to the kitchen. Grandma refreshed my coffee, and I staked out a corner of the kitchen to call my own.

Before long, Grandma summoned us to the table for our midday Thanksgiving dinner. Grandma always had little place cards at the table. I normally sat down at the end with the rest of the cousins, in this case, Abby and David. This year, though, I was sitting up with my uncles and aunts. I did a double take before realizing the message implicit in Grandma's arrangements. I was now the senior representative present of my mother's family. As such, my social rank at dinner was on par with Uncle Mike. Uncle Larry sat at the head of the table in his role as head of the family and stand-in for the late Grand Jack Tolliver. I was wishing I'd spent more time mastering the intricacies of etiquette that Mom had tried, usually without much success, to pound into my skull. Maybe there was a more subtle message involved. In any event, Abby and David glared daggers at me from the far end of the table. I studiously ignored them and made small talk with Grandma and my aunts.

Thanksgiving dinner itself was uneventful. Uncle Larry boasted about the year's achievements at Tolliver Corporation. He'd collaborated with others in the Circle to lobby for carbon tax credits for owners of timber land. "All those trees are sequestering away carbon," he explained. "The owners should get credit for the good work of their investments in preserving our planet's future." As one of the larger private landowners in Eastern Tennessee, Tolliver Corporation was poised to reap a substantial bounty.

"While receiving favorable tax treatment may help the company," Uncle Mike replied, "a focus on the business fundamentals would help ensure there are continuing profits in the long run. Tax credits are worthless without profits to apply them against." No matter what Larry accomplished, the company would be better off if only management were in Mike's more capable hands.

I kept out of the crossfire, making small talk with my aunts and learning far more about the extraordinary achievements of David and his older brother Daniel, and the remarkably eligible young men chasing after Abby than I really cared to hear. I got the impression Grandma didn't get much company. I didn't begrudge lending Grandma a sympathetic ear to learn the latest news about her chrysanthemums, particularly given the feast Grandma and Cookie had placed before us all. It beat hearing more from Abby about how the locally-sourced honey she had selected to grace our Thanksgiving table came from genuine certified free-range bees.

After dinner, Uncle Mike and Aunt Susan departed with David. Grandma and Aunt Nikki were going shopping with Abby – "just us girls." I started helping Cookie clear the table when Uncle Larry walked back in and asked me to follow him. I looked at Cookie.

"Thank you, sir, but you run along with your uncle," she insisted. "I'll take care of everything."

I followed Larry to the living room. "So," he said, "do you have any plans for the summer?"

"I figured on working for Uncle Rob, like I did last summer," I explained.

Uncle Larry shook his head dismissively. "You don't want to waste your talents doing that," he said disdainfully. "Your social justice connections will open doors for you. I understand the Civic Circle will be recruiting summer interns from your class at Georgia Tech. You have a wonderful opportunity to rub shoulders with the elite."

You can tell a lot about a person by how they try to persuade you. Larry was a social climber. For all his power as President of Tolliver Corporation and patriarch of the Tolliver family, he still felt insecure and second-rate compared to the more established members of the Civic Circle. He craved being treated as a peer by them. An opportunity to mingle with the leaders of the Civic Circle was catnip to him – highly attractive and irresistible. By default, he assumed other people would have the same reaction, so his techniques of persuasion reflected precisely the kind of argument that would most appeal to his own sensibilities. I decided not to disappoint him.

"That sounds like a great opportunity to jumpstart my career, sir." I replied enthusiastically.

"Absolutely," he beamed in approval at my recognition of his wisdom. "And you'll have a chance to witness history in the making. This summer, the leaders of the world will come together on Sea Island for the G-8 Summit. A week before the G-8 Summit, The Civic Circle will be holding a retreat to discuss the global situation and prepare recommendations to be presented at the summit. If you play your cards right, you can be in the middle of it."

"I assume this is more than a spectator opportunity for me." I fixed him in my gaze. "What's the focus of the meeting and how does it impact family business?"

"That's what I like about you, Peter my boy: no beating around the bush," he said patronizingly before collecting his thoughts. "You see, the Middle East has been a flashpoint for decades. We had to kick Saddam Hussein's butt out of Kuwait back in 1990, but we didn't have the balls to finish the job. That's finally changing. 9/11 showed how Iraq presents a clear and present danger to the civilized world, and it's about time we did something about it.

"President Lieberman forced the Saudis to turn over the financiers and some of their government officials who had a hand in the plot. Then, we intervened and deposed the Afghan government when they refused to close the terrorist training camps and turn over the ringleaders. The president wanted to make a clean sweep and take out Saddam, too. There's only so much you can do with 'law by stealth,' working within the government to guide policy. At some point you have to have cover from the top. Too many of the new members of Congress were outsiders – they didn't appreciate the threat and wouldn't go along with the leadership. They didn't understand you can't make law from the periphery. You have to be connected with the movers and shakers: the key players who understand where we're going and how to get there. Well, that's finally happening. The outsiders are finally wising up."

"I see." Normally, most every incumbent gets reelected every year. A few outsiders get into Congress each election, but not enough to threaten the Civic Circle's hold on power. What's more, most of the outsiders are probably co-opted – or coerced – before long, anyway. When the 9/11 attack hit the Capitol and killed so many members of Congress, there was unprecedented turnover. Only now was the Circle once again able to exert their customary control. "But why now? Why war?"

"The official line is because Saddam has weapons of mass destruction. He poses a clear and present danger and the threat he poses must be eliminated." He paused. "Unofficially? We have the power to remake the world," Uncle Larry said with the zeal of a missionary. "If we can overthrow Saddam and smash his hollow dictatorship, the dominoes will start falling across the Middle East. Those poor people over there will finally have a chance to live in freedom and democracy, to be true members of the global community. The transition from barbarism to civilization may be painful, but we have a responsibility to make it happen."

The chaos. The turmoil. "Oil," I said, thoughtfully. "All that chaos and conflict will drive up oil prices. In the short run at least. I thought the Tolliver interests were more in natural gas, though, and to a lesser extent coal."

Uncle Larry smiled. "The family's almost out of coal entirely. True, we're more in natural gas, but we own any number of oil leases and we're buying more from small independents who don't have the capital to run their fields in a safe and responsible manner. We stand to profit. Not only will we benefit from rising oil prices, but also, more users will switch to natural gas. It's a win-win."

Another piece of the puzzle. The "Preserving Our Planet's Future" Act not only imposed steep carbon taxes – what opponents called the "Gore Tax" – but also applied onerous regulations on small independents. My father and Uncle Rob had always assumed it was about crushing the competition. Clearly though, part of the plan was to buy out small independent producers at fire-sale prices in time for a boom in oil prices. What's more, Uncle Larry had no idea how Uncle Rob already had his fingers in the business.

"What do you need from me?"

"I want you in the meeting where it's all to be decided," Uncle Larry ordered, "ideally as a representative of the Civic Circle. That internship is your opportunity. Go for it. Tolliver Applied Government Solutions – TAGS – down in Huntsville, they have the IT support contract for the G-8 Summit and for the annual meeting of the Civic Circle the week before on Jekyll Island. That gives us an in already, but the extra perspective you might be able to provide would be helpful."

"It does sound like a great opportunity," I said, trying to get just the right hint of larceny in my voice without overdoing it, "but I may have to cut a few corners to help you out, and it won't be easy. I'm sure there will be added expenses, too," I hinted.

"I'll make it worth your while," he said. He did. We shook on it.

"I'm sure that internship with the Civic Circle will be highly competitive," I pointed out. "There'll be lots of Ivy Leaguers from well-connected families applying. There's no guarantee I'll get it."

"I have it on good authority the Civic Circle will bring in at least one student from your professor's social-justice class," Uncle Larry confided. "I can't pull any strings on your behalf without it being obvious there's a connection, though, so you'll have to win it on your own merit. If you don't get it, TAGS'll be hiring interns, also."

"Thanks, Uncle Larry. I appreciate your looking out for me."

"We'll get you there one way or another," he assured me, "but whether you're directly in the Civic Circle or working for TAGS, don't drop my name or let them know about your connection to the family. You need to keep a low profile."

"Yes, sir," I assured him.

"It's finally going to happen," Uncle Larry added, like a kid waiting for Christmas. "We've been waiting for a long time. You know, if only a few more chads had managed to hang onto those ballots in Florida, we might have had a Republican in the White House leading the way. The Bushes never forgave Saddam for trying to assassinate Papa Bush, and if George W. or Cheney had been in charge, we might have been in Iraq already, enjoying the benefits of peace and stability in the Middle East."

"But then, we probably wouldn't have had the Gore Tax," I pointed out.

"Ratchets," Uncle Larry said. "One step at a time, my boy. With each step, we get closer and closer to the end of history. Each step is inevitable. Universal health care. Universal education. Universal trade and prosperity. A universal global community of free trade and free immigration. All thanks to the benevolent leadership of the Civic Circle. It's all coming, sooner or later. One step forward at a time. Never a step backwards. The end is never in doubt. Only the timing of the individual steps."

I bade Uncle Larry and Cookie goodbye. The dozen-mile drive to Robber Dell was one of the longest of my life. I'd considered just confronting Rob directly, but given the way he'd misled me for so long, I didn't want to let him off the hook that easily. I was determined to given him a taste of his own medicine, and I'd concocted a good way to do it. It was the right thing to do, but I couldn't help feeling nervous. I'd never defied him directly before.

Through the gate, under the sign, up the incline, past the farmhouse, and I arrived to find my uncle waiting for me on his porch. I took a deep breath to steady my nerves and hopped down from my truck.

"Hi Pete," Rob greeted me cheerfully. "I'll take that," he offered, shouldering my bag. I followed him into his steel-sided barn. He and my dad built the barn on top of a buried refuge – a warren of cargo containers and reinforced concrete. The entry was through the bathroom in the barn. A hydraulic lift lowered the floor of the room down a dozen feet to the top level of the refuge. It was nice not to have to pretend to stay in the trailer. Rob carried my bags into my room.

"Take a load off," Rob insisted, "and tell me how Thanksgiving dinner went with the Tollivers."

"Uncle Larry wants me to be his agent to spy on the Civic Circle," I explained, glad for a good excuse to postpone our confrontation a few more minutes. "He wants me to intern with them, or failing that, with his office in Huntsville that works with them. What I still don't get is why he's so interested in recruiting me."

Rob smiled. "I thought I told you about Xanthos Gambits."

I vaguely recalled him mentioning it. "That's when you set up a decision tree so no matter what happens, you can't lose. You box your opponent into a position where no matter what he does it's a victory for you."

"Exactly," Rob confirmed. "He's been working on it since last year. Took me some time to figure it all out. The Tollivers have been successful because they all work together to enhance the family's power, even as they strive with each other for individual dominance. Larry is the eldest brother and head of the family. Mike is his younger rival and at least one of his sons is more or less capable of picking up the reins when the time comes. You tell me, what happens when Larry gets too old and feeble to maintain control? Can you imagine Abby taking over from her father?"

"Hell, no!" The thought was preposterous. Abby was a shallow, arrogant, stuck-up piece of work.

"Can you imagine her marrying someone who could take over Tolliver Corporation?"

My initial reaction was also "hell no," but I considered the question more carefully. "I suppose it's possible that some ambitious young man might decide to put up with her and vice versa."

"From all you've told me, she's enough of a pain in the ass that only someone marrying up would want anything to do with her. The kind of young man with the skill and talent to grow into leading a company like Tolliver Corporation would have far better options than Abby. In the off chance she does find a suitable mate by her father's standards, Larry's son-in-law is unlikely to put up with Abby for long. It will be difficult to truly bring him into the family. The situation is unstable. Even if Larry tried to go that route, enough of the cousins would see the danger for what it was and forbid his son-in-law from exercising real power. So what happens when Larry loses his grip on the company?

"Mike takes over and grooms his son as heir apparent," I concluded.

"Exactly, unless Larry has an ace hidden up his sleeve." Rob looked into my eyes. "You."

"I'm not sure I see," I acknowledged.

"The worst-case scenario is for whatever reason you don't work out for him. Then, Larry finds a way to publically disgrace and humiliate you for your pretension in thinking you could mingle with your Tolliver superiors. By crushing you, he shows his strength and ingratiates himself to the Tolliver cousins who still haven't forgiven your father for eloping with a Tolliver heiress. If Larry gets enough of the family to support him, he may be able to hold off Mike and groom some safer, more distant family member as his successor. That's the worst case, but it's a win for him.

"More likely, you do work out. Maybe you'll be his inside man in the Civic Circle, maybe his catspaw within Tolliver Corporation – just one more distant cousin of the family. However capable you might be, with all the animosity toward your father, you won't get anywhere in the Tolliver hierarchy without your uncle's patronage. That gives him a degree of control over you that he wouldn't necessarily have over one of the other cousins. By the time anyone realizes you might be Larry's ally, you'll be too closely tied to him for any other faction to secure your loyalty.

"That's exactly why he's talking about having you intern at the Huntsville, Alabama, office instead of closer to home," Rob pointed out. "He has someone whisper into HR's ear, and you're hired. It's unlikely anyone learns of your connection to him or his patronage because of the distance from the home office. If they do learn of Larry's influence, you've been exiled to the corporate Siberia, so it looks like some scheme Larry's inflicting on you. He has complete deniability.

"Eventually, he'll be able to place you in the Tolliver hierarchy as his ally, where you're the greatest use to him. You might even succeed him as President of Tolliver Corporation if he has no other safer candidate groomed for the job. You'd be nominally in charge, but he'd be pulling your strings from behind the scenes. No one would expect you to be in cahoots with Larry. When Larry's ready to disclose the connection, it scores points for him for being so magnanimous."

I shook my head in disgust. "I can't believe how ridiculously complicated these dynastic politics can get."

"Larry's counting on that," Rob said with a smile. "The word is 'internecine' – an ugly struggle within a group for power and control. You'll need his help to figure out who's on whose side. That makes you dependent on him. Unless of course you figure out the game and how it's played first."

Rob was being so helpful and so... enlightening. It made my coming confrontation with him that much more difficult to start.

"How's school been treating you?" Rob leapt in, before I could take charge of the conversation and steer it toward the Tolliver Library fire.

"It's been a wild ride." I told him about the zero I got from Professor Muldoon and was gratified at the extent of his righteous anger and the grin on his face when I described the outcome of the hearing. I also described the Introduction to Social Justice class – the essays we were required to do tying oppression into various topics around "justice" and "equality" and "oppression."

Rob was shaking his head in disgust. "That's a classic brainwashing technique," he explained.

"Brainwashing?"

"During the Korean War," Rob explained, "prisoners were subjected to indoctrination classes, just like what you describe. The camps employed a variety of persuasion techniques to try to convert prisoners to communist ideology.

"All persuasion, whether for good or evil, relies on similar principles. I'll run down the list, and you tell me. Reciprocity?"

That one was obvious. "The Social Justice Initiative is paying for my education."

"You have a natural desire to want to return the favor," Rob acknowledged. "There's commitment and consistency...."

"My fellow students and I accepted the mantle of being social justice ambassadors, so we'll have a natural tendency to act and think consistent with that original commitment."

Rob nodded. "What about social proof?" He continued when I gave him a blank stare. "You already told me all your fellow students are writing the same kind of essays and reading them aloud to each other. It's easier to go along with the crowd than to try to buck the consensus."

I'd already figured that out, just hadn't had a name for the phenomenon.

"Authority?" Rob asked.

"I think these terms are loaded with additional connotations for you," I pointed out. "You mean does Professor Gomulka speak as an authority?" I continued when he nodded confirmation. "Of course, he's a professor and we're merely students."

"*Influence: The Psychology of Persuasion*, by Robert B. Cialdini," Rob explained, revealing his source at last. "It's on your reading list." He'd given me a long list of books to read and I hadn't gotten to that one yet. I was coming to the realization that understanding psychology was just as important as military tactics and strategy. "Your professor speaks from a position of authority and his opinions carry extra weight because of it. When in doubt, people will tend to defer to an authority figure. There's... two more," he said looking up and away into space and counting on his fingers.

"There's liking – from what you say he's quite a likeable sort. He's providing positive feedback and boosting your egos whenever you identify yourself as victims of oppression. And there's scarcity – he's made clear that his class is the only source of the revealed wisdom he's providing, that his students are part of an elite few who truly understand what's really going on. There's a natural tendency to value something that is scarce or hard to get. That's part of why hazing is such an effective recruiting tool – the more arduous it is to get into a group, the more highly members value their membership."

There he went again, being helpful. In most every interaction I had with him, he effortlessly became the teacher, the mentor, and reminded me of how much I had to learn as the lowly student apprentice. I had to force the confrontation before he had me too demoralized to go after him. "I need some advice."

"Sure thing," he offered. "What's the problem?"

"You know how we've been speculating for the past year now what organization might have burned down the library?" I began.

It was subtle, but I knew my uncle well enough to detect the understated signs of wariness in his face. "Yes," he replied.

"I figured out who did it," I said confidently. "And I've opened a dialogue with the responsible group regarding future joint actions."

"I thought we'd agreed," Rob responded in an unnaturally level tone, "that you would not take action without my permission."

"Circumstances arose," I explained, "and I seized the opportunity for a conversation. I thought it would be helpful to better understand their capabilities and motivations, and whether they could be trusted."

"I see," he said, neutrally. He stared, prodding me to break the growing silence with further disclosure. He'd already taught me that trick, though. It wasn't going to work. Finally, he relented, a hint of a smile in the wrinkles by his eyes. "Were you going to tell me anything else?"

"No," I replied. "Need to know. The more people who know the details, the less secure the secret."

"Why did you tell me in the first place, then?" he asked.

"I know how much effort I spent trying to track down this information. I'd hate to see you waste your valuable time continuing to pursue the matter," I explained, "when I know who was responsible for the library fire. Don't you agree that's the correct course of action?" I was wondering what he'd do when I backed him into that corner.

"Maybe," he said. "Maybe not. It depends on how much confidence you have in my ability to handle the information in a responsible manner," he explained. "Speaking strictly hypothetically, of course," he added, "if I were the sort to waste my comrade's time with overly-clever schemes trying to expose an imagined hypocrisy, you might be better off keeping me completely in the dark and letting me spin my wheels rather than turning me loose where I might do more harm."

The bastard. He knew. He knew I knew. Now, he was just toying with me.

"Very well," I said. "You prefer directness. I'll be direct. You burned the Tolliver Library down using liquid oxygen as your accelerant, didn't you?"

"Technically, it's an oxidizer, not an accelerant," he clarified, "but yes, I did."

"You led me to believe it was some mysterious third party, so I was filtering or parsing all the data available under the false assumption you left with me."

I'd expected equivocation. Instead, he looked said, "Yes, I did," calmly, looking me in the eye, daring me to call him on it.

Challenge accepted. "You lied to me," I said, doing my best to control the anger growing inside me.

"I kept you in the dark," Rob acknowledged. "I protected you. Would you like to know why?"

"Of course," I answered.

"Do you remember when I picked you up from your parents last Thanksgiving?" Rob asked.

"Yes." It was the last time I saw them. It suddenly struck me: I'd just completed my first year without my parents, but I had to suppress the rising wave of grief and anger and focus on what Uncle Rob was saying.

"Your father gave me a simple charge: 'Keep my son safe.' I knew there were risks, but I thought I was ready to manage them. Then, you told me all you'd learned about the Civic Circle. The likelihood that the Civic Circle was mixed up in this Heaviside secret vastly increased the potential capabilities and the likely danger of our enemies. My risk assessment went from dangerous to critical. I couldn't believe your folks were just waltzing off at a time like that. Remember how I left the next morning?"

"Yes." I'd been working on scholarship essays.

"I left to go persuade your father to grab Kira and bring her back here with your mom so they'd all be safe," Uncle Rob explained. "Your father was headstrong. He'd been planning this second honeymoon with your mom for months. He was convinced the government couldn't do anything over a federal holiday weekend – not an unreasonable assumption under most circumstances, actually. He refused to cancel his trip. Still, he agreed on a contingency I offered. I arranged a safe house with a Nashville friend, and I spent most of the rest of the day figuring out how to smuggle us all into Mexico, if need be."

I had no idea Uncle Rob had been doing all that behind the scenes.

"On Saturday, Amit found that the Circle was moving against your parents and Jim Burleson. He brought over the list of books their Technology Containment Team wanted to seize. I warned your folks to get to the safe house, but it was too late for Jim. We snuck into the library and you and Amit set up your equipment and started scanning the books while I checked the perimeter. The idea was to scan the books and get away with none the wiser."

"But, you changed the plan once we got to the library," I said. "Why?"

"I saw the light from the study room you were using the moment I got to the top of the stairs and surveyed the third floor of the library. You and Amit ought to have known better than to set up your scanning operation in line-of-sight of the stairs. I was wondering if I should have you break down and move to a place with better concealment when I cleared the door and saw what you were doing." Uncle Rob's voice was turning distinctly grim.

"Your gloves were off," he said.

"They were too awkward to handle the pages of the books," I explained defensively.

"You didn't think to bring rubber gloves?" Uncle Rob asked. "You and Amit were leaving your fingerprints all over books that were about to be confiscated by the Circle's Technology Containment Team. I could guarantee you: the very first thing they would do was a forensic analysis to try to figure out who might have handled the books, and you boys... you were leaving your fucking fingerprints over everything."

Amit and I hadn't even thought about that. He was right. We should have.

"I asked you what was going on," Uncle Rob continued, "and you offered me goddamn snacks, spraying crumbs, spittle, and DNA all over the place, like a little puppy dog wagging his tail in front of a steaming pile of dog shit."

Ouch. That was both brutal and true. My uncle wasn't done dissecting our performance yet, however.

"I was furious. I was about to rip into you both, but I caught myself. I realized the problem was not with you and Amit, but with me. Your father had convinced me you two were super-competent. Perhaps you were in your own way, but not in the way I was assuming. I'd figured I was dealing with operators: skilled men who know my craft, who understand basic principles of stealth and infiltration. I was wrong – dead wrong. You were boys. Clever boys, yes, but utterly clueless about what a competent adversary would do with all the evidence you were unwittingly leaving behind. If I chewed you out, I'd only make matters worse. A couple of jittery and flustered teammates wouldn't do. Scanning was a no go. The only way out of that monumental goat rope was to collect all the books and sanitize the room to destroy any traces of DNA evidence. The Circle would know someone grabbed the books, but you'd screwed things up so badly, it couldn't be helped. The books couldn't be left behind to incriminate you boys. I figured I had to get you out of there with the books and clean the place up. I figured I could shoo you on out of there, then find some bleach and take care of it. In a janitor's closet, maybe."

"That's when you told us to take the books and go," I said.

"Right. I made up an excuse about the sheriff coming, told you that we didn't have time, and we'd have to take the books on the list. There were dozens of them, but the three of us could carry them away, no problem. You started to gather your things, when I had a sickening realization. You two had spent your whole summer scanning books. I asked, and you confirmed the total was at least several hundred all throughout the library. No way could we clean them all out and carry them back through the steam tunnels in a reasonable amount of time. Every one of those books was a clue leading straight back to you and Amit.

"We had harvested the kernels of truth, but your fingerprints and DNA remained, strewn throughout a library full of books. We had gathered the wheat, but the chaff remained. This wasn't a mess I could clean up with a bottle of bleach. There was only one way to destroy that vast pile of evidence and save your lives."

Uncle Rob's face was hard as granite and as merciless as Judgement Day. "I had to burn up the chaff with unquenchable fire.

"I sent Amit to take you to his hotel. Surely you two couldn't screw that up. Then, I drove back up here, and cached the loot from the library. I loaded up the liquid oxygen and carried it, Dewar-by-Dewar into the library. I disabled the sprinklers, soaked the books in liquid oxygen, and almost caught myself on fire when I finally set it off.

"Meanwhile you and Amit had the genius idea of ignoring my instruction, and you went back to your house. The Circle's 'FBI' agents caught you. You were damned lucky the sheriff was on top of what was going on and got you away from them. Then, your dad heard about your arrest, and he and your mom rushed back home and straight into an ambush.

"You're a smart kid. You're honest, too. So, you tell me, should I have trusted someone of such demonstrated... inexperience in tactical operations to help me commit and cover up felony arson? Or to undertake any sort of tactical operation against the Circle?" Uncle Rob's eyes bore into mine, as silence enveloped the room.

He was doing it again: trying to use my own guilt against me. That was a ploy he'd tried one time too many. "However inexperienced I may have been or may continue to be," I replied, "I think I've amply demonstrated I'm a quick study when given appropriate direction. I accept responsibility for my actions, the good and the bad, the competent and the inept." I returned his gaze with all the will I could muster. "Can you say the same?"

"How so?" Rob asked.

"Let me run another scenario by you," I hypothesized. "Suppose you had taken me and Amit into your confidence. Suppose we had stayed together and helped you burn down the library. Then, I wouldn't have gone home, I wouldn't have been arrested, my parents wouldn't have left their safe house, and they might still be alive. You were the leader. You are a veteran. You are the man with the experience in tactical operations. You convinced yourself: your two teammates were inexperienced."

I thought better of that.

"No, let's not mince words. Amit and I aren't just inexperienced, we're inept and incompetent at tactical operations, certainly by your standards. Fine. Yet, instead of keeping the team together, so you could supervise and guide us, you left us to fend for ourselves."

"I trusted you to follow a simple order: go to the hotel and hide," Uncle Rob countered. "I thought you and Amit were competent enough to handle that without my micromanagement. Yes, I was wrong. Yes, I am responsible for my mistake in trusting you. Yes, it's possible with the benefit of hindsight that I might have done things differently. Yes, different actions would have led to different consequences and a different outcome. Nothing we say to each other now can change what happened last year. Actions have consequences, for ourselves and others. We must assume responsibility for our own actions, learn from our mistakes, and move on.

"I'm being blunt, because I respect you," Uncle Rob explained. "You're a promising analyst. The way you spotted the clues and pieced together the hidden truth about that Heaviside guy and the Circle – that was truly remarkable. You do have a talent. You do have a part to play. If I'm going to defeat the Circle, I'm going to need your help to figure out what they're doing and why. It's only help I need from you, though. Not the main event. I have no intention of letting you get anywhere near any sort of tactical operation in the future. You're a researcher, not a rifleman. And I will be the judge of what constitutes an acceptable tactical risk in any future operation. We are not gallivanting off to rescue everyone who falls under the scrutiny of the Circle.

"My job is simple: to fulfill my promise to my brother, your father, to keep you safe," Uncle Rob concluded. "Your job is to get your education and prepare yourself."

"No, sir," I said out of habit and instantly regretted it. I needed to stop deferring to him. "Our job is to defeat the Circle. Yours and mine. Anything else is only a means to that end. I can't be the analyst and figure out the Circle if you withhold critical information from me."

"Your role is secondary," Rob countered. "Sure, the Circle's been around a while. Yes, it would be nice to know their history. The sciencey stuff you're working on might be useful. Fundamentally, though, taking down the Circle is a tactical problem – refining our understanding of who they are and what they do, identifying the 'Inner Circle:' the key players who call the shots. Then, I'm going to take them out. That's not something you can look up online or in a library. It requires tactical intelligence, it's not something you can discover from old books."

"You don't understand the big picture," I replied. "Neither do I. We need to know who they are and what they want. Those library books must have some current importance, or their Technology Containment Team wouldn't be so sensitive about hiding them. Figure out what exactly they're hiding and why, and you figure them out."

Uncle Rob was shaking his head. "I'm convinced saving those books was a mistake. They certainly weren't worth your parents' lives. I was expecting some kind of smoking gun. Instead we get folklore and obscure history, memoirs and mysticism with no real direct relevance to hidden technical secrets or to the Circle and their operation. Your study of them? Hardly rises to the level of 'nice to have' and miles away from 'got to have.' Amit's more likely to come up with something of direct tactical relevance than you, reading those dusty books of yours."

"There has to be something in those books, or the Civic Circle wouldn't be engaging in wholesale slaughter every time someone comes close to a copy their Technology Containment Team missed," I pointed out.

"Risk versus reward," Uncle Rob said. "The Circle killed Jim Burleson, your folks, and those people in Houston to keep you from understanding this Heaviside theory. Electromagnetic waves actually bounce off each other. What good is that secret to us? It's certainly not worth the bloodshed. It was a deleted sentence here, a botched index entry there that let you figure out the Heaviside business. Needle in the haystack stuff. The Tolliver Library haystack is vastly bigger – many more books. You've fixated on this MacGuffin for reasons that aren't all that clear to me."

I was convinced Uncle Rob was wrong, but I couldn't prove it. There had to be something in those books – something we just didn't quite understand yet. The MacGuffin book? It was the most puzzling, the most perplexing with its rambling narrative meandering through memoir and mysticism. It was the life's work of someone who'd tried to untangle the mystery of the Civic Circle. It was just a feeling I had, but somehow I was convinced MacGuffin had laid bare secrets that perhaps even he didn't fully understand. Honestly though, Rob had a point. I hadn't made much progress other than to confirm that the Circle had a long and shadowy history, the details of which we still didn't know. Angus MacGuffin was the key to unlock that history. He had to be.

Uncle Rob interrupted my thoughts. "Look, it's not like I've been sitting on my ass since you went off to Tech. I left Bud Garrety and the shop rats in charge of the operation here, and I went up to DC and did some surveillance of the Circle. I talked to some of their staff and figured out what they're doing."

"How did you get past their security to talk to their staff?" Mr. Burke's private investigator had reported extremely high levels of security around their building in Arlington, Virginia.

"The fraternity of smokers crosses all kinds of boundaries," Rob grinned. "The building is officially nonsmoking. There's an alley behind the building where smokers go at breaks and over lunch. You happen to be there when they arrive. You hang out. You share a light. You listen sympathetically as they vent about their job and their bosses."

"I didn't know you smoked," I said.

"Used to," Uncle Rob acknowledged. "Gave it up."

"Because of the cancer risk?" I asked.

"No," he explained. "I figured out how much of the price went to the government in taxes. As far as I'm concerned, government is worse than cancer. You're getting me off topic, though.

"The Circle is hiring lots of those war hawks. They're gearing up for a major lobbying push. You know how President Lieberman was all gung-ho to invade Iraq after we toppled the Saudi and Afghan governments, chasing the 9/11 terrorist masterminds? He was stopped by a coalition of Democrats and Republicans. Too many of the Old Guard in the establishment perished in the attack. The new Congresscritters who replaced 'em were satisfied with avenging the 9/11 attack and wanted nothing to do with further foreign adventures. If Lieberman and McCain had gone ahead, Congress would have slapped them down and prevented them from taking action. Maybe it just took time for the Circle to get enough dirt on enough of the new guys in Congress. I don't know. They're beating the war drums again, though. In a year – maybe less, we'll be at war again."

I was impressed he'd been able to figure all that out, however, his information just confirmed what I already knew. I realized, he'd managed to do it again: slide right back into the mentor-student role. "That confirms what I've already found out from Uncle Larry," I pointed out, trying to regain the initiative. I shared what Uncle Larry told me, particularly his estimate of what the war would do to oil prices.

"That's what I've been hearing from my sources," Uncle Rob acknowledged. "Someone's been trying to buy out the small independents who've been crushed by the Gore Tax regulations. I'll spread the word. Urge them to hold on."

"Would war with Iraq be a bad thing?" I asked. "Uncle Larry insists that by toppling Saddam Hussein, we can bring peace and democracy to the Middle East."

Uncle Rob was already shaking his head ruefully before I could even finish. "Proglodytes," he said. "Progressive troglodytes. I swear half the reason they're so fixated on universal equality and the doctrine that everyone is fundamentally the same is intellectual laziness. Assuming everyone is really just like them saves them the effort of having to figure out what makes other cultures tick. Expecting a stable democratic state to take hold in a low-trust culture is lunacy."

"Low-trust culture?" I wasn't sure what he meant.

"Many Middle Eastern societies are very tribal," he explained. "For instance, cousin marriage runs rampant. It's common over there for young men to marry their father's brother's daughter."

I thought the relationships through and frowned. "Like me marrying Abby."

"Exactly," he said. "Helps reduce sibling rivalries if you're sharing the same grandchildren. Those cousin marriages keep family loyalties much closer than in the West. Over there it's me against my brother; me and my brother against our father; my family against my clan; my clan against my tribe; my tribe against the world. And everyone against the infidel," he added. "Family and local loyalties always trump national ones. Makes for unstable nations.

"The European model is completely different. One thing the Catholic Church did early on in Europe was forbid relatives from marrying. There's an argument that that policy led to a more open society where people would be more trusting of outsiders, more loyal to distant rulers.

"I've seen it argued that these cultural practices reflect actual genetic differences. Or culture reinforcing genetics reinforcing culture. Hard to say. Can't be a good thing genetically to have only seven great-grandparents. There's a greater chance of getting two copies of the same recessive genes that could cause birth defects or similar problems. Maybe the genetic downside is compensated by the survival benefits of enhanced loyalties within family and clan."

"A high-trust society may have weaker family bonds, but makes it easier for people to work together in even larger groups," I pointed out.

"Right," Uncle Rob agreed. "You can see how either approach might work out for the best, depending on the circumstances."

"So you're saying that if we topple Saddam Hussein's dictatorship, the consequence won't be a stable democracy taking its place. We'll see chaos?"

"Exactly." He nodded his head. "People don't understand how unstable the very concept of a nation is when superimposed on competing tribal cultures. The boundaries in the Middle East were drawn by the British and French without much regard for the people being fenced in together within the borders. It may well take an authoritarian government to hold together the competing tribes. Undermine the authoritarians, bad as they are, and the result may well be worse: bloody civil war of tribe against tribe and sect against sect."

I let that sink in. I had a feeling we were missing something. "If there's one thing we've learned about the Civic Circle, it's that they're smart people who understand exactly the consequences of what they're doing," I pointed out. "To understand what they're after, you have to look at the effect of their policies and actions, not just listen to the rhetoric and justifications they use to get their way."

Rob was nodding his head, so I continued. "They promote social programs that don't work, not from any affection for the poor, but to create a dependent class and buy votes. They see families as a threat to their power, so they encourage feminism to disrupt traditional families, suppress the birth rate, and create still more dependents who will vote for more government control and more handouts. Most everything they do ultimately contributes in some way to their goal of a centralized global government with themselves in charge. What are they after here?"

"One consequence of this instability is a temporary shock to oil prices," Rob observed. "That's something your Uncle Larry is counting on. They'll make themselves richer with that advance knowledge."

It didn't feel right. "There must be more to it. The Civic Circle thinks long-term, years or decades ahead. They wouldn't make this a centerpiece of their policy for the sake of a quick profit. What's the long-term consequence of disrupting the Middle East? Chaos? Civil wars?"

"Even more terror?" Rob speculated. "A more visible enemy to make us sacrifice even more liberty in the name of security?"

"That's got to be part of it," I agreed. It wasn't enough. Then, it came to me. "Refugees. Wave upon wave of migrants and refugees, fleeing the disorder in their homelands."

I could see Rob putting the pieces together, too. "An invasion of Europe. Not a military invasion, but a mass migration. Right into the heart of a prosperous, high-trust society. Transplanting their traditional Islamic culture. Terror and unrest everywhere. Necessitating a permanent police state and an abandonment of the liberties and rights made possible by our high-trust society."

"The Circle doesn't want to rule our society as it is now," I concluded. "They want to rule the world, but not our world as it is. They want to rule a world of their own creation, a remade world with a different culture. Somehow, this is part of the overall plan."

"That summer meeting of the Civic Circle and the G-8 meeting are critical," Uncle Rob concluded. "The push for war will come right after the G-8 Summit. We need to get inside that meeting. Figure out how to disrupt it."

He'd done it again. He took the full brunt of my criticism for leaving me in the dark, and here we were again, right back to the status quo with him as boss and me as junior analyst. He was going to keep feeding me those little bits and pieces of data he figured I could handle while continuing to leave me in the dark. I tried again to see if I could break the cycle.

"I want to point out something here." I held Rob in the most penetrating gaze I could muster. "You spent your fall working around the periphery, looking for an opening. You successfully uncovered the Circle's plot to instigate war in the Middle East. I appreciate your efforts," I acknowledged, "and I'm glad you were successful, but I got the same and better intelligence from Uncle Larry. I have a solid opportunity to get myself, and probably Amit, too, inside the Civic Circle's meeting, where I'll be able to uncover even more.

"You've been keeping me in the dark, while I've been doing some heavy lifting, too – accomplishing as much or more than you. I got the same intelligence you collected, and Amit and I managed to expose the whole surveillance program to public scrutiny.

"I haven't told you everything I've been doing," Uncle Rob replied, coldly: "making contacts, building a network, getting ready to move. There's a whole operational side that has to be ready before we make a move. You have no need to know the details."

"Fair enough," I conceded, "but, what kind of move? How do we hurt the Civic Circle? I don't doubt you could lie in wait somewhere and kill someone. What would that accomplish? There are layers upon layers to the Civic Circle. Uncle Larry is on the outermost layer with several hundred other wannabe movers and shakers. The Civic Circle has a structure we're only now beginning to discern. There are hundreds closer in, yet still in the periphery, and many dozens even closer to the top. We don't know who's really running the show – who's actually in the Inner Circle."

"In any organization, there are only a few decision makers," Uncle Rob observed. "A committee only works with no more than five or six people. If there are more, it becomes ineffectual – a hotbed of competing cliques and factions. By the time we can identify the Inner Circle, I'll be ready to take them out."

"Understand this," I explained. "Whoever killed my parents is living on borrowed time. If we can figure out who was responsible, the only problem I'll have with killing them is if you try to cut me out." He started to interrupt, but I kept on talking. "Organizations have a life of their own, though" I continued. "Kill the top dozen people, and more from the lower ranks rise to fill their places. Arguably, that's exactly what happened on 9/11. President Gore and his most senior personnel died in the attack on the White House. President Lieberman assembled an all-new team and was acting within a day or less. Killing the leadership isn't enough. More junior members are promoted and the organization continues on. We have to find a way to kill the organization itself, not just the handful of people at the top."

I paused as Rob digested this.

"I understand I have much to learn from you," I continued, "but, I'm pulling my weight and doing my share. I deserve to be treated as an equal partner, not kept in the dark."

Uncle Rob was unfazed. "We need to find out more about our enemy. To the extent you can do so safely, to the extent you can handle the truth, I have no problem. I am responsible for you and for your safety, though, and I am the judge of that extent. You still have no appreciation of the risks you are running and the dangers you're facing. I do, and I will remain in charge. The time is not yet right to move openly against the enemy. We are in a phase of building our strength and our resources, and we will not take direct action against the enemy prematurely."

I may have figured out the library fire, but here I was, right back where I started with him. "I understand revealing the secrets from Tolliver Library would lead back to us, but we can and should at least warn the Circle's targets – protect them if we're able."

"I know you were bothered by the LeChevalier business," Uncle Rob acknowledged. "Maybe we could have tipped him off. Maybe he could have done something to avoid the Civic Circle's Direct Action Team. That tip could have led straight back to us, though. If we become too casual with Amit's intercepts, we risk exposing how he's penetrated their field operatives' communications. Anyway, LeChevalier appears to be recovering from what was supposed to be a terminal brain cancer, thanks to the Coley's Fluid treatments he's getting at that clinic in Tijuana."

He seemed conciliatory, so I decided a bit of reciprocation was in order. Maybe I could get him to help me on a project I'd been suggesting for months. "Acting directly may well pose a risk, but the Circle is a big organization with plenty of opportunities for field agents or analysts to develop scruples and decide to leak information. We pose as an insider with a guilty conscience, and if the Circle does get wind of our tip, they chase their tails hunting their presumed mole. Win-win."

Rob still wasn't convinced. "It's only a couple of agents with sloppy tradecraft that make Amit's penetrations possible. It wouldn't take more than a handful of your tips before they'd identify those agents as the source. They might even figure out exactly how those agents' communications were compromised, which would lead straight back to Amit and to us. It's way too risky.

"You can carry on your research, provided you continue to access the Internet only through anonymous links, but I have to insist: no operations, and no operational use of Amit's data. Not without my approval." He fixed me in his gaze.

He had me. I may have been getting my tuition and room and board paid by the Social Justice Initiative, but I was still dependent on him for everything else. I couldn't agree not to act according to my own judgment, though. "I'll offer you this. I will not act without first discussing the proposed operation. I will listen to your feedback. In exchange, I expect you will not be unreasonable in withholding your approval."

Neither of us liked the deal. They say a good deal makes both parties unhappy. I had strained my once-close relationship with my uncle. I spent most of my holiday away from Robber Dell so I wouldn't have to be reminded of how he'd deceived and betrayed me. I hung out with Amit at his family's hotel, and I spent time at Kudzu Joe's Coffee Shop just relaxing, taking a breather from the stress of trying to save the world and getting through my fall classes. I ran into Emma at Kudzu Joe's, and we had a private chat about our respective college experiences. She'd put Amit behind her and was dating a boy she'd met at the University of Tennessee.

I even connected with my shop-rat friends. We had lunch together. Apparently, Uncle Rob had coached them not to discuss his business with outsiders, and I wasn't on the cleared list. Fair enough – I could hardly tell them about my own struggles with the Civic Circle. They were all happy to be out of school and making money. A couple of them were still living with their folks, the others had modest apartments. Rick had already bought land and a trailer up in the hills around town. They were carefully banking their salaries and getting on with their adult lives under the guidance of Uncle Rob, Mr. Garrety, and some of the older truckers and contractors in his crew. I felt a bit left behind – still a dependent as a student: not earning my own way and not carrying my own weight. It was a humbling experience.

On my way back to Atlanta, Sunday morning, I went by my old house. The ruins had been removed and bulldozed over. The land was still tied up in the forfeiture and probate proceedings. I visited my parents' graves, sitting by the tombstones Grandma Tolliver had insisted upon, marking the site where we laid two coffins to rest, empty but for a small urn of wood ash in each. I smiled, remembering how my sister Kira had deftly stolen the urns with my parents cremated remains so she, Rob, and I could defy the Tollivers' plans and have our own private remembrance up at Robber

Dell. I wished I could tell my parents how I was doing, see their supportive faces, and hear their encouragement and advice. I was going to have to live my life and avenge their death without the benefit of their counsel and wisdom. They'd done their fair share and more to make me who I was and to prepare me for the demands of adult life, even if those demands were far more extreme than any of us could have imagined. Now I was on my own – I couldn't count on Kira, and I could no longer count on Rob

The rest would be up to me.

CHAPTER 6: THE SECRET KINGS

Amit and I got a couple of surprises in our first social-justice class after the Thanksgiving holiday. The first surprise was when Professor Gomulka returned a backlog of graded essays.

I was used to getting an occasional A, but more usually B's or sometimes a C. "Check your heteronormativity," "uncover the depths of your internalized racism," "engage better with your identity," and "deconstruct your unearned privilege," were a few of the nicer things he had to say about my attempts to parrot back his social justice rhetoric. The opaque jargon of social justice was designed to resist easy interpretation by outsiders. Mastering the argot was the secret recognition handshake by which one member of the collective could recognize another and assess the other's moral status. In this latest batch of graded essays, I'd aced them all. True, I had been working with Amit to hone my rhetoric, but the enhanced "quality" of my social justice propaganda hardly justified the improved grades. At this rate, a good performance on my finals might boost me to an A in the class. With my B in differential equations and C in programming, it would be nice to have another A to pull up my average.

The second surprise came after class. Professor Gomulka invited Amit and me to an off-campus lunch. A couple of days later, we found ourselves dipping chunks of bread in melted cheese at a fondue restaurant with an unexpected guest, the dean.

"Glad to meet you in a less formal setting," the dean said, shaking my hand. "Ah, and you must be the Amit Patel I've heard so much about," he added, shaking Amit's hand. "I'm not sure you realize what you've accomplished," he said, turning his attention back to me. "The way you handled Professor Muldoon was masterful – gave him enough rope and let him hang himself. I thought I was going to have to save you from Muldoon, but you set him up and took him down by yourself. Very cleverly done."

"Thanks," I replied neutrally. It was hardly a clever scheme on my part – more a combination of Muldoon's arrogant stubbornness and the slow-moving academic integrity review process – but I wasn't above taking the credit for it. "I appreciate your decision to drop the charges," I acknowledged.

"How is everything working out with Professor Fries?" the dean asked.

"Very well," I answered. "He's graded the homework Professor Muldoon refused to accept, and given me a couple of additional assignments. And he's going to prepare a final exam for me."

"Excellent," the dean beamed. "You probably don't know what a service you did to the university by so embarrassing Professor Muldoon," he added.

"I suppose I may not appreciate all the implications," I noted, dryly.

"Indeed," the dean nodded his agreement with a smile. "You see, Professor Muldoon is on the faculty senate. He's one of the leaders in the reactionary movement opposing the Social Justice Initiative. You've seriously damaged his credibility among the other faculty. Soon, we may be able to force his resignation and replacement with someone more forward-looking."

"Happy to be of service," I replied, trying to keep the inner turmoil out of my voice. Had I dealt a fatal blow to someone who was actually an ally? "I'm surprised that my little run-in with Professor Muldoon could possibly have such significant consequences."

"You've helped alienate him from potential allies and supporters," Professor Gomulka interjected. "Another pebble. A particularly shiny and worthwhile pebble, but still just a pebble. Alone, it means little. Enough pebbles, however, and before long you get an avalanche." He turned to the dean. "You were telling me about the other little surprise in store for Professor Muldoon?"

"Yes," the dean grinned. "I understand Professor Muldoon is upset that his research funding does not cover all the lab equipment he'd like. He brings in his personal equipment from home to supplement the meager resources of his lab on campus. He feels justified in borrowing some of the lab equipment to use in his ham radio station at home to balance the scales. That's not the way the auditors will see it, though. When the time is right, we will discover exactly how much university property is missing from his lab, file a complaint, and secure a warrant to search his house. If it's anywhere near the amount I suspect, Professor Muldoon will find himself suspended and facing criminal charges, not to mention disbarment from any future research grants or contracts. It will be the end of his career, and the end of his interference in our plans."

I smiled and nodded in honest, wholehearted approval. I really approved of villains who wanted to boost their egos by bragging about their exploits in front of me.

Amit interjected, "I'm delighted to see you taking such an activist approach to social justice. I was afraid it was mostly just words."

"Never underestimate the power of words," Professor Gomulka smiled, "but ultimately, power in civil society derives from money and people. We provided our backers with an update on the progress of the Social Justice Initiative just a couple of weeks ago. They were very pleased at how much we've accomplished." He turned to me with a big smile.

"Your uncle's support for our initiative has been most helpful."

Ah. I began to understand why my grades had improved so dramatically after Thanksgiving. Professor Gomulka only just now realized my Uncle Larry was one of his principal benefactors.

"We have a modest amount of money to serve our needs, and we're using it to fund our people. You two are my star pupils," Professor Gomulka said approvingly. "You have the potential to become more than just social justice ambassadors, you're on track to be..." he paused as if struggling with a new concept "...social justice 'warriors,' to coin a phrase."

"That means a lot to me," Amit replied, "but surely there are others in class who've made even more significant contributions to social justice. Marcus and Ryan made national headlines by standing up for their rights and exposing government surveillance of text messages."

"We certainly took credit for their accomplishments," Professor Gomulka admitted. "But you'll recall how reactionary they both were at the beginning of the semester. You were right, Amit. Marcus' existence, like that of any student-of-color, is protected and made possible by the rules and laws we have set up. We own him. He belongs to us. For him to spout this self-made nonsense undercuts and sabotages all the good we've done for him and others like him. Besides, his conversion is... suspicious. Ryan, too. The way in which their little stunt rapidly escalated into national headlines suggests they have some undisclosed backing and support. They're dangerous. You'll find there are always reactionaries trying to infiltrate their own stooges into revolutionary groups. There's nothing wrong with a government keeping a close eye on its citizens – provided, of course, it's the right kind of government."

"What can we do about them?" Amit asked. "Can't you just drop them out of the program?"

"No," Professor Gomulka acknowledged. "It's not that simple. There's a certain decorum we must maintain. If I just kick them out, questions will be asked. If they happen to be out of class the day we review for the final, miss certain critical hints and instructions, and then fail," he added with a satisfied smile, "why then I will have to regretfully revoke the scholarships of two of my most favorite students."

"Madison's been spreading the word through her column in the student paper," I pointed out.

"Madison? She's an effective tool for spouting feminist propaganda, but she actually believes what she's saying. We can hardly include her in our little patriarchal cabal here," Gomulka pointed out. "We men, however enlightened in social justice, are the 'enemy' in her perception. It colors her perspective and limits her utility."

"Well then, what's the program?" I asked. "What are we doing to advance the cause of social justice, and how can we help?"

"Our power on campus is limited. We have friends and allies in key places," Professor Gomulka said, gesturing toward the dean. "We pick a target, like Professor Muldoon, who stands in our way. We cut him off from his support network and destroy any sympathy for him. That's where you've been most helpful, Peter. Then, we attack the target personally. People hurt faster than institutions, and to get an institution to do what we want, we have to attack the people who are blocking us. Part of that is making sure our enemies live up to their own rules. When we catch him breaking the rules, we make sure he's forced to live up to them and that he suffers the consequences for his refusal to do so. That's what the dean has in store for Muldoon. Saul Alinsky laid out these *Rules for Radicals* in a book we'll be studying in the spring semester."

"It's not as easy as it was in the old days," the dean added.

"How did it work in the old days?" Amit asked.

I saw the dean look to Professor Gomulka for guidance. The professor nodded, "It's mostly public now, anyway. You can tell them."

"Every student entering an Ivy League school for a generation, between the 1940s and the 1970s, was required to strip and be photographed in the nude. 'Posture and scoliosis study,' they were told. Amazing what the more puritanical among our elite will do when threatened with an intimate public exposure. Unfortunately, attitudes began to change." The dean looked to Gomulka.

"Apparently, someone approached Bill Clinton in 1992 to withdraw from his campaign as the rumors of his womanizing began to spread," the professor explained. "They threatened to reveal the picture to the public. Rumor has it he laughed in their faces, 'Hell, I haven't looked that good in years! Go ahead. That'll get me an extra five points from women voters.' The problem was, the threat was empty, because the first time someone actually released a picture the entire elite would unite against the leakers, and the victims would be objects of sympathy. The Clintons arranged for the Smithsonian to take possession of the archive and 'destroy' it back in the 1990s."

"You can bet they have copies squirreled away somewhere," the dean speculated, "just in case."

"Power is not just what you can do," Professor Gomulka concluded, "it's what your enemies think you can do. Unfortunately, once the bluff is called, the threat becomes ineffective. We have to devise more sophisticated means of influence and control for the younger generation.

"We recruited our first social-justice class by soliciting applications," Professor Gomulka described the process. "A couple hundred students applied and we selected you dozen. Next year, every applicant to Tech will have to fill out our social justice questionnaire. We'll be able to screen the entire incoming class for their social consciousness and select a larger group, maybe a hundred or so. Eventually, we'll have mandated social justice classes for the entire student body, using the results of the survey to individualize and optimize social justice education for the masses, while continuing the specialized training in social justice activism for the elite."

"If the social justice curriculum replaces all the humanities electives in the curriculum, won't that leave a lot of professors out of jobs?" I asked.

"Who do you think we're counting on to teach the social justice curriculum?" Gomulka responded, with a twinkle of amusement in his eye. "Most of the humanities faculty are on board already. In many cases, their teachings are already well-converged with social justice ideals. Study literature, you'll learn about the misogyny of dead white males, and be introduced to more modern, more enlightened books and thinking from more diverse authors. Study history, you'll be introduced to the narrative of oppression through the ages. Faculty that aren't on board with social justice won't be able to stand against the enlightened example of their peers. The real challenge lies in getting STEM to converge toward social justice."

"STEM?" I asked.

"Science, technology, engineering, and math," the dean helpfully added. "We're looking to hire a new head for the College of Engineering. She's a real creative gal. She'll shake up the curriculum, make it more relevant to our diverse student body. She'll see to it that our faculty move beyond superficial measures of equality as statistical analyses of headcounts, and toward addressing justice and the genuine engagement of all students as core educational challenges."

"Professor Muldoon stood in our way," Professor Gomulka explained. "Now you've helped us extinguish his opposition. As we expand the program for next year, I'll need teaching assistants to help me. That's how you two fit in. In addition, our backers want to recruit our top students for summer internships. I'll be passing on the details in class, and I encourage you to apply.

"True social justice warriors are hard to find. Most students are wrapped up in their own petty interests. In fact, they don't truly understand what those interests are. They need more enlightened folk like us to figure out what's best for them and then to nudge them in the right direction through our power and our persuasion," Professor Gomulka explained. "Ultimately, we are the secret kings. One day, before too much longer, we will rule the world. But don't worry about all that just now. This little lunch is merely our way of saying thanks to a couple of our valued junior allies. Welcome aboard!"

I had to run off to my chemistry lab final when we got back to campus. I met up with Amit at dinner.

"I know Professor Muldoon is hardly your favorite guy," Amit began.

"That's an understatement," I said, "but I think George P. needs to help him out, anyway. Enemy of our enemy and all that. Let's send Muldoon a letter explaining what's going on, and the usual instructions for using encrypted email. I'm more disturbed by the fact that Gomulka saw right through George P.'s handiwork with Ryan and Marcus. I thought we had them both in the clear."

"George P. can email the details from the social justice review session to them both," Amit suggested. "That should get them through the final. In the long run though, Gomulka will probably find a way to boot them both from the program. We'll have to warn them. They'll need to be figuring out another way to fund their educations for next year."

"The bigger issue is how we can derail the Social Justice Initiative's program of systematic indoctrination," I pointed out. "We need to take a page out of Gomulka's playbook — find some way to discredit him and the program."

"If we're the teaching assistants, we'll have a certain amount of leverage to influence the implementation of the program," Amit noted. "Anything really drastic, however, and we'd be found out. We can't just flunk out the most obnoxious of Gomulka's 'social justice warriors.' He'd see right through that."

"I wonder if we could get inside the selection process for next year's class," I offered. "Gomulka is lazy. I swear half the reason he makes us read our essays out loud in class is so he can listen and score them then and there, instead of having to prepare a lecture and take a stack of essays back to his office to grade. It wouldn't take much persuasion to get him to let us do the evaluation for him."

"Half the reason? You're too conservative, as usual." An evil smile danced across Amit's face. "I'm beginning to think Gomulka needs our help. You know how bad he is with computers and email. Suppose I help him out with his computer, and maybe add a key logger."

"Key logger?"

"It's a program that records his key strokes," Amit explained. "We'll get his passwords and anything he types. We could get his passwords, read all his email." We brainstormed a bit. Amit already had something in the scripts and tools he'd downloaded from the "Dark Web," the online black market of hackers. He installed it on my school computer and we confirmed that everything worked as advertised. Then, we finalized our plans.

* * *

I slid a note from George P. Burdell under Professor Muldoon's office door the next day detailing the dean's plans for an equipment audit and suggesting the professor open an encrypted email channel to us so George P. Burdell could keep him informed of further developments. A few days later, Amit got back a "Thanks, George P." note from Muldoon by encrypted email.

The dean summoned Ryan and Marcus for a meeting at the same time as the review session for the social justice final. We took scrupulous notes of the arcane social justice history Professor Gomulka shared. Somehow, the professor's email inbox had filled up with spam overnight, each email running a long and CPU-cycle consuming script as he attempted to preview the contents. After class, Amit approached him, "Is everything OK with your laptop, professor?"

"No," he replied. "I can't get my email to load."

"I can help you with that," Amit offered. He turned off the email preview mode, did a global search for a keyword he'd embedded in the emails and deleted them. The problem was resolved and the email loaded perfectly.

"Let me check your anti-virus software.... Your definitions are out of date." Amit started the update process. "I can install some software that will help keep that from happening again."

"Go ahead," the Professor Gomulka agreed, delighted at how quickly Amit had resolved his difficulties."

Amit navigated through the professor's Omnibrowser, downloaded Malwarebytes, and started the installation process. "This is a great application for avoiding adware and other more subtle forms of malware that your virus scanner might miss." Part way through the process, he reached up and scratched his left ear. That was my cue.

"Professor Gomulka," I drew his attention, "I still don't understand how Clarence Darrow was able to impeach the credibility of Harry Orchard in the Steunenberg trail." Amit deftly inserted his flash drive in the professor's USB port. "I mean, Orchard confessed to planting the bomb that killed the governor, and he fingered 'Big Bill' Hayward and the Western Federation of Miners' leadership in the assassination." I saw Amit installing his script packages. "That's about as open-and-shut as it gets, isn't it?"

"You have to appreciate the bare-knuckles approach to justice of the era," Professor Gomulka replied, giving me his full attention. "Both sides tried to influence and bribe the jurors. Clarence Darrow and the miners' union managed to out-hustle William Borah, the prosecution, and the Pinkertons."

That was a bit more honest and succinct an answer than I'd expected of him. I had to keep him distracted. "The irregularities of kidnapping Hayward and his co-defendants and transporting them to Idaho must have left a bad impression, too."

"You have to remember, this was before there was an FBI or any other truly federal law enforcement," the professor answered. "That's what gave the Pinkertons their power – filling the void between the competing jurisdictions of the various states." Amit removed his flash drive. "Then they used that power to help business interests try to crush the legitimate interests of the emerging labor movement."

"All set, professor!" Amit said. "Run Malwarebytes every week or so. Let me know if you need any other help."

"Thanks, Amit." Professor Gomulka looked thoughtful. "I have thousands of essays and applications to review," he noted, "and it needs to be done over break so we can be getting the early admissions offers out. I do have some funds. I could pay you for your time."

Amit looked at me. I nodded my agreement. "We could do that for you," Amit offered. "We could do an initial pass and make some recommendations, leaving the final decision up to you, of course. Between the two of us, we could get the job done over the break."

"Excellent!" Professor Gomulka looked relieved at our agreement to take on his workload. "I'll be in touch."

George P. sent both Marcus and Ryan some excellent lecture notes full of the obscure social justice heroes not previously mentioned who nevertheless were prominently featured on the final exam. Amit's penetration worked perfectly. The first fruit of our access was a copy of the final exam which George P. also helpfully passed along.

* * *

Amit headed home right after the exam. I decided to stay on campus through break. I really didn't feel like going home to Uncle Rob. His betrayal, his treatment of me as a child in need of his guardianship, stung. I wanted to be doing something. We had to be so careful with our online research, and with the slow download speeds possible through TOR connections and Amit's VPN, it took forever to get anywhere unless we had a very specific idea what we were seeking. Browsing in the library, on the other hand, allowed for anonymous access to vastly more information. Besides, Professor Chen offered to let me work in the mirror lab over break, and I could use the extra money, on top of what Professor Gomulka was going to pay us.

My winter break began with a bang, the evening after finals.

Bang! Bang, bang, bang! My door rattled with the pounding. I cracked it open. "Where's Amit?" Ashley demanded angrily.

"He's not here. He already left..."

"Amit!" She shoved past me into the room to check for herself. Amit really needed to see the kind of crazy girl he was dating. I walked past her to Amit's camera clock and pushed the record button.

"Why!" she screamed at me. "Why is he flirting with all those other girls, why?!?"

"That's how Amit is," I tried to explain to her. "He..."

"Tell me! Why, why, WHY?" Ashley screamed, trying to get in my face. The top of her head barely came up to my chin.

I stood my ground. "Ashley," I started again.

"He doesn't love me!" She interrupted, looking up at me. She was crying now in hysterical sobs. "He doesn't love me!"

I felt bad for her. I wasn't happy about having to clean up after Amit's mess, but I calmed her down as best I could. We sat down – Ashley on the edge of my bed and me in my chair – and I let her tell me the many ways in which Amit was a jerk. She had some good points, actually, but she was completely overlooking her own very significant role in creating the mess she found herself in. Now was not the time to point that out. I just nodded and let her vent.

Calmer, but still crying, Ashley said, "I need you to hold me." She stood up, approached, straddled my lap and sat on me. She held my head against her chest.

She was upset, and I wanted to comfort her, but this was getting to be too much. "Ashley," I began.

"Just hold me," she insisted, slowly swaying in my lap. Reassuring her was becoming rather... arousing. I was frozen with indecision. On the one hand, her grinding against me felt great. On the other hand, she was seriously unstable. She leaned over and kissed me. What the hell. I reciprocated. Then, she lifted her shirt and pulled it over her head. She reached behind her back and undid her bra.

It was overwhelming. I was dating her roommate, and she knew it. Yet what started as comforting a distraught friend had become a make-out session. A really intense make-out session. What a mess! She and Amit deserved each other. Ashley slowly undulated down my lap and started unzipping my pants. It was too much, too quickly. I reached down and stopped her. "No."

"You don't want it?" she asked incredulously.

"It's too much. We're seeing each other's roommates, for goodness' sake."

She look dumfounded at me for a moment. "Fuck roommates," she blew up at me, pulling herself up and grabbing her shirt. I had just enough time to appreciate the view as she pulled her shirt over her head before she yelled, "and fuck you!" She stormed out, bra in hand, slamming the door behind her.

Great.

I spent the weekend after finals in the library. I'd gotten no further with the Majorana equation Professor Chen mentioned than I did with the Schrödinger or Dirac formulations. I'd simply reached the limit of my ability to understand the math. I might have to set aside my physics research for a year, until I could master quantum mechanics and partial differential equations better. Since I'd hit a brick wall trying to understand the physics, I thought I'd look into the history of Majorana. Amid all the long-lived quantum mechanics, he was clearly an outlier. Ettore Majorana (1906-

1938?). Nineteen thirty eight... question mark? That's when I knew I was on to something.

Majorana vanished under "mysterious circumstances" while traveling by ship from Palermo to Naples on March 25, 1938. Five years earlier, in 1933 he went to study physics in Germany with Werner Heisenberg. He spent time in Copenhagen with Niels Bohr. He returned to Italy a changed man. Suffering from "nervous exhaustion," the formerly gregarious physicist became a recluse, distant from friends and family alike. He became a professor of physics at the University of Naples.

His mentor, Enrico Fermi, a first-rate physicist himself, proclaimed that Majorana was a genius on par with Galileo or Newton. One day, though, Majorana withdrew all his money from his bank account, and he sent the following note to Antonio Carrelli, Director of the Naples Physics Institute:

Dear Carrelli,

I made a decision that has become unavoidable. There isn't a bit of selfishness in it, but I realize what trouble my sudden disappearance will cause you and the students. For this as well, I beg your forgiveness, but especially for betraying the trust, the sincere friendship and the sympathy you gave me over the past months. I ask you to remember me to all those I learned to know and appreciate in your Institute, especially Sciuti: I will keep a fond memory of them all at least until 11 pm tonight, possibly later too.

E. Majorana

Then, he hopped on a ship, and was never seen again. Clearly, this was someone I needed to learn more about.

"Good morning, Peter," Professor Graf greeted me cheerfully when I checked in the Monday after finals. "Glad you'll be joining us here over break. Get the kiln going, and come see me. I have something interesting to show you." I immediately speculated on all the interesting things she could show me, but I had to push those thoughts aside and focus on getting the kiln going without setting anything else on fire.

When I got back, she was waiting for me. "We're ready to conduct a more detailed study of the data sets from the gamma ray observatory. Professor Chen and I have already taken a look through the data, but I'd like you to take an independent look and tell me what you find."

I reviewed their results – beautiful maps of the concentration of various radioisotopes obtained from their distinctive gamma ray energies. Not all isotopes worked well in this kind of study. For instance, one of the decay products is the noble gas, krypton. It's not reactive and merely floats off and disperses in the atmosphere. It doesn't stay put, so it can't be used to localize spills. Chen and Graf had focused on cesium-137. This isotope behaves like potassium, so it gets absorbed by plants – it persists in the neighborhood of where it was deposited in a nuclear event or accident. Their maps of the Chernobyl and Kyshtym disasters showed how decades later the gamma decays of cesium-137 could be used to map the fallout zones from these disasters.

My professors were busy now looking at other isotopes – how they spread from the same disasters and persisted in the environment. I was curious about something Professor Chen had mentioned – the possibility of comparing the concentrations of different isotopes to date when the radioactive releases might have occurred. I looked at tin-121 – not as common as cesium-137, but it has a forty-year half-life and a strong gamma decay. I used the 1986 Chernobyl disaster and the 1957 Kyshtym disasters to check out my idea, comparing the cesium-137 concentration to the concentration of tin-121 detections. Sure enough, the ratio was higher for the Chernobyl fallout zone than for Kyshtym.

When I came in early the next morning, the glass disk I'd slumped in the kiln the previous day was cool. I put in a new disk and started up the kiln again. I carefully transferred the formed glass to the vacuum chamber and began evacuating the air. "Can you take a look at this, Professor Chen?" I asked when he came later that morning. I showed him how the ratios of tin-121 to cesium-137 were different in the different areas, but didn't match the difference one might expect from simply comparing the half-lives of the isotopes.

"The radioactive half-lives don't tell the whole story," he explained. "You have to account for the fission yields – tin-121 is much less likely to be created than cesium-137 in the first place. I tried the same analysis correcting for the yields. The problem is that tin and cesium have different chemical properties, and migrate and diffuse differently through the environment. Different climate, different rainfall, different wind, different erosion, yield different ratios. We won't be able to date the various radioactive plumes very effectively. There simply aren't any fission products where two different isotopes of the same element are strong gamma emitters. What we can do is study how different isotopes spread in different ways into the environment."

Bummer.

I kept working through the data set, using the tools Professor Graf had written to generate maps of the detection frequency for various gamma ray energies. In most cases, each energy level corresponded to a specific isotope, so the maps showed the distribution and density of that isotope. By then, the chamber was evacuated, so I turned on the heaters to melt the little scraps of aluminum wire and generate the aluminum vapor to deposit on the mirror. When the process was complete, I turned off the chamber and the kiln, ready to repeat the process all over again the following day. When I had time to give it my attention, I could crank out a mirror a day, and it only took a couple of hours of actual work.

I'd accomplished quite a bit by the end of the day, but the idea of trying to date the radioactive plumes intrigued me. I thought about the problem overnight. If only I could find two different isotopes of the same element. The chemically-identical isotopes would behave and diffuse in the same way, allowing for a direct comparison of their half-lives. I looked through the fission product tables but only confirmed what

Professor Chen had told me. There were plenty of cases where two isotopes of the same chemical element were created, but they decayed differently. For instance, I'd been looking at tin-121. It had a forty-year half-life and yielded a nice strong gamma ray detection. Tin-126 is another common decay product with a whopping 230,000 year half-life. On human time scales, the decay rate would seem virtually constant. Unfortunately, tin-126 undergoes a beta decay – an electron pops out, as a neutron changes to a proton yielding antimony-126. That beta particle can't be detected from orbit.

It had been a few days since I checked our encrypted email accounts, so I set up the Wi-Fi antenna to hit a remote Wi-Fi connection from a law office high up a skyscraper on the other side of the Interstate, and I connected to Lavabit via TOR. I discovered our friend Petrel had been busy.

Hello Anonymous Patron,

I know you told me I shouldn't look further into the matter of Angus MacGuffin, but the whole event is so clearly just a small piece of a much larger puzzle. Curiosity. Cats. You know.

I suppose I shouldn't tell you the exact way I figured this out for fear someone starts asking about who's been poking around the relevant archives. Suffice it to say that others in the period – like Sweeney – were similarly curious about the demise of the mysterious missionary Mr. Angus MacGuffin and received visits from G-men telling them to leave it alone. One of them looked into the G-men and their background. These G-men seem to have been a most special group of special agents – confidants reporting to J. Edgar Hoover, himself. One in particular came to the FBI as a veteran of the Pinkerton Detective Agency and was a key figure in the National Bureau of Criminal Identification before that. They were an outfit the Pinkertons founded in 1897 with the help of state and local law enforcement officials to create a central library of mug shots, fingerprints, and criminal records. In 1924, one year after the death of William

Pinkerton, young J. Edgar Hoover's new "Bureau of Investigation" took it over. They became the "FBI" in 1935.

Is this who you fear will be after anyone unwise enough to poke into the events surrounding the murder of Angus MacGuffin?

If so, I have more ominous news for you.

I found a couple of vague mentions, speculations really, that "The Circle" was involved. I immediately thought of our own "Circle," the Civic Circle. However, they only became widely known in the post 9/11 era when their members pooled their efforts and resources to help in the recovery from that devastating attack. According to their claims, they've been around as an informal gathering of the high and mighty since the 1950s or so. There have been rumors and speculations that the organization dates back even earlier. I believe those rumors are true.

I believe these mysterious G-men or FBI agents are part of an organization that dates back to the earliest days of the FBI and possibly even to the Pinkerton Detective Agency. The Pinkertons not only served as Lincoln's intelligence agency during the Civil War, they also pioneered the art of infiltrating criminal groups and labor unions.

Another of the "G-men" involved in l'Affaire MacGuffin has a most curious past. Eyewitness reports from 1910 place him on Jekyll Island, a junior member of the team providing security for a group of bankers who met together to hammer out details of what would come to be known as the Federal Reserve System. Details are in G. Edward Griffin's The Creature from Jekyll Island. This gathering sounds suspiciously like the Civic Circle's better documented meetings on the island from the last decade or so. The data point troubles me, because it suggests that both the Circle and their mysterious protectors and enforcers have been active over a hundred years. How old are they really?

That's what I've been trying to find out. I understand you've been keeping me in the dark for my own protection, and I'm beginning to appreciate why. Call me terminally *curious, but I intend to keep poking into this. If they are still active today, I figure they may be less sensitive about these dusty old records. All events leave fingerprints and echoes in the archives if only you know where to look and how to put the pieces together.*

I've passed on what I've learned in hopes you'll reciprocate with more of what you know.

Stay safe. I'll try to do the same.

Petrel

Amit and I certainly got our money's worth hiring this Petrel character. I forwarded his note on to Amit and Rob with a recommendation we share what historical background we'd uncovered about the Circle's crusade against electromagnetic scientists.

The next morning I was back in the lab with an overnight inspiration. What about antimony-126? That's the isotope that results from the beta decay of tin-126. After switching out glass disks and starting up the vacuum chamber again, I took a look and discovered that antimony-126 decays relatively quickly and emits a high energy gamma ray. I looked back through the data set for the characteristic decay energy of antimony-126. There it was – a ghostly outline that looked exactly like the maps I'd generated of the tin-121 decays. We couldn't see the beta decays of tin-126, but I could use the gamma rays emitted by the decay of antimony-126 decays as a proxy for the concentration of tin-126. For all practical purposes, the two isotopes of tin would be chemically and environmentally identical.

Now I had an accurate comparison. I used the ratios for the Chernobyl cloud to normalize for the different isotope fractions. A fission tends to produce more tin-126 than tin -121. Then, I used the technique to try to date the Kyshtym disaster. It came up 1955, two years off. Not too bad. Soon, I was dating all kinds of Cold War nuclear incidents. Some were obvious. The Nevada test site had multiple overlapping results from different tests. My analysis averaged out to the late 1950s, which made sense because they'd stopped testing above ground in 1963. A few locations were a bit surprising. I found a big hotspot along the Iowa-Minnesota border that dated to 1960, for instance. Fallout from some test further to the west? By then it was getting late. I set up an analysis to sift through our entire global database using the tin ratio to date the most significant radiation fallout events.

My grades were finally available. I pulled them up. I ended up with B's in Differential Equations and Introduction to Programming. This first was a disappointment, but the way I struggled with the material, it was a reasonable outcome. That last really annoyed me – a valuable lesson, though, in distinguishing between knowing the material and jumping through the instructor's arbitrary hoops. I earned my A's in Linear Circuits and Electromagnetics, thanks in large part to Dad's patient tutelage in the basics. Mom's relentless insistence on memorizing atomic weights and ionic states in my high school chemistry class gave me the foundation to excel in my university class – I earned an A in Chemistry. From here on out, though, I was on my own. I'd just managed to squeak out an A in Introduction to Social Justice, too.

I exchanged a few notes with Rob and Amit. The details of Heaviside's work might lead back to Mr. Burleson and ultimately ourselves if the letter were uncovered or if Petrel had been compromised or was working against us. My recent work on Majorana? I'd been careful, but Professor Chen and Professor Graf both knew I'd been looking into him. Best not to mention that. Still, Petrel had shared some valuable insights. Rob and Amit agreed that I should reply to Petrel with some additional information, in hopes of learning still more from him. He hadn't asked for more money, and he appeared to be motivated by his own curiosity, so we didn't offer any payment. I drafted the following note, trading our insights for his.

Greetings Petrel,

Thanks for the note and for the risks you are running in your research. I share your interest in uncovering the hidden truth of our history, and I would be delighted to share what I know and suspect in hopes my insights provide you with leads and clues useful in your own investigations.

I believe you are correct regarding the deep historical roots of the Circle and their agents operating under the cover of FBI agents. They are still active today, seeking out forgotten books that might reveal the truth behind their schemes. Be careful in your research to leave no trace and always have a plausible, innocuous subject of research available to alibi your investigations. Leave no fingerprints or DNA on the papers, documents, and books you examine, and no record of your interest in them.

L'Affaire MacGuffin, as you called it, highlights a connection between the Circle and events in Chinese history. As you noted, MacGuffin had a wealth of information and artifacts he brought home – some of which he may have hidden or entrusted to his "thorny friend." The Circle was clearly very sensitive about the secrets that MacGuffin might have been able to reveal. I'm confident they'd be just as violent in suppressing the same secrets today. Now, they have even greater resources– the full might and power of a surveillance state that monitors all but the most encrypted and secure communications in the name of preventing "terror." Be careful.

Identifying MacGuffin's friend and tracking down the MacGuffin cache would be of great potential value. We do not fully understand the Chinese connection, although many of the Circle's overt actions today appear to run in parallel to those of Imperial China – aiming for harmony, order, social stasis, dripping with contempt for commerce, and centralizing power in the hands of an educated elite all professing the same homogenous doctrine. The Circle may well have a long pedigree stretching back hundreds of years.

We believe the Circle, or an allied or precursor organization, was equally violent in suppressing certain scientific truths. Three of the five pioneers of electromagnetics – Maxwell, Hertz, and FitzGerald, met premature deaths. The other two, Heaviside and Lodge were sidelined. Each death was caused by cancer of the jaw or stomach. We suspect an ingested radioactive poison as the means by which this happened. Interestingly, Kaiser Friedrich of Germany died by a similar affliction after only ninety days on the throne of Imperial Germany, thus paving the way for Kaiser Wilhelm and the First World War.

Your research pointing out a connection between the Circle and the creation of the Federal Reserve was very illuminating. We would welcome any further insights you might share.

Stay Safe

Your Anonymous Patron

* * *

The mirror lab was a lonely place. Professor Chen dropped by once and was pleased with my results. "Maybe you could present a paper at GammaCon," he suggested.

"GammaCon?"

"The annual conference on gamma ray physics and phenomenology," he explained. "This year, it's up in Chattanooga at the Choo Choo."

I'd been there before. The Chattanooga Choo Choo was the city's old train station, converted to a combination train museum, hotel, and conference center. They even had guest rooms in the old Pullman cars, although most of the rooms were in a more traditional hotel building.

I worked a few more days on compiling the most interesting of the gamma ray results. The Friday before Christmas, Amit drove down to Atlanta for an overnight trip to consult with me on Gomulka's data.

"I can't believe he just gave us all the admissions data," Amit marveled at the shocking breach of privacy. "We have everything here on next year's class – grades, scores, essays, applications, and the social justice psychological profile results. I can't believe the administration just gave it to him."

"I can't believe he got the administration to add this psychological profiling questionnaire to the admissions process," I added. "He must really have a lot of influence."

We analyzed the candidates according to the criteria Professor Gomulka gave us. Some of them appeared to make sense – for instance he preferred candidates who scored high on compliance with authority and came from single parent homes without fathers. Membership in Boy Scouts or Junior ROTC was a negative, in his scoring. Other made little sense – for instance, he preferred candidates who scored high on conflict avoidance and didn't play team sports.

Amit and I began developing our own set of evaluation standards. We included good grades and high test scores, but by and large looked for the psychological opposite of Professor Gomulka's criteria. We wanted the strong-willed, independent rebels.

Amit had already discussed the plan with Uncle Rob who surprised me by giving it his blessing. We eliminated almost all of the strongest candidates according to Professor Gomulka's criteria, and filled two-thirds of the class with mediocre social justice candidates who seemed fairly innocuous. The remaining third of the incoming social justice slots we populated with our candidates.

"That ought to derail the program without being completely obvious," I noted.

"I'll modify the applicant database so our candidates appear to be the winners according to Professor Gomulka's criteria," Amit volunteered. "Then, I'll upload our modified file to Gomulka's computer, and overwrite his. I think I can use Gomulka's credentials to modify the original copy in the Admissions office." He drove home Saturday morning, the day before Christmas.

Christmas fell on a Sunday. I'd considered going home, but I simply didn't feel comfortable hanging out with Uncle Rob. I understood he had good intentions, but for now, I just wanted space and solitude. Trying to learn more about the mysterious missing scientist, Ettore Majorana, I looked into the life of his mentor, Enrico Fermi, the man responsible for the first nuclear reactor and a key contributor to the Manhattan Project. His wife, Laura Fermi, wrote an interesting memoir of her life with Enrico, *Atoms in the Family*. Early Christmas morning, I found the critical passage in Laura Fermi's book:

> *A short time after his [Majorana's] return to Rome a tragedy occurred in the Majorana family. A baby, a little cousin of Ettore's, was burned to death in his cradle. The baby's nurse was suspected of setting the cradle on fire. One of the baby's uncles was accused of having instigated the nurse. Ettore refused to believe that his uncle could have committed such a depraved, coldblooded crime. Ettore wanted to prove his uncle's innocence, clear him of a suspicion that could not fail to taint the entire Majorana family. He hired lawyers; he took personal charge of all details in the defense. His uncle was acquitted.*

Angus MacGuffin's mysterious Mr. Bini. The scientist who "derived the Heaviside theory they thought they had hidden." The man MacGuffin quoted, saying: "They burned my poor little cousin to death when I refused, and they threatened others in my family." The timing seemed right. MacGuffin was in Buenos Aires in 1939. Majorana vanished from Italy in 1938. According to *Atoms in the Family*, Enrico Fermi had delivered lectures in Argentina and Brazil in 1934. Might he have been able to provide contacts and introductions to his young protégé? In the 1930s, Argentina was still one of the most prosperous places in the world, on par with many European countries, and an excellent place for a young Italian speaker to make a fresh start.

I'd made solid progress, and I was confident I had identified Mr. Bini. What a wonderful Christmas present! I decided to treat myself to a lunch out by way of celebration.

Every place I stopped at, though, was closed for Christmas. My frustration mounted. Finally, I found an open Waffle House. I made a late breakfast of it with an omelet and hash browns, scattered, smothered, chunked, and covered. Coffee, black. The thrill of my discovery faded and my mood began to match the bitter brew. This was a mistake. Oh, the food was tasty enough. With each bite though, I couldn't help but compare it to Mom's usual Christmas dinner – a savory ham, green beans, and cornbread. I'd never taste that again – at least not seasoned with the same sense of maternal love and family and contentment. I'd never have a Mom-cooked meal again. Never sit respectfully waiting for my father to say grace. My parents were dead. I was estranged from my sister and my uncle. I'd made yet another minor breakthrough, but I had no one with whom to share it. All thanks to the Civic Circle. Sure, I was chip, chip, chipping away at their secrets. Ultimately, though, what did it matter? What was I doing? Was I only fooling myself? How could I possibly overturn the Civic Circle and their reign of terror?

"Y'all right, honey?" asked the waitress as I paid my tab.

"Yes," I lied. "Merry Christmas."

I made my way home, back to campus, and I took a long walk to clear my head. The goal I set for myself seemed insurmountable. Destroy the Civic Circle. Change the world. Impossible. "The journey of a thousand miles," Dad's voice came to mind.

"Begins with a single step." I filled in the rest myself. I know, Dad.

"How do you eat an elephant?" Dad was also fond of asking.

"One bite at a time," I answered.

"To master the world..."

"You must first master yourself," I completed Dad's thought. Back to work.

Sadly, I finished *Atoms in the Family* without any other major epiphanies. I was no closer to figuring out the how "the curious yin-yang symbol followed from the calculations of a Russian mathematician and an American named Smith." The only Smith in *Atoms in the Family* was Cyril S. Smith, a British metallurgist and colleague of Fermi's on the Manhattan Project. I could find no evidence of his collaboration with any Russians.

Petrel was right, though. All events leave fingerprints and echoes in the archives if only you know where to look and how to put the pieces together. It's genuinely hard to hide the truth. It's out there. A hint from here, a suggestion from there, and soon you have enough pieces to fill in the rest of the picture. I had to keep searching for the little pieces and figuring out the big picture. I had to trust that in doing so, I'd also figure out the appropriate course of action.

"Go get 'em Pete!" I could imagine my father's voice with the same tone and cadence he used when he was coaching my fourth grade basketball team.

"I'm proud of you, Peter," I could almost hear my mother's voice, as well.

I'd internalized my parents, their ideas, and their teachings to the point where I could almost hear their words and feel their presence. Looking back, I think I actually did end up with what I most wanted for Christmas that year – one last Christmas with my folks, if only in spirit.

CHAPTER 7: IN PLAIN SIGHT

"Oh, this is so hot," was Amit's reaction as Ashley's video tirade transitioned to pornography. "I never did get her back to our room, you know." He was enjoying the show far more than I enjoyed the actual event. "Oh, yeah, look at her go! That girl is fine!" Then, he saw me stop her and the final eruption. "What?!?" He turned and looked incredulously at me. "Why did you stop her?"

"You were dating her," I explained, "and I'm dating her roommate. It didn't seem right. And in case you haven't noticed, she's crazy."

"Of course, I know she's crazy. Crazy is hot," Amit opined. "She was about to educate you on that very principle. She wanted to get even with me and re-establish her self-esteem by seducing you. You should have let her have her revenge sex with you – the perfect no-strings-attached hook-up. You should know I'm not going to mind."

"I'm dating her roommate," I pointed out.

"You're too young to settle down with one girl," Amit counseled me. "The best way to be confident with girls is to have lots of them in your orbit. If you don't care about any particular girl, you adopt an abundance mentality. Girls love confident men with options."

"But I do want to care. At least about one particular girl. And Ashley didn't appear to appreciate you for your confidence and your options," I pointed out.

"Some girls are just... needy," he countered. "That's why you need more than one – so your dating doesn't suffer when one flakes out on you. If you keep enough plates spinning, you don't need to worry when one crashes and breaks."

I thought about Amit's notion of running up his score with girls. Something troubled me about it. "I can see there are advantages to confidence. Certainly practice and experience breed further success at anything, including dating, but it's like your goal is just to run up the score and sleep with as many girls as possible, though. You're focusing on the persuasive techniques and dating methods that let you hook up with the most receptive girls, the easiest girls, the least discriminating girls."

"You mean the sluts," Amit nodded. "Yes, of course. That's the goal."

"Are those the girls you really want, though?" I asked. "The ones you can really care for?"

"Depends on how hot they are," he flashed a lecherous grin. "Too many years of sleeping around really wears them out fast, though. They get nasty diseases, too, so it's better to get them young," he said smugly.

"I'm serious," I replied. "If you perfect your game toward quick scores and easy sex, doesn't that become all you get? At the expense of a deeper and more meaningful relationship?"

"Yeah..." he nodded. "So?"

We were going to have to agree to disagree.

With one semester at Tech under my belt, the second semester seemed easier. If anything, the material was more difficult, but I'd developed the appropriate study habits and support network to make the experience much less stressful than starting from scratch. Even social justice became more interesting, because Professor Gomulka was transitioning from theory to practice.

"Welcome to Applications of Social Justice," he greeted us on the first day of classes. "Good to see you all back after your break." I saw him glance over at Ryan and Marcus. Was that a hint of displeasure in his voice? Marcus and Ryan had both aced the Intro to Social Justice final, thanks to their mysterious friend, George P. Burdell. I didn't know how Amit and I were going to be able to keep them in the program in the long run, what with Professor Gomulka deliberately trying to fail them. We'd won the first round, though, and we'd just have to do our best the next time around.

"Last semester, we learned about the theory and history of social justice and what it means in our personal lives," Professor Gomulka continued. "This semester, we're going to put that theory into practice. I see most of you already have our text." He held up a copy of *Rules for Radicals* by Saul Alinsky. "We're going to apply the principles and teachings of this book to effect social change right here at Georgia Tech. We've made great progress aligning the faculty in the College of Liberal Arts toward an emphasis on social justice. For too long, however, the science, computing, and engineering faculties have maintained a narrow focus on their subjects without critically examining the broader applications and implications for society at large.

"That changes now," he insisted, "and you are going to be the agents of that change." I could feel the excitement ripple through the class. Gomulka had berated, browbeaten, and shamed everyone there for an entire semester. We'd come through his social-justice boot camp, and now the class was eager to show their beloved professor that his confidence in them was well placed.

He flashed a professional portrait of a smiling woman "Meet Dr. Cindy Ames. Dr. Ames is a thought-leader in social justice pedagogy. She will revise the engineering curriculum to make it more relevant to a more diverse population of students. The mission of the College of Engineering must converge to put social justice first – above all other concerns. Dr. Ames is the social justice warrior who will make that happen."

I noticed he was becoming more comfortable with the term he coined – "social justice warrior."

"This man is a threat to our vision and our community." Professor Gomulka flashed a photo of Professor Muldoon on the screen. The lighting was poor. Muldoon wore a scowl on his face, and he looked sinister and evil. "Professor Harmon Muldoon's reactionary obstructionism in the Faculty Senate is single-handedly blocking our prospective head of the College of Engineering. Worse, he's been rallying opposition to Dr. Ames from faculty and influential alumni."

"Boo!" Amit was really getting into it, and the class was following his lead.

"No," Professor Gomulka held up a finger to silence the class. "No. This is a good thing. Individuals are easier to hurt than organizations. Muldoon has made himself the champion of the reactionaries. Now, in order to defeat the reactionaries, all we have to do is defeat Muldoon – the rest will fall in line. We have picked our target. We will isolate him – 'freeze it, personalize it, and polarize it.' We will keep the pressure on and never give up!"

Gomulka had challenged Muldoon to a "Dialog on Diversity," and apparently, Muldoon had accepted. I could see exactly what Gomulka was thinking. Destroy Muldoon's credibility with a surprise audit and all opposition would collapse. He'd win by default.

In the meantime, though, the social justice warriors of Georgia Tech would organize for victory. "Of course, it wouldn't be appropriate for us to use class time to organize for specific political action," Gomulka observed, "so let's discuss, hypothetically of course, the kinds of steps students at other campuses have taken to effect social change, within the general framework that underlies all activism."

He wrote, "**TARGET**," on the board. "First we have to ask ourselves, who is the target of our activity. If our targets are individuals, we want to change their attitudes or behaviors. If our target is a group or organization, we may want to change the group structure, redirect one or more vectors in the network of power relations, or secure greater participation and control for our allies. If our target is a community, we want to change intra-group relations such as discrimination, or attitudes, or beliefs. Finally, if our target is the society-at-large, we want to impact policies like globalization, education, the economy, health care, the environment, and so forth. Campus activism can take on any of these targets. Our focus is on a group, the administration, and to a lesser extent, the public whose support they require, and the individual reactionaries who oppose social justice."

He added, "**AGENT**," below it. "Then, we have to consider who the agents of social change are. The agents of social change can be leaders, directors, politicians, the people in charge. Or it can be the supporters or backers on whom the target relies. Or it can be the grassroots volunteers, employees, or interested citizens." He smiled benevolently at the class. "That's you – the idealistic student advocates for social justice. You need to keep it simple, maximize cooperation by maintaining good relations, and be ready to show how change benefits the target. Which brings us to..."

Then, he wrote, "**AGENT → TARGET**," on a third line. "How does the agent relate to or impact the target? The target may already be well-converged toward social justice and only require a modest nudge. Pre-converged targets are in the grasp of reactionaries and require a change in beliefs, attitudes, or values. Finally, anti-converged targets are actively opposed to social justice. They may dominate and oppress the agents, requiring more forceful measures.

Finally, he wrote, "**SUPPORT**," at the bottom of his list. "What actions are required to gain public support for your goal? Social change is easiest when the target is already well-converged: acknowledges the problem, agrees change is needed, is open to assistance, and willing to change. That's the case in most campus advocacy. We already have allies and fellow travelers in the administration who recognize that true equality requires more than head counting and quota checking. Equality requires fundamental changes in beliefs and attitudes that can only be achieved through changes in how and what we teach our students. The administration needs our help to overcome and silence the determined opposition of reactionary voices. Well-converged targets only require empirical evidence – information journalism, reports, and studies. They can transform that information into the right action." He wrote, "**CONVERGED = RATIONAL / EMPIRICAL**," on the board.

"Pre-converged targets need re-education. They need to be taught to adopt new values and new norms, either through the carrot of rational or emotional means, or the stick of facing the consequences of their poor choices. The holdouts, the reactionaries, the opponents of social justice," he smiled, "and no campus is without a few of those, they respond best to non-violent methods – strikes, protests, rallies, sit-ins, publicity, advocacy journalism, public shaming, boycotts – those are the principal tactics." He added "**PRE-CONVERGED = NORMATIVE / RE-EDUCATIVE**," on the board.

"Anti-converged targets require coercive strategies and raw power, up to and including riots, guerilla warfare, revolution, and terrorism." He added "**ANTI-CONVERGED = POWER / COERCIVE**," on the board.

"Campus advocacy will typically employ rational / empirical and normative / re-educative strategies for social change. Power or coercive strategies are rarely appropriate. Why?" He pointed at Madison.

"Because the administration is, like, on our side already and we want to cooperate with them," she answered.

"Exactly!" He beamed. "You're providing cover for them, giving them a justification to do what they want to do already because 'the students demand it.' Alinsky tells the story of radicals who lobbied FDR for a particular policy. 'OK,' he agreed with them, 'you've convinced me. Now go out there and put pressure on me to do this, so we can make it happen!' You have to keep the pressure on to help the administration overcome the opposition to the social justice changes we all want to implement.

"Of course, all I've been saying is true of campus activism most everywhere, including here at Georgia Tech. As I said, it would be highly inappropriate of me to organize activism here in class. I've covered all I need to say today, so class is over." A few students started to gather their things. "However," he loudly interrupted them, "if you find yourselves gathered here and want to take advantage of the opportunity to organize outside of class time, why, I see no reason why anyone would object. I'll see you next time."

The message was loud and clear. Everyone sat back down, afraid that a failure to demonstrate a proper commitment to the ideals of social justice might jeopardize their scholarships. Gomulka had already coordinated with Amit and me regarding precisely the kind of campaign he wanted. After Gomulka left, Amit stepped up to the board and began soliciting ideas. The class was well-trained. They suggested most of what Gomulka wanted. I filled in the few aspects of Gomulka's strategy that the rest of the class had overlooked. Finally, Amit went around the room seeking commitments – "What will you do for social justice?" He put everyone on the spot trying to out-do each other for the cause.

After class, I caucused with Amit. "He's making Muldoon the focal point of all the opposition to Professor Ames. That "Dialog on Diversity" should prove interesting. He's anticipating a win by default. Muldoon is... formidable, ruthless. Gomulka wouldn't be so eager to take on Muldoon directly if he didn't have his audit ambush waiting in the wings."

"I just hope Muldoon took George P.'s warning to heart," Amit muttered.

I'd considered looking ahead at my textbooks over the break, getting a head start on my spring classes. Like so many vague desires to accomplish something, I'd put no thought into how to make it happen, so it didn't. Instead, I'd spent my entire winter break working in the mirror lab, generating isotope maps, studying Majorana, trying to understand the physics, and when my physics background failed me, investigating the history surrounding Majorana's mysterious disappearance.

Turns out, I should have been hitting the textbooks, too.

That spring, I still found myself straddling the line between physics and electrical engineering. So far, I could still choose either subject, and the courses from the other would fulfill my requirements for technical electives. By the end of the semester, however, I would need to choose whether to commit myself to electrical engineering or physics. Professor Fries convinced me to sign up for his microwave circuits class, saying that my physics electromagnetics class would be adequate preparation.

On the first day of class, he handed out his syllabus and a strange sheet of graph paper with a curious, circular sort of graph. It looked like this:

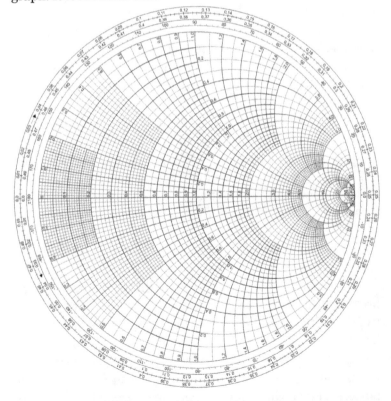

Those circles... those arcs... I tilted the center line. It looked remarkably like the background on MacGuffin's yin-yang diagram. I raised my hand. "Professor Fries, what is this graph?"

"That is a Smith Chart. You'll need to make copies of this sheet," he announced to the class. "We'll be using it to solve impedance matching problems graphically."

I remembered the words from MacGuffin's manuscript – that "Mr. Bini" (Majorana) said the yin-yang diagram followed from the work of an American named Smith and a Russian mathematician. I may have finally found the elusive Mister... Doctor? Professor? Smith. I couldn't believe my good fortune. I'd been searching the library for the last couple of weeks looking for a physicist named Smith, and here he was in my microwave circuits textbook: Phillip Hagar Smith. Only, apparently he was an electrical engineer, which explained why I hadn't found him.

My eagerness to solve the rest of the mystery overcame my discretion. "Is there a Russian mathematician known for his work with Smith?"

"No," Professor Fries paused, searching his memory. "I don't recall Smith collaborating with anyone in particular let alone a Russian mathematician. Of course, Schelkunoff came up with the concept of impedance in the 1930s, so Smith's work followed from Schelkunoff's."

"And Schelkunoff was Russian?"

"I believe he was American." Professor Fries seemed amused at my sudden interest. "He may have come from Russia originally, though. We'll be discussing him today, so hold your questions for now."

Every electrician and electrical engineer knows Ohm's law: voltage equals current times resistance ($V = I\,R$). A little algebra tells you that resistance is the ratio of voltage to current ($R = V/I$). Heaviside, along with Lodge and a few others, extended Ohm's law to cover AC or alternating current circuits. In the modern representation, voltage, current, and resistance become complex numbers, only the resistance gets called "impedance" and it has two parts: "resistance" (R) is the real part and "reactance" (X) is the "imaginary" part ($Z = V/I = R + jX$). Of course, there's nothing truly imaginary about it. Both parts are physically real – complex numbers are just a bookkeeping method – keeping track of a voltage wave and a current wave, for instance, that may have different amplitude and phase.

Don't ask me how impedance got denoted by the letter "Z" and reactance by the letter "X." Maybe it's because current already took the letter "I" and resistance had adverse possession of "R." And don't get me going on how electrical engineers use "j" to denote the square root of negative one instead of "i" like physicists and mathematicians. They certainly didn't disclose such sensitive information to mere undergraduates.

Anyway, this Schelkunoff had the brilliant idea that if impedance was the ratio of voltage to current, then maybe there was an analogous kind of impedance that could be defined as the ratio of electric to magnetic field. The units make it really clear: electric field is volts per meter and magnetic field is amps per meter, so the ratio of electric field to magnetic field works out to volts over amps, just like voltage over current. Now, maybe we'd covered all this briefly in Professor Graf's emag class, but where impedance was an afterthought to physicists, it was the main event to these electrical engineers. This entire microwave circuits class was all about applying AC electronics ideas to electromagnetic waves not simple enough to be mere voltages and currents, but caught up in transmission lines so they couldn't be treated as waves in free space.

It may not excite everyone, but was I looking forward to understanding this stuff. After Professor Fries' introductory lecture, I could see how Schelkunoff had a big hand in the theory behind the Smith Chart, the theory of impedance, but I still didn't see where the actual yin-yang curve came from.

"Is there some reference I could look at," I asked Professor Fries after class, "to check out Schelkunoff's work?"

I followed him back to his office. He opened his Omnibrowser and Omnied his search query to come up with a reference: "The Impedance Concept... Bell System Technical Journal, January 1938." He turned his monitor to show me. "Shall I email this to you?"

If it were a crucial clue, the last thing I needed was an electronic trail connecting it to myself. "Could you just print it out for me?" He did, and he handed me the copy.

I thanked him for the Schelkunoff paper and left. I read through it as best I could while taking notes during my next class. It really didn't seem that complicated or difficult. I was itching to try plotting out some of Schelkunoff's equations, but I didn't want to risk working on them in public on my thoroughly compromised school laptop. Instead, I got an early start on my homework between my classes, and then, I had an early dinner.

I saw Jennifer leaving the dorm as I was returning to work on my Schelkunoff calculations. "How was your..." I began to ask when she cut me off.

"How dare you?" she said. "Ashley told me all about how you were making moves on her. I never want to speak with you again!" Jennifer stormed off.

Great.

I really needed to get a copy of Matlab on my secure laptop for work like this, but all I had installed was an old DoD release of Microsoft Office. I just used an Excel spreadsheet, instead. I opened my microwave circuits book and worked through the equations to plot a Smith Chart in the x-y coordinates Excel could display. It took over an hour before the Smith Chart canvas was ready on my laptop's screen. Then, I took the equations Schelkunoff provided for the impedance of the fields around a dipole – an elemental source of electromagnetic radiation. I'd heard people talking about the beauty of mathematics before, but I'd never really felt it until that night. Here are the equations Schelkunoff provided for the impedance of an electric and a magnetic dipole, respectively.

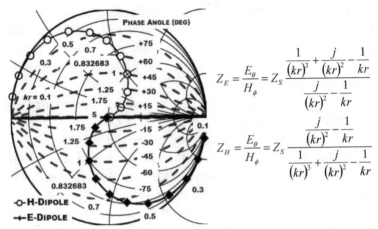

$$Z_E = \frac{E_\theta}{H_\phi} = Z_S \frac{\dfrac{1}{(kr)^3} + \dfrac{j}{(kr)^2} - \dfrac{1}{kr}}{\dfrac{j}{(kr)^2} - \dfrac{1}{kr}}$$

$$Z_H = \frac{E_\theta}{H_\phi} = Z_S \frac{\dfrac{j}{(kr)^2} - \dfrac{1}{kr}}{\dfrac{1}{(kr)^3} + \dfrac{j}{(kr)^2} - \dfrac{1}{kr}}$$

Plotting them was not straightforward. I had to split each into real and imaginary components. Then, I had to translate them into x-y coordinates to superimpose on the Smith Chart. I got a kind of distorted curve on a 50 ohm Smith Chart, so I recalculated, normalizing the Smith Chart to the Z_s = 377 ohm impedance of free space. There it was: MacGuffin's yin-yang diagram glowed on the screen. When the wave number times the distance, "kr," was small, the curves started at opposite end of the real axis. They spiraled into the center as kr got big, hitting the 377 ohm bullseye as kr reached about 5. All that mystic mumbo jumbo about yin and yang and how the yin-yang symbol, the "taijitu," symbolized harmonic balance in some vague manner – it wasn't mystic at all. It was a description of the impedance, the balance of electric to magnetic field intensity in the creation of an electromagnetic wave, starting from either pure electric field or pure magnetic field. I opened up my scan of MacGuffin's manuscript and took a closer, second look at his "mysticism."

Non-polarity and yet Supreme Polarity! The Supreme Polarity in activity generates yang; yet at the limit of activity it is still. In stillness it generates yin; yet at the limit of stillness it is also active.

"Polarity..." a dipole? "In activity" it "generates yang..." an electric field? "At the limit of activity it is still." OK. "In stillness, it generates yin." As the dipole reaches maximum excitation it generates a magnetic field... yin? "At the limit of stillness, it is also active."

Activity and stillness alternate; each is the basis of the other.

MacGuffin's mysticism described an oscillation creating activity and stillness... magnetic and electric potential? Yin and yang... magnetic and electric fields? Each transforming back and forth, one into the other.

When the Supreme Polarity is Non-Polar, there is a balance of yin and yang. Each contains its own beginning and its own ending and together they flow harmoniously.

In radiation, the electric and magnetic fields form closed loops – in that sense, each contains its own beginning. That's just Gauss' Law for electricity and the corresponding law for magnetism – two of the four fundamental Maxwell's equations that describe how electromagnetics works. They oscillate together in harmony with the precise ratio of 377 ohms between the electric and magnetic field intensities.

In imbalance, yin exceeds yang or yang exceeds yin. Yin no longer begins at the end when there is stillness without activity.

In static fields, the impedance is no longer 377 ohms. There is an imbalance. And, although the static magnetic field still forms closed loops around currents, the electric field no longer forms closed loops, no longer "begins at the end" because it now begins and ends on charges: Gauss' Law for electricity.

There it was: right under my nose all this time. It wasn't mysticism. I was reading a primer in electromagnetics, dating back hundreds of years before Maxwell was thought to have been the first to discover it. The concepts were tricky, slippery, not exactly the way I was taught in class. It was challenging to interpret the flowery mystical language into precise mathematical terms. MacGuffin was no scientist, and his translations connected analogous English words to the original Chinese without regard to the precise, underlying mathematical relationships. "Stillness" seemed a metaphor for electric potential, "activity" for magnetic potential. "Yin" meant an electric field, and "yang" meant a magnetic field.

I split the screen on my laptop – the scan of the MacGuffin manuscript on one side and a Word document on the other. I kept translating MacGuffin's mysticism into modern terms. "Twistings?" Somehow that seemed to correspond to what we called "curl" in vector calculus. The next section I quickly realized was describing the other half of Maxwell's laws – the Faraday and Ampere relations. I was reading the Tao of Maxwell, written hundreds of years before Maxwell himself had discovered, or rather, re-discovered it. I'd managed to translate less than a page of MacGuffin's prose into modern physics. What mysteries lay hidden in the rest?

Amit finally showed up. "I got three more numbers, today," he bragged.

"Well, I'm down one." I told him about Jennifer.

"Sorry, dude, but that's why you've got to get over your oneitis," was his attempt at consolation. "You should have done Ashley, anyway."

I decided not to waste my time pointing out the alternate scenario in which my roommate hadn't pissed off my girlfriend's roommate. I shared my result with him.

He grasped the significance immediately. "No wonder the Circle's so paranoid about MacGuffin. That's why they shut down the Maxwellians – Maxwell, Hertz, and Fitzgerald were killed before they could figure out the implications. There's over a hundred pages there, and you haven't finished translating page one. The Circle knew where it was going, and they acted to stop anyone from finding out."

I also showed Amit some of my latest research from over the break. It was amazing to me how – long before the development of quantum mechanics in the 1920s and 1930s was supposed to have "forced" physicists to abandon classical causality – key figures were already actively pushing in that direction. For instance, in 1921, noted physicist Walter Schottky argued that elementary acts of emission and absorption of radiation were indeterminate, "without direct cause and without direct effect," and that they were "outside the relation of cause and effect."

I was particularly fascinated by the 1924 collaboration of a young American physicist, J. C. Slater, with the famous physicist Niels Bohr at Bohr's Institute in Copenhagen. Slater brought to Copenhagen an interesting idea. It was already well-established that electromagnetic radiation could sometimes be thought of as particles. Slater's idea was that these corpuscles of radiation or "photons" were guided and directed according to the familiar laws of electromagnetism. He viewed them as real entities obeying causal laws.

Bohr and his other collaborator, Kramers, insisted that Slater recast his theory in non-causal form. They argued in favor of modifying Slater's theory so that energy was not conserved in the individual acts of emission and absorption of radiation. These individual processes were viewed by Bohr and Kramer as random and not subject to the law of cause and effect. Under Bohr's and Kramers' modification, the law of energy conservation was only satisfied on average.

"So that's like a theory of gasoline consumption that might correctly predict a certain car consumes on average a gallon of gas in travelling 30 miles," Amit asked, "but also predicts that once in a while the car would end up the trip with more gasoline than the amount with which it started?"

"Right."

Slater's idea, as modified by Bohr and Kramers, came to be known as the "BKS" theory (after the authors' initials). The notion that energy and momentum were not conserved in individual atomic processes, but only in the aggregate, statistically averaging over many individual processes was soon proven false. To colleagues in later years, Slater recounted being led on a "dubious adventure" by Bohr and Kramers.

"You think Bohr and Kramers sidetracked Slater?" Amit asked. "They were in on the conspiracy?"

"It sure looks like it," I concluded. "Bohr, at least. You see exactly how Alinsky uses Bohr's concept of complementarity to justify any number of political and philosophic contradictions, that all good requires evil, and that's OK 'because quantum mechanics.'"

"I still don't get this whole observer-dependence thing," Amit shook his head ruefully. "It's confusing. An entity isn't real until it's detected and measured. It's like the tree doesn't make any sound when it falls if no one's there to hear it?"

"Exactly," I agreed. "Bohr's followers claim he's such a deep thinker despite his notorious obscurity. They've never actually observed this profound wisdom, yet they're confident it's there. They forget his dictum that no phenomenon is actually real until it is observed!"

Amit chuckled. "This Majorana, he worked with Bohr?"

"Majorana was working with either Heisenberg in Leipzig or Bohr in Copenhagen when he rediscovered or came across the Heaviside theory," I explained. "I can't be precisely sure of the timing. Apparently Schrödinger visited Bohr in Copenhagen, too. Schrödinger fell sick due to stress and overwork. So there he was, lying in his sick bed, and Bohr came in and kept badgering and harassing him until he got Schrödinger to renounce causality and accept the Copenhagen interpretation."

"Man, that's hard core. I remember when you first suggested someone was trying to guide the course of scientific discovery by diverting, distracting, even killing scientists," Amit recalled.

I nodded, "Dad pointed out the logical problem – the people responsible would have to be much further along.

They'd have to know what the answers were going to be in order to try to hide them."

"They really did know the answers," Amit pointed out. "That's what you've found in the MacGuffin manuscript." He looked thoughtful. "That still begs the question – how did they know? Profoundly deep thinkers who sat in a monastery somewhere and came up with all these clever ideas without any experiments?"

That made no sense. "I don't see it. Maxwell's discoveries were the result of a synergy between theory and application. Faraday based his ideas on lots of direct experimentation. Maxwell built his theory on the foundation provided by Faraday and his contemporaries. Heaviside did a lot of the most critical work, for goodness sake, and he was a telegrapher, interested for professional reasons in how transmission lines behave. I just don't see how they could come up with the right theory if they weren't using it or applying it."

"Ancient high tech civilization?" Amit speculated. "Atlantis, all the traces of which were lost beneath the sea?"

"Hard to hide all that," I pointed out. "You'd think there'd be more evidence lying around, even with the Circle doing their best to hide it." Each step forward only led to more questions.

Amit set up a secure connection, and I sent my findings to Uncle Rob. We also sent another note from George P. Burdell to Professor Muldoon warning him a second time about the audit and explaining how we thought Gomulka was planning to discredit him.

Amit recounted his day. He'd sounded out the Japanese graduate student who was TA for his data structure class. "Satoshi is amazing – really knows his stuff. He gave this lecture on open source software. You need to read this book, *The Cathedral and the Bazar*, he recommended. It's all about the difference between centralized control and a more robust, more distributed approach. I think it's relevant to how the Friends of George should operate. We need to act as independent cells, each improvising and adapting to meet the same end goals." Amit thought his TA seemed a promising target. "George P. needs to reach out to him. The FOG thickens, once again!" he proclaimed as he customized our encrypted email tutorial and call for action we'd been distributing as we came across likely candidates.

Gomulka was right about most students being too focused on their daily lives to get involved in activism. The Friends of George had the same problem, without the carrot of offering a full-ride scholarship. Even students whose opinions appeared to align with ours rarely troubled themselves to sign up and contact us. I'd had only a few successes among my engineering and physics acquaintances out of a couple dozen invitations sent.

Before we turned in that night, George already had his answer from Professor Muldoon, "I heard you the first time. Keep me posted if you have any actual updates. Thanks." Arrogant bastard.

While homework, note taking, studying, and tests had become routine by my second semester, one aspect was new – job interviews. Neither Amit nor I had ever done an actual job interview before. We looked up long lists of interview questions online and spent several hours one weekend taking turns playing interviewer and interviewee. We'd learned from long experience in high school debate that the best impromptu answers are the ones carefully prepared in advance!

The first surprise was how little help the career center offered. Both Amit and I spent a good bit of time getting entered in the system and submitting resumes. Many of the top employers, however, including Omnitia, Tolliver, and even the Civic Circle, interviewed outside the formal career center bureaucracy. Omnitia and Tolliver both advertised in the *Technique*. I signed up through their websites and each held off-campus interviews. One afternoon in February, I found myself walking over the Interstate to a conference room in the Renaissance Atlanta Midtown for my first interview.

I swear the interviewer for Tolliver Applied Government Solutions must have used the exact same list of questions I'd practiced with Amit. "Can you tell me about yourself?" "How did you hear about us?" "What do you know about Tolliver?" "Why do you want to work for us?" "What is your greatest achievement?" "Where do you see yourself in five years?" "What's your dream job?" "Who else is interviewing you?"

My practice with Amit paid off, and I had a smooth, well-thought-out answer to every question. I'd studied their website, and could speak with genuine enthusiasm about their work. TAGS worked for NASA supporting the International Space Station, they did classified work on missile defense, and they did contract research for any number of government clients. It sounded interesting. I played up my IT expertise and networking experience aiming to get into whatever group was responsible for networking the Civic Circle meeting and the G-8 Summit. Uncle Larry had instructed me not to mention my connection to the family, so I didn't. I suspected he'd be pulling the strings for me anyway, but I left the interview feeling I was likely to get an offer even without his assistance.

I landed one of the highly sought after interview slots with Omnitia a couple of days after my experience with TAGS. That was the highpoint of the experience, however. I walked over to the Crowne Plaza Midtown and showed up ten minutes early. Then, I had to wait twenty minutes for my interviewer to show up. She started the interview with a question about my high school background. I explained that my high school only offered an introductory course in programming and that I'd had to supplement it with online training. She was busy looking for something on her laptop and didn't appear to be listening to me. She must have found what she was looking for, because she suddenly asked me some Java-related questions. They were pretty easy, and I think I answered them correctly. That was the last of the technical questions. Then, the interview transitioned to a series of logic puzzles.

"Suppose a couple has two children and I tell you that at least one of them is a boy," she asked. "What's the likelihood the other is a boy?"

That one's a basic exercise in conditional probability. There are four possibilities: boy-boy, boy-girl, girl-boy, and girl-girl. The information that at least one offspring is a boy eliminates the girl-girl case, but leaves the other three. Since two of the three cases are a boy and a girl, and only one case is both boys, the answer is straightforward.

"One-third of the time the other child is a boy," I explained.

"No," she replied smugly. "It's something called a "conditional probability" and the answer is two-thirds."

Somehow, she'd gotten it backwards, I started to explain. She interrupted me. "These are very tricky problems, and we don't have much time, so let's move on to the next question. What is logically wrong with this statement – 'In 1925, Madame Jolie told her friend that her husband died in the First World War.'"

"It was usually referred to as the Great War or perhaps just 'The War' until after the Second World War," I replied. Then, I made the mistake of adding, "Although a prescient observer may well have called it the First World War if they were expecting another."

That set her off. "No," she lectured me. "It's logically impossible to have called it the 'First World War' until there was a second." She smiled triumphantly.

That's when I knew I was wasting my time. I felt like standing up and asking, 'Is this the first time someone has walked out of one of your interviews or merely the Great Walkout?' Instead I decided to play it out for the sake of the experience. I put on my best friendly face and said, "That's a fascinating perspective," as if she'd enlightened me.

She grinned in pleasure at my recognition of her cleverness. Suddenly, I realized that the interview wasn't about my suitability as a job candidate, but rather all about helping my interviewer demonstrate to me how clever she was.

The rest of her logic puzzles really weren't that complicated. I gave her the superficial answers she wanted and took every opportunity to compliment her on her insightful questions as if she'd thought them all up herself, instead of finding them in a list somewhere. On the few that stumped me, I emphasized how tricky they were and implied how smart she must be to understand the answers.

The final phase of the interview included all the standard questions I'd prepared for with Amit. I nailed them.

Finally she asked me, "What do you see as your greatest weakness?"

"I get frustrated sometimes when I don't understand things," I acknowledged with a straight face, "but then I dig in, and I do my best to figure them out." I don't know why interviewers bother with that question, since the trick is always to turn the weakness into a hidden strength. The only challenge is not being completely obvious about it.

My final interview was with the Civic Circle. Amit had helpfully volunteered to assist Professor Gomulka with all the arrangements for the interviewer. Unfortunately, the interviewer refused to stay at the Berkshire Inn just south of campus, where Amit and I could monitor their Internet traffic. Only a suite at the Westin Peachtree Plaza downtown was good enough. Professor Gomulka had arranged for me, Amit, Madison, and a couple of his other social justice students to interview. It was a couple of stops down from the North Avenue MARTA station to get there.

A few days later, Amit used Professor Gomulka's password to access the professor's email. "What is it with these Civic Circle goons and hookuplandings.com?" He asked, sifting through Viagra ads and the email updates the adult relationship site had delivered to the professor's Omnimail inbox. Finally, he found the report from the Civic Circle interviewer.

The interviewer recommended Amit for the internship at the Civic Circle, and the rest of us were rejected. I was rated as "too idealistic." I must have overdone it. Madison was "vacuous." Curiously, Amit refused to share his evaluation with me. "I gave them what they wanted to hear," was all he would say. We got the official notice a few days later.

I was surprised to receive a summer internship offer from Omnitia. I'd figured it for a long shot, particularly after how my interview went. The job was in Silicon Valley, and even though the offer was excellent, the high cost of living would make it tough to save any money. I turned them down, and accepted the offer I got from TAGS. Even though the money wasn't as good, the cost of living in Huntsville, Alabama was much lower, and I'd have the opportunity to get to the Civic Circle meeting and the G-8 Summit in the summer.

By the middle of February, Professor Gomulka's "Engineering 4 Everyone" campaign was in full swing, but the results were not what he'd expected. His "social justice warriors" – the term was getting awkward to use, so by then we usually just abbreviated it: "SJWs" – had no idea what hit them. Amit and I had unleashed the Friends of George. We encouraged the "FOG" to get involved and fed them a steady stream of updates through our encrypted emails. When the SJWs teamed with a bunch of proglodyte student groups to post flyers, the FOG was right behind them, tearing down "Diversity Now!" flyers and replacing them with "Earn Your Place!" When the SJW's were up half the night scrawling and scribbling "Engineering 4 Everyone!" in chalk on the sidewalks, the FOG were up early in the morning wiping the sidewalks clean and writing "Engineering 4 Engineers!" everywhere.

That last stunt amazed me, because we had nothing directly to do with it. Marcus sent George P. an encrypted note saying he'd take care of it. Somehow he managed to wipe out the SJW chalk scribbles nearly a dozen of us spent four hours creating. He replaced them with twice as many FOG chalkings. Unlike the scrawls or scribbles of the SJWs, the FOG chalkings looked like works of art.

"It's exactly like the one in front of the dorm," Amit commented as we stood admiring the three-color "Engineering 4 Engineers!" doodle outside the Student Center. The precise craftsmanship made the SJW slogans look like the inept scribblings they were. "That's got to be some kind of stencil or template."

"It looks machine drawn. Even so," I noted, "it would take quite a team to pull that off. Marcus couldn't have done it all, even if Ryan is helping him."

"George P. Burdell has friends," Amit smiled, "and apparently, his friends have friends, too."

The impact was demoralizing. None of the SJWs were expecting the pushback. Professor Gomulka was convinced – correctly – that someone was funneling information to the counter-protesters. Marcus and Ryan were his prime suspects, but even when he didn't share flyering plans with them, somehow the Friends of George – thanks to Amit and me – stayed a step ahead. We didn't even have to dispatch the FOG to tear down flyers once Muldoon and some of his other engineering professor allies announced an extra-credit bounty on their exams for every SJW flyer turned in by a student. "This is my way of inspiring you to help these so-called social justice warriors be environmentally aware and recycle" one professor told several hundred of his freshman students. With that encouragement, the campus was immediately stripped of SJW flyers and they stayed down. By the time Gomulka discovered what was going on and complained to the dean, it was too late.

The social justice campaign was centralized and sclerotic. We had to wait until Professor Gomulka found out what was happening and told us – usually in class a day or two later – what to do in response. The FOG thrived on improvisation, making tactical decisions at the grassroots and reacting instantly. By the time Professor Gomulka thought to emulate FOG tactics and encourage the SJWs and their allies to tear down FOG flyers, an enterprising Friend of George came up with a way to tack or tape flyers up high, using a ten-foot pole – out of reach of the ill-prepared SJWs. Another had an older brother in a band who taught him how to paste posters directly to surfaces so they were next to impossible to remove. He passed his insights on to the rest of us. The SJWs surrendered. The dean encouraged the campus police to arrest anyone caught posting flyers. That put an end to the aggressive flyering, but the campus remained peppered with FOG flyers simply due to the difficulty of removing them. The Friends of George and our allies won the Battle of the Flyers decisively.

The rallies and protests were a different story. Professor Gomulka's allies on the faculty gave extra credit to their students for participating in the protests and rallies. Any number of psychology, or history, or literature, or philosophy, or public policy undergraduates made up the SJW contingent. What really surprised me was the fact that some Friends of George managed to organize counter-protests at all. FOG was always outnumbered, but never outdone when it came to protesting. Even though the FOG contingent was always much smaller than the SJW crew, they made up for it with their creativity. A few even brought poster and sign materials and made up rebuttal signs on the spot.

The SJWs would chant, "Two, four, six, eight! End misogyny and hate!" That would prompt a chorus of "You're a disgrace! Everyone should earn their place!" An SJW held up a sign reading "This is a Hate-Free Zone!" One of the FOG maneuvered into place beside them with a "Logic-Free Zone?" sign. Another took a photo. The picture was all over the Internet.

Another enterprising FOG got wise to how few actual engineering students cared enough to protest on the SJW side. He put on a "Diversity Now!" T-shirt to look at home among the SJWs, and he circulated among them shooting video and asking them why they were there and what their major was. A surprising number acknowledged outright that they were only there for the extra credit and that they weren't engineers at all. The video went viral, and really reinforced the "Engineering 4 Engineers" theme of the counter-protests.

One of our social justice classes was actually interrupted by a handful of protestors chanting "No more indoctrination in our education!" from the hallway, and Professor Gomulka had to call the campus police to remove them.

Professor Gomulka remained calm, insisting that the opposition "only demonstrated how desperately the campus needed our advocacy." It was hard to keep up with the mandatory social justice protests, coordinating and sharing ideas and information with FOG, and with homework. The SJWs were feeling the pressure, too and morale began to suffer. They thrived on consensus and were particularly discouraged to discover that that not everyone agreed with them. "We put up all the flyers and those Nazis just tear them down." One girl was near tears. Amit and I sabotaged morale further with defeatist remarks. "There's too many reactionaries – we can't expect to be able to keep up with them," and, "We just have to keep trying, even though it's not working, because it's the right thing to do." The protests and rallies got smaller and smaller.

One day after class, Professor Fries called me aside.

"Have you heard about Professor Muldoon?" he asked.

"No what?"

"Apparently a team from the administration is busy auditing his lab," Professor Fries replied. "They think he may have stolen some equipment."

So, Gomulka finally decided to spring his ambush. I gathered all the contempt I could into my voice. "Couldn't have happened to nicer guy." Then, I realized we had no "Friends of George" among the faculty, except, possibly, for Professor Muldoon. Might Professor Fries be willing to take a stand in support of his colleague?

"I understand he's one of the leaders opposing Professor Ames, that new professor who's going to reform the College of Engineering." I hoped he'd take the bait.

"Yes, I know," Professor Fries said, shaking his head sadly. "The dean asked me to speak with him about it – how his opposition only makes us appear to be sexist and misogynist. Muldoon simply has no concept of academic decorum – spent too much of his career in industry. I told him he was headed for disaster. It's going to happen. You can't fight city hall, let alone university administration. I told him he needed to leave it alone and just go with the flow. You know what he told me?"

"What?"

"Only dead fish go with the flow, my dear Fries." He actually had a pretty good imitation of Muldoon's voice.

I suppressed a grin and tried my best to appear outraged. "He simply has no respect for authority. Who is he to question the dean when it comes to selecting a new head for the College of Engineering?"

"You wouldn't believe the vicious things he says about Professor Ames in private," Professor Fries said, apparently eager to share his concerns with someone who might appreciate them.

"I understand completely," I replied. "He tried to have me expelled, after all."

"You don't know the half of it," Professor Fries confided. "Muldoon really has it in for you. 'Look out for that Burdell kid,' he told me. 'He's more cunning than the usual social justice viper, and if you don't watch out for him, he'll bite you in the ass, like he tried to do to me.' He was convinced that your academic hearing was some kind of setup, and you were in cahoots with the dean. Can you imagine that?"

"Wow." Professor Muldoon was way more clued in than I'd given him credit for. That was shockingly close to the truth. Was that why he'd been so hostile? Had he been extra hostile all along because he realized I was involved in the Social Justice Initiative? I learned an important lesson: never underestimate someone just because you don't like them.

"I know," Professor Fries was shaking his head. "Isn't it incredible? The man is paranoid. Almost certifiable."

"So you're on board with social justice and with Professor Ames reforming the curriculum?" I asked.

"Actually," Professor Fries replied, almost guiltily, "I do share a few of Professor Muldoon's reservations. There isn't enough time in the curriculum to teach our students everything they need to know to be good engineers. Taking more time out for social justice, well it just isn't a good idea, no matter how noble or worthy those ideals are. Also, the proposed curriculum seems so – so very one-sided. Maybe we can compromise and have a more balanced treatment of the subject?"

I could see Professor Fries was useless. Worse than useless. He might agree with many of Professor Muldoon's fundamental objections, but he was more interested in decorum and compromise than in standing up and fighting for his beliefs. Allies like him were as bad as outright enemies.

"Social justice is all about balanced treatment," I regurgitated. "It's about equity. It's about making sure that previously marginalized voices finally get a chance to be heard." I was shocked how easy it was getting for me to play a vacuous social justice minion and spout the appropriate jargon.

"I suppose so," Professor Fries acknowledged, happy to concede my "point" with no objection.

After my last class, I swung by the physics building. Professor Graf was inundated with her pre-med students again, but I found Professor Chen in his office.

"Peter! What brings you in this afternoon?"

"I was just wondering what you thought about all the protests."

His happy mood evaporated. "I have not been a citizen for long," he explained in a neutral tone, "and I continue to think of myself as a guest in your country. As a guest, it is not my place to tell my host how to run his house." He was clearly a bit uncomfortable, but we needed more allies on the faculty. I pushed him.

"Free speech is part of how we run the place," I said with a smile. "Everyone's entitled to their own opinion."

"Indeed," he replied, relaxing a bit, "but wisdom often lies in doing what one should, not what one can."

"How do you mean?"

"You have no real history in your country," he explained, "not like in China. The Manchu persecuted the Han when the Manchu-dominated Qing overthrew the Han-dominated Ming. The Han resented that treatment and returned the favor, slaughtering Manchu when they overthrew the last Qing Emperor. The Japanese, they persecuted everyone. During the Cultural Revolution, the least comment could be misinterpreted as disloyalty or regressivism and result in a sentence to a reeducation camp – or worse. That's just the last few hundred years. Our history goes back for thousands." He paused as if pondering something.

"Would you be offended if I told you how American student protesters are viewed by some in China?"

"No," I assured him.

"There is a term for these student protestors and their supporters. We call them 'baizuo.' It literally means 'white-left.' The perception is that they are hypocritical humanitarians who advocate peace and equality only to satisfy their own feelings of moral superiority. They care only about equality and do not understand the real problems facing the rest of the world. They are arrogant Westerners who pity the rest of the world and think themselves saviors. At least, that is the perception." I couldn't tell him, of course, but he – or his countrymen – had my fellow social justice warriors nailed.

Professor Chen paused, looking me straight in the eye. "The lesson of history is one should keep quiet or risk offending the powers that are or the powers that will be. I know you are involved in what's going on. You should think through the consequences, carefully. Newton told us every action has an equal and opposite reaction. Already, you can see there is a reaction forming against your protests. You should ask yourself, 'what form will the reaction take and what will happen to you?'"

I thanked him for his advice. He seemed to have the right ideas about what was going on. I still didn't know exactly where he stood, but it was very clear he had no interest in activism of any flavor. In any event, it was getting too late to recruit more Friends of George for the current battle. Professor Gomulka's showdown with Professor Muldoon was right around the corner.

CHAPTER 8: A FAILURE TO DE-PLATFORM

Professor Fries filled me in on the details later. The audit showed exactly what Professor Muldoon wanted it to show. All equipment was present along with a surprising amount of cobbled together, second-hand, and hand-built hardware that was not on the official books. "You see what good stewards we are with what we've been given to work with," Muldoon told the investigators. "We have to take good care of what little we have and improvise the rest. Now about that increase we requested in our equipment budget..."

I think Professor Gomulka would have backed out of his "Discussion on Diversity" if he could have. His knockout blow missed. The protests had been a fizzle and actually inspired additional opposition. No way could the administration justify hiring Professor Ames by claiming it met with the universal approval of the student body. Not anymore.

It was too late for Professor Gomulka to withdraw. Professor Muldoon had doubled-down, inviting important alums, donors, and even a couple of the regents to the discussion. A state senator had agreed to moderate the discussion. The auditorium was packed to overflowing. Professor Gomulka won the coin toss, so the program began with his opening statement.

"For too long we have refrained from interrogating power structures and investigating social possibilities in engineering. We uncritically replicated patriarchal authoritarian attitudes and dismissed as naïve the idea of providing students with a genuine voice in their own education. For too long, we have excluded many of our best and brightest from the benefits of an engineering education. We in turn have missed out from the fruits of their labors, and the contributions they may have made to society.

"That changes next year, and Professor Cindy Ames will be the agent of that change as the new head of the College of Engineering. I regret she was not able to share her vision in person with us this evening, but I have had many conversations with this dedicated, hard-working scholar, and I'll attempt to provide you with a small sample of her innovative ideas.

"Each student is unique – an individual snowflake – requiring the correct culturally-aware engagement and respect for their personhood in order to thrive and flourish. Professor Ames' scholarship focuses on culturally inclusive pedagogy that makes historically underrepresented students feel more welcome in the classroom. She has taken the best practices from women's studies and ethnic studies to engage students in a more inclusive and democratic classroom that encourages all voices.

"She will be the catalyst to implement the new paradigm these more open and comprehensive pedagogies demand. She will reposition us away from the bean-counting status quo in which we superficially evaluate equality in terms of headcounts. She will de-center Western civilization, and move us toward a more genuine engagement with all students, letting all students equalize their reality to what they deserve by emphasizing justice and ethical behavior as the concrete that binds together the engineering curriculum.

Professor Gomulka went on and on about synergy and diversity and mutual respect and embracing differences and welcoming change. I was wishing Amit and I had put together some buzzword bingo cards. We'd heard it all before in class. Finally, Professor Gomulka began running out of steam.

"Change may be frightening to some, as the disruptions of the past few weeks have amply demonstrated," he concluded, "but Professor Ames is the ideal person to guide us through this beneficial change. How appropriate it is that such a talented woman will lead the effort to ensure that women's voices and those of other underrepresented groups are finally heard in the engineering curriculum!"

On cue, Amit and I stood with the rest of the SJWs and gave him a standing ovation.

Professor Muldoon rose as the clamor began to subside, shaking his head. "I'll believe you're sincere about wanting women's voices in our curriculum when you start discussing Ayn Rand in literature, philosophy, and political science."

He waved an arm over the audience. "Look around you at this facility. Civil engineers designed the water and sewer systems that keep us safe from disease. Mechanical engineers keep the structure from falling on our heads. Electrical engineers design the power, lighting, and sound system to work without electrocuting anyone. I've just barely scratched the surface.

"A doctor who makes a mistake can kill a patient. An engineer can wipe out a hundred people in the wink of an eye. Engineering is pervasive. It's all around us, everywhere, every day. It's here. It's real. It works. Almost all the time. Whether you realize it or not, you bet your lives on the judgment of engineers many times every day. If you wonder why we engineers may tend to be a bit more conservative than usual, it's because our profession teaches us not to mess with what works. Failure has consequence.

"Professor Gomulka and his social justice clique aren't satisfied with that success. They want to change all that. They want ideas included in the curriculum for reasons other than engineering relevance, voices heard for reasons other than merit, and standards applied other than engineering truth.

"Are there obstacles in the way of our students' success? Certainly. Do some students have greater obstacles to overcome than others? Of course. Should we remove those obstacles? Hell, no! Sweat expended in training avoids blood spilled in battle.

"How will a timid student, afraid to raise a hand and speak in class when all that's on the line is a grade, ever summon the courage to look their boss in the eye, the person controlling their paycheck, their livelihood, their future, and say, 'These O-rings won't take the cold, and were going to have to tell NASA to scrub the launch even though it may cost us millions in penalties,' or 'We can't put the gas tank there; it may explode in a rear-end collision; we're going to have to delay the product launch and redesign the car,' or 'Those levees have to be fixed or else the city will flood during the next hurricane, and I'm going to tell the public even if you fire me.' The best engineers, in my experience, are the ones who've overcome obstacles, who have the gumption to stand up for themselves, who have the discipline to dig in and solve problems themselves, instead of waiting for some authority figure to tell them what to do.

"Heaven help us if some coddled social-justice snowflake is all that stands between us and the next disaster. God as my witness, we should be making our classes less welcoming and cuddly! We should be making them more intimidating and more demanding, placing more obstacles in our student's paths, making sure our graduates are worthy of the responsibilities they will face in their careers! If Professor Ames is allowed to run amok, she will corrupt our curriculum, debase the value of our degrees, and produce graduates with dangerous delusions of adequacy.

"We engineers take time-tested principles and impart them to our students in time-tested ways to yield the time-tested results you see around you. When we make a change or an incremental improvement, we test it. We check it out. We make sure it works as advertised before inflicting it upon the public. We already are diverse. We already are inclusive. We will include anything, any idea, or anyone that works. Period. De-center Western civilization? We are the guardians of Western civilization! Our civilization rests on how well we engineers do our job. How well tomorrow's engineers do their job depends on the choices we make in the coming weeks.

"Educating tomorrow's engineers in the practice of engineering – that is our business. Researching and testing improvements to improve the engineering state of the art – that is also our business. Overthrowing the civilization that made this institution and most of what we teach possible, indoctrinating students in the currently fashionable political claptrap, those are not our business." Professor Muldoon's conclusion triggered a remarkable thunderclap of applause. His backers rose and gave their champion a standing ovation as well. I was surprised to see almost as many in support of Muldoon as had risen for Gomulka. When the crowd had quieted, the moderator announced that the opening statements were concluded, and we would have an open discussion, beginning with Professor Gomulka.

The professor rose slowly, defiantly, as if taking possession of the platform. "Humanity is our business!" He countered triumphantly, as if he'd just refuted Muldoon's argument. Professor Muldoon looked... puzzled? No that wasn't it. Smug? He always had a touch of arrogance to him. I didn't have time to decipher his expression before Gomulka continued. "Dickens," he added haughtily. "Marley to Scrooge... *A Christmas Carol*. Behind all your posing and protestation that you're some kind of champion of 'Western Civilization,' you have not the least idea of the simplest basics of our culture – where it's come from, its history of systemized oppression, and where it's going. Your 'engineering truth' is a racist narrative employed by hegemonic institutions to perpetuate systems of white hetero-patriarchal dominance and to project their bigotry and misogyny! We 'social justice warriors' are the next chapter in what you call Western civilization. We progressives will overturn your reign of oppression, correct historic injustices, introduce culturally inclusive pedagogies, and allow the voices you and yours have marginalized to be heard at last!"

Muldoon smiled condescendingly at Gomulka's diatribe ran down. "Mankind," he said with a smug smile, as if he had just rebutted Gomulka's case in turn. There was a long pause.

"What archaic, patriarchal point do you think...," Gomulka began.

"You heard me," Muldoon countered. "I said 'mankind.' 'Mankind is our business,' said Marley to Scrooge," Muldoon corrected Gomulka. "Not 'humanity.' You and your real-life Ministry of Truth twist and pervert language and facts and truth, rewrite literature, history, and culture, trample and spit upon the genius and the hard work that made this institution and all we teach possible, all to acquire power. You proglodytes have as little respect for culture, as little respect for engineering, as you have just shown to the inestimable Mister Dickens. You're only interested in power and how to acquire it."

"You have held the reins of power long enough!" Gomulka insisted.

"And how did we in what you like to call the patriarchy acquire that power in the first place?" Muldoon asked. "By delivering success. By engineering the society in which we live. By providing the infrastructure for individuals and families to thrive and prosper and a safe place for mothers to raise their children."

"Thanks to us, women are no longer confined by your narrow patriarchal standards of old," Gomulka proclaimed. "Thanks to the suffragettes, and the civil rights workers, and the activists, and the feminists, and today's social justice warriors, women don't have to squander their talents in domestic roles – they now have the freedom to pursue the same careers in engineering as men!"

"You say that as though it's a bad thing your mother chose to squander her talent in your upbringing, although on second thought, I shall concede the point." That prompted a laugh, although some of the chuckles seemed awfully guilty.

They bantered back and forth. I thought Gomulka was getting the worst of it, but he kept drawing cheers from the crowd with his every attack on the oppressive white hetero-patriarchal hegemony. Finally, the moderator reined them both in and called for closing statements.

"The bottom line is this," Muldoon summarized. "Do you want free and open discussion in your classroom? Or must we and our students alike forever walk on eggshells, timid and afraid lest something we say can be twisted or construed so as to offend the sensibilities of some proglodyte? Do you want the true diversity of opinion and thought dueling on a level playing ground? Or do you prefer the pseudo-diversity of race and sex quotas? No to the thought police. No to the would-be commissars of culture. No to Professor Ames." He sat down to hearty applause, taking Gomulka by surprise with the brevity of his comments.

That was a trick Amit and I loved to pull in debate. Take less time than the other team expected, so they wouldn't have the prep time they anticipated to collect their thoughts and be ready when it was their turn. Gomulka made a weak closing statement meandering around and around his buzzwords and catch phrases. The SJW contingent gave him the obligatory standing ovation, and then it was over.

It was difficult to tell exactly what happened and why. Professor Ames "was appalled at the bigotry and narrow-mindedness on display at Georgia Tech" and withdrew her application to head the College of Engineering. We got the real story by reading Professor Gomulka's emails. A critical mass of influential donors and alums had pressured the administration to rescind Professor Ames's offer and her withdrawal was a mutually agreed upon face-saving measure. For all the vitriol and contempt unleashed at Georgia Tech, I think they'd have been better off making it clear the school rejected her rather than giving her the chance to pretend she was rejecting us.

It was amusing seeing Gomulka rationalize his failure to "Bernard," his superior at the Civic Circle. "More challenging than anticipated," he explained. The Georgia Tech community was "full of racists and misogynists," and we

Southerners were "hardly a generation away from Jim Crow, after all." Ominously, though, Bernard castigated him for agreeing to the debate. "There can be no free speech for hate speech. You never should have let it get to a discussion. In the future, you must de-platform reactionaries instead of giving them a forum from which to spread their hatred and misogyny."

There were many glum faces in social-justice class the Friday morning before spring break. Most of us had taken several midterms, and all the time out for social activism couldn't have been helping with studying or grades. All week long there'd been an atmosphere of gloom and failure which Amit and I had reinforced as best we could. "Bigotry and misogyny are deeply embedded in our culture," we explained in private conversations with our classmates. "We'll be fighting this same fight all our lives, over and over, again and again, making incremental progress at best against the pervasive forces of reactionism." For some reason, our classmates seemed turned off by the prospect of a perpetual struggle for incremental progress.

Professor Gomulka gave us a pep talk. "Ours is a deeply flawed institution," he began, "and change doesn't happen overnight. We exposed Professor Muldoon in particular and Georgia Tech in general as a haven for intolerance, xenophobia, ethnocentrism, and hostility against women and minorities." He tried to encourage us by claiming that our defeat had a silver lining. Then, he asked us to self-critique our social justice campaign. I'd already read the Civic Circle's critique, so I came out strong.

"With respect, sir," I replied, "I think it was a mistake to debate Professor Muldoon. You gave him a platform. You treated him as an equal. You legitimized his hatred and misogyny by treating it as just another opinion instead of something to be shunned, suppressed, and silenced."

I saw looks of surprise. No one challenged, questioned, or disputed Professor Gomulka on questions of social justice, not that directly. The few who'd tried in the fall semester quickly learned they'd be assigned an essay to deconstruct their deviationism.

The neutral look on Professor Gomulka face burst into a smile. "Exactly," he beamed at my insight. "Peter has it exactly right. There can be no free speech for hate speech. Reason and persuasion are only for well-converged targets. Those tactics only made sense when we were thinking in terms of the campus administration as the target. Muldoon on the other hand... he's as anti-converged as they come. We should have applied power and coercive tactics against him." He spent the rest of the class discussing the need to de-platform reactionaries, and the tactics to disrupt their presentations, shout them down, intimidate them, and silence their voices.

"Enough with the 'could have dones' and the 'might have beens,'" he concluded. "Have a great spring break and come back refreshed for the second half of the semester."

* * *

Having carefully consulted his pick-up artist blogs for the destination with the "hottest and easiest" girls, Amit was off to some Gulf Coast destination for spring break. "I could use a wingman," he offered. "I'm paying for the hotel room and driving down anyway. You're welcome to join me." I appreciated the offer and thanked him. For all his flaws, he was thoughtful about the fact I had nowhere near the money he was making from his software business. I also didn't have anything against picking up girls, but the way Amit went about it just seemed... distasteful. I didn't really want the kind of girl who'd sleep with me on the basis of a few glib lines and some psychological power projection.

Furthermore, I hadn't clocked near enough hours at the mirror lab, what with my involvement in protests and studying for my midterms. Sarah was off with her friends on a camping and climbing trip out west, so the lab would be deserted. Spring break gave me an opportunity to earn some extra money and spend some quality time on my translations of MacGuffin's mystical prose into modern physics. Besides, Professor Chen and Professor Graf's paper on their gamma ray breakthroughs had been accepted, and the physics department scheduled a big press conference for the Monday after spring break. I'd been there at the beginning and I'd contributed to the discovery. I wanted to help the team get ready and see it through.

I got an early start Monday morning by slipping a glass disk in the kiln and firing it up. I didn't already have a slumped disk to coat in the vacuum chamber, so instead I went back to the data I'd been looking at over winter break. "Interesting technique," Professor Graf acknowledged. "Maybe we can get your results into the conference paper we're presenting for GammaCon. The deadline's coming soon. We already know when Chernobyl and Kyshtym happened, and all this Cold War testing took place, though, so I'm not sure it adds much to the conversation." She and Professor Chen were more interested in understanding the environmental and biological impacts of radioisotopes – seeing which ones went where, how they were taken up by plants and animals and diffused through the biosphere.

I revisited my calculations from winter break, and updated them with the latest satellite data. There were a few anomalies that really bothered me. For instance, there were more than a dozen significant plumes with gamma ray detections from antimony-126 significantly above background levels all over the world. In each case there were very low levels of tin-121 – so low that my dating technique was yielding ridiculously old dates for them. Finally, I asked Professor Chen to take a look. He pointed out the hits in China and England and in the Andes Mountains of South America. "That's a tin producing region," he pointed out an area in southeast China. "A small amount of tin-126 occurs naturally. Take a closer look at your hits, and I bet they will correlate to tin deposits." He looked thoughtfully. "Your results suggest we might be able to look through the data for deposits of valuable minerals. Keep working on your tin analysis. I want to take a closer look to see if there are any other valuable ores or minerals that might show up in this gamma ray data." Sure enough, some online research showed that I'd really just generated a map of the world's tin deposits, more or less. I spent the rest of the day correlating my detections with known tin regions.

The next morning I loaded a fresh plate into the kiln, fired it up, and placed Monday's slumped disk into the vacuum chamber to be coated. I was feeling burned out by the gamma ray data, so I worked a bit more on translating MacGuffin's mystic prose into the physics notation I'd been learning in my classes. One section of it talked about "qi" which translated as "energy," but MacGuffin talked in terms of "bounding the fields" of yin and yang to get their energy. I had to run to the library at lunch time to hunt down an ancient Chinese math text, *The Nine Chapters on the Mathematical Art*, or the "*Jiuzhang Suanshu*" to make sense of it. I found a hundred-year-old translation by Florian Cajori. "Bounding fields" meant measuring the area of literal fields – pastures, farmland and plots. MacGuffin's bounding the field of yin meant the "area" of the yin? What did that mean? I was stumped for a while on that one, until I remembered that the energy density of the electric and magnetic fields depended on the square of the respective intensities. Yes, this bounding language referred to area, but more generally, the text must be describing taking the square of the field intensities.

That led me to a lengthy example in MacGuffin's text – the case of an exponentially decaying dipole. It threw me for a while, until I realized it was the same thing as the discharging capacitors I'd studied in my class work. The problem was simple, yet fascinating. The induction component of the magnetic field goes as inverse distance squared and dominated near the discharge. The radiation component of the magnetic field goes in the opposite direction and went as inverse distance. On a spherical bubble whose radius was the speed of light times the decay constant time, they exactly cancel out, meaning there is no magnetic field on that bubble. No magnetic field means no energy flow. The energy inside the bubble is absorbed by the discharge. The energy associated with the radiation came from outside the bubble. That really blew my mind. I'd thought that radiation came from accelerating charges. Accelerate a charge and out pops a photon moving away, carrying the radiation energy. That was – more or less – what Professor Graf had taught me – at least as best I understood it. MacGuffin's manuscript had a different story.

In MacGuffin's telling, accelerating charges were only "the fount of yin and yang," the source of the fields. The "qi" or the energy was only loosely coupled to the fields. At any given point, there was a local energy density proportional to the square of the field intensity, but from moment to moment, fields could be going one way and energy the other. That's what was happening in the case of the dipole. Radiation fields propagated outward through the in-falling energy – the energy being absorbed by the dipole. The radiation fields only became associated with out-flowing energy past the zero-magnetic-field bubble. They picked up the energy associated with the original static field outside the bubble. I compared the result of the Larmor formula for the radiation energy and integrated the energy density for the static fields outside the bubble. They matched perfectly. That took most of the day to work through what with my babysitting the vacuum chamber and prepping the next glass disk.

I returned to analyzing the gamma-ray data the next day. Once I'd accounted for naturally occurring tin deposits, three major anomalies leapt out at me. I had a radioactive hotspot that dated to the 1600s in southeast China, Fujian Province, and two more hotspots that dated to around 1900, one in England, and the other... the other was right along the Georgia coast centered on Jekyll Island – three mini-Chernobyls that dated to decades, even centuries before the invention of nuclear reactors. "What's that?" Professor Chen startled me. I hadn't realized he'd come into the lab – one of the problems trying to work with a vacuum pump running.

"I was trying to date some hotspots and I found some curious anomalies," I explained. "There are hotspots that look to be just over a hundred years old in England and here on Jekyll Island, and there's another hotspot that dates back to the 1600s in Fujian Province in China. The dating on that one is a bit..."

"Where in Fujian?" Professor Chen demanded. I zoomed in the map to show him the location. His eyes got big. He whispered something I didn't understand in Chinese, his voice full of emotion. "Peter." He looked at me. "You must drop this immediately and forget you discovered it." He must have seen the confusion on my face. "I am deadly serious," he continued. "There are certain secrets that must remain so. They will kill you, and me, too, if they know that we know."

That sure sounded like the Civic Circle. "Who are 'they,' and what are these secrets?"

"There are questions that must not be asked, and answers that must not be given," he replied solemnly. "I am truly sorry to put you in this place. I did not realize where your work might lead and what it might reveal. I can only ask you to trust me and remain silent." He paused, thinking through the next steps. "I will get a CD for you to burn a copy of the data and analysis. Then, you must delete everything from your machine."

Naturally, I made a complete copy of the data set to my secure flash drive while he was out of the lab. When he came back, I copied the data over to the CD. "Deleting" a file from a drive merely frees up the space to be rewritten upon – it doesn't actually remove the data. Before I could point that out to him, he had me download a program that not only deletes, but also rewrites the sectors several times so the data will be – in principle – irrecoverable.

He cautioned me again. "You are young. You are... idealistic. You must forget this and not look into it further. I have done all I can for you. The rest is up to you."

"Yes, sir," I acknowledged.

Amit showed up late Sunday night. "What happened?" I asked. "I haven't heard anything from you."

"You don't think I'd actually describe my exploits over the phone or by email do you?" he countered. "They're listening, you know. To everything." He regaled me with stories of his conquests. "Two!" he exclaimed. "Two different girls!" He gave me a blow-by-blow account. Literally. Then, exhausted from his vacation, he collapsed. I left early for class and didn't see him again until lunch time.

"My professor is announcing our big discovery this afternoon," I told Amit. "Want to come?"

"I have a date with Madison," he replied. "We're brainstorming ever more creative ways to enhance equality by promoting messages of universal inclusion and diversity."

I thought about that a moment. "If everyone's truly equal, why do we need diversity?"

Amit glared at me. "You're doing it again – bringing facts to feel-fight."

"Bring her along," I suggested with a smile. "It's a legitimate news story. Maybe you can get her to do real news for once."

"Not likely," he said. "She's only interested if there's a social justice angle. I don't suppose your professors' gamma rays are complicit in the institutionalized oppression of historically underrepresented portions of the electromagnetic spectrum by any chance?"

"Sadly, no," I replied, "but Professor Graf was a key contributor to the discovery. Maybe she could do a 'heroic woman overcoming systemic male hegemony to succeed in science' piece?"

"That angle might work," he said nodding. "I'll see what I can do."

I didn't need to worry about trying to pack the audience, after all. The auditorium at the Student Center held a healthy crowd. The start of the press conference found Amit and Madison sitting beside me. Amit had a hand on Madison's thigh and she leaned against him. They seemed awfully friendly. Then, Professor Graf took the podium.

"I'm Professor Marlena Graf of the Georgia Tech Physics Department. Thank you for the opportunity to speak to you this afternoon about a remarkable discovery. Our Gamma Research Group studies gamma rays – the most intense electromagnetic radiation known. Lately, we've taken an instrument designed to peer into the deepest reaches of the cosmos and turned it back at our own Earth with surprising results of great scientific, environmental, and commercial significance. It's my honor to introduce my collaborator, our Principal Investigator, Professor Wu Chen." Professor Graf stepped down, and Professor Chen approached the podium. I was surprised to see he was wearing one of his trademark Hawaiian-style print shirts, instead of something more conservative.

"I'd like to thank Marlena for her introduction," he began. "We have discovered we can detect, locate, and analyze terrestrial sources of gamma radiation from space." He walked the audience through the Chernobyl and Kyshtym results, and showed maps of the fallout from Cold War nuclear testing in such places as Nevada, Kazakhstan, and Algeria. "These maps provide an unprecedented level of detail to show how and where man-made radioactive materials have entered the environment." He showed examples of how the data could be used to find previously-unknown deposits of uranium and other radioactive ores. Finally, he announced the team's discovery of antimatter production in lighting storms.

"These are some sexy, sexy results – they did not come easy. Our results were a team effort from a fantastic group of hardworking researchers, graduate students, and even undergraduates. I'd also like to acknowledge the support of our sponsors."

Professor Chen answered a few questions. Just as the press conference was breaking up, Madison approached the podium. "Professor! Oh, Professor!" she squealed.

Professor Chen had an indulgent look on his face. "Yes?"

"That's like such a cool shirt!" Madison gushed. "May I get a picture of you?"

"Certainly," he beamed back at her.

She whipped out a camera. "Right next to the podium with the Georgia Tech logo," she insisted.

He complied. I took a closer look at the shirt as she was taking her pictures. Sexy, buxom women struck provocative poses, straddled motorcycles suggestively, and, adding insult to social justice injury, wielded firearms with a near orgasmic look of pleasure on their faces. I'd noted it was awfully garish, and I honestly thought, inappropriate for a formal event. However, it was also exactly the kind of shirt Professor Chen made a habit of wearing. I hadn't much thought about it. Only now, it was too late. What was she up to?

"Don't wait up for me," came the text from Amit later. I spent the evening on homework, and I didn't see him until lunch the next day.

"How'd your social justice date go?"

"Jackhammered her like the Berlin Wall!" he proclaimed. "She worked on some column she wouldn't show me while I did my own homework. Then, I persuaded her she should reject the outmoded mores of patriarchal oppression, assume autonomy of her own body, and express her sexual independence. She found it 'empowering,'" he said smugly.

"Wait... you encouraged her to exercise her autonomy and empowerment by complying with your demand for sex?"

"Complying with my demand for sex? See," Amit explained, "when you say it like that, it's verbal assault and sexual harassment. When the timing is right, though, and I say it – it's sly and sarcastic. Social justice chicks get wet for dominant social justice dudes who are only acting out traditional hetero-patriarchal roles out of a sense of irony."

I really didn't need to know that. Wait a moment, chicks? Plural? "How many social justice 'chicks' are you dating?"

"Well," he looked sheepish, "just the one, but really, you've seen the rest of the chicks in our class. Would you want to bang any of them?"

This was getting badly off topic. "You didn't know what Madison was writing?"

"It was about your professor, but she wouldn't tell me the details. She seemed pretty excited about it, though."

I handed Amit the copy of the *Technique* I'd picked up earlier. Madison's picture of Professor Chen and his shirt made the front page – a symbol of the pervasive sexism in science and engineering by the "Ramblin' Wrecks at Georgia Tech" made clear by the institution's previous disgraceful reaction to a woman heading the College of Engineering. The highlight, though, was Madison's column.

END THE TOXIC HYPER-MASCULINITY OF SCIENCE

Yesterday morning, wearing a shirt featuring scantily-clad women, Professor Chen of the Georgia Tech Physics Department announced a discovery to help make the world "safe" for even more deadly radiation. Professor Chen's technique for finding where radiation is and where it goes helps proponents of nuclear technology argue that it can be safely managed and controlled, thus encouraging further proliferation. Proclaiming his results "sexy" and declaring "they did not come easy," Professor Chen perpetrated the patriarchal narrative that science is the figurative rape of nature. Not content with emboldening those who want to make dangerous nuclear technology more readily available, Professor Chen demeaned and objectified half the human race in the process with his outrageously sexist shirt.

Could any shirt possibly be as bad as all that? Yes it can.

Imagine buxom button-bursting bosoms breasting boobily, amid guns, motorcycles, and other icons of patriarchal domination and violence. Professor Chen may say he respects his female colleagues and students, but his shirt says otherwise. His shirt says, "I have no respect for you as a professional." His shirt proclaims that science is a boys' club where women are merely sex objects for the visual pleasure of men. Professor Chen's shirt visually rapes every woman who sees it, reducing women to pieces of meat that men get to utilize for their sexual pleasure. His shirt marginalizes his female colleagues just to show how laid back he is. Professor Chen isn't the least bit stuffy, and he's prepared to throw his female colleagues under the bus to prove it.

Most disturbing of all, no one in the physics department, not even his intimidated and browbeaten female colleagues, thought his shirt was inappropriate. By their failure to take action, they are complicit in his phallic imperialism. The physics department in particular and the so-called "Ramblin' Wrecks" at Georgia Tech in general have once again exposed their flagrant hateful misogyny to the world.

Despite our best efforts, bigots and sexists like Professor Chen thrive in our society. The systemic patriarchal hegemony of science and engineering provides a breeding ground for their chauvinism. Their rampant sexual objectification triggers an environment wherein sexual harassment is commonplace. This pervasive atmosphere of toxic hyper-masculinity deters even strong, independent women like me from careers in science. Little girls watching Professor Chen get the message loud and clear – science is not for you; stay home, have babies, and bake cookies.

We need to send a different message – a message to Professor Chen and any other scientist who harbors such sexist and ostracizing attitudes. Get out of science. There is no place here for you to demean half of humanity with your archaic bigotry. We need to root out these sexist attitudes so scientists and engineers alike can be taught to think as critically about socially important issues like *race and gender as they do about their test tubes and telescopes. This overt sexism is unacceptable, and the perpetrators must be held accountable. None of us can stand on the sidelines. If you're not part of the solution, then you're part of the problem.*

I waited for Amit to finish reading. "Wow...." He looked up at me in honest amazement. "No wonder she was so enthusiastic last night. She really outdid herself this time: 'buxom button-bursting bosoms breasting boobily?'"

Figured he'd focus on that line. "Breasting boobily? Are those even words?"

"They are now," he replied dryly. "Your professor is in trouble. You know what Gomulka will do with this."

"He's going to restart the fight we just won." I should have made that connection sooner.

"We're all woman-hating, patriarchal, reactionaries here," Amit confirmed. "That's exactly what he'll say. His first defeat becomes fuel for the fire. First we reject the nice lady professor because we're all misogynists, and then mean old Professor Chen objectifies women, further illustrating the systemic institutional sexism of Georgia Tech."

"It's worse than that." I explained the results I'd found in Professor Chen's data.

"Jekyll Island ties in," Amit nodded. The timing seems reasonable. "But England? And four hundred years ago in China?"

"More like three hundred fifty," I corrected him, "I think. It's hard to date it accurately, that far back."

"Still... it's not just electromagnetics, then," Amit said slowly. "They were doing nuclear physics, too, centuries ago, and all this scrutiny..."

"Is likely to draw enough attention to bring the implications of Professor Chen's work to light." I completed the thought. "We have to stop it. Somehow."

Amit shook his head. "It's too late. If we can see how the social justice warriors could use this, I'm sure Gomulka does too."

Amit was right. It was "Engineering 4 Everyone" Part 2.

"This is a prime example of the hetero-normative oppression that we must root out of our school," Professor Gomulka explained triumphantly to the class. "Right here on this very campus is a physics professor who epitomizes the toxic masculinity of science. We have to draw a line. To tell the Professor Chens of the world that they cannot demean half of humanity with impunity. This time, we have the advantage. Why did Engineering 4 Everyone fail to achieve its goals?"

It was a Bueller moment. I wasn't about to volunteer the truth: because Amit and I and the rest of FOG completely out-thought and out-fought him and the rest of the SJWs.

"I should think the answer is obvious to the veteran social justice warriors in the class," he continued.

That probably wounded Amit's pride, because he was quick on the uptake. "We lost the momentum. We took too long. We gave the reactionaries time to see what we were doing and to counter it with activism of their own. We lost the initiative. And we failed to de-platform their hate speech."

"Exactly," Professor Gomulka beamed at his star pupil. "This time, we will not make the same mistakes, and we will leave nothing to chance. I have it on good authority that the dean will demand Professor Chen apologize at a press conference on Monday. Between now and then, we will put so much pressure on him that his apology will be a prelude to a resignation. If he doesn't resign, we will see to it that his tenure is revoked and he is fired for his misconduct and the shame he has brought to himself and to this institution. This time we have an advantage! We have a source close to the professor! Peter Burdell actually works in his lab!"

Oh, no. Oh no, no, no, no. I'd done such a good job of partitioning my phony social justice activism from my work with Professor Chen that I had forgotten the first social justice lesson from my first day in class – to pretend to be them was to become them.

"Peter?" Professor Gomulka asked expectantly.

Professor Chen. The man who hired me. The man who mentored me. I had no choice. "Professor Chen must resign," I said calmly, "and we're going to make it happen."

Professor Gomulka grinned. He was so eager to get going that any attempt at subtlety or working behind the scenes through student cut-outs was forgotten. He laid out a four-day campaign culminating in a Friday noon rally by the Campanile and a weekend-long hunger strike for equality. The professor took me aside after class. "Do you know anything that might help us take him down? Any questionable habits or behaviors?"

"Other than his quirky taste in shirts, Professor Chen is actually a nice guy," I couldn't help but defend him.

"The fight for social justice may entail certain aspects that in other circumstances we would deplore," Professor Gomulka offered his friendly counsel. "The sacrifices we must make – and those we must ask of others – are a small price to pay when weighed against the benefit of a just and equitable society, don't you agree, Peter?"

He dressed it up in flowery, abstract language, but the message was clear. The ends justify the means. Because our social justice ends are just, we can form a lynch mob to hound an innocent man from his job just to score some political points. I finally understood the social justice perspective: when your end is achieving ultimate power, so you can enact what you perceive to be ultimate good, the ultimate in evil means are justified. I suddenly realized why I'd had such trouble with social justice rhetoric. The goal was not to convey a message. The goal was to hide the true meaning behind a cloak of euphemism and cloudy vagueness. He couldn't very well say, "I believe in killing any who oppose us and stand in the way of our quest for power." Instead, he would say something like, "We deplore the extreme measures that may prove necessary, but a certain temporary curtailment of normal rights are an inevitable consequence of the evolution to social justice." You could defend any atrocity, conceal any crime...

"Can I count on you to help us out?" Professor Gomulka interrupted my reverie.

"Yes. Yes, of course, Professor," I assured him. "I understand. I understand it all, perfectly."

"You'll approach Professor Chen about resigning?" Professor Gomulka forced me to commit myself.

I took a deep breath. "Yes, I will," I said, betraying Professor Chen a second time.

I swung by the physics building and waited around the corner while loud voices talked behind the closed door of Professor Chen's office. The dean and a couple of others left, walking past me. One corner of the dean's mouth quirked up as he passed – a subtle acknowledgement of his junior ally in social justice. Professor Chen appeared shell-shocked.

"Peter," he welcomed me warily. "What brings you here to see me?"

"I understand you are in trouble, Professor," I began.

"Peter," he said softly but with a burning intensity. "You must not reveal what you know. They will kill you, and me, too, to keep their secrets safe."

"I understand the danger we're both in," I assured him. "I will keep your secret. They will not hear of it from me. My concern is that all the publicity and attention you are about to receive will draw more attention to your work. If they scrutinize it, if they realize what can be done with the data set you and Professor Graf have assembled..."

"I know," he nodded sadly.

"I think," I drew a breath to calm myself as I prepared to complete my sin by disowning my professor a third time, "I think you may need to resign."

He looked at me a moment. "I have already decided to resign," he explained. "Professor Graf will be a good steward of our research group. Can I count on you to continue to help her out and make sure she does not ask the wrong questions or draw dangerous conclusions from our data?"

"Yes, sir."

I'd done it again. Just a couple of years ago, I cluelessly poked around old books at the Tolliver Library. I started a chain of events that led to five deaths, including my parents. Now I'd managed to destroy a professor's career and put him, Professor Graf, and maybe the whole research team in jeopardy.

Amit and I alerted the FOG, but Professor Gomulka was right – by acting quickly, the SJWs had the initiative. Amit and I joined the SJWs handing out flyers along Tech Walk, as was expected of us. Professor Gomulka called in a favor with CNN and they interviewed Madison. She explained how shocked and traumatized she felt. "I felt unsafe. I was literally shaking with fear and rage," she explained. "Literally!"

The dean opened up a "Safe Space" with cookies, coloring books, and Play-Doh for students who had been "traumatized" by Professor Chen's terrifying shirt. "It's not just a shirt," the dean insisted. "It's the pattern of institutionalized sexism and systemic oppression that the shirt so vividly illustrates. Our counselors are standing by to help any Tech student who feels threatened or alienated," he assured the student body.

"These sexist attitudes are precisely why so many women are turned off careers in science," proclaimed Professor Gomulka at the Friday noon rally by the Campanile. "We demand that Professor Chen apologize for his disgraceful behavior and resign!"

I showed up to Friday's lab meeting early. Sarah was already there. "I can't believe what your friend wrote. 'This pervasive environment of toxic hyper-masculinity deters even strong, independent women like me from careers in science?'" She rolled her eyes as she read from the article. "Like that journalism freshman taking business math would so totally be doing quantum mechanics if only Professor Chen's scary shirt hadn't frightened her away."

Defending the indefensible is never fun, but I'd had to do it countless times before in high school debate.

"She's trying to help the cause of women in science," I offered.

"She's certainly not helping the cause of women in science, or journalism, for that matter," Sarah insisted indignantly. "Professor Chen and Professor Graf make a great scientific discovery, and instead of focusing on their achievement, your friend wants to critique a shirt? A fashion critique is the extent of the analysis that alleged journalist can 'perpetrate?' Besides, any more 'help' like that and I'm going to be out of a summer job, because this research group will be shut down. I've already been accepted to grad school, but I was hoping to work here over the summer. Now that's in jeopardy."

"What's going on?"

"Apparently they're pressuring Professor Chen to issue a formal apology on Monday and resign," she explained. "They're hinting to Professor Graf that she should take over the research group and how wonderfully enlightened it would be to have a woman in charge to show the physics department isn't really a bunch of mean, nasty, sexist bigots after all. Professor Graf turned them down. She's standing behind Professor Chen one hundred percent! She told me she thinks they're going to try to force him to resign, and if he doesn't, they'll fire him."

"You wouldn't prefer working for a woman?"

"How can you be for equality and justice and say something like that?" Sarah asked, incredulously. "Being a good boss and mentor depends on the person, not their sex. Professor Chen is wonderful. You know, he helped me get my gamma ray sensor module completed." She popped open the Styrofoam cooler and pulled out her sensor package. "We're going to test it in the vacuum chamber, cold soak it, and if it works, launch it in a couple of weeks using a high-altitude weather balloon." She gestured toward a helium cylinder and what looked like some folded sheets.

"How will you get the data back? Won't you lose the balloon and payload when it drifts away?"

"I'm using a cellphone with GPS. That was the expensive part of the payload. It'll send text messages with its location.

"I thought cell phones won't work at altitude."

"Neither will GPS," she noted. "The cell phone is really only to help us locate and recover the module as it's drifting down by parachute. We're using a 70-cm ham-radio data link for real-time telemetry to the chase vehicle. I've been working on this all year for my senior project, and I wouldn't have gotten this far without Professor Chen."

"I'm sure Professor Graf could help you." I felt like such a disloyal weasel.

"That's not going to happen," Sarah shot back at me, defiantly. "Professor Graf and I are not going to stand by while you social justice types throw Professor Chen to the dogs!"

Wow! Sarah had always been so mild-mannered and even-tempered – completely apolitical. The persecution of her professor had pushed her over the edge, and she was determined to fight back. Good! The Friends of George needed to reach out to her.

Just then, Professor Graf arrived with some of the graduate students.

Sarah looked suspiciously at me and then asked Professor Graf, "Did you...?"

Professor Graf smiled. "It's all arranged."

Professor Chen entered the lab, his head held low, not meeting our eyes. "I have been suspended, pending the outcome of the dean's investigation. The dean has scheduled a press conference for Monday. He demanded I make a formal apology."

"Don't do it," Professor Graf stood defiantly, her hands balled into fists as she leaned forward against the table. "That's exactly what they want you to do. Your apology won't help anything. They'll just twist it around as an admission of guilt. You're handing them the excuse they need to break your tenure."

"I honestly think you and the team will be better off if I apologize," Professor Chen insisted, finally raising his head to meet her gaze. "It's the only way we can put this controversy behind us and let you get on with your work. I have to resign."

"Nonsense!" Professor Graf would have nothing of it. "It's our work, yours too! Your apology is an admission of guilt. The next step will be to use your apology as ammunition to force you to resign. Your only hope, the team's only hope is if you stand firm and fight."

"You don't understand." Professor Chen was clearly taken aback by the intensity of Professor Graf's insistence. "If it's not this, it will be something else. They are going to shut us down one way or another."

"Then, we will fight them at the press conference, and we will fight them at your tenure hearing, and on the peer review panels, and at GammaCon, and we will never surrender!"

I was torn between fear Professor Graf was making matters worse and risking drawing the attention of the Civic Circle, and the realization that she was seriously hot when she was worked up to a high temper, leaning over, giving an excellent view of... I really had to stop my mind from wandering in inappropriate ways!

Professor Chen wilted under the intensity of Professor Graf's assault. "Is there nothing I can say to persuade you to give up? To just let it go?"

Professor Graf relaxed a bit. I think we all realized she'd won. "You have to fight," she said simply. "That's all there is to it. For yourself, and for your team. We will be right behind you, all the way." I could see the heads nodding around the table. Everyone was with her.

"Very well," Professor Chen acquiesced. Sarah leapt to her feet and started applauding. Everyone else joined in. I pretended reluctance, but inside I wanted to cheer. Finally, people were starting to fight back against the cry bullies. Professor Chen looked a bit overwhelmed by the burst of emotion his words had unleashed. He looked a bit misty eyed as he shook his head. "I fear you may have cause to regret your stand."

"You just leave it to me, sir," Professor Graf assured him with a bright smile. "Sarah and I have an idea to turn this around." She looked at the rest of us, avoiding any eye contact with me. "Will the rest of you please leave us?"

She knew, or suspected, there was a mole on the team. Good for her. With my "social justice" connection, I was a likely suspect. I'd have to wait until the press conference Monday to learn what she and Sarah had in mind to save Professor Chen and the research group. I had to let Professor Gomulka know that Professor Chen might not apologize at the press conference after all. I waited until Saturday morning to pass on the news, and I slipped the invitation letter from George P. Burdell into Sarah's box at the physics building.

I'd put on a few pounds since arriving on campus, so I figured participating in the Hunger Strike for Equality wouldn't hurt me, not that I planned to be an absolutist about it. I hadn't been camping since I was in Boy Scouts, and the experience was nostalgic. It was surprisingly satisfying spending the night out on the green near the Campanile in my DEET-coated mosquito net, surreptitiously consuming an energy bar and listening to the whining, hungry insects feast on the even hungrier and hopelessly unprepared SJWs. That's how I found myself right there at ground zero chanting, "Hey, hey! Ho, ho! Sexist science has got to go!" Sunday at lunchtime when those magnificent bastards in FOG unveiled their surprise: a "Barbeque in Support of Professor Chen" just upwind. The SJWs called off the hunger strike a few hours early because, "we'd made our point," and we went out together for some food at the Varsity. I treated myself to my favorite pick-me-up: a frosted orange.

CHAPTER 9: ON DEATH GROUND

I showed up early Monday morning to be sure I got a seat at the press conference. The place was packed. I was watching the back door to the auditorium when she entered. No one else had noticed yet. Professor Graf walked forward at a slow but deliberate pace, taking ownership of the room one row at a time. The audience quieted from the back to the front as she walked past. She looked gorgeous, even more so than usual, turning every head and quieting every conversation in her wake. If I weren't so intimately familiar with how she looked, I wouldn't have been able to tell she was wearing makeup.

"Good morning," Professor Graf began. "I'm Professor Marlena Graf of the Georgia Tech Physics Department. Not long ago, my colleague, Professor Wu Chen, shared a momentous discovery with the world – an innovation that will save lives by identifying areas of radioactive contamination, a new technique that will enhance quality of life by making deposits of nuclear fuel easier to find, and the realization that anti-matter exists in nature, right here on our own planet. As a member of his team, I'm proud to have contributed to these remarkable scientific breakthroughs.

"Unfortunately, our team's incredible discoveries were overshadowed by concern about Professor Chen's poor judgment in attire. I speak for all the women on Professor Chen's team when I say we find it highly inappropriate of him to wear a print shirt depicting sexy, attractive women wielding firearms or driving motorcycles," she said, her voice conveying a stern schoolmarmish disapproval. "This is a place of science, a research laboratory, not a shooting range or a motorcycle rally. So I have collaborated with Professor Chen's other female colleagues and with the artist of the original shirt to commission something a little more appropriate for Professor Chen to wear to this and any future scientific press conferences and events."

Professor Graf held up another print shirt – similar in style to the one that got Professor Chen in trouble. The shirt depicted women in science and engineering. Astronaut Sally Ride floated weightless above the right pocket. Across the back, Madame Curie showed a rather attractive calf as she dueled with a kettle of radium. Hedy Lamarr gazed out with smoldering eyes past a sketch of her spread-spectrum radio design. Sexy, attractive women in lab coats examined test tubes, peered into microscopes, and wrote formulas on blackboards. And was that Professor Graf and Sarah wrestling with a vacuum chamber just below Madame Curie's kettle? I could hear the crowd beginning to murmur, chuckles and laughter merging with gasps of horror and outrage. Professor Graf handed the shirt to Professor Chen who calmly put it on, a serene look on his face... or was it just resignation to the inevitable?

Whatever. The shirt was simply awesome.

"Professor Chen's critics complained that his shirt sent the wrong message," she continued. "They complained that we 'browbeaten and intimidated' women in science are wilting violets and that the least display of sexuality would have us cowering in fear from the rapacious male overlords of our hetero-patriarchal profession. They proclaim that the power differential between teacher and student or between boss and employee leaves us no choice but to submit without protest to off-color jokes, degrading workplace behavior, or inappropriate advances. They trivialize the horror of rape by equating it with images on a shirt. These fainting-couch feminists and modern-day puritans demand we institutionalize their neuroses by insisting that the least hint of sexuality be purged from the workplace. They would take us back to the Victorian era when table legs had to be covered lest they arouse inappropriate thoughts. Well, we have a different message to send his critics. We say, 'No.'

"Autonomy means personal responsibility, not crying to authority figures for help at the least provocation. If we have a problem with a co-worker's behavior, we accept the responsibility to stand up for ourselves and say so. Mere offensiveness is not harassment. If someone offends you by their speech, you must learn to defend yourself by the same method. To run crying for outside help is to send a message that women are too weak to work with men. Appealing for outside help must remain a last resort, not first aid.

"It's true that science has long been male-dominated for the simple reason that science is largely a creation of males. Science was largely devised by men, but now has been augmented and is co-owned by women. Men invited us in as their guests, and now we work together as partners. A sex-free workplace is neither achievable nor desirable. Demanding that men redefine themselves to suit feminist dogma is no more acceptable than demanding women redefine themselves."

Professor Graf defiantly defended her boss from the witch-hunt. She proclaimed her independence from the would-be social justice white knights who wanted to reduce her to the status of anointed victim under their protection... and control. They'd offered her Chen's research group, and she contemptuously spurned the offer of social justice patronage as she would an improper advance from an unclean thing. I'd seen flashes of it before, but she'd kept it well hidden. Now at last she turned on the full force of her personality and her feminine presence. She radiated a power I'd never seen before. I was simultaneously in love, and a bit intimidated by her. The audience sat silent, shocked by the unexpected intensity of her remarks.

"I stand with Professor Chen against his critics, against the world if need be. You don't intimidate me, and neither does a silly shirt." She began to leave the podium.

The reporters present leapt to their feet and began yelling questions. "Doesn't Professor Chen's behavior discourage girls from pursuing STEM careers?" shouted one reporter. "Shouldn't you be encouraging girls, not turning them away?"

"I think it's a good idea," Professor Graf countered, "to expose more students, male and female alike, to the possibility of a STEM education. I am concerned, however, that those who succumb to the high-pressure sales tactics used in promoting STEM studies may lack the inner drive to succeed. STEM degrees are difficult. If you need to run and hide in a safe space when a professional colleague wears print shirts featuring pin-up models, STEM is not for you."

"You're not being very welcoming to female students, are you?" asked another reporter accusingly. "Why should Professor Chen be allowed to wear sexist and misogynistic clothing? Doesn't that deter women in STEM?"

"I can assure girls, or boys for that matter, who may be considering STEM that there are far more challenging hurdles to overcome in your studies and potential career than the dubious fashion sense of your future colleagues," Professor Graf added dryly. "As someone who has worked closely with Professor Chen, I can attest that I regard his questionable attire as an amusing idiosyncrasy, not a cause for alarm.

"The unknown won't discover itself," Professor Graf concluded, "and we need to get back to our work. We will have no further comment." She stepped down from the podium.

Professor Graf's press conference had burst the narrative bubble. The designated victim had refused to accept her victimhood and had thrown it right back at them. Having denied the administration an apology and resignation, Professor Chen remained on paid leave, "pending the outcome of an investigation." That meant he could come in and work as much or as little as he wanted. The ordeal was not over, however.

The following week, Professor Chen's program manager flew in for an unannounced review. Citing inadequate progress and insufficient results, Professor Chen was advised that his research grant would not be renewed for the following school year. His remarkable discoveries counted for nothing, because they were not the stated goal of his grant application. We were behind on creating mirrors, and thus demonstrated ourselves unworthy of support. Professor Graf had been promised tenure on the strength of her work with Professor Chen. Now she was told her appointment would not be renewed either. In class, Professor Graf was close to her usual self, but she seemed more preoccupied and distant. She no longer smiled.

Professor Chen and Professor Graf were not the only ones under pressure. Students who were not previously interested in social justice or my involvement in the movement, now discovered that social justice was nevertheless deeply interested in them – and that social justice wanted to make an example of a couple of their favorite professors. My fellow students had learned that previously ignored ideas and slogans had dramatic real-world repercussions.

Word got around the physics department that I was one of the SJWs who'd been hounding Professor Chen and now, Professor Graf. My physics friends were suddenly "too busy" to discuss homework. Conversations stopped when I approached people I thought were friends. Replies were perfunctory and dismissive.

I went to see Professor Graf during her office hours. She wore a poker face, and was clearly glad to be rid of me once she'd answered my questions. Sarah dealt with me the bare minimum she had to for us to accomplish our work, and no more. She found another place to study and no longer hung out in the mirror lab as before. Sarah made clear she blamed me for the persecution of her professors.

I continued my work in the mirror lab, but it was obvious time was running out for the research group. One evening, I'd finished early with my homework, so I thought I'd take a moment to download the latest satellite data. "Permission denied," came the error message. I tried a different data set. "Permission denied," the database portal insisted again. Then, I went way back to the original data from last year that I'd used to establish the technique in the first place. "Permission denied."

I asked Sarah to take a look. "Permission denied."

"They've cut off our access to the earth-observation data," she concluded. "Hey! They cut off our access to the astronomy data as well!" She glared at me. "If you want your data, you'll have to ask your SJW friends for it!" Sarah gathered her things and stormed out.

Some unexpected guests delayed that Friday's lab meeting. They were speaking in private with Professor Chen and Professor Graf. "They want us to pack up and go to work for them in Nevada," Professor Chen said. "Enough of that, though. Let's get an update on the mirror inventory and review the papers we'll be presenting at GammaCon."

I cornered Professor Graf afterward. She looked haggard and stressed – not her usual cheerful self. The pressure of having the rug pulled out from underneath her and losing her job was weighing heavily on her. "What did you tell them?" I asked her.

"I told them, 'no,'" she replied. "I will remain 'mistress of mine own self and mine own soul.'"

That sounded familiar, somehow. "Shakespeare?"

"No," she smiled sadly. "Tennyson."

* * *

Amit was busy "entertaining" one of his young ladies in our room, so I spent my Friday night in the mirror lab, trying to make further sense out of MacGuffin's manuscript.

I could follow MacGuffin's description of the energy density as the sum of the electric and magnetic energy density: $\frac{1}{2} \varepsilon_0 |\mathbf{E}|^2 + \frac{1}{2} \mu_0 |\mathbf{H}|^2$. Then, he started to talk about the difference between them as well: $\frac{1}{2} \varepsilon_0 |\mathbf{E}|^2 - \frac{1}{2} \mu_0 |\mathbf{H}|^2$. MacGuffin described something about how the quantity changed in space and how it was the same as the rate of change with respect to the velocity? Somehow the whole mess of relationships seamlessly segued into a discussion of ebbs and flows of qi and something called the great circle. It seemed some kind of physical manifestation of a universal great circle or wheel of life. The whole thing sounded vaguely Buddhist. I'd dismissed that particular section as incomprehensible mysticism the first time I'd read it, but I'd deciphered enough of MacGuffin's mystic prose by then to become confident there must be some deep physical meaning to it all.

I'd worn myself out trying to translate the mystical prose into some kind of mathematical sense. I simply didn't understand it. I had the equations strewn all over the chalkboard. I sat back and stared at them, as if I could intimidate my scribblings into revealing their hidden meanings to me. I was deep in a sense of futility and frustration when the door opened behind me.

Professor Graf entered. "I saw the light on in the lab," she explained "I was heading out to a club, stopped by to pick up..." Wow she looked hot! She was wearing a low-cut blouse that really accentuated her cleavage. I couldn't take my eyes off them. "Hey!" she interrupted my reverie. "My eyes are up here."

Going out to a club while I was working late doing physics? I was tired. I was frustrated. I looked up at her eyes. Then, I deliberately looked back at her cleavage. "So that's why you're wearing that low-cut blouse," I asked her, gesturing as if I were cupping her breasts in my hands, "to draw attention to your..." I looked her in the eye, "...eyes?"

She looked shocked, then smiled guiltily and looked away. Finally she giggled and looked back at me. "You'd best not let your social justice friends hear you objectify me like that," she replied with a delightful smile – the first I'd seen from her in weeks. She looked past me at the blackboard, full of my notes and equations from the MacGuffin manuscript – ideas that the Civic Circle would happily kill us both to keep secret. "What's this?"

"Some electromagnetics ideas," I grabbed an eraser and moved for the board.

"Hold on a minute," she said, pointing at one of the mathematical tangles. "That's the electromagnetic Lagrangian."

"The what?"

"Lagrange reformulated Newtonian mechanics, taking the difference between the kinetic and potential energy as his starting point," she explained. "And that's the Hamiltonian." She must have perceived the look of bewilderment on my face because she hastened to add, "It's another way of approaching mechanics that takes the total energy, kinetic plus potential, as a starting point."

In her enthusiasm, Professor Graf forgot any concept of personal space. She squeezed between the desk and the blackboard to join me, her delicate fingers teasing the chalk from my hands. She added "$H =$" in front of my "$\frac{1}{2}\, \varepsilon_0 |\mathbf{E}|^2 + \frac{1}{2}\, \mu_0 |\mathbf{H}|^2$". "That's the Hamiltonian," she said, standing so close to me a few stray strands of hair swept under my chin as she turned back to the board. "See, that confusion between $\mathbf{H}$ for magnetic field and H for Hamiltonian is yet another reason why you ought to be using the $\mathbf{B}$-field instead of the $\mathbf{H}$-field. You've been picking up bad habits from your electrical engineering friends!" She smiled indulgently at me.

"You may come to appreciate the advantages," I said confidently, although I still really didn't understand the point she was making. Maybe there was a benefit to the bad-boy mystique Amit tried so hard to cultivate, but I doubted any of his pick-up artist blogs ever suggested seducing a physics professor by throwing electrical engineering notation at her and confidently asserting the superiority of the approach. It was a bit like what Amit called a "neg," an attempt to puncture self-esteem and create...

Professor Graf interrupted my musing by appending "$L =$" to "$\frac{1}{2}\, \varepsilon_0 |\mathbf{E}|^2 - \frac{1}{2}\, \mu_0 |\mathbf{H}|^2$." "That's the Lagrangian... but this..." she looked up at me, "Whatever were you trying to do by dividing the Lagrangian density by the Hamiltonian density?"

I had no idea what MacGuffin was up to, of course. I was just trying to follow the poorly marked path he'd laid out. Fortunately, she didn't wait for me to answer. "Oh, I see," she bubbled forth excitedly from her delicious-looking ruby-red lips, "you're using the Hamiltonian to normalize the Lagrangian. That's what this is!" she brushed against me again as she pointed to a jumble of symbols. "Clever," she turned again and smiled, gazing intently in my eyes before returning her attention to the board. "For radiation, the electric and magnetic energy balances, so your normalized Lagrangian goes to zero. In static cases, it goes to +1 for electrostatic fields and to −1 for magnetostatic fields."

Now that she mentioned it, I could see how the math was analogous to the way the microwave reflection coefficient went to +1 for an open and -1 for a short. "It's analogous to the way microwave reflection coefficients behave," I confidently asserted, but her attention was already drawn to the other side of the board.

She pressed her back against me as she squeezed past me in the enclosed space, her hair tickling against my mouth and nose...

"This here," she pointed to another tangle of symbols, "you must mean the Poynting vector, but it looks as though you were writing it as a scalar product instead of a vector product... but you appear to be assuming the fields are orthogonal, so it doesn't matter. And then, you're dividing by the Hamiltonian, or more generally, the total energy density, and you're dividing by the speed of light." She placed a hand on her hip, her sleeve sweeping the board and collecting chalk dust. She turned back to me, her other shoulder brushing against the board. "You're trying to write an expression for the energy velocity? The Poynting vector divided by the energy density? And you're normalizing it by the speed of light?"

Is that what I was doing? "That's what I was doing," I said confidently, "but I'm not sure it's working out correctly."

"Your notation is just... clunky," she said. "Look, let's call this normalized energy velocity, 'gamma,'" she wrote out "$\gamma = S / c H =$" in front of one of the mathematical tangles. Then, she slid past me again to go back to the other side of the board. I placed a hand on her shoulder to guide her strategically past me. She didn't appear to notice my touching her. "And let's use script ell for the normalized Lagrangian." She added "$\ell = L/H =$" in front of the mathematical tangle she had dubbed the normalized Lagrangian.

All the worries and tension of the last few weeks seemed to evaporate as she put them out of her mind to focus on the problem. I watched as she deftly manipulated the symbols, dancing back and forth, brushing against me, becoming more excited as she teased out the hidden meaning behind MacGuffin's relations. The chalk dust mingled with the smell of her hair. Finally, the blackboard full of mathematics reduced to a simple relation: $\gamma^2 + \ell^2 = 1$, the equation for a unit circle – a circle of radius one.

"It all works out to a circle, after all," I murmured. "The 'great circle'..." I added, recalling MacGuffin's words.

She looked at me, nodding, "That's amazingly elegant." She stared at the board as if reverence, soaking up the meaning and the implications of what she'd derived. "You could say the electromagnetic energy velocity is in a kind of quadrature with this normalized Lagrangian of yours."

She looked at me as if really seeing me for the first time. I could see her finally realize she was standing right next to me and I was blocking the way out. She took a step back. "I'm covered in chalk dust," she said, looking at her fancy clothes.

"Looks good on you," I replied, holding my ground and maintaining eye contact. There was a long pause as we looked into each other's eyes.

She blinked first. She looked at the chalkboard, then back at me, shaking her head in disbelief. "How did a smart guy like you get tangled up with those social justice freaks?"

"It pays the bills," I shrugged.

"There have to be easier ways to pay the bills," she countered.

"You might be surprised how little effort it takes to string together the appropriate jargon in the approved fashion," I replied.

"I meant easy on your conscience," she chided me, "not easy on your effort."

There wasn't much I could say in answer to that.

She looked at the board again. "I'm so frustrated with... with everything. I wanted to get away from it all, just for one evening. This isn't exactly what I had in mind," she smiled, "but I honestly haven't had this much fun in ages. Thanks." She looked into my eyes.

The moment was right. I leaned in to kiss her.

"No, Peter," she turned her head. "We can't. I'm your teacher. And I'm your boss, at least while Professor Chen is still under his ridiculous suspension. And it's late."

I so wanted to... I took a deep breath and stepped back. "Shall I walk you to your car?"

"Yes," she smiled. This time she noticed my hand on her shoulder as I guided her past me, but she didn't seem to mind. I locked up the lab.

"Haven't you ever wanted to do something crazy?" I asked when we got to her car.

"Yes," she smiled, opening the door. I took a step toward her. She turned to face me and interrupted my progress with a slender chalky finger on my lips, her fingers on my cheek, her forearm against my chest. I lit up from head to toe, aching to pull her the rest of the way against me.

She paused a moment, in thought. "No." She pulled her finger down yet remained tantalizingly close, looking up into my eyes. "Everything that's been happening lately. You're in the middle of it. You're not what you seem. I can't figure you out." She paused, looking straight through me. "I don't trust you." She gave me a sad smile and got in the car.

"I could..." I started.

"No, Peter. Not tonight." She added with a hint of a smile, "I'll see you around," and she drove off.

My head was spinning so fast I could hardly walk. Was this what Amit felt with all his girls? I went back up to the lab. I needed to copy down the formulas and erase the board before I got someone else in trouble for knowing pieces of the hidden truth. That thought reminded me I needed to have a chat with Professor Graf before she shared her work with anyone else. I caught her after class on Monday.

"About the other night..." I began.

"I've been thinking about that interesting result," she replied. "About how energy propagates at the speed of light for radiation where the impedance is 377 ohms but slows down when the balance is disrupted and you have an excess of electric or magnetic field intensity."

Not exactly the part I'd found most memorable, but it segued nicely into what I had to ask. "Would you mind keeping all this confidential for the time being? It's part of a project I've been working on for a long time, and I'd hate for it to get out before I've had a chance to complete my study and write up the results."

"I understand," she smiled. "Let me know if I can lend a hand. It's an interesting approach, and I'd love to help, even after I'm gone."

That sounded disturbingly fatalistic. "Have you decided what you're going to do next year?"

"I have a class to teach here over the summer. After that... well, I have applications out. These things are usually not so rushed, or so late in the academic year." Her uncharacteristically cheerful expression quickly dissolved. She was back to the neutral, resigned look that had become her new baseline the last few weeks. "I'll have a chance to network at GammaCon in a couple of weeks. There may be an opening at the University of Alabama at Huntsville. Professor

Glyer wants to speak with me at the reception. I may find a lead on other new jobs there, too. It's finals week, but if you're done early, you should attend. It's right up the road in Chattanooga. Our budget can cover a room and gas for you."

"I'll see what I can do about finals." I took a deep breath. "You know, we could go out some evening, if you'd like to talk. I know a nice fondue restaurant..."

She held up a finger, interrupting my proposition. "Peter, I'm sorry about the other night. That was... inappropriate of me to lead you on or give you the wrong impression."

"Have you heard me complain? What happened to sexual autonomy in the workplace?"

She smiled. "I'm your teacher and your boss. That's all... I did enjoy working on your physics problem with you, though. Maybe we could do that again sometime. During business hours."

Shot down. The next class was already coming into the room, and I needed to be going anyway.

The remaining weeks of the semester were a grind. With everything that had been going on, I was behind in too many classes and working too hard to notice how I'd been ostracized by my physics classmates. They'd accepted my social justice activities as a fellow student's amusing quirk, like Sarah's participation in the climbing club, or the group that dressed up in period costumes and went to the Atlanta Renaissance Festival together. Now though, the stakes had become clearer and lines were drawn. The people I most liked and valued wanted nothing to do with me. What troubled me even more were the creepy sorts who suddenly wanted to be my friend, latching on to me as if by association they could exploit my patronage in the coming social justice order. At least Professor Gomulka had no more brilliant time-sucking ideas for implementing social change on campus. He seemed a bit subdued after his two defeats.

Professor Fries kindly let me take my microwave circuits final early, so I could take off for GammaCon on Thursday. I had the truck packed and was ready to head up to Chattanooga when I got the text from Amit.

"Coffee with cream at the Varsity?"

Oh, no. "On my way," I texted back.

Amit knows I always drink my coffee black. Early on, we'd realized we might need a way to warn each other over open channels. "Coffee with cream" was Amit's way of telling me it was an absolute emergency. I ran to my truck and made sure my go-bag was accessible. The black backpack had basic tools, a couple of burner phones, change of clothes, cash, food, water bottle, first aid, survival gear – enough to get by for a couple of days nearly anywhere. I drove to the Varsity and was there in just under fifteen minutes.

Amit was in the Varsity's glass-walled seating area over the parking lot with a beautiful view of the sun setting behind the Tech campus across the Interstate highway. The directional Wi-Fi antenna was artfully concealed in a backpack on the table beside him. "What is it?"

He pushed a frosted orange across the table. "You'll need it. You remember Agent Wilson?" Of course I remembered the bastard – the Civic Circle's direct action expert. The troubleshooter they sent in to figure out who to kill and how to do it. The man who killed my parents. "He was on a job in Austin, Texas, last night when he got the message," Amit continued. "His team is on the way to Atlanta. They're after Professor Chen and Professor Graf."

I took a sip from the frosted orange. "They found out about the radiation maps?"

"I don't think that's it. Apparently, Professor Chen emailed an encrypted file to a contact in San Francisco. They couldn't read the file, but the contact is a member of a 'known terrorist group.'"

Known terrorist group? "But they're not sending in the police or the FBI..."

"Exactly. I think your professor's tied in with some kind of anti-Civic Circle group. Remember the tattoo you told me about? The one that matched the diagram in the MacGuffin manuscript?"

I hadn't thought about it in months. "We have to get to him first. Why are they roping in Professor Graf?"

"They figure she's working with him, somehow, after the way she stood up for him. After the 'shirt storm,' they're both listed as subversive persons."

Amit showed me the note he'd already sent to Uncle Rob. "URGENT! Technology Containment Team on way to detain Pete's professors. Pete and I will attempt exfiltration of the professors to Robber Dell. Can you assist? Come here, soonest."

Then, I read Uncle Rob's answer: "Negative. Stand down. Exfiltrate yourselves on up here, soonest. Do not attempt rescue of those professors."

"Maybe we can persuade him..." I began.

"There's no time," Amit insisted. "They're on the way now. We have a couple of hours tops. Rob couldn't get here, anyway, even if he wanted to. And he's demanding we pull out, run home, and hide."

Damn. It was Robb LeChevalier all over again. Uncle Rob insisting we step back and let the Circle have their way with someone. Except I knew these two someones, and really cared about...

Amit looked up from his laptop. "Pete..." he began.

"What is it?" I said softly.

"There's something else you should know. It happened last week, apparently." Amit spun his laptop around. On his screen was an obituary: "Local Engineer, Inventor, Succumbs to Cancer."

Robb LeChevalier was dead.

Another life extinguished. Another creator destroyed. Another destiny altered. Another bright and shining future smothered at birth by the Circle's quest for power. Next on their list was Professor Chen. They'd probably kill Professor Graf, too. How widely would the Circle's devastation fall this time? The professors' other colleagues? Their graduate students? Sarah? Professor Graf's freshman lab assistant?

Can you perceive a Nexus directly? Sense first-hand the tipping points in the course of human events as you stand at the crossroads and weigh the alternatives? I may have been imagining things. Somehow, though, deep down, I felt the same way I did that awful night in the hotel room after my parents' funeral. My thoughts raced. The possibilities and options swirled wildly around in my head and converged to a singular point.

No.

This will not stand. This will not happen. The Circle will not win. Not here. Not today. I will not stand by, do nothing, and let the Circle have their way. Again. I have the power to shape my own destiny, I realized. I can impose my will on events. I can save Professor Chen and – I could admit it to myself now – the woman I loved, Professor Graf.

Amit was looking at me, a puzzled expression on his face.

"I... I am going to save Professor Graf and Professor Chen," I said, slowly.

"Your uncle?" Amit asked.

"I don't care," I said flatly. "He made his decision. Now, I'm making mine. Are you with me?"

A smile slowly formed on Amit's face. "Hell, yes! Let screw those Circle bastards over so hard they turn inside out."

I started to envision that gruesome topology applied to Agent Wilson before getting my thoughts back on track. "She's already in Chattanooga at GammaCon. I'll go there," I explained. "I'll find Professor Graf. I'll have to persuade her to go into hiding... Dr. Krueger. He'd be willing to help us out. You'll have to go to the physics building, find Professor Chen, and get him up to Chattanooga. Then, we'll take them both on up to Dr. Krueger's place in Knoxville."

"Hello, Professor Chen," Amit play-acted without dropping a beat. "You don't know me, but I'm a friend of your freshman lab assistant. An evil conspiracy bent on your destruction follows in my wake, so will you please drop everything you're doing, abandon your life, your career, and everything you own, and come with me into a new life as a fugitive?"

"Your persuasion needs some work," I acknowledged, thoughtfully.

"I'm slick, Pete," Amit asserted confidently, "but there's no dialectic nor rhetoric possible that would let me persuade your professor. Not in the time we have left to us."

"Chen is the key," I noted. "If we can persuade Chen, he can persuade Graf." I really wanted to go after Graf myself, but the logic was clear. "I'll save Chen. I have the best chance with him. He's their first target. They'll have acted, and it will be obvious to him my warning was correct. He'll help us persuade Graf. Then, I'll help you save Graf."

"You could use help," Amit observed, "a lookout, a diversion, someone to help you hide the bodies."

"I know," I agreed. "But it's just you and me, and Chattanooga is a long way away. You need to head up there now, so once I secure Chen, you'll be ready to save Graf, without delay." Why was it Amit always ended up with the girl? It wasn't fair. "Improvise, adapt, overcome, drive on."

Amit slowly nodded his agreement. "For once it would be nice not to have so much improvisation, though."

We packed up and headed back to the dorm. "I'll take your phone," he offered. "I'll leave both our phones in our room safe and snug in case anyone's checking, and I'll be sure to make a good alibi for us. We'll be sleeping off our finals."

We double checked burner phone numbers. "I'll turn mine on once I have Chen secure," I offered. "You turn yours on once you get to Chattanooga." There wasn't much more to say. Amit was right. We were both really winging it.

He pointed at my Firefly T-shirt with Adam Baldwin as the mercenary, Jayne, saying: "Time for some thrilling heroics!" Amit smiled. "I see you managed to dress for the occasion!"

"One more thing," I said to Amit as we prepared to go our separate ways. "Thanks for being my friend."

"It's been a wild ride," Amit acknowledged. "Whatever happens though, I wouldn't have missed it for the world." We shook hands deliberately, and parted.

CHAPTER 10: THE ENEMY OF MY ENEMY

The physics building seemed deserted, but I found Professor Chen in his office. "They're after you," I explained. "They're on their way now to arrest you, or worse." I was expecting him to ask me who "they" were. Instead, he surprised me.

"I see," he said matter-of-factly as he shut down his laptop and began packing his bag. "I've been expecting this, but I thought I had more time. How do you know?"

"It's a long story, and there's no time to explain. I can take you somewhere safe," I offered.

"Yes," Dr. Chen agreed. "They will be looking for my car. Yours is safer. However, I already have a place I can go. Can you take me there?"

"Where?"

"Somewhere nearby," he explained, vaguely.

"OK," I agreed.

He yanked his hard drive out of his computer and finished packing his backpack. We headed out of his office.

"Bang!" I heard a crash and the tinkling of broken glass from the direction of the main entrance downstairs. It was too late. They were already here.

"The lab!" It was the only other secure room nearby I could open. I pulled Dr. Chen along the dark hall and he followed. "Quick!" I unlocked the door to the mirror lab and closed it behind us. Dr. Chen reached for the light switch. "No!" I said quietly, but insistently. I felt my way over to the vacuum chamber. "Come over here," I said to him as I turned on the vacuum pump. I saw Dr. Chen groping his way over to me, illuminated by the glow of the LEDs on the instrumentation. The dome of the chamber stood four feet above the base. "Get in," I ordered Dr. Chen.

"But the air..." he began to protest.

"It's not actually sucking air out of the chamber," I explained. "Get in quick, and make room, because I'm about to join you."

Dr. Chen climbed in as I found the control for the hoist we used to lower the heavy dome into place. I saw the light in the hallway turn on through the crack under the door. I grabbed the control and climbed in after him, lowering the dome in place over the two of us and our backpacks. The sturdy cable for the hoist control made a narrow gap between the dome and the base. As I noted the air sucking in through the gap, I saw the light penetrate through the silvery film on the glass window. Someone was in the room! I could hear them even over the racket made by the vacuum pump.

"Clear!" shouted a hostile voice. I heard them moving around on the other side of a fraction of an inch of steel.

"Clank-clank!" I heard someone bang on the steel chamber.

"What's this?" a voice asked.

"I don't know," another voice answered. "But there's no way to get in."

"Can you shut that damn noisy thing off?"

"Hell if I know. It might explode or something. Secure the computers, but never mess with the lab equipment. That's the containment team's job."

The agents spent the better part of an hour rummaging through the lab while Dr. Chen and I crouched uncomfortably inside the chamber with our backpacks. What would have been... interesting... if only I'd been with Professor Graf was instead awkward and uncomfortable as hell. As usual, Amit gets the girl, and life isn't fair. Finally, a voice said, "Chen's gone."

Someone else said something about "checkpoints," "fugitive," and "deadly force." Within minutes, the room became quiet, except for the vacuum pump. Before long, the lights went out and I heard someone close the door. I wiped a tiny bit of the aluminum from the inside of the glass and peered out. The coast appeared clear. We waited another ten minutes before I used the control to make the hoist lift the dome.

We stumbled out and stretched our cramped muscles. We both had swaths of aluminum on our hands and clothes where we'd touched the inside of the vacuum chamber. We cleaned ourselves and our bags up as best we could, then donned rubber gloves from the lab supplies so we wouldn't leave any additional fingerprints. I began to load an already coated mirror into the vacuum chamber. Dr. Chen gave me a puzzled look.

"We left marks and fingerprints all over the inside of the chamber," I explained. If I re-run a mirror with extra aluminum, it should cover up the evidence. It will explain why the chamber was running, too. Would you wipe the aluminum off the cable to the hoist controls?" With Dr. Chen assisting, the work went quickly. The lab was pretty thoroughly ransacked, and we had to be careful to leave the mess the agents made alone, while cleaning ourselves up and leaving the chamber running for the Technology Containment Team to find.

Now, we needed to create a diversion. "Do you have a phone?" I asked Dr. Chen.

"Yes," he replied, "but I turned it off. I think I will not be turning it on again."

"Don't be so sure of that," I advised, thoughtfully.

The Circle and their government and law enforcement allies could track and locate cell phones. At the very least, they knew which cell tower any given phone employed. That gave them a rough idea of the phone's location. There'd been talk of a more precise location capability for 911 use, but that was a way off yet. I was betting their ability to locate

Professor Chen's phone wasn't good enough yet for them to figure out what I was about to try.

Sarah had left a few of her high altitude balloons in the mirror lab. One, her backup rig, was already equipped with an insulated foam gondola – perfect! "Dr. Chen, your phone is going for a ride," I explained. I gathered the supplies we needed into a spare garbage can. I saw she'd left her climbing bag, too – perfect! We had to hope no one would notice the missing cylinder or duffle bag.

We carefully opened the door to the lab and stepped under the "Crime Scene – Do Not Cross" tape, and carried our load up the stairs. Dr. Chen used his master key to get us onto the roof. "Hey! Mind if I keep your master key?" He passed it over with a smile. We got the balloon inflated, turned on Dr. Chen's phone, and watched it soar into the sky as the winds carried it in the general direction of the BellSouth tower just east of campus. They'd get some good tracks on his phone as it drifted east across Atlanta before rising out of range.

Then, I opened Sarah's climbing bag and showed Professor Chen the ropes. His eyes got big. I assured him it was perfectly safe, or at least safer than trying to go out the front door. "We need to move fast, before someone notices us up here." I got the professor and myself in harnesses. Then, I doubled up the rope, looping it around a railing that seemed secure. The figure-eight rappelling devices were designed to work off a single rope, so they'd be particularly slow with the double-rope configuration I was using. Slow was fine for a novice at rappelling like Professor Chen. I coached him, clipped him in, and then went down first, so I could belay him from the ground. By pulling on the rope, putting tension on it from the ground, I could slow or stop him from sliding down. Once he scrambled over the edge, though, he did fine without needing my help. We ended up nicely concealed behind some shrubs along the side of the building. With the rope looped around the anchor point on the roof, all I had to do was pull one end to retrieve the rope. It made a satisfying thump on the ground as the loose end fell beside us.

Dr. Chen eyed me suspiciously as I packed up the harnesses and coiled up the rope. "You're no baizuo. Who are you? Albert Shun?"

Albert Shun? "What do you mean?" I asked. "I'm Peter Burdell."

"That's not what I mean," Dr. Chen insisted. "You hide us in the vacuum chamber, you send my phone flying off by balloon, and now you get me down from the roof. You are too good at this to be just a student.

"The rappelling? I picked that up in Boy Scouts. The rest? Let's just say this isn't my first rodeo," I replied. He looked confused. "I've run into these people before," I explained.

Dr. Chen looked at me. "I have some friends you need to meet," he said, pulling out a pen and a card from his pocket. "If we get separated for any reason, go to the restaurant at this street number – note I transposed those digits in case this card is found. It's on Peachtree. You will need to ask for my uncle, Mr. Hung."

I took his card and agreed. "I'll be back in a few minutes with my truck," I assured him.

I left Dr. Chen in his hiding place with my go-bag while I jogged back to the Varsity for my truck. My truck was packed. It was going to be tricky to make room for Professor Chen. I might have to dump out some stuff and abandon it at the Varsity. There was no time to mourn my lost possessions, though. Campus police were everywhere. I passed a couple of cops guarding the entrance to the physics building. Good thing we didn't try to go out that way! I saw even more officers entering the physics building as they continued their search, but at least Dr. Chen was outside their initial search perimeter. For now. I had to hurry before they discovered the helium cylinder on the roof or decided to take a closer look around the outside perimeter of the building.

I was jogging along Atlantic Avenue when I saw a Chevy sedan parked just off the street with a familiar face. Marcus?

What was he doing here? He looked the other way as I approached, studiously ignoring me. I knocked on his window. He looked and rolled it down. "What brings you here?" I asked him.

"I got nothing to say to you," he insisted. "Why don't you..." I caught him staring at T-shirt. His eyes got big. This had to be Amit's doing – calling out the Friends of George to lend a hand.

"Can a Friend of George P. get some help?" I asked.

He looked skeptical. "A friend of who?" He was still inspecting my T-shirt.

"George P. Burdell," I insisted. "By the way, I never got to tell you how impressed I was at the 'Engineering 4 Engineers' chalking. That was incredible work."

"You?" Marcus looked incredulous. He blew up at me. "You goddamn lying piece of shit. You and your fucking SJW friend fucking me over all the fucking time. I've been hanging out here for an hour, and you're the fucking friend of George P. with the Firefly T-shirt I'm supposed to help?"

"Yes," I acknowledged. Marcus was shaking his head in disgust. "I'm sorry," I apologized, "for fooling you, for everything, but friends of George P. do what they have to do for George P. and for the good of Tech," I explained. "And I don't think their mommas would approve of that kind of language," I added.

Marcus cracked a thin smile. "Damn, but you did fool me and good," he admitted. "You," he said, "you got George P. the answers for the social justice final, didn't you?"

I nodded. He may have been fooled before, but he was figuring it out quickly, now.

"You... you're not just a friend of George P. You... you are George P. Burdell, aren't you?" Marcus dared me to deny it.

I thought about that a moment. "Yes," I acknowledged, "I was George P. Burdell," I said, savoring the words, "but right here, and right now, Marcus, you are George P. Burdell. This is Georgia Tech, and when a friend of George P. needs our help, we are – each and every one of us – George P. Burdell."

"I am George P. Burdell?" Marcus thought about that a moment. "Me? I don't know if I'm tall enough for this here ride," he admitted. "I... am George P. Burdell?" he said tentatively, mulling it over, getting used to the idea, nodding his head. "I am George P. Burdell," he said decisively. "George P., he kept my ass in school, and if a friend of George P. needs my help, this is Georgia Tech. We can do that."

I got in the Chevy. Marcus drove me around to where I'd hidden Dr. Chen. I got him into the trunk of Marcus's Chevy without Marcus getting a good look at him. It was surprisingly spacious, and certainly more comfortable than doubling up in the vacuum chamber. Then, I explained to Marcus what I wanted. "Me? You want me to get this dude past a ton of cops?" He laughed at my naivety. "You gotta be kidding me. They see me, they be pullin' me over. It like a reflex for 'em. See black dude. Pull over black dude. Search black dude's car for drugs. Throw all our asses in jail when they find dude in trunk."

"They're too busy looking for the guy in your trunk," I explained, "to have time to hassle you or me tonight. No one will want to waste the time to search a couple of harmless students. You've got the Tech parking stickers on your car and a Tech ID. We balls it out if they stop you. And, the dude in your trunk? You're way better looking than he is. No way are they going to mistake you for him."

Marcus rolled his eyes at that.

"Besides, I'll be with you," I assured him. "I'll vouch for you to the nice officers and explain to them what fine upstanding young men we both are."

He was still skeptical. "This dude in the trunk better be George P.'s own home boy for what you're asking." I guaranteed Marcus he was, and he finally acquiesced.

Sure enough, the campus police stopped us twice at their checkpoints. Each time, they asked Marcus for his ID, took a good look at the two of us, and waved us on through. We got out on to Techwood Drive and were stopped again by city cops. Finally, we got across the Interstate on North Avenue with no further problem. I guided Marcus to Dr. Chen's Chinese restaurant off of Peachtree. I was tempted to drop off Dr. Chen and return with Marcus, but Dr. Chen's friends intrigued me. He implied he knew the agents after us. Did he and his friends know about Xueshu Quan and the Civic Circle? Also, I needed to get that letter from him to help persuade Professor Graf.

It wasn't too far to the nearest MARTA station, and I could make my way back to campus by myself, if I had to. I got Dr. Chen and both our bags out of the trunk, and then I told Marcus he could head on back.

"You sure you don't need me to hang around?" he asked.

"I'll take MARTA back," I explained. "I'll leave this duffle bag with you though," I pointed to Sarah's climbing gear. "I'll be in touch with you where to drop it off."

"Good luck, man," he said.

"You, too. Thanks, George P." I shook his hand. Marcus snorted and drove off.

I opened the door for Dr. Chen and followed him in. Dr. Chen said something in Chinese to the girl at the reservation stand. Her eyes got big. She looked suspiciously at me and she headed back into the kitchen. "My family will want to thank you for your help," Dr. Chen assured me, "but first they will have to find someone to verify who I am."

The girl came back, trailing behind an older man in a tux. "I am the manager," he explained. "We are honored to have you as our guests. If you will please wait here," he said to me, "while I have some tea with you, sir," he said to Dr. Chen.

Dr. Chen spoke to him in Chinese. They were having a disagreement of some kind. Finally, the manager relented. "Please leave your bags here," he said, "You may both follow me." He led us back through the kitchen to his office, and brought an extra chair for me into the cramped room. A waiter brought in a tea pot with four cups.

The manager eyed Dr. Chen suspiciously as Dr. Chen poured the tea into the four cups. He appeared angry as Dr. Chen arranged the cups in a pattern. The tension in the room was rising as the manager glared at him. Dr. Chen glared right back at the manager, deliberately chose one of the four cups, and took a sip. The manager exploded in a shout, and the door burst open.

Things got confusing. A man grabbed at me. I was still sitting, so I had the perfect angle to land a solid uppercut to his groin. He let out a bellow and delivered a vicious blow to my face, as I attempted to stand. He knocked my head into the drywall behind me. I hadn't been hit that hard before. The blow stunned me, dropping me back into my seat long enough for a second man to pile on, knocking me and the chair to the ground and then pinning me underneath him. He was just too big and too strong for me. As they dragged me out, I heard Dr. Chen and the manager screaming Chinese at each other. I was dragged out the back door of the restaurant down the alley behind, into another door, and up some stairs. I heard keys rattling as they opened a door. They searched me, confiscating my knife, my keys, and my phone. Then, they shoved me into a room where I stumbled and fell across a bed.

"You stay!" said one of the thugs in broken English. "Boss decide about you. You make trouble, you make noise and..." he gestured cutting his throat. His pal flicked a switchblade ominously. They shut the sturdy door with a solid "thud." I heard the jangling of keys as the deadbolt slid into place.

I hurt all over, but waiting passively for "the boss" to decide whether or not to kill me didn't strike me as a winning plan. I could hear the low hum of people talking in the vicinity and the occasional high-pitched giggle. I could shout out and probably be heard, but if no one was troubled by the ruckus in the restaurant, I wasn't confident about some Good Samaritan phoning 911, let alone the police arriving in time to save me from the thugs and their switchblades.

I took stock of my surroundings. One bed with a well-worn cover. Sheets? I looked out the window. The parking lot was a good thirty, maybe forty feet below, but if I could make fifty feet of improvised rope, getting down would be easy. I tried the window. It was painted shut. The only way out was to break the glass. I could hear the thugs talking outside the door. I might be able to break the glass and climb down, but I wouldn't have much of a head start, and they'd be right behind me. I wasn't in any condition for a sprint, let alone a marathon. Maybe after I'd recovered a bit. Let's make that Plan B, for now.

I continued looking. There was a small bathroom, adjacent. I washed off the blood, helped myself to a sip of water, and began to feel a bit better.

Back in the bedroom there was a small sofa, a table, and two chairs. I searched the sofa and found a quarter, a nickel, and a couple of pennies to add to my inventory.

Weapons? I could smash the bathroom mirror or the window, and use a shard of glass as my defense against two professional knife-wielders. That didn't seem prudent. I might be able to use a table leg or a chair as a club. Perhaps I could electrocute them somehow? There were no lamps or appliances, from which I could scavenge a power cord to improvise a 120V cattle prod.

I took a closer look at the wall. Behind the sofa was a phone jack. Of course, the thugs weren't thoughtful enough to have left me a phone to call for help.

Or, so they thought.

That moment when you finally see how to solve a tricky problem? When a plan comes together? There's nothing like that feeling of satisfaction and pride in your own capabilities. It makes you feel on top of the world. I didn't have time just then to savor it, though.

I got to work stripping the bed: I tore the sheets into long strips to fashion a rope, then, I carefully and quietly rearranged furniture to barricade the door. It would take them a while to get in, buying me more time. I placed a chair adjacent to the window, so I could use it to break the glass. The bed cover I set nearby ready to cover the sharp edges of remaining glass. I secured one end of the rope to the bed. My escape was prepared. Plan B ready, I got to work on Plan A.

I used one of the pennies I found to unscrew the faceplate to the phone jack, and I peered inside. A red and green wire connected to the jack – a standard, single-line setup.

The basic technology dates almost all the way back to Alexander Graham Bell. The green wire is connected to ground through a thousand-ohm load. The red wire is hot with -48V DC potential. When you pick up the handset, the phone shorts the red wire to the green wire, through a small transformer to let the local exchange know you want to place a call. The exchange confirms it's ready by modulating the current with a dial tone that's picked up by the transformer in the handset and delivered to the speaker. The newer phones use "dual-tone multi-frequency" (DTMF) signaling to dial. Each of the twelve buttons generates a unique pair of tones to let the exchange know what number you want. Older "rotary-dial" phones used a different scheme. A user would rotate a dial to a particular number and the dial would spin back to its rest position, opening the electrical connection with a sequences of "clicks" for a particular number. Dial 1, and the phone would click once, dial "6" and it would open and close the connection six times. Support for the old rotary phones was being phased out, but there were still enough of them around that most exchanges would support rotary dialing.

I licked my fingers, shorted the red wire to green, and felt a tingle, so I knew the line was live. I had no way to detect it, but after a few seconds, I'd probably be receiving a dial tone. Then I dialed 911. Open-open-open-open-open-open-open-open-open... pause... open, pause... open, pause.... The line may have been ringing. I had no way to tell, and I had no way to talk with the emergency dispatcher on the other end. Sure, I could have tried Morse code, but how many people know Morse? I gave it a twenty count and then opened the wires to break the connection. I repeated the process again. And again. And again. See, I figured if I called 911 often enough, maybe they wouldn't interpret it as an emergency, but at least they could use caller ID to figure out where I was, and they'd send someone out to tell the obnoxious phone customer to cut it out. When the police arrived or if the thugs tried to enter, I'd execute Plan B, break the window, climb down, and run for it.

I'd made well over fifty calls before I saw blue flashing lights through my window. I peeked out the window, and I saw a police cruiser pulling into the lot below. I grabbed a chair and broke the window, the glass shattered and tinkled on the lot below. I heard shouting outside the door as I spread the bedcover over the remaining glass in the window frame, and the jingle of keys as I threw the rope out the window and climbed through. I straddled the rope between my legs, around my right thigh, and over my left shoulder to rappel down without any harnesses or hardware. It's called the "Dülfersitz" technique. I was already out the window climbing down before the thugs got the door unlocked, and I'd made it almost to the ground before I heard a shout, "POLICE! HOLD IT RIGHT THERE!"

Don't throw me in that ol' briar patch Br'er Fox!

I dropped to the ground and held my hands open and high to look as unthreatening as possible.

"Hands against the wall!" shouted one of the officers. I complied and the other pulled the rope free, kicked my legs wider, and frisked me while his partner kept me covered. The officer expertly pulled one hand down after the other to secure me in handcuffs. I could hear the thugs banging furiously against my barricade through the open window above me as the cuffs bit into my wrists.

"What the hell is going on here?" asked the officer. Just then a couple more thugs came running full-tilt around the corner.

"Stop! Police!" the officers yelled.

The thugs were completely surprised. For a moment, I wasn't sure if they were going to keep coming at us or if they'd turn and run. They lost their initiative and split the difference by standing still. The officers handcuffed them as well.

"What's going on here?" one of the officers asked the thugs. They replied with an incomprehensible stream of Chinese.

Out of the corner of my eye, I could see a crowd gathering around the two officers and the three of us handcuffed and facing the wall.

"Excuse me officers," an accented but cultured voice called out. "I'm the manager of this establishment. Is there a problem here?"

"Yes, there's a problem," the officer insisted. "We got a bunch of 911 calls from here, we pulled up to check it out, and we find this kid breaking through your window, and these two chasing after him."

I turned my head a bit to see the elegantly dressed Chinese gentleman speaking, "I'm sure it's all just an innocent misunderstanding, officers. Our doors sometimes get stuck and with the noise, it can be difficult to hear someone calling for help. I'm sure the young man was just trying to get attention so he could get out, and we can hardly blame him for breaking our window and calling you for help." He sounded so smooth and eloquent he was convincing me. Then, I noticed Dr. Chen standing just behind him. We made eye contact, and he nodded his head, urging me to play along.

"Is this true?" the officer asked me.

"Yes, sir." I said. "Somehow I got locked in the room upstairs. I kept banging on the walls, but no one heard me."

"We are very sorry for placing you in this awkward situation," the elegant Chinese man assured me.

"911 is for emergencies only," the officer lectured me. "What if you tied up the line while someone called in with a real emergency?"

"I'm very sorry officer," I said as sincerely and contritely as I could. "But I thought it was an emergency. I was trapped and couldn't get out."

"Well why didn't you say so on the call instead of dialing in and hanging up?" the officer grilled me.

"The handset wasn't working properly, officer," I explained.

"Did you get in a fight?" the other officer asked, referring to the blood on my clothes and what was probably an emerging black eye.

"Oh we were just horsing around," I assured him. I don't think he bought it.

"My name is Mr. Hung," the Chinese gentleman said to the officers. "I'm very sorry for this misunderstanding. We're prepared to overlook the damage Peter caused to our establishment, if he'll forgive us for accidentally trapping him upstairs."

Of course it wasn't that easy to get out of trouble. I got my wallet and things back from Mr. Hung. Once the officers decided they couldn't pin a drunk and disorderly charge on us, they cited me and the thugs for disturbing the peace.

One of the officers took me aside and said quietly, "This is no place for a college kid. You need to find some place to dip your wick on campus, not go looking for action around here."

"Yes, sir," I said, though I wasn't exactly sure what he meant.

"My nephew has told me all about what happened, Peter," Mr. Hung said, alluding to my rescue of Dr. Chen, who had since slipped away with the crowd. "We are both deeply sorry for the misunderstanding and for how you were treated. If you care to join us for dinner we will try to make amends."

The officers clearly thought I should leave. My job was only half done – I still had Professor Graf to rescue. I needed to hurry up to Chattanooga. On the other hand, Amit was already there by now, and at this rate, I wouldn't be there until the wee hours of the next morning, anyway. Furthermore, I'd been too busy to get a note from Dr. Chen explaining the danger. I'd need his note to help me persuade Dr. Graf to take my warnings seriously.

"I accept your gracious invitation, sir." I replied.

The officer who'd talked to me shook his head in disgust. "Your funeral, kid." He said as they departed.

We walked around the front of the building – the storefront proclaimed it an oriental massage parlor – and continued on to the restaurant where the adventure had started an hour or so ago.

The same manager greeted us at the door. I locked eyes with his. He broke eye contact and hung his head in shame. "I'm so sorry, sir," he said. "Please forgive me."

I let his question hang in the air for a moment, then I replied, "I will consider it."

He led us to a different table in a back room. Mr. Hung spoke brusquely in Chinese to the manager who cringed, bowed deeply, and exited the room, closing the door behind him.

"We owe you an apology, Peter," Dr. Chen said. "It is... unusual for an outsider to be present when we discuss family business. The manager was suspicious that I was not who I claimed to be and that you and I were trying to deceive him. When I gave him the recognition signal, he was upset that I would do so in front of an outsider. He ordered my brothers to detain us until Mr. Hung could arrive, and they were – overly enthusiastic in the performance of their duties. I regret the... inhospitality we showed you. Those responsible will be severely disciplined. Thank you for letting our family make amends by treating you to dinner."

I got the impression that Dr. Chen's "family" was a bit more loosely defined than usual.

"Professor Chen is my nephew," Mr. Hung began. "You helped him in his work, and you brought him here when he was in danger. We owed you gratitude and thanks but we compounded the debt we owe by treating you poorly. For this, I must apologize on behalf of my family. Please accept this dinner in partial repayment of the debt we owe you."

"Thank you for your hospitality, gentlemen," I replied. "Even in the best families... misunderstandings can arise. You are making amends, and there are no hard feelings."

"I appreciate your understanding, Peter," Professor Chen thanked me. "It is fortunate you learned they were on the way to arrest me, and capture our work. You were very ...skillful. Few of my brothers could have performed as well under such challenging circumstances."

Mr. Hung said something to Dr. Chen in rapid Chinese. Of course, I couldn't understand him, but I could swear he'd said "Xueshu Quan." That was the name of the Circle's rare book collector. Had I fallen in with allies of my enemy? Mr. Hung must have seen my shock. He jerked his head and glared at me. "Xueshu Quan," he repeated. "You have heard of Xueshu Quan," he said, daring me to deny it.

I was caught. I was also going to have to do a better job on my poker face, but for now I needed to get out of the hole I'd dug myself.

"A wise man does not speak certain names where they may be heard," I replied, trying my best to be cryptic and ambiguous.

Mr. Hung's eyes narrowed at the implied insult. "You are in the Red Flower Pavilion, surrounded by heroes," he explained, gesturing at the lavish surroundings of the private dining room. "Here, one may speak forbidden names and hidden truths without fear they will be overheard. How come you to know the name of our enemy?"

They regarded Xueshu Quan as an enemy? That was a good sign. Or maybe a clever trick to find out where I stood with respect to Xueshu Quan. I knew Xueshu Quan was tied into the Circle somehow and the Circle was after Dr. Chen, but I wasn't yet ready to acknowledge Xueshu Quan was my enemy, too. Not without more information.

"Xueshu Quan," I said neutrally, trying to avoid any hint of intonation or emphasis. "How did you come to acquire so dangerous an enemy? You have said you are in my debt for my service on behalf of Dr. Chen. May I have your answer in partial payment?"

Mr. Hung looked thoughtfully at me. Then, he nodded at Dr. Chen. "Very well."

"Many years ago in Fujian Province, in the southeast of China, there was a monastery," Dr. Chen began. "For over a thousand years, the monks there studied in secret, learning the mysteries of science, developing arcane technology, perfecting themselves through meditation and discipline, and above all, studying the art and science of war. Their greatest teacher was an immortal, some say a god, who today goes by the name, 'Xueshu Quan.'"

"The gamma ray results from Fujian province. They are related to this monastery?" I asked.

Dr. Chen smiled. "Indeed. The exact site had been lost for centuries. Our brothers in China have been investigating the site since you identified it.

"It came to pass that foreign invaders attacked China and inflicted serious losses on the Emperor's finest armies. The Emperor called upon the monks to help defend the nation. The one hundred twenty eight brothers hurried to the imperial palace, where the Emperor offered them whatever men or money they might need. On behalf of the brothers, Xueshu Quan accepted the Emperor's charge, requesting only fresh horses and food for the warrior monks. They tarried a few days until the timing was auspicious then rode out to attack the enemy.

"In three months' time, they had wiped out an army of many thousands, struck deep in the enemy's country and forced the enemy to pay a vast ransom."

"How could a hundred-odd monks prevail against such overwhelming odds?" I asked.

Mr. Hung took over from Professor Chen. "Know the enemy and know yourself; in a hundred battles you will never be in peril. He who knows when he can fight, and when he cannot fight shall be victorious. Invincibility lies in defense. The brothers took up a position in which they could not be defeated, and they allowed the enemy to waste their strength."

"Like the Spartans at Thermopylae," I said, nodding.

"Indeed," acknowledged Mr. Hung. "But the possibility of victory lies only in attack. So as the enemy withdrew, the brothers skirmished ahead, destroyed the enemy's camp, and captured the enemy's treasure. The enemy soldiers lost the will to fight, and the brothers spent months chasing and harassing them back to their country.

"But it was the brothers' learning that made their warlike skill so effective. They used their art of divination to find and foretell the... the 'turning points.' Places where critical people and crucial decisions can alter destiny, where the will of Heaven is revealed."

I felt a chill run up my spine. "A Nexus," I offered. These ancient Chinese monks had Nexus Detectors?

"Nexus," said Mr. Hung, eying me suspiciously. "Yes. That's a good way to describe it. A Nexus. The monks found each Nexus and got there first, striking swiftly as a falcon strikes its target. Time and again, they broke the back of the enemy for they always knew the perfect moment to strike."

"I see. But if they had such power, what became of them?"

"The Emperor was grateful, for the warrior monks had saved the nation," Dr. Chen explained. "The Emperor offered whatever rewards were in his power to bestow, but the monks wished only to resume their studies. Before the brothers left the court to return to their monastery, the Emperor insisted on bestowing three gifts: the first, a tablet inscribed 'Imperial Favor, Kindness, and Honor,' the second, a scroll proclaiming the monks 'First in Bravery, Matchless Heroes,' and the third, a scroll stating 'It was not by learning that they got to court, through warlike skill they saved the Emperor.'

"Xueshu Quan, however, was not content to resume life teaching the monastic scholars. He elected to remain at court. The Emperor showered gifts upon Xueshu Quan and made him general of all the armies. Now despite all his wealth and power, Xueshu Quan was angry, for he had hoped to lead the brothers to overthrow the Emperor and take the throne for himself. The monks were not interested in worldly power, however. They were devoted to their studies, and they had returned to their monastery. Xueshu Quan knew that he had taught the brothers too many of his secrets, and while the brothers lived, he could not hope to overthrow the Emperor and maintain his power for long.

"So, Xueshu Quan bided his time until the Emperor had begun to forget the service the warrior monks had done for him. Then, Quan whispered in the Emperor's ear that none could stand against the warrior monks – which was true – and that the brothers were a threat to the Emperor – which was a vicious lie. The Emperor took Xueshu Quan's advice and assembled his army in secret, dispatching it to the monastery. The Emperor's army surrounded the monastery, burning it down, but five of the monks escaped with the order's most sacred scrolls and relics.

"The surviving brothers led a revolt against the Emperor and his secret advisor, Xueshu Quan, but they were too few, and they ultimately failed. The brothers exchanged signs that they and their successors would know each other, and they vowed to come together again when the time came to overthrow Xueshu Quan, the teacher who betrayed them.

"Many of our brothers have now forgotten our sacred mission," continued Mr. Hung, "but we remember. Among our brothers are scholars like Dr. Chen who seek to understand and recover the secrets we have lost."

"Xueshu Quan," I said. "You said he was an immortal teacher. Today's Xueshu Quan is the same being?"

"Indeed," said Dr. Chen. "He uses different names in different ages. He remained behind the scenes in the Imperial Court for over a century, but without the Brotherhood to support him, he had difficulty acquiring power and controlling events. The Brotherhood lost track of him during the Opium Wars as the power of the Imperial Court began to fail. Apparently he somehow removed himself to England."

"The signs in England," I observed as pieces of the puzzle began tumbling into a coherent whole.

"Indeed," Dr. Chen acknowledged. "We believe at some point Xueshu Quan realized the trajectory of the West would overtake that of China, and so he came to England to better control events.

"And now Xueshu Quan operates out of Jekyll Island," I concluded.

"We believe so. His associates have operated from there since colonial days. He transferred himself there in the 1890s. He hides behind the scenes," Dr. Chen agreed. "But that is clearly his current base. He remains at a distance from the center of power, yet exercises control through his associates."

Just then the waiters brought in dinner – a dozen dishes placed on the rotating center of the table. We served ourselves as the waiters withdrew again.

"His... 'associates,'" I began. "How much do they know about Xueshu Quan?" I asked.

"Very few know that name," Dr. Chen explained. "He uses it rarely, almost on a whim. Lately, he has used it when posing as a collector of antiquities and rare books, as he who secures forbidden knowledge and hidden truths. He has other names he uses elsewhere. His is a name you would be wise to keep to yourself lest he hear you."

He who must not be named? OK. "And he provides his secrets, like his art of divination, to his associates to aid them in their missions on his behalf," I offered.

Dr. Chen and Mr. Hung looked gravely at each other.

"You know more than you should. You used the name earlier," Dr. Chen said gravely. "His minions employ divination to alter destiny and shape history to serve their ends." I was beginning to think I had revealed too much.

"You obviously know far more about Xueshu Quan than is safe or proper for one outside the Brotherhood," Mr. Hung said intently. "Now you will tell us how it is you came to know our enemy."

I could hear a veiled threat behind Mr. Hung's words. He and Professor Chen had offered their secrets, it was only fair that I exchange a few of my own.

"Very well," I agreed.

"I came across the name in a bookstore in Houston, Texas, last year," I explained. "A girl named Nicole gave me a secret list of books sought by this Xueshu Quan. I looked into the books on the list. Xueshu Quan found out. They killed Nicole and her boss."

"Mr. Rodriguez," Mr. Hung said.

"Yes," I confirmed, wondering how he was so well informed.

"So, you were an associate of the late Jim Burleson?" Mr. Hung asked.

How the hell... Jim Burleson was my father's friend. He'd been fingered as the culprit behind my research and killed. I forced my face into a neutral expression and said levelly, "It appears you, too, know far more than you should of my own secrets."

I saw the light bulb turn on for Dr. Chen. "Burdell. This Burleson had an associate named Roy Burdell."

"My father," I acknowledged. "So you see, your enemy is also my enemy. I have sworn vengeance against Xueshu Quan and his associates who killed my father, and my mother, and countless others. Xueshu Quan's agents used their Nexus Detector to find our house."

Mr. Hung appeared to relax, slightly. "You are lucky to have learned such secrets and still be alive."

Rob taught me that the enemy of my enemy is not necessarily my friend. Of course that was the lesson he kept emphasizing when he was doing his best to keep me from figuring out he was the mysterious third party who burned down the old Tolliver Library. And my enemy was powerful. I needed allies. Like Dr. Chen and his "brothers." Was this another moment of decision? A turning point? A Nexus? Perhaps not, because my best course of action seemed obvious.

"I appreciate your honoring me with your secrets," I acknowledged. "I am prepared to offer you some of mine in in hopes you may be able to make use of them against our mutual foe."

"What secrets do you have to offer?" Mr. Hung asked.

"I can confirm that Xueshu Quan is allied or associated with the Civic Circle," I offered.

I saw Dr. Chen lift an eyebrow in surprise. "We had suspected as much," Mr. Hung agreed. "Your evidence for this connection?"

"Mail to Xueshu Quan is collected by a woman who works in the same building occupied by The Civic Circle in Arlington, VA," I offered. "And my Uncle is a junior member of the Civic Circle. When the associates of Xueshu Quan realized the connection, they became... less aggressive in investigating my connection to Xueshu Quan's secrets."

"I see," Mr. Hung acknowledged.

"What is your evidence for the connection?" I asked.

"The Civic Circle arose from meetings of the rich and powerful on Jekyll Island more than a century ago," Mr. Hung pointed out. So they knew about that connection, too. "They still meet there, every few years, to set the course and direction of their plans."

"Indeed." I was learning more about my enemy in a few minutes than I had been able to uncover in months. We'd been exchanging minor facts. I was coming to trust Mr. Hung. It was time to up the stakes and offer Mr. Hung something more significant, in hopes of him reciprocating with something of comparable value.

"Your tattoo," I gestured to Dr. Chen. "It is a symbol of your Brotherhood?"

"The taijitu, the 'yin-yang' sign, it denotes the dualism of the Tao, or the way," Dr. Chen explained.

"But your version is slightly different from the usual," I noted. "You tilt it at an angle and have a single line running across it. That particular version in your tattoo is the original as taught by Xueshu Quan to the Brotherhood, is it not?"

Mr. Hung narrowed his eyes. Dr. Chen looked puzzled but agreed, "Yes. It is said to have been taught by Xueshu Quan."

"But, the secret meaning has been lost," I said confidently.

"It denotes the dualism of the Tao," Dr. Chen reiterated. "And the line indicates the straight and true path to the center, the point of harmony."

"It denotes the dualism of the electromagnetic field," I explained. "In radiation, there is an equal balance of electric and magnetic energy. When one disrupts the balance, one creates an excess of one field or the other. The act of making one field creates the other, and the balance is restored. A changing electric field makes a magnetic field, and vice versa. The taijitu is what electrical engineers call a "Smith Chart." The line is the axis of real power transfer, and the center point denotes the characteristic impedance of free space – where the fields are in balance and propagate as a pure electromagnetic wave. Your symbol is not a mystic metaphor. It is a physical diagram of the electromagnetic impedance for a dipole."

I explained to Dr. Chen how I calculated the impedance of a dipole from Schelkunoff's equations and plotted it on a Smith Chart to derive the Brotherhood's sacred symbol. Apparently physicists don't use Smith Charts, because he was unfamiliar with the concept. Another deliberate misdirection by Xueshu Quan? Dr. Chen may not have seen a Smith Chart before, but he caught on quickly.

"The Supreme Polarity..." Dr. Chen said, his voice full of awe and wonder, "it's a dipole."

"Exactly," I confirmed. "Your ancient writings do not describe a mystic philosophy. In their original version, they are a primer of physics, disclosing physical principles not discovered by Western science until the last couple of centuries – principles that, in some cases, Xueshu Quan will keep secret by killing those who threaten to disclose them. Maxwell, Hertz, and Fitzgerald all died in their prime before they could complete their work. Heaviside and Lodge were suppressed and distracted. Later scientists who began down the path of truth like Ettore Majorana vanished under mysterious circumstances."

"This is all true?" Mr. Hung asked Dr. Chen.

"I think so," Dr. Chen confirmed. "I will need to double check the details against our surviving fragments of the scrolls to be sure. He's given me much to think about."

"You know too many secrets," Mr. Hung observed. "You have told us many things that Xueshu Quan would never disclose. It is good you are so clearly an enemy of Xueshu Quan. We can respect a son's vow to avenge his father's death." He said something to Dr. Chen in Chinese.

Dr. Chen pulled a small dictionary from his pocket. "Filial piety," he translated. "Respect for one's parents, elders, and ancestors." He replaced the dictionary. "It is a fundamental principle in our philosophy."

"Honor thy father and thy mother," I replied. "It is a fundamental principle with us as well. If I were not an enemy of Xueshu Quan?" I asked.

"Why then, the two brothers outside the door would kill you," Mr. Hung explained matter-of-factly. "It would be quick and merciful, in light of the service you have rendered our order, but our vows to keep our secrets and destroy Xueshu Quan and his supporters transcend even the service you have performed on behalf of Dr. Chen."

He was deadly serious. I suppressed a chill and remained impassive.

"As it is, we are now even deeper in your debt. You have faced peril to bring my nephew, Dr. Chen, back safely to our family. We answered your questions about our Brotherhood and we will trust you with our secrets as you have trusted us with yours. We will ensure your safe return for your service to Dr. Chen. We have offered our hospitality," he gestured at the feast the three of us had barely eaten, "to repay our poor treatment of you on your arrival. Now, you have unbalanced the scales again by showing us the meaning of our own secrets. You must allow us to repay the debt."

"I need a letter." I explained to Dr. Chen how Professor Graf was in danger, and how I stood ready to protect her.

"Indeed," he agreed. "I will write such a letter to help you persuade her."

I thought as Dr. Chen wrote. I had a favor I could call upon. By now, I was sure Amit would be up in Knoxville to look after Professor Graf. That appeared under control, and I hated the thought of squandering the favor Mr. Hung's family owed me if I didn't need it.

Dr. Chen handed me the letter. Perfect. And an idea began to form.

"There is a scholar at Georgia Tech," I explained to Mr. Hung. "He is an agent of the Circle, and thus of Xueshu Quan. He seeks to impose the will of Xueshu Quan upon the school, its faculty and students. He tried to get Dr. Chen fired, and now he has succeeded. He needs to be stopped."

"An assassination is a serious step," Mr. Hung noted. "Uncomfortable questions will be asked – questions that may lead back to us or to you."

"No, not an assassination," I explained. "I don't want the man dead. If we make a martyr, another would take his place, and Xueshu Quan would emerge even stronger. We need him – and the Circle – discredited." I explained what I had in mind.

For the first time since I met him, I saw Mr. Hung crack a wide smile. "Yes," he said, clearly enjoying the thought of what he was about to do. "We can do this. I understand you have much to do as well. You must depart, but we should meet again, soon. We have much to discuss."

CHAPTER 11: THE EYE OF THE STORM

I had Mr. Hung's driver drop me off at The Varsity, then I drove back over the Interstate and back toward campus. A couple of cops eyed me as I drove past them. I could see more out on adjacent blocks.

I parked illegally next to the dorm, taking the chance I could be in and out before I got ticketed and towed. As I approached the dorm, a heartrending scream startled me. It was answered by a piercing cry of fear. A rising chorus of terror split the night air. Midnight. It was time for the traditional finals week "midnight scream." I surprised myself, and let loose with an inarticulate shout of rage and defiance! One down, one to go, I thought to myself. Take that you Circle bastards. I beat you once, and I'm going to beat you again. Or so I hoped. It was time for me to check in with Amit. I pulled out my burner phone and called his.

"How's it going?" he asked. We'd have to keep it vague. While it was an anonymous phone, we couldn't risk sharing details or specifics that might trigger more attention to our call.

"I got my friend safely where he belongs," I said. "He won't be coming home with me or going to work tomorrow. Also, I got that note from the doctor we discussed."

"I see," Amit replied. "Yes I could certainly use a doctor's note, too, right about now. Your boss doesn't believe me."

"Ah. I understand," I replied. I was afraid of that. Damn. Professor Graf was a sitting duck just waiting for the Circle to swoop down on her.

"And there was some confusion," Amit added. "Seems your boss ended up in the wrong room. Go figure."

"What a curious event," I acknowledged in mock irony. Amit may not have been able to persuade Professor Graf to take his warning seriously, but at least he'd managed to rejigger the hotel's records so they'd be looking for her in a different room. "Maybe she'll think differently when I show her the note. Anything else you think I should bring?"

"Nah," Amit insisted, "but you should know they're very, very angry at your friend. He should probably stay out of sight for a good long while."

"I figured as much. Oh, and thanks for letting you-know-who know I was in a bind. His friend was extremely helpful."

"Just one? I thought more might be on the way, but I'm glad one was all it took. Tell me all about it when you get here."

"On my way."

Our plan to leave my phone with Amit's in our room by way of an alibi was pretty much shot when I got cited outside the massage parlor and had to show the police officers my ID. I dashed into the room and grabbed my phone. I looked bad - an obvious black eye. I felt worse. I wanted to lie down on the bed and rest, but I had miles to go before I could sleep. I confirmed I had all my stuff cleared out of the room. Amit hadn't had a chance to finish packing, but I couldn't help that now. I rushed back to my truck. The police were still out in force, but apparently too busy to worry about parking violations. They stopped me twice at checkpoints before I got on I-75 heading north.

I turned on the local AM talk station, WSB, to help me stay awake. There was a manhunt underway for Professor Chen, "the Georgia Tech professor accused of espionage." The public was advised to be on the lookout for him. Homeland Security and the FBI were confident that he would soon be in custody and the nuclear secrets he stole would be recovered. Now that he was with Mr. Hung, I had a feeling the FBI and more importantly, the Circle, would be disappointed.

I pulled in at a truck stop halfway to Tennessee and filled up. Not that I needed the gas, but I had to get some coffee to keep going. I also got some ice to help the swelling around my eye. I finally arrived at the Chattanooga Choo Choo just after 2am. The old train station had been converted into a hotel and conference center. I parked in the adjacent garage, and entered the old station lobby to check in. I hadn't arranged anything in advance with Amit, but I figured if he was rejiggering reservations for Professor Graf, he'd have taken care of mine as well. Sure enough, he was asleep in my room.

"You look like hell," he yawned sleepily.

"Glad to see you, too."

"So, what happened to you?"

"Some of Professor Chen's 'family' play rough. You remember when I was telling you about Chinese tongs? We eventually reached an understanding. How'd it go with Professor Graf?"

Amit couldn't stop staring at my face. Finally he said, "I was persistent. She didn't believe me. Eventually I got a door slammed in my face. Wasn't the first time, probably won't be the last. I figure she'll be more receptive if she's had more sleep. We'll all need some to get through the day we have ahead of us. Breakfast isn't until 6 am. Let's get up at 4 am and go wake her up, then, too."

I got nearly two hours of sleep. Glorious.

Amit woke me up at 4 am. It was too soon. "I got up early to check if there was any news." He handed me a cup of coffee. "You want the good news or the bad news."

"How about some good news for a change?"

"The only good news is at least we know what the bad news is. Agent Wilson is in Atlanta coordinating the search for Professor Chen, but there are agents already here in the hotel. They plan to interrogate your professor this morning. They're supposed to see if she knows anything about

Professor Chen's disappearance and what happened to his research data. They plan to poison her at the conference reception tonight. They say they have some kind of super toxin to spike her drink. Sounds like nasty stuff. Then, they're supposed to follow her around for a couple of days until she dies."

"Great. Any details on the poison?"

"It's radioactive. They have a couple of doses in gel caps that will dissolve when placed in a drink. They say it isn't dangerous, though, until the gel caps dissolve. They say they got it from some Russian friends."

"Sounds like an alpha or beta emitter. Must have a very short half-life to be radioactive enough that such a small dose can be toxic." I'd have to study to figure out what it was. "Let's call Professor Graf to let her know we're coming."

Amit gave me her room number – next door to ours. I could hear the phone ringing through the wall. "Hello?" came a sleepy voice on the other end.

"Good morning." It was probably internal to the hotel and not likely to be recorded, but I didn't want to say anything over the phone. "I'll be at your door in a minute. It's really important. I need to speak with you." I hung up. "Give us a few minutes," I told Amit, "then join us."

I knocked. I assumed she saw who it was. She opened the door with the chain still attached. "It's four in the morning. What do you think you're doing waking me up like this?" She took a look at my face. "What happened to you?"

"Long story," I said. "Let me in and I'll explain it. Also, I have a letter you need to read. It's from Professor Chen."

She looked suspicious, but let me in. I asked her for her cell phone and laptop, and I put them in the microwave to deaden the sound and prevent any possible transmissions. Then, I handed her the letter and turned on the news. "It will be on soon," I explained. Also, I figured the noise would help cover our conversation if anyone was listening. Professor Graf read Professor Chen's letter:

My dear friend and colleague,

I very much regret the trouble you are now in. I would have spared you, if I could. We have discovered secrets they wish to remain hidden. One way or another, your old life and career are now over. If you do nothing, they will soon have you. I do not believe they will let you survive, knowing what you now know.

For my part, I am glad in a way that my old life is over. My family will hide me and allow me to spend much of my time uncovering and understanding the hidden truth. Without the distractions of grant writing, committees, and campus politics, I believe I will make better progress, particularly with the new leads our young friend gave me.

The young man who gives you this letter knows much about who they are and what they want. He is on my side and yours. He believes he may be able to save you as he has saved me. I suggest you trust him, listen to him with an open mind, and follow his guidance. If you do, there is a chance you may survive these troubled times. If you do not listen to him, they will kill you and any they can find who have helped you. He is taking a great risk to help you. Please take advantage of the opportunity he has to offer you.

The unknown will not discover itself. I must close now so our young friend may deliver this to you. I hope our paths will cross again sometime. I look forward to collaborating once again, some day.

Yours in Science,

A Friend

There was a knock on the door between the adjoining rooms. Professor Graf looked up in alarm. "That will be Amit. I'll get it." Amit had good timing. "I believe you've met my friend?"

"We meet again!" Amit said brightly.

Professor Graf looked at Amit, a decisively neutral look in her face, then back at me. "Who are these mysterious 'they' that are after me and Chen, and what's this secret they wish to remain hidden?"

I explained. It took a while. Part way through the news cycle, the story came up about the manhunt for the missing Georgia Tech professor suspected of espionage.

"It's true," she said softly. "They are after him."

"A couple of 'FBI agents' who are actually working for the Circle are waiting to talk with you," I explained. "They'll want to know where Professor Chen is and what happened to his data."

"Well that's easy. I don't know where he is, and if he has data that's not on the server in the lab, I don't know where it is."

"They are probably going to take your computer and phone."

She looked dismayed, but nodded.

"They plan to kill you at the reception tonight, by dropping some deadly radioactive poison in your drink," Amit added, far more cheerfully than was warranted. "It's supposed to kill you within a few days. They'll be following you around to make sure."

"How did they know I was going to the reception?"

"You're supposed to be meeting a Professor Glyer about a research position in Huntsville?" Amit asked.

"That weasel!" She looked pissed. "He's in on it?"

"I can't be sure," Amit acknowledged. "They may have just been monitoring your emails and phone calls."

That didn't make her any happier. "So, I don't drink or eat anything at the reception," she began, thinking it through, "but then they'd just come up with an alternate plan once poisoning failed."

"We have to let them think they've succeeded," I explained, "make them think you've been poisoned."

"They'll be watching you pretty carefully," Amit said, thoughtfully. "You order a beer," he suggested to Professor Graf. "A bottle will be safer to handle than an open cup or glass. We swap out your beer and dispose of the poisoned bottle. You wander around socializing, obviously drinking from the 'poisoned' beer. Once they're convinced, we smuggle you out of the hotel."

"How do we get a bottle of beer? We're underage," I pointed out.

"They never check IDs at these receptions, if you have a conference badge," Professor Graf assured me. "There are two problems with that scheme, though. Amit has no business being in the reception or talking with me. You're my student, Peter. You're signed up, already. That gets you a badge to get into the reception. And there's nothing strange or unusual about my hanging out with a student of mine at a conference."

Damn, she was right, and Amit was going to get the girl. Again. I'd swap the bottle, but he'd get to take her to safety.

"The second and more serious problem is the vultures will be following me around, waiting for me to drop dead," she added dryly. "If I vanish, or worse, just go about my life and refuse to cooperate by dropping dead, they'll be after me. They'll try again and keep trying until they succeed."

"I've been thinking about that." I looked her in the eye. "Good thing you're such an outdoorsy type."

She lifted an eyebrow curiously, her attention focused on me. I liked it.

"See, if you vanish, they'll just keep looking for you. You'll be a wanted terrorist or evil foreign espionage agent, you'll make the FBI's top-ten most wanted list, and they'll never give up looking for you. You have to convince them you're dead."

"So we fake a suicide by driving my car into the Tennessee River," she suggested.

"Too obvious," I countered. "Too tough to arrange it so once they recover the car and you're not in it, the evidence is convincing that your body somehow washed away. What if you decide to go hiking in the mountains, and just never show up again? Happens all the time. You get 'lost,' you wander about, you 'die' of exposure, search parties find shreds of evidence that link to you months later. It'll be particularly convincing because they'll figure you got sick and became too feeble to make it out on your own."

"I don't have any gear," she said.

I dictated a shopping list for her: water bottle, first aid kit, sun protection, flashlight, all the scout essentials. "We'll need your dirty laundry. That conference T-shirt would be perfect." I pointed to the shirt she was wearing. "Put it in a plastic bag so we avoid any cross contamination. Also, I need you to get a new pair of boots, too. You'll have to tell Amit what kind. He'll buy an identical pair and attach the treads to my boots – instant Graf prints. I'll have to shorten my stride to make it convincing to trackers. You stop at a gas station a few miles from the trail head – fill up the tank, then park next to Amit's car in some shadowy corner behind the gas station. You get a snack, and chat up the clerk, so he'll remember you. Everything's on their security video, except where you've parked. I wear a wig so a casual observer thinks I'm you, and I drive up to the trail head. Meanwhile Amit will drive you to safety. I'll leave a false trail – wander around a bit dropping off your clothes and gear here and there. Then, I'll make for a different trail head, so Amit can pick me up the next morning."

"I can drop hints and comments with colleagues about this hike." Now she was getting into it. "Where will I be going?"

"Cades Cove. Up in Great Smoky Mountains National Park. My family used to have a homestead there, before the government expropriated it back in the 1930's." I gave her the details on the location of the trailhead I had in mind. Amit and I hashed out the supplies we'd need and further details.

We had the beginnings of a plan, but for it to be successful, I needed a place for Professor Graf to hide. Amit could stash her in his family's hotel for a while, but her face would be all over the news when she went "missing" and they started looking for her in earnest. It was too risky, and not even close to a long-term solution. With Rob's refusal to cooperate, that limited my options. I had only one friend who could help, but I was going to have to see him in person to arrange it.

"I'm going to head up to Knoxville this morning," I told Amit. "I have to call in a favor to arrange a refuge for Professor Graf to stay."

"Herr Doktor Krueger?" Amit asked.

"Yes," I nodded.

"My mother will be worried sick about me, when I go missing," Professor Graf was beginning to think through the implications of her pending disappearance, "All my stuff in my apartment, and my cat! Sarah is checking on Tigger over the weekend..."

"I'm sure Sarah will take care of your cat," I assured her. "If you can trust your mom to keep your survival a secret, we can probably arrange to tell her, maybe even get some of your things from your place for you." I had a feeling that Sarah, one of the FOGs newest members, was going to come in handy on this one. "First things first, though. We need to get you out of here alive, and convince the Circle their plan worked."

We finalized the details of the plan – how to swap out the beer bottle, how to dispose of the poison, when Professor Graf would leave the hotel, the switch-off at the gas station. We had to be careful to make sure we covered everything. Sure, Amit and I still had our burner phones. We could call each other with last minute changes in plan. The more calls you make on a burner phone, though, the more vulnerable you are – the more of a trail you're leaving behind. You can't start calling people with your burner phone without giving away your connections. For instance, suppose I tried to call Dr. Krueger, and suppose Amit ran into an emergency and had to call Professor Graf for some reason. Then, Amit and I might still be anonymous, but anyone reviewing the phone records would realize there was a connection between Professor Graf and Dr. Krueger. That's why the fewer calls you make, the more secure you are. And if you leave your phone on, you're leaving a record of your travels. Amit would leave his burner phone on, just in case I needed to contact him. I would leave mine off, unless I needed to update him on my plans. One way or another, I should be back to Chattanooga hours before the evening's reception.

Now I had to get to Knoxville to arrange the last part of the plan – a safe place for Professor Graf to hide. I could have phoned ahead, but Knoxville was only a couple of hours from Chattanooga – no sense risking a call when I couldn't disclose any sensitive details or even my identity. This early in the morning, he would probably be at home. I needed to call in my favor from Dr. Krueger.

Dr. Krueger ran an automobile plant near Knoxville. He'd contracted a lot of the electrical work to my father and my father's associates while the plant was under construction. They'd butted heads in the negotiation and the subsequent work. Their business relationship had flowered into a friendship. Dr. Krueger asked my father to design and build an underground refuge beneath his house, similar to the one Dad and Rob had built under Rob's barn. With Rob refusing to help, Dr. Krueger's refuge became the logical place for Professor Graf to hide.

When my parents were murdered, Dr. Krueger had promised he would be there for me, if I ever needed help – a job, a place to stay, even money for a down payment on a house or to start a business. It was a debt of honor he felt he owed my father, an obligation he could only discharge by helping me. I hoped his generosity extended to sheltering a fugitive scientist.

By seven in the morning, I pulled into his neighborhood. The once-barren subdivision was now largely complete. Only a few empty lots remained, and a couple of houses were under construction. The subdivision still had that "new" look

– scrawny, freshly planted trees, and lines in lawns where the fresh grass had not yet grown out to disguise the strips where sod had been laid down in rolls. I parked in front of Dr. Krueger's home, walked up, and rang the doorbell. Nothing. I waited a minute, and rang the doorbell again. Finally the door opened.

"Mein Gott!" Dr. Krueger exclaimed, standing there in his bathrobe. "Come in, come in."

I followed him in.

"Wer ist das?" came a woman's voice.

"Peter Burdell," he announced me to Frau Krueger. "Would you please make some coffee for our young friend?" He turned and looked at me, a benevolent half smile on his face. "He appears to need it." Dr. Krueger gestured me to the kitchen. "Tell me," he gestured at my face, "what happened to you?"

"My parents were murdered," I explained. "Last night, the murderers tried to do the same to one of my professors. I got him to safety and acquired this," I gestured to my black eye, "in the process. Now they're after another professor. I think I can save her, but I need a place for her to hide. I thought you might be able to accommodate her."

He took a deep breath. "Your parents? Ja. Was crazy with that car accident and talk of cyber terror. Never made sense. You sure it was murder? It was the government agents who did this?"

"Not exactly government agents," I explained. "They were working for some of the same people behind the Civic Circle. I uncovered some of their secrets, and they thought Mr. Burleson was responsible. They killed my parents just to make sure the secret was safe. Now they figured out one of my professors at Georgia Tech is part of a group working against them. I saved him, but the Civic Circle thinks the other professor is also in on it. They're going to kill her."

"The Civic Circle?" He looked skeptical. "I heard about this professor on the news last night – this Chinese spy at Georgia Tech. You are involved with him?"

"Yes," I acknowledged, "but he's no spy."

Frau Krueger brought over some coffee, and offered us a plate with bread and cheese.

"Perhaps you'd best begin at the beginning," Dr. Krueger suggested.

I described the clues I found in the Tolliver Library and how they led me to Heaviside's theory of wave interaction. Dr. Krueger's eyes lit up as I walked him through how energy slows to a stop when waves interfere, and how the waves exchange energy. "Macht sinn," he said nodding. "Of course. I never looked at it that way before. Why did I not learn of this in school?"

I noted the death toll of scientists the Circle left in their wake – Maxwell, Hertz, and FitzGerald, all dead in their prime. "Three of the five Maxwellians," Dr. Krueger nodded. "The pattern, it is obvious once you point it out like that. They just kill scientists? What about your parents?"

"They kill anyone who gets too close to their secrets. Probably even political figures." I shared our speculation that they may have had something to do with ninety-day reign of Kaiser Friedrich III in 1888. His death by cancer of the larynx set the stage for Kaiser Wilhelm and the militarists to take power.

"That dummkopf Wilhelm," Krueger muttered. "He led Deutschland to ruin and set the stage for Hitler."

I explained what we'd discovered from the books we saved from the library – about Angus MacGuffin and how he was murdered to cover up additional secrets, about Ettore Majorana and his flight to South America, and about how the Circle had been influencing events in the United States for at least the last hundred years.

"You know for a fact it is Civic Circle men kill your parents?" Frau Krueger asked me.

"Yes, ma'am," I replied. Frau Krueger looked sternly at her husband.

"Scheisse," he said with disgust. "My own boss, the CEO of my company – he is one of them."

"I doubt all the members of the Civic Circle know everything that's going on," I cautioned. "My own uncle, Larry Tolliver, is involved with them, and I'm confident he knew nothing of the plan to kill my father. He's not a good enough actor to hide it, if he were involved. There's a small group within the Civic Circle that's responsible for the murders and blackmail. The rest are just patsies who go along to get along, to feel important, and to trade favors."

"That doesn't make me feel much better," he said. "Tell me. What do you need of us?"

"I need a place to hide my professor," I explained. "Maybe I can find another solution, another place for her to go, but she'll need shelter for weeks at least, maybe even months or years."

"Your Uncle Rob," Dr. Krueger suggested, "he cannot help? He has many friends, many connections."

"Perhaps, eventually. For now though, he has refused to help. He thinks it's too dangerous, too early to make any move against the Circle. He wanted me to come home and hide until this all blows over."

"Did he now?" Dr. Krueger asked, disapprovingly. He looked at Frau Krueger. She gave her husband a nod. "Your professor can stay with us as long as she is in danger."

Just then, I heard footsteps behind me. "Papi, wer war an der ...eek!" Eva shrieked when she saw me.

"Sorry to startle you," I started, but she had already turned and left.

"Machts nicht," Dr. Krueger said with a smile. "It doesn't matter."

"Can you join us for a proper breakfast?" Frau Krueger asked. "I'm sure Eva and the boys would love to see you."

"No," I declined as politely as I could. "I have to go save my professor. I'll have time when she's safe. I'll be back tomorrow morning."

"I understand," Dr. Krueger said. He and Frau Krueger rose and walked with me over to the door.

"I have to warn you," I added. "What I've told you must remain a secret. If the Circle and their agents knew what you now know, the consequences for you and your family..."

"I know," Dr. Krueger said, giving my hand a firm shake. "I understand. We will keep your secrets. For your sake and for ours."

Frau Krueger stretched up and kissed me on the cheek. "You come back safe to us, ja?"

"I will." I hoped that was a promise I'd be able to keep.

I hit the road. My mood improved the closer I got to Chattanooga. It wasn't even lunchtime, yet. I had all afternoon to make sure the plan was all set and ready to go. Maybe I'd even have a chance to take a nap. I ran through the plan over and over again, looking for flaws: swap the drinks, ditch the poison, save the girl, fake the hike. We had a simple plan – not exactly foolproof, but close to it. I was back with four or five hours to spare before the reception – plenty of time to make sure Amit had everything all set. I pulled into the parking garage beside the Chattanooga Choo Choo, feeling on top of the world.

Maybe Rob was correct about my lack of tactical experience. He always emphasized I should maintain situational awareness at all times. So help me, I did see the van coming. It did register as suspicious. I took off at a sprint as it drove up and the door opened. The masked guys who hopped out were too fast for me, though. The last thing I remember was a hood put over my face. When I came to, I was tied up in a chair, blinded by the hood. There was a bit of dampness and a smell of stale air. I was in a basement? I heard the distant rumble of urban traffic from above. I had a notion where I might be.

Chattanooga has always been a city with something to hide. As a river port, it had its share of smugglers. Before the Civil War, it was a major stop on the Underground Railroad. Fugitive slaves would come to Chattanooga to be smuggled north on riverboats and barges. Not many people realize that the Tennessee River dips south into Alabama, then back north, crossing Tennessee and Kentucky before joining the Ohio River near the southern tip of Illinois. From Chattanooga, a fugitive slave could float downstream to freedom in the North.

After the Civil War, floods devastated the city. The City Council proposed raising the level of the streets, but never officially funded the project. Undaunted, citizens took it upon themselves to raise the level of their streets. Ground floors became basements, and the old downtown acquired a hidden substratum – Underground Chattanooga, they called it. Old underground railway stations and smuggler's lairs connected via a network of old tunnels. Moonshiners and the mob expanded the network further during prohibition to make secret warehouses for their product. I was probably somewhere in somebody's old sub-basement deep in Underground Chattanooga.

I slowly flexed the bindings around my wrist to test them. Not slowly enough.

"He's awake," came a woman's voice, far too perky for the circumstances.

I heard heavy footsteps approaching. I prepared myself to throw my bound body in the most advantageous direction. "Who are you, and what do you want?"

"I think I should soften the punk up some before we talk," a gruff voice barked.

I couldn't see either Perky Girl or her friend, Bulldog. As a rule, kidnappers and other evildoers prefer their victims not to be able to identify them later. The fact they weren't allowing me to see them was probably a good sign they intended me to survive this encounter. I paid close attention to my other senses: a distant hum of traffic, the dampness, the mustiness, and... a hint of perfume?

"I'm sure that won't be necessary," said Perky Girl. "Besides, I saw that black eye you gave him! You must have been awfully rough with him. No wonder he punched you."

"Nah. He got that shiner a while ago," Bulldog pointed out. "Punk could stand a matched set though."

"Really, haven't you put him through enough already?" Perky Girl said with an excellent imitation of genuine empathy and affection, despite completely ignoring my question. I heard motion behind me – a door opening? A deep voice behind me said, "Investigare."

I could hear Perky Girl and Bulldog move to face the newcomer. They replied, "Cognoscere," in unison, almost like some kind of ritual or countersign?

The deep voice responded, "Defendere."

Ah ha! Investigare, cognoscere, defendere. To investigate, to learn, to defend. The motto of the Ordo Alberti, the Dominicans with whom Ettore Majorana found refuge in Buenos Aires. Interesting.

"I regret the enthusiasm with which my colleagues arranged our meeting," the newcomer said. You may call me Brother Francis." Bulldog and Perky Girl seemed to withdraw behind me. "We would not have taken such liberties were it not for the urgency of the situation. Your professora, she is in danger. Unless you help us, she will be killed, probably tonight."

Fortunately, Brother Francis interpreted my stunned silence as disbelief of the threat to Professor Graf, and not amazement that yet another team had joined this dangerous game. They'd kidnapped me, preventing me from saving Professor Graf... so they could warn me that I needed to save Professor Graf. I'd have found it amusing were it not for the fact they were making me late to my very clever plan to save the same professor they were trying to convince me was in danger.

"I know this is hard to understand," he continued, "but there are dark forces at work in the world. They are pursuing Professor Chen and will likely soon find him. Now their eye has turned to Chattanooga and to Professor Graf. They will kill her this very evening, unless you help us help her."

I decided my best course of action was to feign ignorance and play along. "I know she annoyed a lot of people by standing up for Professor Chen, but is that any reason to want to kill her?"

"Professor Chen's research may have uncovered secrets they want to keep hidden," Brother Francis explained. "The location of their places of power. The fact that those places have existed for centuries, operating at a level of technology our civilization has only reached recently. If those secrets were revealed, there would be obvious questions asked – questions that would lead to the discovery of their existence."

Brother Francis' explanation came disturbingly close to the truth I'd already uncovered. As far as Amit had been able to determine, though, the Circle didn't actually know the details of Professor Chen's research, only that he had communicated something of great importance to a known associate in the Brotherhood. They wanted Chen, because they'd figured out he was in the Brotherhood, and they were after Graf because, after her spirited defense of him, they figured she was his accomplice. It was getting tough keeping track of who knew what.

"Whose locations of power?" I asked, wondering how much more they knew. "Whose existence?"

"I will answer you, if you wish," he replied, "but know this first: knowledge is power. Power may be used for good or for evil. If the forces and followers of evil learn that you possess certain knowledge, you, too, will be at risk, just like your professors, and we may not be able to save you from the consequences. There is danger from evil, and yet considerable opportunity for you to do good. If you want, we can end our conversation now. We will return you to the streets of Chattanooga, and your professor's death will be on your conscience. Or, I will answer your question, and, for better or worse, you will know the truth.

This scene was familiar. "I'll take the red pill," I told him.

Apparently, Brother Francis had never seen The Matrix. Bulldog broke the awkward silence – "Kid means he wants you to tell him."

"Very well," Brother Francis continued. "Do you understand that there is weakness and waywardness enough in the hearts of men acting according to their own free will to account for much of the evil in the world?"

I nodded yes, before realizing he might not be able to see me under the hood. "Yes," I verbalized.

"How much greater is the danger if these human foibles, follies, and weaknesses were directed, guided, channeled, by a vigilant and hostile intelligence. The Great Tempter. The Father of Lies. The Prince of Evil. That is the enemy – ours and yours."

That sounded like... "You mean... Lucifer?"

"The bringer of light," Brother Francis confirmed. "Although that's more the job title he had before his fall from the heavens, than a proper name, or a description of his fundamental nature or essence."

"A literal, supernatural angel of evil." I hoped my skepticism wasn't too obvious.

"Christ, in the Gospel, called him the Prince of this World," Brother Francis explained. "He and his followers have many masks they wear in presenting their face to the world as they seek dominion over us. One mask is that of the Civic Circle."

Suddenly this abstract theological discussion of evil had acquired some very practical implications. "The Civic Circle is out to get Professor Graf?"

"Indeed." Brother Francis paused. "There is more. Your father's friend, Mr. Burleson: he stumbled across some of the Civic Circle's hidden truths. They killed him. Then, they killed your parents to keep the secrets Mr. Burleson found. They will kill your professor, too, unless you help us to save her."

The distant rumble of a truck passing on the street above punctuated the silence. It was getting spooky exactly how many people were aware of my history. "I believe you," I told him, "but what can I do?"

"We can offer sanctuary to your professor – a place where she can work with other scholars to uncover and understand the secrets the Civic Circle would prefer remain hidden."

"Sanctuary? What sanctuary?"

"Somewhere safe," Brother Francis answered vaguely. "It wouldn't be a sanctuary if it weren't secret."

"A place of research working to unlock these secrets – surely if such a place existed, their work would be well known," I pointed out. Perhaps it was that convent in Buenos Aires that sheltered Majorana? I had to be careful to keep such speculations to myself.

"Their work is kept in darkness against the day the Civic Circle is overthrown and all can be brought into the light."

"But aren't you merely doing the Civic Circle's work for them?" I asked. "Helping the Civic Circle keep secret the ideas they want to suppress? Why wouldn't you trumpet your discoveries to the world? Can't you do so in a way that doesn't give away the details of your location or identity?"

There was another long pause. Had I pushed too far, too fast? I kept deliberately silent and waited for Brother Francis to fill the void. Listening intently, I was confident I was somewhere below downtown Chattanooga.

"This is not the way I envisioned this conversation going," Brother Francis acknowledged.

"I can extend your offer to Professor Graf," I confirmed, "but she's a smart woman – not easily persuaded. She'll need more to go on than my second-hand say-so of your claims."

"If she ignores our warning, she will be dead soon enough," Brother Francis intoned solemnly. "Tonight. They plan to poison her at the GammaCon reception."

Wow. These guys had hooks into the Civic Circle every bit as good as Amit's. "Then, why don't you approach her directly? Warn her. Why use me as an intermediary?"

"We tried last night," Brother Francis explained. She was not in her assigned room when we went to bring her here for..." he paused, "an involuntary interview."

Ah ha. Amit's plan worked, though not against the opponents we'd anticipated. "Is that the euphemism for kidnapping people off the street these days?" I asked. "Involuntary interview?"

"We are trying to save your professor's life," he insisted, firmly. "Now, she is being watched. If we approach her, they would know. You, however, can convey to her our offer – arrange for her to meet us outside, so we can deliver her to safety."

"I'm telling you right now, while she might be as inclined as me to believe in the possibility of a threat, that's not enough to make her turn her back on her life and career and trust in you. What is the point of this Sanctuary if all it does is help the Circle keep secrets from the rest of us? Why should she want to go with you to work there?"

I could hear Brother Francis weighing his words in silence. Finally he spoke. "After the Second World War, it became obvious that science had incredible military potential. The Manhattan Project, a government-funded research effort, developed weapons of unimaginable power. The Civic Circle had no trouble persuading our temporal leaders that the power of science had to be tamed. Their argument was economic – if we don't fund science, no private business will, because the benefits of scientific discovery are general – they cannot be monopolized and monetized. Scientific discoveries will spread to the benefit of others who did not fund them, and thus there is no incentive for any individual or business to perform scientific research. Of course, they also argued that science could not possibly spread across borders, and if our country did not fund science we would fall behind those that did.

"No one picked apart the contradiction, because the real reason for the government to fund science was to control it. The Civic Circle has... some kind of a roadmap of discovery. A path they want us to follow. They fear that if we stray from that path they may have difficulty controlling the consequences.

"They have carefully engineered the sociology and mechanism of scientific research so as to slow down discovery. Even the most talented researchers now spend half their time or more writing proposals and beseeching agencies for funding instead of conducting productive scientific work. The funding agencies serve as the guides and gatekeepers, making sure that research progresses only in approved directions and squelching any signs of true innovation off the Civic Circle's desired path. When a researcher goes too far off the path and brings to light what the Civic Circle wants kept in the dark, they arrange a promotion or an alternate position to distract them, or they recruit them into the world of classified research, so their discoveries can never see the light of day. In more extreme cases where a determined researcher cannot be distracted or deterred, they arrange a convenient accident or a death by apparently natural causes.

"We can offer Professor Graf an opportunity to work on whatever research she desires. Our accommodations are necessarily modest, but she will never want or worry for how she will fund her work. She will have the opportunity to work on whatever problems she desires, to engage with like-minded scholars, learning from their discoveries and sharing with them her own results. Complete scientific freedom."

"It does sound like an attractive offer," I acknowledged. "I'll pass it along, but you still haven't answered why the discoveries of your Sanctuary are kept secret."

"Our founder said 'I shall not conceal a science that was before me revealed by the grace of God.... What worth is a concealed science; what worth is a hidden treasure?' We have since learned, though, that some secrets are too dangerous to disclose to those without the prudence and judgement to apply them wisely.

"We must keep our secrets from the Prince of this Earth," Brother Francis insisted, "for He would twist the tools we have discovered and use them for evil purposes. Decades ago, servants of the Civic Circle found one of our sanctuaries. They stole from us the secrets of a device of unimaginable power and potential – a device that can sense when history is being born and where subtle events are changing its course. It literally senses a Nexus where free will is exercised in such a way as to have lasting and profound consequences. We call it a Nexus Detector."

The Albertians discovered the Nexus Detector? Or rediscovered it from MacGuffin's descriptions?

"The Civic Circle uses these devices to sense when and where history is changing," Brother Francis continued, "so they can get on top of events, control the outcome, and shut down potential threats to their power before they are made real. They are in town now. Our own detector shows we are nearing a Nexus. I should warn you, however, that our decision to contact you hardly appeared to register at all. It is as if Professor Graf's fate is already ordained for better or worse even without our intervention."

"Something will happen to her whether we act or not?"

"We all have free will," Brother Francis clarified, "and we will choose to exercise it – or not – according to our nature. If we chose to stand by and do nothing, events will take a different course than if we intervene. Your professora is an outstanding scholar and would be a great benefit to our work. We failed in our first attempt to save her. That's why we have chosen to risk contacting you as an intermediary. Time is running out. We pin our hopes on you. I hope you will forgive us, now that you understand our motives."

I thought about that a moment. "I can forgive you," I agreed. "I will convey your warning and your offer to Professor Graf. How will I contact you again when it is time?"

"My associates will make the arrangements. Time is running out. We have spoken long enough." Brother Francis cut short our conversation. "As I have already explained to you, knowledge is power. We have shared with you secrets that will cost you your life, if you reveal them to the wrong persons. God bless and keep you."

CHAPTER 12: THE FINAL SHOWDOWN

Bulldog pulled me roughly to my feet. "You gonna behave yourself?"

"Unless you give me reason otherwise." I could afford to be a smart ass, since clearly they wanted me on their side. Bulldog and Perky Girl guided me along some long tunnels. I tried counting steps and keeping track of turns. It did me no good though, because they directed me up some rickety stairs and they bundled me back into a van. I think Perky Girl was driving. Bulldog kept me company in the back.

"Here's a phone," he said. I felt something sliding into my back pocket. "When your professor is ready, give us a call and we'll provide further instruction. Push and hold the number 1 to dial us. We'll let you off here," Bulldog said. "They've got security all around the hotel. You'll have to walk your way in past the cops." He untied my hands.

"Go!" said Perky Girl.

The door slid open and Bulldog shoved me out, grabbing the hood at the same time. The sudden sunlight blinded me. By the time I looked back, I saw a dark van speeding off. I oriented myself, and walked to the hotel. I could see what Bulldog meant. A couple police cars were positioned around the front. There was a security checkpoint at the door. I looked at my watch. The reception was already under way, and I was supposed to have checked in with Amit long before now. He'd be worried sick. I must have been out for a while.

I quickened my pace and approached the GammaCon registration desk. I picked up my badge and a GammaCon logo bag with the conference program. Swap the bags, get a beer, swap the bottles, save the girl. Easy, peasey, lemon squeazy.

I saw Amit waiting for me in the lobby of the old train station, just outside the reception. He looked relieved. He'd staked out a spot in the crowded lobby and had a GammaCon bag beside him on the window sill. I set my bag down next to his. "What happened?" he asked softly. "No. No time. You're late. She's already in there."

"This place taken?" a couple of older men squeezed in next to us.

"No, I need to be going anyway," I said, picking up Amit's bag and leaving my own.

Amit looked at me. There was clearly something else he wanted to add, but he wasn't comfortable with the strangers yakking right next to us. "Our friends are here," he said.

"OK," I replied. Did he mean that ironically, as in our friends the agents of the Civic Circle? Or did he have some other friends in mind? I pondered it as I walked into the reception. He'd let me go ahead, so whichever it was, it didn't change what I had to do.

The reception was in a bar and lounge area just off the train station lobby. I walked past the man checking badges, noted Professor Graf, and took a roundabout path through her field of view. Our eyes met momentarily, and I saw a hint of a smile dance across her face. I walked up to the bartender. "Sam Adams," I ordered.

"You got ID?" the bartender asked with a thick accent. Russian? Oh, no. No ID, no bottle, no swap. I tried a bluff.

"Left it in my room," I explained. "Look, I'm with the conference, and they said all I'd need is my badge." I helpfully held my badge under his nose for him to inspect.

"Aren't you young to be gamma-ray astrophysicist?" the Russian bartender asked.

"Well, gamma ray astrophysics is a young science," I replied confidently.

"Sorry kid, no ID, no beer." I was too frantic to appreciate the irony of poisoners being all scrupulous with underage drinking rules. Professor Graf was going to be dead at their hands if I didn't figure something out. Fast. Like, now. Think! I froze under the pressure. Nope. No brilliant insights miraculously came to me.

"OK." I walked off slowly, my thoughts racing. Damn. Now what? I took a deep breath to calm myself. I had to have a bottle of beer. I surveyed the room. There was a tray in the corner where conference-goers stacked their glasses, plates, and bottles. This might be easier than I feared. I saw where someone had left a plate on one of the tables. I picked it up and walked over to the tray. I deposited the dirty plate on the tray, and picked up a bottle of Sam Adams that still had some dregs left, carefully holding it in a napkin so as not to leave fingerprints. I tried not to be too obvious about it. Then, I found a table with good visibility of the entrance and the bar. I was getting hungry, but I wasn't about to leave my precious bottle unattended. They were being all scrupulous about looking out for under-age drinking. There was no way I should risk walking around with my bottle, if I didn't have to. I hid the bottle in my lap between my thighs and pretended to examine the conference program while I checked in the bag. I found the rubber gloves on top, and I put them on. Then I fumbled about, inventorying the contents of the conference bag, making sure Amit had included the supplies we'd discussed. I set the cork where I wouldn't lose it, opened the plastic bag Amit provided, and placed it carefully inside the conference bag in my lap. When I was ready, I grabbed the bottle of beer and held it under the table with my gloved left hand. I hid my gloved right hand under the conference program and continued pretending to study it intently.

A couple minutes later, I saw Professor Graf get up from her talk with Professor Glyer and approach the bar. The first bartender removed the cap from a bottle of beer and turned his back. His partner said something to Professor Graf – a distraction while the first bartender poisoned the bottle? The first bartender handed her the bottle. I could see them watching her intently as she walked away. Professor Glyer was watching her intently, too. I averted my eyes so they wouldn't see me watching them or her.

I sensed her approach. "Hi, Peter!" She stood next to me and pointed at the program with her left hand. "Peter, did you see that interesting paper on the latest gamma ray burst detection results in the Finely Lecture Hall?" She held her bottle under the table with her right hand.

"No, I was... detained." Shielded by the tablecloth, I deftly swapped my bottle for hers under the table as she sat down.

She raised my bottle and set it down on the table in front of her, frowning slightly. "The gamma ray pulse was 200 seconds long," she said, adding softly, her lips hardly moving, "You're late. You saw Amit?"

"That's a really remarkable gamma ray burst." I added quietly, "Yes, I saw him."

"And the furthest detection yet. Imagine seeing an event that happened 13 billion years ago." She pretended to take a sip of the from my bottle, even made a show of arcing her lovely neck and swallowing, then casually set the bottle on the table in front of her. She looked at me and frowned slightly as if to ask why I'd consumed virtually all the beer. I cringed about her drinking someone's stale, second-hand beer, but it was healthier than the alternative. "I'm sorry I'm going to be missing tomorrow's talks, but I have plans to go hiking."

I doubted anyone could hear us, but I wasn't taking chances with lip reading. "Sounds like fun. I have a week off before I head to Huntsville to start my summer job."

"I want you to know, I do appreciate everything you've done for me."

"No problem," I assured her. "See you around."

Professor Graf stood up and wandered off.

She started walking around, nursing her beer, talking to her professional colleagues one last time, and telling them all about the hike she planned. I couldn't hear exactly what she was saying, but her voice carried, bright with enthusiasm and full of light – a light the Circle was trying to extinguish. Not on my watch, I vowed silently. I tried to stay relaxed, the toxic bottle of beer feeling remarkably heavy in my left hand. I could see the bartenders and Professor Glyer keeping an eye on her.

When I figured I'd waited long enough for the Circle's attention to be off me, I reached my gloved hand under the table, retrieved the cork and sealed the bottle. Holding the conference bag between my knees, I cautiously slid the toxic beer in the plastic bag. Finally, I sealed the plastic bag, being careful that it would sit upright in the GammaCon bag – no sense taking chances with the cork.

There was a fair bit of choreography to the rest of the plan. I had to empty the toxic bottle and deposit it in the women's restroom. That would be Professor Graf's cue to dispose of her phony bottle. I assumed the Civic Circle's agents would be standing by to whisk the toxic bottle safely away, so mine – the real empty toxic bottle of beer – had to be in place first. I checked my watch. It was time. If all had gone well, there'd be a "closed for maintenance" sign on the ladies' restroom door, placed there by Amit five minutes earlier. I carefully slid the bottle in my conference bag to hide it. I made my move for the restroom.

"Hey!" the man at the entrance checking badges stopped me. "What's that in the bag?" He took a closer look, apparently seeing the impression of the bottle through the cloth GammaCon bag. "Drinks stay in the reception area," he said. I started to head back into the lounge area. "Wait a moment. How old are you?" I was busted.

"I thought I got in with my conference admission?" I stalled for time, considering whether I should try to make a run for it. I could probably get to the women's restroom, but I couldn't risk the bad guys knowing something was going on. I also couldn't risk the guy opening up the bottle and handling it either, if the radioactive poison were as toxic as Amit indicated.

"Looks like we got ourselves an underage juvie trying to steal his self a drink," came an intimidating drawl from behind me. I turned to look.

Sheriff Gunn? What the...

"I'll handle this," the sheriff said to the badge man. He walked me around the corner toward the restrooms.

"That the toxic brew?" he said softly once we were out of earshot.

"Yes."

He guided me to the restroom and gestured me to continue on toward Amit, waiting just down the hall from the ladies' restroom door, pretending to read the conference program. I joined him. Sheriff Gunn knocked and opened the door to the women's restroom. "Security. Is anyone in here?" He ushered a couple of women out. "Sorry, ma'am, security check. Anyone else in there?" Finally, he motioned for us to join him. "It's clear. Do your thing," he ordered. "I'll cover for you here." I followed Amit in. He donned gloves of his own and laid an extra pair on the counter by the sink. Then, he opened a plastic garbage bag and left it on the counter.

That morning, we'd realized we couldn't just make the radioactive bottle of beer vanish. We had to make sure we left behind an empty radioactive bottle so the Circle's agents would be convinced that Professor Graf had consumed the contents. Amit argued that if we flushed it down the toilet, anyone who detected the radioactive poison would conclude she'd excreted it in her urine. He hoped that being diluted in thousands of gallons of sewage would render the radioactive poison less harmful. Professor Graf and I both lacked his blithe confidence in the metabolic ease with which the radioactive poison might be excreted. They'd have chosen something that lingered long enough to kill her, not something that would pass right through her. Also, we were concerned a detailed investigation might be able to figure out the entire radioactive dose had gone down the toilet instead of into Professor Graf. We'd agreed on an alternate plan.

He held an open glass jar inside a big plastic bag with one hand and the lid with the other. I placed my GammaCon bag inside Amit's plastic bag. Then, I removed the plastic bag with the toxic brew. I uncorked it, and slowly poured the contents into Amit's waiting bottle, trying carefully to avoid any splatters or turbulence. He sealed the jar, then took hold of the bottle with his free hand. I stripped off my rubber gloves and let them drop into Amit's plastic bag. Then, I went over to the sink and washed my hands as thoroughly as I could. I dried my hands, and I donned the new set of rubber gloves Amit had left for me. I retrieved the radioactive bottle from Amit's bag, grasping it in my left hand. Once I had it, Amit sealed the bag, and placed the first bag inside the second plastic bag on the counter. He removed his gloves, dropped them in, and sealed the second bag over the first. Finally, he put the double-bagged jar in his own GammaCon bag.

I left the toxic bottle in the trash and joined the sheriff at the door. "We need to distract that badge guy to give the professor a chance to slip to the restroom and give the decoy bottle to Amit," I said, affixing the "Closed for Maintenance" sign to the door to deter anyone from walking in on Amit.

"Figured as much. Come on." He marched me back down the hall to badge man at the entrance to the reception room. "You..." the Sheriff continued ominously, "how is it that your establishment is allowing underage drinking?" I heard the man stammering something as I looked past him. It took a minute to find Professor Graf. I caught her eye, and she gave me a modest nod of her head, the decoy bottle held in a red cocktail napkin in her hand. I saw her disengage and move toward the restroom. Badge man never saw her. The sheriff continued to give badge man an ear-blistering dressing down. A moment later, Amit walked right past us, carrying Professor Graf's decoy bottle.

"This is your lucky day," Sheriff Gunn was telling the hapless badge man. "I'm supposed to be focused on the security of this establishment from terror threats, so unfortunately, I don't have time to run you all in. You tell your boss to see to it that nothing like this ever happens again."

"Yes, sir," badge man replied.

"And you," he said turning his stern attention my way, "get out of here and don't try a damn fool stunt like that again."

I exited the station and walked through the Glenn Miller Gardens, past the old Pullman Cars, and into the hotel building at the far end. Somehow your nose is always itchier when you don't want to touch it. Technically, my right hand was clean and it ought to be OK, but I really didn't want to take chances with something so radioactive a tiny grain could strike you dead.

Amit was waiting for me at the door and escorted me back up to the room. He helped me remove and bag my gloves and then my clothes, just in case. I kept my wallet, keys, and pocket knife figuring the risk they'd been contaminated wasn't worth the hassle in replacing them. Naturally I kept my pair of burner phones, too. I stripped, naked. Everything else including my underwear went into the trash. Next, I hopped in the shower. I was just finishing up when I heard the door open. I threw on my change of clothes, thoughtfully provided by Amit, and came out.

The gang was all there: Sheriff Gunn, Amit, and... I saw Rob dressed in a sheriff's-deputy uniform.

"Deputy Rob," I said dryly. "Thanks for joining us."

"Damn good thing, too," he added sternly, gesturing at my face. "Go running off without a word to me, get the hell beat out of you and then, for want of a fake ID, your mastermind plan goes down in flames, and you need the grown-ups to rescue you. Kids these days don't show near the initiative my friends and I did in our youth."

"In the kid's defense," the sheriff pointed out, "it's much harder to fake an ID now than it was in our day."

"Thanks for the save sheriff," I said extending my hand to him. "How've you been?"

He clasped my hand firmly. "Why, I'm finer than a toad hair split four ways," he proclaimed, "now that you've arranged this here opportunity to twist the Civic Circle's tail some. Wish you'd called me in sooner, son."

"Events moved quickly," I apologized.

"Piss poor planning, and then you run off without a word of coordination...," Rob began.

"You made clear your decision not to help," I interrupted him. "We were too busy executing... and accomplishing the mission to..."

"A mission which would have failed without..."

"Gentlemen!" the sheriff silenced us both. "I'm a traditional sort, in case you haven't noticed, Deputy, and we'll be holding the after-action review in the time-honored place. That is to say, after the action is over." I liked the way he was emphasizing their relative rank in the current hierarchy and putting Rob in his place. I was still angry with Rob for forcing us to act alone and even angrier that he didn't seem to care I'd saved...

The sheriff interrupted my thoughts. "We got us a genuine level-red terror attack imminent alert right here in Chattanooga," he continued. "I got the word from Amit this morning, explaining what was really going on, and an earful from Dr. Krueger. The governor was mighty pissed with this Special Agent Wilson running roughshod over the state troopers' investigation of your parents' 'accident,' last year. I made sure the governor knew that Wilson's buddies were up to something here. He called up lots of us locals to provide extra security for the "terror alert" until he could get the National Guard rousted and turned out. Knowin' how sleepy things always are up in Lee County," he said without a trace of irony, "I figured I could call up a few of my reserve deputies," he gestured at Rob, "and lend 'em a hand. I got put on security for the Choo Choo and the transit center here."

"Another of their phony cover stories," Rob added. "They don't want to look inept when Professor Graf dies from this spooky radiological poison, so they're running another terror-theater production. It'll look like they're proactive and doing something. It's a two-fer. Need to be careful they aren't planning another false-flag operation while they're at it."

"I haven't picked up any chatter," Amit said. "The Circle's agents here seemed to be focused on Professor Graf. Not that they couldn't have farmed some other operation out to other players."

"Where is she, by the way?" I asked.

"Showering," Amit said with a satisfied grin gesturing to a second trash bag next to the one with my clothes. What!?! Did she? No.... Amit gets the girl, again? "By the way, where did you get that extra phone?" he asked me.

Damn. I forgot about that. Were they listening in on the phone? "Where is it?"

"In the microwave with the rest," Amit explained.

Just then there was a knock on the door from the adjoining room. Professor Graf entered wearing a bathrobe and a towel over her head. There was a subtle motion throughout the room as suddenly everyone was standing just a bit straighter. "Oh my," she said at the sight of the law enforcement officers.

"These are the friends I was telling you about," Amit said.

"Oh," she said, relaxing with obvious relief. "Then if you'll excuse me, I'll finish getting dressed and be back in a minute."

Rob gave me a questioning look with a raised eyebrow. I returned his gaze levelly. "Let's wait for the professor to rejoin us. This concerns her most of all. I'll give you a sneak preview, though. You know how I stopped looking for the mysterious conspirators who burned down the Tolliver Library once I realized who was really responsible." I looked at Rob.

"Tarnation..." Sheriff Gunn looked at me and at Rob, his eyes widening in surprise. "I got me an honest-to-goodness firebug among my reserve deputies? I knew that fire was hinky, but..." he clearly suppressed a curse with some effort, shaking his head in amazement.

"All unsupported hearsay, of course," Rob replied levelly.

"Of course," the sheriff added, "and my hearing just ain't what it used to be, so I maybe missed what the kid was saying." He kept shaking his head in disbelief. "Still... you did that all by your lonesome? Hypothetically, of course. To save the kid and keep the Civic Circle goons from getting the books?"

Rob gave him a subtle nod.

"I declare. That's slicker than greased lightning," he added in obvious respect. "You were saying, kid?"

"I was saying I stopped looking for mysterious counter-Circle conspiracies who could have burned down the Tolliver Library to keep it from falling into the Circle's hands. Apparently, I was a bit premature in closing down that investigation. In the last day, I've found not one, but two of them.

Just as I had captured everyone's attention, I immediately lost it as Professor Graf reentered the room.

"Professor Graf," I took the lead at making introductions. "This here is Sheriff Gunn."

"Ma'am," he said politely, gently shaking her hand.

"And over there is my uncle, 'Deputy' Rob Burdell."

He grasped her hand as if he were about to kiss it. "A pleasure to meet you, Professor." His eyes remained fixed on hers.

"I was just explaining that matters have become much more complicated than we anticipated." I could see I hadn't yet recovered everyone's attention – all eyes were on the professor. "In addition to the Civic Circle, there are two other groups seeking the same secrets. One of them wants to extend you a job offer, Professor."

That got everyone's attention back.

This," I said pointing at my face, "was the consequence of a little misunderstanding I had with Professor Chen's Brotherhood. The Brotherhood is a secret Chinese society that apparently broke from whoever – or whatever – is really behind the Civic Circle back in the 1600s."

"You've established this?" Professor Graf asked.

"I believe them. Their stories align with what we found in another book by Angus MacGuffin. He was murdered, probably by the Circle, so the Circle certainly took his stories seriously. Professor Chen's gamma ray results hinted at a three-hundred-fifty-year-old reactor meltdown in China. That was the aftermath of the fight. I don't think the Circle knows that we know about that. They seem to be keying on the fact that they caught Professor Chen communicating with his Brotherhood, and after your... vigorous defense of him, they're convinced you're his partner and ally. Professor Chen is safe with the Brotherhood, now. They've agreed, in principle, to help us in certain ways, but I need to work through the details with them."

"This Brotherhood is some kind of Chinese Tong or Triad? You've been making deals with organized crime?" Rob was clearly skeptical.

"Anyone firing in the direction of the enemy is an ally, by my book," the sheriff offered.

"I'm still trying to figure it all out," I confessed. "If the Brotherhood's stories are to be believed, there's a Chinese deity or some kind of immortal being behind the Brotherhood's origin. They claim our mysterious book dealer, Xueshu Quan, is that very same entity. Quan, or whatever he was calling himself back then, taught The Brotherhood his secrets and tried to use them to overthrow the Emperor. The Brotherhood refused, so Quan betrayed them, and tried to take over China directly. It's hard to tell what happened next. Maybe Quan succeeded, at least in part, maybe not. The Brotherhood believes that Quan realized Europe was on a path to overtake China. He moved to England to better control events, and eventually settled on Jekyll Island for a base of operations."

"Right where the Circle meets," Rob nodded, "and near where the G-8 Summit will be held this summer."

"Exactly," I agreed. "The Brotherhood thwarted Xueshu Quan once, but they were nearly wiped out in return. They appear to be the friends of our friend, Professor Chen. And apparently they're the enemy of our enemy, the Civic Circle. There's a basis for us to work together."

"Professor Chen wants me to work with him and this Brotherhood?" Professor Graf asked.

"No. The reason I was late is on my way back here, I was kidnapped by the Albertians. They wanted me to warn you about the danger from the Civic Circle and arrange for you to go into sanctuary with them."

"Holy shit," Amit said. "The Ordo Alberti? They're here, too?"

I nodded. "They knew all the details about what the Circle was up to and how they were going to attempt to poison Professor Graf. They even knew the details of Professor Chen's research, so they probably have sources in the Brotherhood, too."

"We might be able to ID them," Amit suggested. "You could pick them out through surveillance video or maybe mug shots."

"No," I acknowledged. "They kept me hooded. Couldn't see anything. There was an older man who called himself Brother Francis. There were also a younger man, and a younger woman. I'd recognize their voices. I didn't see any of them, although the woman had a distinctive perfume."

"We can work with that," Amit said enthusiastically. "Those would be the base notes of the fragrance, unless she'd put it on just before kidnapping you, which doesn't seem likely. There are only seven principal olfactive families in traditional perfumery. We'll figure out which one, then we ought to be able to narrow it down from there to identify the precise scent..." Amit paused as he noticed us all staring in amazement at his impromptu lecture.

"How do you know so much about perfume?" I asked.

"The girls who work at department store perfume counters tend to be really hot, and if you're buying perfume, that prequalifies you as having attracted the interest of a girlfriend. You return the order a few days later saying that your girlfriend got too serious and started talking about wanting your babies or something, so you broke it off with her, and then you ask out the perfume girl on the rebound."

I should have known it would be something like that. "This actually works?" Professor Graf asked, skeptically.

"I'm two for five, which is a great success rate for a cold approach, and once I started being more careful to pre-qualify..."

"Not to interrupt this fascinating lecture on the creative use of applied perfumology in dating," Sheriff Gunn drawled, "but could one of you eggheads tell me what the heck an Albertian is?"

"Near as I can tell, they're a secret branch within the Dominicans," I answered. The sheriff looked puzzled.

"They're an order within the Catholic Church?" Rob asked. "Like the Jesuits?"

"Similar in a way," I agreed. "Both were originally created to combat heresy. The Jesuits were formed to confront Protestantism. The Dominicans were created with the mission to combat the Albignesian heresy."

"Can't say as I've run into any Dominicans before," Rob noted.

Sheriff Gunn lifted an eyebrow. "Can't say as I've run into no Albignesians, neither."

"Exactly," Amit pointed out. "Don't underestimate the Dominicans."

"The Albertians take their name from Albertus Magnus, Albert the Great, patron saint of science," I explained. "Their motto is: 'Investigare, cognoscere, defendere,' investigate, know, defend." I explained MacGuffin's report of how

Majorana was sheltered by the Albertians in Argentina after he fled Europe in 1938.

"Ettore Majorana?" Professor Graf asked, wide-eyed.

"You've heard of this Majorana?" Rob asked Professor Graf.

"Of course," she replied. "He was a student of Enrico Fermi, one of the most brilliant physicists of the twentieth century. He compared Majorana to a Galileo or Newton – a world-class genius." She looked thoughtful. "No telling who they might have working with them now."

Another piece suddenly snapped into place. "The Albertians said they have a Nexus Detector. That they invented it. That the Civic Circle stole the technology from them." His name would never be on a patent application, but I was pretty sure I knew who invented the Albertian's Nexus Detector.

"Judas Priest," Sheriff Gunn exclaimed. "They're givin' those freaking things out in Cracker Jack boxes, now?"

"What's a Nexus Detector?" Professor Graf was having trouble keeping up. I explained.

"And they seem to exploit the physics of neutrinos?" she asked. "Oh," I could see her reach the same conclusion. "Majorana must have invented the Nexus Detector technology."

"Or rediscovered it from MacGuffin's description. That's what I was thinking, too." I saw any number of puzzled faces, so I explained. "Before he vanished, Majorana developed a theory that explains... well, it describes how neutrinos work. The Albertians said the Civic Circle stole Nexus Detector technology from them. Nexus Detectors work from neutrino physics in some obscure way, so..."

"Majorana probably invented them," Amit completed the thought. "So now we're one of three groups fighting the Civic Circle: Professor Chen's Brotherhood, The Albertian Order, and us. And only the Albertians and the Civic Circle are fighting with their blindfolds off."

"Yeah, more or less," I confirmed. "Unless the Brotherhood has a Nexus Detector and just didn't say anything. They're very coy. Oh, and the Albertians have sources of information at least as good as our own. Like I said, they seemed to know all about the plot to poison Professor Graf," I added. "I was supposed to get you out of the reception before you ate or drank anything, then give them a call and arrange for them to pick you up."

"This is all moving so fast." Professor Graf sat down. "The last couple of months, I've felt I've been in a race – that someone, something was right behind me, about to catch me. The quiet sense of something lost. Now that I know what's happening... There's so much going on that I was blind to – a darkness consuming the heart of the world... about to devour me as well."

"It's a lot to take in," I said, sitting on the dresser across from her. "If you go with the Albertians, I doubt you'll have an opportunity to change your mind. Come with us. You'll be safe. You'll have time to think, time to decide."

I saw her thinking about it. "The world is vastly more complicated than I thought... Survival first. I need to escape from the Civic Circle." she said. "Time to weigh the alternatives once I'm safe."

"That other burner phone," Amit made the connection. "What are you going to tell the Albertians?"

"I need to buy time with them," I concluded.

"Tell them she's safe, you've got her in hiding, and you'll be in touch tomorrow," Rob agreed.

"The Civic Circle thinks I've been poisoned," Professor Graf noted. "Maybe they'll be less vigilant now that they expect I'll be dead in a few days."

"Not likely, ma'am" Sheriff Gunn shook his head. "They'll follow you around until they're sure you're dead."

"Unless, of course, their cars don't work for some reason," Amit said. "The bartender guys aren't actual Circle agents. Hired contractors. Soon as that reception's over, they'll be out of town and heading for who knows where. The

Circle has a pair of agents – the same ones who spoke with you – staying in the hotel. Their car is outside in the lot. They probably have your phone set to broadcast your location to them, alert them when you start moving. Maybe they've got a bug on your car, too."

"I get the basics," the sheriff said. "Now that they think the lady's been poisoned, we need her to vanish. The 'lost in the wilds' idea is sound. We'll use it. When I spoke with Herr Doktor Krueger, he was a bit put out at the lack of assistance you were receiving." Was that a hint of guilt on Rob's face at being called out? The sheriff continued. "He was happy to volunteer his place, but we agreed Robber Dell would be a better choice." He turned to the professor. "Rob's place is up in the hills and the next neighbor's the better part of a mile off. Krueger's in a subdivision. You'd have to stay inside all the time."

"I built a new barn a couple of years back with an apartment – you can stay there until you figure out what you want to do," Rob explained. "I'll stay in my old trailer."

"I suppose that makes sense," Professor Graf agreed.

"My deputy also agreed to be the decoy," the sheriff added.

"I know a few escape and evasion tricks I haven't taught the kids yet," Rob confirmed. "The trackers and their bloodhounds will be convinced you wandered off the trail, got lost and blundered around for a day or two. I've got a long day ahead of me. Let's you and me go through that gear you bought. I need you to handle it so I don't risk leaving fingerprints or DNA on anything."

"There's a military police battalion, should be moving in any time now," Sheriff Gunn said. "The governor has had a word with their CO. The MPs will help us keep the Circle agents out of our hair. The State Troopers? They'll be creatively uncooperative if the Circle asks for their assistance. If the Circle agents here or Wilson call in the locals? Well, I'll be right there and I can take the call."

The sheriff took charge and began running down the tasks as Rob and the professor worked on her camping gear. "The Circle and the Albertians may be able to trace the lady's car, but so long as we can delay them, knowing the car's location only reinforces the story we're trying to tell."

"The gas station switch-off is a good idea. Then Rob will drive the lady's car to the trailhead and take off from there with a light pack full of debris from the lady's equipment for the searchers to find. Should make his weight comparable to what the lady's would be with a full pack. I'll take the lady up to Rob's place in my cruiser."

"What about me and Pete?" Amit asked.

"Peter's been compromised. These Albertians are the wild card," the sheriff pointed out. "They're standing by here to rescue the professor. They kidnapped Peter once, and might not hesitate to do it again. Peter stays with me. I'll have one of my other deputies drive his car home, tomorrow. Amit, you'll wait here monitoring the situation until we get the professor safe at Rob's place. Pete can take over monitoring them from there, and you can drive on home, yourself. Pete, why don't you make that call to the Albertians? She's considering their offer and will get back to them in the morning. Better yet, get Professor Graf on the line, and put the call on speaker so we can all listen in."

A couple of minutes later, Rob had finished preparing his pack full of debris – mostly soiled clothing to leave a scent and a few recently purchased items that could be traced to her shopping spree. He kept the receipt with the professor's name on it to make it easy for the searchers to draw the intended conclusions. The team assembled, and I made the call to the Albertians.

"You failed," barked Bulldog, "and it's too late for your professor. We saw what happened."

They were watching? They saw Professor Graf drink the "poisoned" beer? They saw me being arrested by the sheriff? They were there? And they were fooled by our little production? Good! I could work with this. I held up a finger for silence.

"There's... there's nothing that can be done?" I asked plaintively, trying to get the right tremble in my voice.

"Nothing," replied Bulldog in obvious disgust at my incompetence. "She's good as dead – just hasn't finished dying, yet."

I heard some commotion on the other end. Then, Brother Francis spoke up. "If we take to anger to intimidate, in time anger will overtake us." His voice seemed distant – admonishing Bulldog? A moment later he continued, his voice clear through the speakerphone. "I'm sorry, my son. We were too late. Make your professora comfortable, and help her to find her peace with God."

He hung up.

"They're going to throw away that burner phone and there'll be no way to contact them." Amit was perplexed. "You didn't even try to get another phone number or set up a way to follow up with them."

"That was the right call." Rob acknowledged. "Last thing we need is to risk them trying a rescue or interfering with our plan. It's going to be challenging enough getting away from the Civic Circle. I think we'll be hearing from these Albertians again soon enough, once Professor Graf 'disappears,' and they begin to realize they've been had."

We went through the details of the next day's plan one last time and got to sleep.

The alarm broke my slumber too soon. Again. Quietly we gathered our things. Amit made a few last minute adjustments to the hotel's video surveillance computer – it would rerun a ten minute section of video of a side entrance twice for the next twenty minutes to give us a chance to depart unnoticed.

Sheriff Gunn and I left first, carefully depositing garbage bags of deadly radioactive cargo in the trunk of his cruiser. I watched from the back of his cruiser as he stopped a moment with the MPs who'd taken over security at the transit center.

One of the MPs climbed into a Humvee and parked it by the Circle agents' rental car. The sheriff was back a minute later. "That'll fix 'em," he muttered.

Rob joined us a few minutes later. "She's ready. Let's roll."

Sheriff Gunn turned over the engine and the cruiser slowly rumbled out of the parking lot.

We figured Professor Graf's phone and laptop had been bugged to alert the Circle agent's rental car when she awoke, so she'd left them in her microwave until the last minute. From our vantage point across the street and down the block, we saw her emerge from the hotel, start her car, and drive off. The two Circle agents emerged a minute later and ran to their car. One ran over to the MPs. I saw an MP make a show of searching his pockets and shrugging. "That's our cue," Rob said. We took off after the professor.

I fell asleep in the back of the sheriff's cruiser. When Rob woke me up, a hint of dawn was evident in the sky over the Smoky Mountains to the east. We stopped at the 24-hour gas station we'd designated for the rendezvous, just off US-411. She pulled in a couple of minutes later. I helped Rob with his wig and rubber gloves, as the professor gassed up her car. Then, she parked beside us and went into the convenience store to buy some trail food. Rob hopped out of the cruiser and into the driver's seat of the professor's car. When she came out a couple of minutes later, she handed off the purchase to Rob, and got in the back of the cruiser with me. Rob started up the professor's car and drove off south toward the trailhead. His disguise wouldn't fool anyone from up close, but in the dawn's early light and from a distance, the wig and matching shirt sure looked a lot like the professor. We waited a few minutes, and then drove off the other way.

I began to get that same feeling I had the previous afternoon – that feeling that it was all going too well, too smoothly. I'd begun associating the feeling of impending victory with impending doom. I mentioned it to the sheriff.

"Believe it or not," he grinned, "when the right people execute the right plan, it usually works out. Not that y'all don't have to stay on the bounce ready for the..." he glanced up at the professor in the rear-view mirror, "...for trouble," he concluded.

We drove on up into the hills above Sherman. I unlocked Rob's gate. The sheriff drove the cruiser through, and I locked it behind us. He drove us under the Robber Dell sign, up the familiar narrow incline, past the ruins of the old farm house, and over to Rob's barn. I got out again, and opened up the door to the barn.

We were home.

CHAPTER 13: EPILOGUE

I spent the day keeping an eye out for any intercepts from the Circle and educating the professor on the Heaviside wave theory and my translations of MacGuffin's mysticism into electromagnetic physics. Teaching was rewarding. Seeing her face light up as she understood a concept and raced through the implications sent tingles up and down my spine. It took her minutes to grasp what had taken me hours to figure out. I gave her a tour of Rob's underground refuge. She was suitably impressed, and started sharing her ideas for cleaning up the living quarters and putting together the lab she'd need to start applying the MacGuffin physics.

Rob had spent the entire the day leaving Graf tracks and spreading pieces of her gear and clothes up and down the trails around the Cove. After dark, he'd removed the improvised sandals with the tread from the boots Professor Graf had just bought. Then he followed one of the main trails through the darkness, out to a trailhead where Sheriff Gunn met him and brought him back home in the early hours of the following morning, waking us up. I scrambled some eggs for him as he recounted the twists and turns of the trail he'd left. "It'll look like a classic case of disorientation, an attempt to reach the high ground for a better view, then stumbling about in the dark along the path of least resistance," he explained before we all turned in to get some much-needed rest.

Professor Graf and I were both up early the next morning. The rate at which she absorbed ideas and information was amazing. Rob woke up just before noon, and came into the study. I'd been bringing Professor Graf up to speed all morning on the implications of MacGuffin's "Great Circle" and how the normalized Lagrangian was related to the energy velocity.

"I see you've made yourself at home," Rob said to Professor Graf. "If you're ready to take a break from all the books, I'd be happy to make you lunch and give you a tour of my place."

"You're a very generous host," she replied, "and this place is simply amazing, but Peter already gave me the basic tour. I'd just as soon keep working to understand these marvelous concepts." Her face was radiant with excitement. Ah, the way to this woman's heart was through physics books. "I'd be delighted if you could provide me with a bite to eat, though."

"Peter?" he asked, clearly intending me to help him make lunch. For some reason, I found his attitude annoying. "Yes, I could use a bite to eat, too, thank you." I chose to interpret his question as extending the same offer to me.

He looked at me a moment, letting me know that he knew exactly what I was doing. Then, he left, returning a few minutes later with a plate of sandwiches and some chips.

"How goes the research, Professor?" Rob asked.

"This is simply amazing," she said, her face bright with joy and enthusiasm. "That's exactly the right way to describe it – simple, yet amazing. That Heaviside came up with this... it's the culmination of the whole Maxwellian paradigm – Faraday's notion of fields reduced to energy flows in space as waves interact with each other."

"I'll have to take your word for it, Professor," Rob said with a smile.

"Please," she said, "you can stop calling me 'Professor.' That job is behind me, now. My name is Marlena." She looked at me. "You, too, Peter," she added in an afterthought.

"Well then, Marlena," Rob took quick advantage of her request, "what I want to know is: can you make us a Nexus Detector?"

"Not yet," she acknowledged, "but... I have a sense that... that there's something there. I know what Majorana knew when he vanished, at least what work of his he published. I have the benefit of decades of mathematical physics techniques, and, thanks to Peter here, MacGuffin's complete translation where Majorana had only fragments to work from. Yes. I think given time, I can figure it out, too. There may be some implementation and engineering difficulties. If we're working from the same notes Majorana used, then yes, I probably can. I just wish we had the complete source material that Peter says this MacGuffin hid somewhere before he was killed."

"That was sixty-five years ago," Rob observed. "MacGuffin's thorny friend has almost certainly long since gone to his reward, apparently without revealing his secrets. Whole neighborhoods in Atlanta have been bulldozed for highways and development. The likelihood we can find MacGuffin's hidden cache is low to nonexistent."

The professor nodded in sad agreement.

"I'm glad you think you can construct one of these Nexus Detectors without it, though," Rob added on a more cheerful note. "If we had access to one, it would help us pick the time and place of our battles and counter the Circle's interventions with some of our own." They were both smiling at the thought of that particular collaboration – a little too comfortable together for my liking.

"Aren't you glad we didn't abandon Marlena to her fate?" I asked Rob.

She looked at me and then back to him in shock. "Abandon me?"

"'We're not ready to fight back yet?'" I reminded Rob. "Abandon Professor Chen and Professor Graf, run home and hide out here until it all blows over?" I wasn't about to let him forget it, particularly in front of Professor Graf.

Rob had the good graces to look guilty. "I may have underestimated the advantages of bringing Marlena in to our fight," he turned to face her. "The boy lost his parents last year. His safety is my responsibility, and despite his best efforts, I try to take that charge seriously. He took a mighty big risk to save you and Professor Chen – a risk I didn't think he was ready to take. It was poorly planned, it was sloppy," he paused a moment and smiled, "but it was successful. That's what counts... with a bit of an assist from the grown-ups at the end."

"I understand." She was far less outraged than I thought she should be. "If you gentlemen will excuse me?" She took her leave and headed for the bathroom.

"Brains and beauty," Rob said softly to no one in particular after she'd closed the door, "and lots of spunk." He turned to face me. "I saw that press conference of hers. She's a real firecracker."

I didn't like his tone, so I changed the subject. "I asked Amit and the sheriff to come on over for dinner. Thought we'd review our plans and maybe have a bonfire to celebrate."

"Good thinking," he agreed. "Let's head up and get ready. I still don't want Amit or the sheriff to know about the underground refuge."

He looked me in the eye. "We'll have a chat later about what you did wrong, and how you screwed up. I won't be sparing your feelings. That was rash, impetuous, and foolish, but you were the man on the spot, and it was your decision to make. Success counts for a lot. Tangling with a tong, saving your professors, contacting some secret order of monks," he was shaking his head, "I wouldn't have thought you could have pulled all that off, but you did. Now, well let's just say I can see you were well-motivated." He held out a hand. "No hard feelings?"

"No hard feelings, Rob." I stood and shook his hand, facing him man-to-man as a peer. Then he ruined my moment of manly independence by engulfing me in a huge bear hug.

I'd made my point. I'd defied him, and I won. It was time to bury the hatchet and work together. We managed to get

Marlena to put the books aside, and we went topside to prepare our celebratory dinner and build the fire.

* * *

"Success!" Amit showed up with a smile on his face, not long after the sheriff arrived. "The Circle is combing the trails around Cades Cove looking for you under the theory that you may be rendezvousing with the sinister Chinese spy, Professor Wu Chen."

The surprised Marlena. "They really think Chen is in the Great Smoky Mountains Park, too?"

"No," Amit confirmed, "it's an excuse to look for you. I think they're trying to find your body to forestall any autopsy that might give away the radioactive poisoning. They think they got away clean with your murder, and if they're careful with the cover up, they may be able to use this 'polonium' poison again."

"That's nasty stuff," Marlena pointed out, thinking through the implications of her narrow escape. "I don't recall the half-life, but..."

"It's 138 days," Amit said smugly. How did he become such a nuclear physics expert? I stared at him. "I looked it up," he confessed.

I felt the hairs rising on my spine. The sooner we got those garbage bags sealed in a 55 gallon drum and buried, the happier I'd be.

"What do they think happened to Chen?" I asked.

"The balloon trick of yours has them thinking he took back roads through to South Carolina. They're convinced he's in the Charleston area trying to sneak out of the country."

"I'm worried about my Mom," Marlena acknowledged. "I sent her a text that I'd be out of touch a few days, but when I turn up missing..."

"We can arrange to get a note to her, ma'am," the sheriff offered. "They'll be keeping an eye on her, though. Expecting you to contact her, if they think you're still alive."

"My mother is a level-headed woman," Marlena assured him. "She can be trusted to keep a secret. Sarah is checking in on Tigger and keeping an eye on my apartment, but that was only for the weekend."

"I need to get a note to Sarah anyway about borrowing her climbing gear and the balloon," I explained. "I'm sure she'll keep an eye on your place for you."

"We may be able to get your cat and your belongings for you," the sheriff offered. He looked at me. "When the time comes, suggest to Sarah she should reach out to the professor's mother, they make arrangements to pack and ship her things home. We make a switch and bring them up here."

"I want to hear more about this deal Peter made with the tong," Rob changed the subject. "How are they going to help you get this Professor Gomulka?"

I explained what I had in mind.

"That might work...." Rob nodded his head thoughtfully. "It's a start. We need to refine it some. Not tonight, though." He turned to face Marlena. "Tonight, we're going celebrate the newest member of The Resistance."

The Resistance? That rubbed me the wrong way. "I don't like that term – resistance. It suggests all were going to do is slow them down, not stop them."

"Kid's got a point," the sheriff agreed. "It's like conservatives only slowing down the inevitable progression to tyranny, never stopping and reversing it."

"What would you call it then?" Rob put me on the spot.

I thought about it a minute and realized why the term bothered me. Resistance made me think in terms of direct current, DC, slowing down a one-way flow. We needed something more dynamic, something alternating current, AC, pushing back the flow and making it going in the other direction. Impedance? No. Then I had it.

"Reactance," I proposed. "They call us reactionaries already. Let's own the term. We're 'The Reactance.'"

"The imaginary resistance?" Marlena asked skeptically.

"Or the resistance with imagination," I offered, "or the complex component of the resistance, if you prefer."

"I like it," Marlena smiled. "I think Oliver Heaviside would approve. I'm delighted to be the newest member of 'The Reactance.'"

Rob grilled some steaks for dinner. We roasted marshmallows over the fire. Finally, as the sun began to set, we pulled up our chairs around the fire. How long had it been? I remembered a July 4 bonfire – one of the last happy times I'd had with my folks before we'd found ourselves in a fight for our lives. Now, we could relax, celebrate our victories and plan our next steps. Rob offered me and Amit some beer. I took it to be polite, but I didn't much care for the taste.

"It's been a good year," Rob stoked the fire and a burst of sparks rose to the heavens. "We've made some progress, learned more about them, acquired some new allies, even bloodied the Circle's noses a bit, and gotten away with it, with them none the wiser."

"True," I agreed, "but we're no nearer understanding who's really behind the Circle. Was there an unknown ancient civilization discovering electricity, wrangling with electromagnetic theory, and developing advanced technology? Atlanteans? Lemurians? How could they have discovered so much without leaving a trace?"

"Ancient batteries have been discovered," Marlena noted. "They're thought to have been used in electroplating."

"But, that much technology would leave some trace," I pointed out.

"Extraterrestrials?" the sheriff suggested.

"I don't see how," Marlena was skeptical.

"The Brotherhood thinks it's a Chinese deity," Amit noted.

"Maybe the Albertians are right," speculated Rob. "Fallen angels seeking to tempt us with the forbidden fruit of dangerous knowledge? Or Satan himself, seeking dominion over the Earth?"

The flames danced in front of us as we continued to ponder what we learned. "We have some intriguing clues, but we simply don't know enough yet to figure out who they are and what they really want," I concluded.

"They seek power?" the sheriff speculated. "Control?"

"But to what end?" I asked. "We don't really know." No one care to dispute me. Who are they? I stared into the fire. What do they want? No deeper answers were forthcoming.

Finally, the sheriff lifted his bottle in a toast, "To Amanda," he took a swig. "Gone, but never forgotten." I drank to my mother's memory.

"To my brother, Roy," Rob offered a toast. "You're..." He started to say something, more, but couldn't. He took a deep breath, and simply added, "Roy." Then, he took another sip of the bitter brew in my father's memory.

"To James Clerk Maxwell," offered Marlena in toast, "To Heinrich Hertz, and the other pioneers struck down by arrows in their backs before their days were finished. You will be avenged." I drank to that with a smile. She had a bloodthirsty twist to her. Good. She'd be needing it.

"To Mr. Rodriguez, Nicole, Jim Burleson, Robb LeChevalier, and the other forgotten victims of the Circle," Amit proposed. "May they rest easier when our work is done."

Hear, hear. I gazed into the flickering flames as the silence grew. I realized we'd forgotten a critical someone who'd been with us at the beginning and at the end of our first year at Tech, but was no more.

"Angus MacGuffin." I held my bottle up and observed the dancing flames refract through the bottle. "They struck you down, but not before you accomplished what you set out to do. Now we know. We will share your story, we will recover your legacy, and we will avenge your murder."

Everyone drank to that. The sky darkened to black. The gathering was winding down. The pause stretched ever longer. Finally, Marlena broke the silence. "You realize that

'MacGuffin' is a term used in drama to denote the goal for which the hero seeks," she pointed out.

I smiled. "Yes, that was one of the first things we uncovered in our research. Alfred Hitchcock popularized the term in the 1930s. How he came across it, I'm not sure. Maybe he was a member of the Circle, or maybe he just associated with them and overheard some stray mention of the name. In the 1930s, 'MacGuffin' was the ultimate goal, the man of mystery being sought by half the world's elite."

"Heh," Marlena snorted in amusement at the irony of it. "The man the Civic Circle tried so hard to get everyone to forget," she was shaking her head with a sad smile.

"Will be remembered forever as the goal of every hero's quest." I completed her thought.

It was late. We'd continue building on MacGuffin's legacy, in the morning.

The End.

Look for Pete's continuing adventures in
The Brave and the Bold: Book 3 of The Hidden Truth.

AFTERWORD: ABOUT *A RAMBLING WRECK*

This is a work of fiction, but *A Rambling Wreck* draws heavily on real-world history, science, philosophy, and events within our own timeline. Here are a few of the more interesting examples.

The writings of the quantum physicists are quoted accurately, and Paul Forman makes a compelling case that the intellectual revolt against causality, determinism, and materialism, in Weimar German culture contributed to the philosophic foundation of the Copenhagen Interpretation of quantum mechanics.

John A. Wheeler, a contemporary of Niels Bohr, told me the story of how Bohr harassed Schrödinger to adopt the Copenhagen Interpretation while the later lay in a sickbed. Wheeler further described details of Slater's "dubious adventure" with Bohr and Kramer. I have verified these stories against other historical sources as well.

The brilliant Italian physicist, Ettore Majorana, really did disappear in 1938, and there is considerable evidence that he lived out his life in South America. The quotations from *Atoms in the Family* are correct – Majorana's nephew really did die in a mysterious fire, his uncle was charged with the crime, and Majorana successfully worked for his uncle's acquittal.

Widespread government surveillance of domestic communications became known in the fall of 2005 in our own timeline as well, and the Electronic Frontier Foundation (eff.org) reacted as described. Erin McCracken really did write an amazingly prescient article in the fall of 2005 about the dangers of Facebook and the threat to civil liberties posed by the NSA's Echelon program. I found this and other incidents of Georgia Tech campus news in back issues of the *Technique*.

The Ivy League Nude Scandal is real. A wide variety of Ivy League and other "elite" schools really did mandate that all incoming students be photographed in the nude. Boxes of abandoned photos have been found, so it is not impossible that some photos may have found their way into the hands of those who may have used them for nefarious purposes. Anything beyond that is completely fictional. I hope.

I offered a fictional reinterpretation of the controversy surrounding Rosetta scientist Matt Taylor's rather casual attire. Professor Graf's "Shirt Storm" advocacy borrows heavily from the "Amazonian feminism" of Camille Paglia. Like Cassandra, her decades-old essay, "No Law in the Arena" (collected in *Vamp and Tramps*), was as prescient as it was ignored.

The fictionally suppressed electromagnetic discoveries attributed to Heaviside are my own. The curious behavior of the exponentially decaying dipole was the subject of my doctoral dissertation. The electromagnetic impedance of the fields around an elemental dipole source really do form a yin-yang diagram when plotted on a Smith Chart. A more technically rigorous discussion and the application of these ideas in antenna theory may be found in my text, *The Art and Science of Ultrawideband Antennas*, 2nd edition, 2015.

One of my Alpha Readers cautioned that the social justice rhetoric of *A Rambling Wreck* sometimes sounded like parody. He had a point. I helped myself to the catch phrases and jargon of a wide variety of social justice warriors from Saul Alinsky to his more modern successors. The typical social justice diatribe is devoid of dialectic meaning. Instead, SJWs typically employ rhetoric, to signal their own perceived moral virtue, to emotionally assault a perceived enemy with trigger words (Nazi! Racist! Fascist! etc.), or to camouflage and obscure some deeper true meaning – not only from the audience, but often from the author xyrself. That makes for long, meandery, and frankly, boring rants. By placing social justice rhetoric in the concise dialectic form required by the narrative structure of my story, the inherent illogic and vacuousness of it become far more apparent. To that extent, I acknowledge I do an injustice to social justice advocates.

While I was writing my fictional account of an attempted social justice coup at Georgia Tech, it all actually happened in real-life. My alma mater, Purdue University, hired a new head of the School of Engineering Education, Professor Donna Riley. Her "scholarship" and philosophy are similar in many respects to that of the fictional Professor Cindy Ames. See Rod Dreher's account "Queering Engineering at Purdue," from *The American Conservative*, March 30, 2017 for details.

If you'd like to learn more about social justice and understand SJWs, Alinsky's *Rules for Radicals*, is a great starting point. I also recommend Vox Day's *SJWs Always Lie*, and *The Evolutionary Psychology Behind Politics*, by Anonymous Conservative. The Chinese opinion of 'baizuo' is as described by Professor Chen.

Finally, the legend of George P. Burdell continues to be told where ever George Tech alumni and students congregate. I enjoyed the opportunity to offer my own contributions to the existing mythos.

ACKNOWLEDGEMENTS

Robert E. (Robb) LeChevalier really did die of brain cancer in 2014 in our real-world timeline. His life was prolonged by the remarkable efficacy of Coley's Fluid (see http://coleyfluid.org/), an overlooked and nearly forgotten nineteenth-century immuno-therapeutic treatment that – for a time – regressed his aggressive glioblastoma. At the time of his death, Robb was seeking funding to commercialize his revolutionary particle-accelerator-on-a-chip technology that has the potential to make interplanetary ion propulsion and fusion power feasible. For details and contact information, see http://www.robertlechevalier.com/donation). Robb's remarkable wit and wisdom will be made available in a forthcoming book, *Robbservations*, edited by Monica Hughes, Ph.D. I'm indebted to Dr. Hughes for permission to use her husband's real-life story in this fictional context.

Sheridan Brinley, son of the late Bertrand R. Brinley, generously granted permission for Harmon Muldoon to appear in *A Rambling Wreck*. I grew up on the tales of *The Mad Scientists' Club* and I'm thrilled to be granted free reign to incorporate a small part of Brinley's fictional universe in my story. Harmon was originally the club's radio expert, but was kicked out for "conduct unbecoming a scientist." He became the worthy nemesis of the Mad Scientists' Club. It seemed deeply appropriate that he should prove to be a nemesis – of sorts – to my characters as well.

If you haven't read these young adult stories – you should! Originally a series of short stories that appeared in Boy's Life in the 1960s, *The Mad Scientists' Club* features clever, independent-minded young men who overcome an amazing variety of challenges through cleverness, teamwork, and, of course, a healthy dose of mad science! If you're a fan of my writing, you'll really like Brinley's.

Peter's undergraduate research experience drew on my own experience at Purdue University. I'm indebted to my Purdue classmate, Professor Dale Litzenberg, now of The University of Michigan, who explained for me the work he and John Ayres did in Purdue's mirror lab.

Thomas Eiden provided me with some nuclear physics consultation, including the critical observation that some of the low-energy gamma rays Professor Chen's team detected from orbit, would have been completely attenuated by the time they reached even a low-Earth-orbit gamma ray observatory. Terrestrial gamma-ray flashes were in fact discovered in 1994 by BATSE, the "Burst and Transient Source Experiment," on board the Compton Gamma-Ray Observatory. I took the liberty of appropriating the discovery for Professor Chen's team. We live in a world in which antimatter (in minute quantities) occurs naturally, a result that would have seemed like science fiction when I was starting my graduate training in physics.

Paul Blair provided suggestions on topics ranging from Latin grammar to the events surrounding Ettore Majorana's fictional stay in Buenos Aires.

My Alpha Readers gave generously of their time to review my early drafts and provide their suggestions and corrections. Alpha Readers included Brandy Harvey, Francis Porretto, Jay Garing, Jack Gardner, Jeff Koistra, June Coker McNew, Daniel Stratton, and Robert Tracy. Foremost among my Alpha Readers is the amazing Barbara McNew Schantz, whose talents, not only in managing our busy household, but also in editing and proofing my novels are much appreciated by her husband.

The vector diagram of Chapter 2 and the "yin-yang" Smith charts originally appeared in my *The Art and Science of Ultrawideband Antennas*, 2nd edition, 2015. If you are interested in the electromagnetic physics of my *Hidden Truth* stories and how it can be applied in practice, you may want to check out my ultra-wideband antenna book. The Smith Chart of Chapter 7 is by "Wdwd" (Own work) [CC BY-SA 3.0 (http://creativecommons.org/licenses/by-sa/3.0)], courtesy of Wikimedia Commons.

In conclusion, I am deeply grateful to all the readers of *The Hidden Truth* who took a chance on an unknown author. You joined Peter Burdell and Amit Patel on their fictional journey to discover the hidden truth and unmask the Civic Circle, and now you have joined my heroes in their first steps to outwit and defeat their formidable enemies.

Your support through your reviews and word-of-mouth have been critical to the success of *The Hidden Truth*. You are wonderfully engaged, and a remarkably high fraction of you volunteered your time to review my work and help bring it to the attention of more readers. If you enjoy my latest story, if you think it deserves a wider audience, I hope you'll let your friends know, and post reviews on Amazon and elsewhere to help spread the word.

Thank you.

ABOUT THE AUTHOR

I'm a radio frequency (RF) scientist with a Ph.D. in theoretical physics. My research aims at understanding how bound or reactive electromagnetic energy decouples from a source or an antenna and radiates away. This theory has been helpful in understanding and designing not only antennas, but also near-field wireless systems. I "wrote the book" on *The Art and Science of Ultrawideband Antennas*. In addition, I'm an inventor with about forty patents to my credit, mostly antennas or wireless systems, but I was also a co-inventor (with my wife, Barbara) on a remarkably effective baby bowl. Barbara's Baby Dipper® bowl and feeding set (see http://babydipper.com) helps parents feed infants and helps toddlers learn to feed themselves through a clever, ergonomic design. With Bob DePierre, I co-invented Near-Field Electromagnetic Ranging. I conceived the idea and Bob reduced it to practice and made it work.

I'm an entrepreneur, as well. I co-founded The Q-Track Corporation. Our company is the pioneer in Near-Field Electromagnetic Ranging (NFER®) Real-Time Location Systems (RTLS). Q-Track released the first NFER® RTLS a few years ago. Q-Track products provide precise (40cm rms accurate) location awareness that enhances the safety of nuclear workers. In other installations, Q-Track products let robotic overhead cranes know the location of workers to avoid collisions. Q-Track's new SafeSpot™ systems help keep people safe from collisions with forklifts. NFER® RTLS provides "indoor GPS" by providing location awareness to the most difficult industrial settings. See http://q-track.com.

Furthermore, I'm an amateur radio operator (KC5VLD), and a Webelos den leader in Huntsville, Alabama, where I live with my wife, Barbara, and our four children: twin boys, and twin girls.

I was deeply honored by the reviewer who suggested that *The Hidden Truth* was a great book to tide a reader over until the next Larry Correia or Jim Butcher release. May I suggest some other authors you might want to investigate to tide you over until the release of *The Brave and the Bold: Book 3 of The Hidden Truth*? I listed a number of recommendations in *The Hidden Truth,* but more appear all the time. There's a growing fraternity of independent, self-published authors busy changing the culture one story at a time with their tales of adventure and heroism. Here are a few of my more recent discoveries.

C. J. Carella's *Warp Marine Corps* series blends small unit action with interstellar warfare and politics in a particularly satisfying manner. Russell Newquist's story, *Who's Afraid of the Dark?* is a fast-paced, clever, horror short, and he promises more tales of Peter Bishop are to come. *Chasing Freedom* by Marina Fontaine is a rare upbeat and hopeful dystopian novel, full of exciting action. Peter Grant gives Louis L'Amour a run for his money with his Ames Archives series. The latest installment, *Rocky Mountain Retribution*, is superb.

I very much enjoy the *Girl Genius* web comic as well as Jim Butcher's *The Cinder Spires: The Aeronaut's Windlass*. Now, there's a new steampunk contender, Jon Del Arroz's *For Steam and Country*. Speaking of webcomics, Big Head Press hosts a number of great titles. I enjoyed *Roswell, Texas*, and Scott Beiser's current strip, *Quantum Vibe* is excellent as well. Declan Finn's *A Pius Man: A Holy Thriller* is the kind of historically-illuminated thriller I enjoy. Francis Porretto is the author of the Spooner Federation trilogy. I appreciated his poignant *Love in the Time of Cinema*. Richard Paolinelli's

Escaping Infinity offers a creepy yet strangely satisfying tale that reads like something out of *The Twilight Zone*. JP Mac makes the Lovecraft mythos accessible to non-fans like me in *Hallow Mass*. A college student must rise to the occasion when an unspeakable evil threatens, not just her campus, but also all of existence in this brilliant, clever mix of horror, ironic humor, and modern-day campus political correctness. *Atlas Shrugged* meets *Invasion of the Body Snatchers* in Justin Robinson's *The Good Fight*.

Daniel Humphreys examines what happens after the zombie outbreak, when the greatest enemy the survivors face is themselves in *A Place Outside the Wild*. Kurt Schlichter has written some excellent dystopic military thrillers set in a future in which the U.S. has split into two countries. Check out *People's Republic*, and *Indian Country*. Finally, a reviewer of *The Hidden Truth* pointed out that Michael Flynn's *In the Country of the Blind* adopts a similar trope of a shadowy conspiracy in control of history with a bit of a steampunk twist. I had trouble following all the characters, but my readers might find it of interest.

Where do I find all these wonderful books? The Conservative Libertarian Fiction Alliance on Facebook is a great place for readers and authors to mingle and learn about the latest great releases. The Ace of Spades HQ Moron Horde Sunday Morning Book Thread is full of good suggestions, as is the Book Horde blog at http://www.bookhorde.org.

For more current suggestions and updates on my progress, check out my blog at http://aetherczar.com, or follow me at https://twitter.com/AetherCzar on Twitter or on Gab at https://gab.ai/aetherczar.

Thanks again for your interest in *A Rambling Wreck*.

CPSIA information can be obtained
at www.ICGtesting.com
Printed in the USA
LVHW011010280121
677610LV00003B/416

9 781949 891805